END IN TEARS

By Ruth Rendell

Ruth Rendell

END IN TEARS

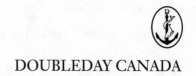

DOUBLEDAY CANADA

Doubleday Canada and colophon are trademarks.

LIBRARY AND ARCHIVES CANADA CATALOGUING IN PUBLICATION

Rendell, Ruth, 1930–
    End in tears : a Chief Inspector Wexford mystery / Ruth Rendell.

ISBN 0-385-66202-5

I. Title.

PR6068.E63E53 2005   823'.914   C2005-904927-8

Printed and bound in the USA

Published in Canada by
Doubleday Canada, a division of
Random House of Canada Limited

Visit Random House of Canada Limited's website: www.randomhouse.ca

BVG   10   9   8   7   6   5   4   3   2   1

Chapter 1

When he lifted it off the seat the backpack felt heavier than when he had first put it into the car. He lowered it on to the soft ferny ground. Then he got back into the driving seat to move the car deep into a cave made by hawthorn bushes and brambles, and the hop vines which climbed over everything in this wood. It was late June and the vegetation very dense and luxuriant.

Getting out again and standing back to take a good look, he could barely see the car. Probably he only saw it because he knew it was there. No one else would notice it. He squatted down, hoisted the backpack up on to his shoulders and slowly stood up to his full height. The movement reminded him of something and it was a moment before he realised what it was: lifting up his little son to sit on his shoulders. A hundred years ago, it seemed. The backpack was lighter than the boy but felt heavier to him.

He was afraid that if he stood upright the pack would jerk him backwards and break his spine. Of course it wouldn't. It just felt that way. All the same, he wouldn't stand upright, wouldn't even try it. Instead, he stooped, bending almost double. It wasn't far. He could walk like this the two hundred yards to the bridge. Anyone seeing him from a distance in this half-light would have thought him a humpbacked man.

There was no one to see. The twisty country lane wound round Yorstone Wood and over the bridge. He could have brought the car right up to the bridge but that way it would have been seen, so he had driven off the lane along a ride and then through a clearing to find the hop-grown cave. In the distance he thought he heard a car, then something heavier with a diesel engine. They would be on the road below, Brimhurst Lane that ran from Myfleet to Brimhurst Prideaux, passing under Yorstone Bridge ahead of him. It wasn't far now but it seemed like miles. If his legs gave way he wouldn't be able to get up again. Would it be easier to drag the backpack? What, then, if he met someone? Dragging something looks much more suspicious than carrying it. He pressed his shoulders back a little and, surprisingly, that was better. There was no one to meet. He could see the lane through the trees and the little stone bridge no one had reinforced with steel or replaced with a brightly painted wooden structure.

Its parapets were low, too low for safety, according to the local paper. The paper was always on about this bridge, and the dangers of the lane and the low parapets. He walked out on to the bridge, squatted down and let the backpack slip off his shoulders to the ground. He undid the flaps and then the zip. Inside, now revealed, was a lump of concrete, very roughly spherical, a bit bigger than a soccer ball. A pair of gloves was also inside the pack. To be on the safe side, he put them on. Though it would never come to anyone examining his hands, it would be stupid to scrape or bruise them.

What light remained was fading fast and with the coming of the dark it grew cooler. His watch told him that it was nine fifteen. Not long now. He lifted up the lump of concrete in his gloved hands, thought of balancing it on the parapet in readiness, then thought again. It wasn't beyond the bounds of possibility that someone would come along the path he had used and cross the bridge. Wait for the call, he thought. It won't be long now.

No traffic had passed along the road below since he had come on to the bridge but a car came now, going towards Brimhurst Prideaux, most probably all the way to Kingsmarkham. He closed his hand over the mobile in his pocket, worried because it hadn't rung. Then it rang.

'Yes?'

'She's left. You want the number again?'

'I've got it. A silver Honda.'

'Right.'

'A silver Honda. Should be along in four minutes.'

He heard the line close. It was dark now. A car passed under the bridge, heading towards Brimhurst St Mary and Myfleet. The road dipped where the bridge passed over it and then twisted to the left, almost a right-angled bend. There were tall trees on the corner with thick ancient trunks and a black and white arrow sign opposite, pointing traffic to the left. A minute had passed.

He moved across to the other side of the bridge, dragging the backpack behind him, and there he bent down, heaved up the lump of concrete, his arms straining, and set it on the parapet. Just as well it wasn't far to lift it. Another minute gone. A white van with headlights on at full beam came from the Myfleet direction, a car following it, to pass, just behind him, a motorbike coming from Kingsmarkham. He was momentarily blinded by the headlights, held in them, which made him curse. No one should see him. The silver Honda with the number he had memorised would be along soon, very soon. The third minute passed. A fourth.

He hated anticlimaxes. The silver Honda could have taken another route. It was all very well to say it never did but you could never say that, not when it came to the way people behaved. He was facing the way it would come, towards

3

Myfleet. It would pass under the bridge but before it reached the left-hand bend . . . He could see lights in the distance. The lights appeared and disappeared as a hedge or a tree trunk cut them from his view, and appeared again. Two sets of lights, not one car but two, both of them silver, quite close together. One was the Honda but he couldn't tell which, not from here, not in the dark, but he could read the number or the last three digits.

As soon as he had given a great push to the lump on the parapet and felt it drop, he knew he had aimed at the wrong car. The crash was huge, like a bomb. The first car, the one he had hit, ploughed into a tree trunk, its bonnet burst open, its windscreen gone, half its roof caved in. It seemed to have split and exploded. The car behind, undamaged until this point, crashed into its rear and its boot lid sprang open. That was the silver Honda which had been his quarry. As its driver got out of it, screaming, her hands up in the air, he knew he had failed.

He waited no longer but picked up the backpack and moved, looking back once to see the leading car burst into flames. In the brilliant light which illuminated everything he saw for the first time the woman he had tried to kill.

Chapter 2

George Marshalson had slept badly. He always did when she was out. Going to bed soon after she had left the house, he had slept for an hour or two, then woken and lain awake, no longer comforted by the presence of Diana next to him. It was August and the night was warm, humid and sticky in spite of the wide-open windows. He lay listening to the sounds of the night, the trickle of the sluggish river, a bird, its name unknown, giving its eerie wail.

Pressing the button on the clock which lit up its display panel, he saw that it was still only eleven forty-one. The bathroom summoned him, reminding him with a twinge that, as with most men of his age, his prostate gland was no longer in perfect working order. He parted the floor-length curtains an inch and felt a breath of air on his face. The sky was cloudless and the moon had risen. Weeks of heat had dried the foliage on the trees that arched above the lane but now only their abundance could be seen, their heavy luxuriance, hanging utterly still in the warm air. He thought how wonderful it would be if something had happened to send her home early. That wretched club closed, for instance, or even a police raid, though he hardly supposed Amber did things to attract police attention – or did she? You never knew with the young these days. Still, it would be wonderful to close these curtains, part them again and see her walking down the lane . . .

There had been nights when he had gone out into the lane to look for her. A fruitless business, too stupid to confess to anyone. Even Diana had never known. He had gone out and walked up to the corner – two or three hundred yards? – looked up and down the road that ran from Myfleet to Kingsmarkham, then walked back. There was no point in it, there never had been, but it was what anxious parents or lovers did. Even if he considered doing it tonight, now was too early. She would be inside that club, an underground place he thought it was, with her friends doing whatever they did. He dropped the curtains and stood looking at Diana. She slept silently, one hand up against her cheek. Youth came back to her while she slept, as it is said to come back to the newly dead. I wonder if she's got someone, he thought, 'someone else', as they say. It suddenly seemed obscene to him to share a bed with a man when you had some other lover. But perhaps she hadn't, probably she hadn't. She was just indifferent to him, as he was to her. In any case, he didn't care. On the rare occasions when he thought about it, he realised he didn't really care much about anyone or anything except Amber.

He fell into a restless sleep. A sound woke him. A car in the lane? That boy might have brought her home. He usually dropped her at the corner but he might have brought her home. Once more he lit up the dial on the clock. One fifty-six. This was the sort of time she came home. She was usually very quiet about it, as much to avoid waking the child as disturbing him and Diana. Perhaps she *was* home. Perhaps the sound he had heard was the front door closing. He lay there and listened. Silence. Then that bird, whatever it was, let out its sad cry. Two o'clock, half past, ten to three . . . He got up and went out on to the landing. If she had come home she would close her bedroom door. It was wide open.

The chaotic untidiness, the unmade bed, the clothes scattered, tossed about, abandoned, confronted him, the offence they usually gave him softened by the moonlit dark. She wasn't home. Three was very late and it was after three now. He went downstairs, barefoot across the wide wood-floored hall, the only cool surface in the place, telling himself he would find her in the living room, in the kitchen, eating something, drinking that sparkling water they all poured down all the time. She wasn't there. He thought, what's the use of going back to bed, I'll never sleep. But what was he to do if he didn't go back? There was nothing to do in the night because that time was set aside for sleep. As he climbed the stairs a cry came to him that wasn't from that bird but from the baby. If it had been left to George he would have let the baby cry, though he had never let Amber cry. He went into the bedroom and saw Diana sitting on the side of the bed, stark naked. She slept like that. She always had. Of course he had liked it when they first knew each other, when they were first married. Now he thought it . . . unseemly. At his age and, come to that, at hers. She stood up without speaking to him, threw on the blue silk robe she had taken off at bedtime and went to see to the baby.

It took her about ten minutes to calm him. When she came back he had the light on and was sitting up in bed.

'She hasn't come in,' she said.

'I know.'

'You're going to have to put your foot down, aren't you? You're going to have to tell her this sort of behaviour is wholly unacceptable. If she wants to live under our roof and enjoy the advantages of living here, she'll have to be in by midnight at the latest. She's only just eighteen, for God's sake.'

'She's going, isn't she, in November?'

She made no answer. She'll be relieved, he thought. He turned off the light and in the renewed darkness heard the blue silk slide off her naked body. The smooth warm skin of her thigh brushed against him. It made him shiver in the heat.

The moon had gone, the dawn not yet come. He lay wakeful for an hour, then got up, went to the bathroom and put on his clothes. Old men's clothes, Amber said they were, flannel trousers, a shirt with a collar and cuffs, socks and lace-up brogues, but he didn't know what else to wear. Probably he had slept a little after Diana came back to bed. It was said that you slept, you dozed, even if you were sure you hadn't. While he had drifted off into that fitful sleep she might have come in. He stood waiting by the bedroom window, giving it five minutes, ten, before going out on to the landing, postponing the joy of seeing her door closed at last or the horror of finding it still open.

It was open.

He thought now, putting his long-held fear into words, something must have happened to her. The thing that happens to eighteen-year-old girls out alone at night. It was ten to five and growing light. The sky was pale and glowing, of that colour that has no name and no description unless it is to be like a pearl. Outside the air, which for hours had been heavy and close, felt fresh and cool. He thought, I will walk down to the corner, I will walk along the road, miles if necessary, until I find her. And if I don't, at least I won't be at home in that bed beside that woman, hearing that baby cry.

The only houses in Mill Lane were his own and, a hundred yards from it, on the other side, a terrace of three small villas. Why they had been built there a hundred and fifty years ago, to house whom, no one seemed to know. Outside the middle one a car stood parked by the grass verge. Briefly, George wondered why John Brooks left his car there overnight when there was room for it on his driveway. The thought was fleeting, carrying him back inevitably to Amber who had been assisted by Brooks in her efforts to use Diana's computer. Why not ask Diana herself? They had always disliked each other, those two, from the first. How could anyone dislike his little Amber?

But where was she? What had become of her? Walking on the Jewel Terrace side, he came to the end of Mill Lane and looked up and down the Myfleet Road. It was long and straight at this point, a single carriageway with fields and woods on either side of it, cats' eyes down its centre but no traffic signs or road markings apart from the signpost 'To Brimhurst St John', which pointed down Mill Lane. Walking along that road was pointless. He would do better to go back and fetch the car. Or he could phone that boy, that Ben Miller. Of course, it was outrageous to phone anyone at five in the morning and Miller wasn't Amber's boyfriend, she had no boyfriend, but he cared very little about that. Oh, the relief if she were at the Millers' in Myfleet – except that she wouldn't be. Why would she be?

He turned round and began to walk back on the other side. She might have stopped over with one of her Kingsmarkham friends, Lara or . . . was she called Megan? Or Samantha or Chris. He was clinging to straws and he knew it. He felt them float away from him downstream. The sun was coming up, already bringing a touch of heat. He stepped on to the grass verge, preferring its soft feel underfoot, looked to the left of him into the shade of the trees and saw something white gleaming there, half hidden by the tall attenuated weeds. A hammer knocked at his heart and a tide of terror tore through him. For a moment he couldn't move, only stand there with blindness enclosing his eyes. He took a step towards the white thing. Trying to see was the most painful thing he had ever done but he had to do it, he had to look. He saw her outflung hand, that stupid white watch with the Gollum face, and he fell forward. In a faint, perhaps, he didn't know, or just because lying across her body was the only place to be.

How long he lay there he was never sure. He wanted to die.

He thought that if he willed it hard enough he would die and they would be found together. It wasn't so. The delivery man bringing newspapers to his house and Jewel Terrace left his van at the corner and, walking down the lane, found him and her. When he refused to move, the delivery man phoned the police and waited for them to come.

Chapter 3

The woman who emerged from the house as they came up the drive had a child of about a year in her arms. Wexford and Detective Sergeant Hannah Goldsmith introduced themselves and the woman said, 'He's asleep. Our doctor has him under sedation.'

'I'd like to talk to you,' Wexford said. 'You are Mrs Marshalson?'

She nodded. Wexford had never before known a case of a father finding the murdered body of his daughter, never thought to see a bereaved parent prone over his child's corpse. He had daughters of his own but he could barely imagine himself in George Marshalson's position.

Once the man had been persuaded to go home, had been taken home, the pathologist had come. The photographers had come, the scene-of-crime officer, the whole panoply of those who attend a murder scene. For his part Wexford had needed to register only that she was very young, still in her teens, very good-looking, and that death had come through a violent blow to the head with a brick or piece of masonry.

He questioned the paper man who had found him and her, then he and Hannah had walked down the lane towards Clifton, the Marshalsons' house. Already the heat they were so used to that it had begun to feel normal was closing in. You could almost feel the temperature rising. The air was as still and heavy as at noon. Mill Lane was overhung with densely foliaged trees through the branches of which shafts of glare penetrated.

Clifton's front garden was flowerless, its shrubs wilting and its lawns yellow. The front door of the house opened and the woman came out before they were in talking distance. Politically correct to a degree Wexford thought ridiculous, Hannah said to him in the kindly and forbearing tone she often used when speaking to him, 'That will be his partner.'

'His wife, most likely.'

Hannah gave him the sort of look she kept for a middle-aged man who still called the woman he had married his wife. They followed Mrs Marshalson into the house. The child, a little boy, looked heavy to carry and she set him down. Not yet able to walk, he crawled rapidly across the polished wood floor, saying, 'Mama, Mama.'

Diana Marshalson took no notice of him. 'Come in here. I don't know what I can tell you. When he came back he was speechless. He's absolutely broken.' Their expressions must have told her the misapprehension both were under. 'Oh, I'm not her mother. I'm George's second wife.'

Wexford had learnt to detect signs of satisfaction on DS Goldsmith's face and in what she would have called her body language. He saw them now, the approving set of the mouth, the relaxation of her usually tense shoulders. That would have been brought about by Diana Marshalson's revealing she was the dead girl's stepmother. Hannah liked complex family arrangements. In her world they signified freedom of choice and self-assertiveness. A bunch of children, thought Wexford, each with a different father and some with different mothers, all living under one roof with four or five unrelated adults would be her ideal.

They went into a spacious living room, its french windows

wide open. He had already learnt that the Marshalsons were interior designers, based at Marshalson's Studio, Design and Restoration, in the Kingsbrook Centre of Kingsmarkham, but he would have known without being told. Such people's homes are always unmistakable, beautiful, the taste displayed impeccable, the ornaments just right and not too numerous, the colours exactly what one would have chosen if one possessed the gift for it, and at the same time the reverse of cosy, not the kind of place in which one would feel like curling up with a book and a glass of wine. Wexford sat down on a dark-grey sofa, Hannah on a pale-grey armchair, Diana Marshalson in another, which looked as if it had started life in a palace in Mandalay. Carved faces of angry gods glowered from its high arched back.

'What made your husband go out into the lane first thing this morning, Mrs Marshalson? What time was it exactly?'

'I don't know,' she said. 'I was asleep. He worried terribly when she was out at night. I suppose he realised she hadn't come in.'

'He went out to look for her?' Hannah sounded incredulous.

'I suppose so. He must have known – well, either that she wouldn't be there or that something awful had happened. But I don't know. He went out. I woke up when the child cried. That was at six thirty.' She listened as if for just such a cry. 'I must go and check on George. Do you mind waiting a minute? I'll be back with you as soon as I can.'

As she went out the little boy came in, still on all fours, but managing to pull himself up by holding on to the edge of an inlaid table that looked as if made of ebony and some pale blond wood. He was a handsome boy, olive-skinned but with red cheeks, his hair dark and curly, clustering in those rings only seen in very young children.

'Hello,' said Wexford. 'What's your name? Let me guess.

James? Jack? The most popular name of the moment is Archie, they tell me.'

'He's too young to know what you're saying, guv.'

Resisting the temptation to tell her he knew that, he'd had two of his own and four grandchildren, he said mildly that small children like people to talk to them, they like the sound and the attention. It doesn't much matter what you say. Hannah achieved a minimal shrug, a favourite gesture of hers. Diana Marshalson, he thought, looked young enough to be this child's mother but only just. Maybe forty-five or forty-six, a second wife who had perhaps never been married before and wanted a baby before it was too late. He rather admired her looks. Tall, handsome, dark-haired women with full figures were his type. His own wife was such a one.

She came back. 'He's fast asleep. It's the best thing for him, though I dread what it will be like when he wakes. He'll have to wake some time. He adored Amber. She was only just eighteen. What happened?'

'Early days to say,' said Hannah. 'She's dead. She was attacked. Really, that's all we know.'

The little boy tried to climb on to Diana Marshalson's lap. To Wexford it seemed that she hauled him up wearily and without much enthusiasm. 'Amber went out last evening? What time would that have been and where did she go?'

Amber's stepmother was choosing her words carefully. 'She went clubbing. To a place called Bling-Bling in Kingsmarkham. Between eight thirty and nine, I'd say. It sounds awful, I know, but they all do it. The friend who brought her home would have dropped her at the end of Mill Lane. It's happened before, she went to the club regularly and she was always all right.' The child caught hold of the pearl string she was wearing and began tugging at it. 'No, Brand, no, please.' She prised his fingers apart. 'Amber was waiting for her A level results. She'd just left school. Look, my husband's asleep but I think I should be with him. Sitting with him, you know. In case he wakes. I can't leave him alone any longer.'

'We'd just like . . .' Hannah began but Wexford stopped her.

'We will come back later in the day, Mrs Marshalson. Then perhaps you or your husband can give us the name of the friend and a few more details about Amber herself. We'll leave you now.'

Diana Marshalson stayed just long enough to open the door for them, the little boy seated on her hip.

'We could have got the friend's name, you know, guv,' said Hannah. 'It's not like she was the woman's mother.'

Although he knew it was accepted practice in police forces all over the country, Wexford very much disliked being called 'guv'. He didn't expect 'sir' these days but he would almost rather she had called him by his given name than that awful abbreviation. When she first joined his team he had gently asked her not to do it but it was as if he hadn't spoken. If she had been in any way disrespectful he would have had reason to reprove her but she hadn't, she never was. He was sure she liked, even admired, him – apart, that is, from his old-fashioned speech patterns and terminology.

Now she repeated what she had said because he hadn't replied. 'She may have been very attached to the girl,' he said. 'We don't yet know how long she had been her stepmother. Maybe from Amber's early childhood.'

Returning to the crime scene, Hannah said no more. It irked her that Wexford used the word 'girl'. Amber was a woman, she was eighteen. He would have to learn correct terms, she thought, or the rapidly changing world would simply leave him behind. Only the other day she had heard him talk about 'people' when he meant 'community'.

The body had gone. There were still several uniformed officers standing on the grass, half a dozen cars filling the entrance to the lane and the scene-of-crime officer stretching blue and white crime tape round the place where Amber Marshalson had lain. DS Karen Malahyde was standing next to a woman of about forty wearing jeans and a white T-shirt.

'This is Miss Burton, sir. She lives in one of those houses opposite. She was out last night and came home about midnight.'

'Lydia Burton,' the woman said. 'I live at number three Jewel Terrace. I was out with a friend. He brought me home in his car and after he'd gone I took my dog for a walk. Not for long, you know. But you have to walk them or they make a fuss.'

She was pretty rather than beautiful, with healthy pink skin and curly fair hair, her face without make-up but for mascara on her long eyelashes. This and the dangling silver dog-face earrings she wore gave a frivolous note to her austerity.

'Oh, yes, of course,' she said in answer to his question as to whether she had known Amber Marshalson. 'I'm the head teacher of Brimhurst Primary School. Amber was there for two or three years when her father first came to Brimhurst.'

'You saw her last night?'

'I only wish I had.'

'What happened?'

'I'm afraid I'm not a very observant person.'

Hannah Goldsmith disliked hearing people, women especially, belittle themselves. A sign of low self-esteem perhaps. It was surely by now a well-known fact that everyone was as valuable as everyone else. All had skills and gifts, and each was uniquely her (or just possibly his) own person. 'You took your dog out at – what? Twelve thirty?'

'I suppose so. About that. It was very dark down the lane because of the trees and I hadn't brought a torch. There was a bit of a moon and I walked the other way, up to the Myfleet road, and went along perhaps two hundred yards.' Metres, thought Hannah, metres. Why did it take people so long to learn? 'When I was coming back – back to the corner of Mill Lane, I mean – I saw a man. He was standing among the trees, in there.' Lydia Burton pointed into the woodland where Amber Marshalson's body had been found. 'It gave me quite a shock. He had his back to me. I don't think he saw me. I crossed the road. I was anxious to get home – I mean, seeing him there made me want to get home.'

'Can you describe this man, Miss Burton?'

Hannah shook her head impatiently. Why couldn't Wexford remember to say 'Ms'? 'I didn't see his face. He was wearing a hood. I mean, he was wearing a fleece with a hood. Well, mostly it's the young that wear them. I don't think he was that young. He wasn't a boy.'

'Tall or short? Fat or thin? How old?'

'Tallish,' she said. 'Quite thin, I think. I wish I'd taken more notice. But people always say that, I expect, don't they? I don't think he was that young, though I couldn't say how I know. Forty, I think. At least forty.'

'A pity you can't be more precise,' said Hannah. 'You didn't see Amber? No, I suppose not. Do you know if she often went clubbing?'

Wexford wished Hannah could bring herself to sound less censorious. She was a beautiful woman in any man's eyes, tall, slender, with the face of an El Greco saint and raven's-wing hair, but he wondered if she had ever been clubbing or possibly been up after eleven p.m. except in the course of duty.

'I really don't know,' Lydia Burton said. 'I was never close to Amber. We just said hi when we saw each other.' Wexford asked her who lived in the other houses in Jewel Terrace. 'The elderly man at number one is Mr Nash, then Mr and Mrs Brooks at number two, they're called John and Gwenda.'

They watched her let herself into the first house in the

terrace, a neat cottage as each of them was, red brick with a slate roof. Her front garden was a small square lawn surrounded by lavender bushes, Mr Nash's a plantation of huge sunflowers, ten feet tall, their sun-shaped faces turned skywards, the Brookses' stone paving within a rectangle of closely trimmed box hedges. The morning was already very hot with that heat which is peculiarly English, the air heavy with humidity, the sun scalding where it touched. Hannah Goldsmith looked to Wexford as unruffled as ever, her pale smooth skin as white as in winter, not a hair out of place.

'You can start on Jewel Terrace, Hannah,' he said. 'Before the occupants go to work. Take Baljinder with you.'

They made a beautiful couple, he thought, as Hannah and DC Bhattacharya crossed the road, the woman so slender, her hair streaming down her back like a dark waterfall, and the tall very upright man, impossibly thin, his cropped hair making hers look brown, his own was so pitch-black. Their profiles were somewhat alike, regular, classical, utterly Caucasian. They might have been brother and sister, offspring perhaps of a father from Iran and a mother from Iberia. Thinking how this area had changed in the short time since the Simisola case, when there had been no more than twelve people from ethnic minorities, he walked with Karen Malahyde back to his car where Donaldson waited at the wheel.

'Going to be a hot day, Jim.'

Donaldson said, 'Yes, sir,' in a stony way, treating this deeply banal remark with the contempt it deserved.

'You know, I don't think I've ever been here before. To Brimhurst, I mean.'

'It's not the sort of place you come to unless you know someone. All there is is the village hall and the church, and that's been locked up since the vicar went. The shop closed ten years ago.'

'How do you know all this?'

'My mum lives here,' said Donaldson. 'People like it because it's quiet. Nothing ever happens – well, not till this.'

'No. Can you turn up the air-conditioning?'

Post-mortems held no attractions for him but he attended them, looking the other way as much as he could. Detective Inspector Burden was less squeamish than he and fascinated by forensics. They sat and watched or, in Wexford's case, pretended to watch, while the pathologist opened Amber Marshalson's body and examined the dreadful damage to her head where she had been struck by some heavy object. He had asked the time of death and been told between midnight and three in the morning. More precisely than that she wouldn't commit herself.

'A brick was the weapon, I should think,' said Carina Laxton, 'but of course you won't take my word for that.'

'Certainly not,' said Burden who disliked her. Apart from her name and her lack of a thyroid cartilage, he had said to Wexford, she might as well be a man, and perhaps she once had been. You never knew these days. She had no breasts, no hips, her hair was crew-cut and no scrap of make-up had ever settled on her virgin face. He had, however, to admit that she was good at her job, less sharp-tongued and plain rude than Mavrikian and her attitude a far cry from the pomposities of Sir Hilary Tremlett.

'She died from that blow to the head, as I don't need to tell you,' she now said. 'It's not of course my place' – this said with an old-fashioned primness barely concealing arrogance – 'to identify the weapon. No doubt you will need the services of a plinthologist.'

'A *what?*'

'A brick expert.' Carina enunciated the words slowly and with great care in case he had difficulty understanding plain English.

19

'No doubt,' said Burden.

'Because a brick is not just a brick, you know.' Once she had left this to sink in, Carina said, 'There was no sexual assault. It'll all be in the report. She'd had a child, as I expect you know.'

'I didn't know,' said Wexford, astonished. 'She was only eighteen.'

'What's that supposed to mean, Reg?' Carina Laxton shook her head at him and pursed her lips. 'If she'd been twelve, that might have been cause for comment. Just.'

Brand, he thought. I wonder. Is he Amber's child, not Diana's? And is it Brand as in Ibsen or Brand as in Brandon? He said to Burden, 'Come up to my office, Mike, and later on we can go back to Mill Lane and see the Marshalsons together.'

They worked as a team whenever they could and particularly when Wexford felt that another hour or two in the company of Hannah Goldsmith might make him say things he would regret. They got on, he and Mike. If they couldn't quite say everything that came into their heads to each other, they got as near to doing this as two people ever can. He liked Mike better than anyone he knew after his own wife, children and grandchildren – and perhaps not exactly after them. For those seven people he loved and no one knew better than he that liking and loving are two different things. Even the Catholic Church at its most stringent had never attempted adjuring the faithful to *like* each other.

Up in his office with the new grey carpet, which was the gift of the grateful council-tax payers of Kingsmarkham, and the two yellow armchairs which were not but his own property, Burden took his characteristic perch on a corner of the rosewood desk. This large piece of furniture also belonged to Wexford, who kept it there along with the armchairs to show to the local media when they came nosing around, looking for evidence of police profligacy and corruption. Burden, always a sharp dresser, had lately taken to the kind of clothes known in the trade as 'smart casual'. The beautiful suits had gone to the back of the wardrobe or, in the case of the older ones, to the charity shop, and the detective inspector appeared in jeans and suede jacket over a white open-necked shirt. One of the things that came into Wexford's head which he couldn't say aloud was that his friend was just a fraction too old for jeans. Still, it was only a fraction and Burden was thin enough to wear them with elegance.

He had laid out on his desk the things that had been found in the pockets of Amber Marshalson's jacket. This white cotton garment, heavily stained with blood, had gone to the lab, as had her pink miniskirt, black camisole and bra, and pink and black thong. The contents of her pockets lay on the dark-red leather top of the desk.

'They don't have handbags any more,' said Wexford.

Burden was looking at a front-door key on a Gollum-faced ring to match her watch, a tube made of transparent plastic holding some bright pink substance, presumably a kind of lipstick, the packet with two cigarettes in it, the half-melted chocolate, still wrapped in foil, and the condom. Still a bit of a prude, he let his eyes linger on this last object and his mouth tightened.

'Better have one than not, surely,' said Wexford.

'That depends on how you intend to spend your evening. Wasn't she carrying any money?'

Wexford opened a drawer and brought out a transparent plastic bag with notes inside. Quite a lot of notes and all of them fifties.

'It still has to be checked for prints,' he said. 'There's a thousand pounds in there. It was loose in her right-hand jacket pocket along with the key and that tube of what, I believe, is lip gloss. The contraceptive, the cigarettes and the sweet were in the other pocket.'

'Where did she get hold of a thousand pounds?'

'That we shall have to discover,' said Wexford.

Chapter 4

The car turned into Mill Lane. Along the grass verge uniformed policemen – jacketless and without caps – were searching the ditch and the field on the other side of the hedge for the weapon. Crime tape, stretched along the pavement edge, isolated the area. On the opposite side of the road an old man stood among the sunflowers, leaning on a stick, staring at the searchers.

'It's been so dry for so long,' Wexford said. 'The killer could have parked a car anywhere along that verge without leaving a mark.'

The house called Clifton seemed to lie among its trees and shrubs peculiarly still and passive. It had that look of resting, of shutting down, buildings have at times of great heat. Alert expectancy would be for the bitter cold of deep winter. Windows were wide open but no one was to be seen. Though it was early evening, they got out of the car's cool interior to be met by a wall of heat.

'It feels like stepping out of the aircraft when you go away on holiday to Greece,' said Wexford. 'You can't believe it, it feels so good. In the middle of the night, as likely as not. But we hardly ever have warm nights here. Why don't we?'

'Search me. Something to do with the Gulf Stream, I expect. Most weather things are.'

'The Gulf Stream makes things warm, not cold.'

This time there was no one to meet them. Wexford rang the doorbell and Diana Marshalson opened the door. Again the little boy was with her, managing to stand if he clutched at the side of her loose trousers.

'I took it for granted this morning that he was yours,' Wexford said. 'But Amber was his mother, wasn't she?'

'I suppose I should have told you.'

Neither Wexford nor Burden made any comment on that. 'Is Brand short for anything or is that his name?'

She made a face, wrinkling her nose and drawing her mouth down. 'I'm afraid it's his name. Still, considering the names that are available these days, it's not too bad, is it? My husband has got up. He'll speak to you – but go easy with him, won't you? He's had a terrible shock.'

She took them into the big living room where her husband was lying on the grey sofa, propped up with grey-and-white cushions. Wexford had discovered that he was not yet sixty. With his wispy white hair fringing a bald patch, his deeply lined face and sagging belly, he looked much older. Allowances must be made, of course. He had just suffered an appalling loss. When the policemen came in he turned his head, his eyes falling on the child.

'Oh, God, he's so exactly like her,' he said. 'Just as she was at that age.'

He was holding a framed photograph in his hands. He thrust it at Wexford. 'Isn't he the living image of his . . . his mother?'

Wexford looked at the pictured face of a young saint seeing visions. 'Yes. Yes, he is. He's a lovely little boy.' He added, 'She was beautiful.' The expression on Diana Marshalson's face almost shocked him. If he had had to describe it he would have called it exasperated. Perhaps she had heard rather too much lately of how beautiful Amber had been and how good-looking Brand was.

He introduced himself, put in a word of sympathy. 'Do you feel up to answering a few questions, Mr Marshalson?'

'Oh, yes. I must, I know that.'

'This is Detective Inspector Burden who is a senior officer in my team. Mrs Marshalson, if you wouldn't mind leaving us for, say, fifteen minutes and then I'll come and talk to you, if I may.'

She picked Brand up and once more slung him on her right hip. It was a very convenient way, Wexford thought, for a woman to carry a child – difficult for a straight-up-and-down man – but, unlike a hug or a piggyback, it allowed few opportunities for demonstrative affection. Sitting there, the little boy couldn't lay his cheek against hers or she hold him close against her breast. Did he miss his mother? He must. Insofar as he could, he must have asked where she was. Then Wexford remembered from the morning his saying, 'Mama, Mama.'

'Sit down, why don't you?' said Marshalson in an empty voice.

'Thank you. I am sorry I have to question you at such a time but I'm afraid it's inevitable. What time did you expect your daughter home last night, Mr Marshalson?'

'I didn't exactly expect her at any particular time. I knew she'd get a lift home. Well, say, I thought she'd be in by two.'

Wexford struggled hard to stop himself showing violent disapproval. Burden didn't struggle at all and showed it plainly. 'Was this a frequent occurrence?'

'Amber had left school – well, sixth form college. She left after she'd done her A levels. She went back to school after Brand was born.' His voice wavered and cracked, and he cleared his throat. 'Her A level results have come. They came in the post this morning, three As and a B. She could have gone to Oxford.' The tears came into his eyes and shone there. 'I thought . . . I thought it was hard on her, stopping her going out to enjoy herself after what she'd been through.'

'Been through?'

Wexford shot his friend a warning look, which Burden took care not to see.

'Becoming pregnant, I mean, having the baby. Breaking up with her boyfriend. Well, seducer is what I call him. Corrupter.'

'Would that be Brand's father, Mr Marshalson?'

'Oh, yes, there was never anyone else,' said Marshalson, defending his dead daughter. 'It's my belief he raped her. Well, the . . . the first time – if there were other times, which I doubt.'

As if parents knew . . . 'May we have his name?' This was Burden, struggling, Wexford could tell, to keep a puritanical distaste out of his voice. 'Is he a local?'

'He's called Daniel Hilland and he's a student at Edinburgh University but of course he won't be up there now, it's the long vacation. His parents live locally, in Little Sewingbury. I've got their phone number somewhere.'

'Don't trouble, sir. We'll find it. Now how about the friends Amber met last night? And the one who brought her to the end of the road. If we could just have their names we'll leave you in peace.'

'Peace!' said Marshalson and the floodgates of speech opened. Tears poured down his face and his voice shook. 'Peace! I can't remember what that was. A long long time ago. Maybe not since I married Diana. No fault of hers, I'm not saying that, no fault of hers at all. Amber – well, she got pregnant and that was terrible, a terrible shock. She had the baby and brought it home for us to care for. For Diana to care for. That's what it amounted to.' His lip trembled. 'Diana had to leave her work at the studio. But all that was nothing, nothing, to this. How am I going to bear the sight of him now? He looks so like her. He looks like her when she was a little girl.'

Wexford thought Marshalson was going to begin sobbing but he made a tremendous effort to control himself, breathing deeply and laying his head against the grey-and-white cushions. His eyes closed, he said, 'I'm sorry. I'll get a grip on myself. The friends – ask Diana. Diana will know.'

'You came out to look for Amber, sir,' Burden said. 'Why was that?'

Marshalson shook his head, not in denial but perhaps in sorrow. 'I never slept well while she was out. Never. And I was right not to sleep, wasn't I? It wasn't needless worry, as Diana said, was it? It was all justified.'

'Perhaps it was, sir, but what did you hope to achieve by going out in the street at – five, was it? – at five in the morning?'

'I don't know. Things you do at that hour are irrational. I thought I might see her getting out of that boy's car. Time means nothing to them at that age. They don't get tired. I thought I might walk her home, take her arm, my princess, my poor little angel . . .'

Burden said what Wexford felt he wouldn't dare to say or wouldn't, at this stage, have the ruthless single-mindedness to say. 'Did you go out into the lane earlier? Did you go out at two, say, or three?'

If George Marshalson understood the purport of Burden's questions, he didn't show it. 'Only once. I only went out at five. I'd walked about the house earlier, I'd seen her bed was empty, but I only went out at five . . .' A sob cut off his last words.

Out in the hallway, Wexford looked around for signs of life. One of the doors, pale wood, flush and with a stainless steel tube handle, was ajar. From behind it Wexford suddenly heard the child's voice saying, 'Mama, mama.'

The words 'they pierce my heart' came into his head and he told himself not to be a sentimental fool. He pushed the door wide open and went in, Burden following. Brand, who seemed to gain more walking skills by the hour, as children of his age do, turned round from the window where he was standing and, disappointed, repeated his sad mantra: 'Mama, mama.'

Diana Marshalson was sitting on the floor amid wooden toys, a fluffy dog on wheels, a welter of coloured bricks. 'I hope it won't go on. I mean, I hope he'll forget her, for his own sake.'

Wexford waited to hear some show of sympathy for the little boy and sorrow for his mother but none came. Brand dropped on to all fours and crawled towards her, his expression puzzled. It looked as if she would take him in her arms and comfort him but she didn't. She got up.

'Do sit down. What can I do for you?'

They were in a kind of study with a desk, a filing cabinet, a computer on a work station, but soft furniture too, upholstered in pale-grey and orange tweed. The single glass door through which Brand had been looking, hoping to see his mother, gave on to a large garden, mostly lawn and shrubs. The excessive heat of the past weeks had turned the grass the yellow of California hills. Burden asked Diana Marshalson the question he hadn't cared to repeat to her grief-stricken husband.

'I only know her friends by their first names. Well, except the one who brought her to the end of the road. He's called Ben Miller and I think he lives in Myfleet. Yes, he does, that's right. Does that help?'

'Very much so,' said Wexford. 'Perhaps you'll tell us the friends' names that you do know.'

'As I said, I don't know any surnames. There was a Chris and a Megan and a Veryan. She came here once or twice. Oh, and Sam – I don't know if that's Samuel or Samantha – and Lara. I think Lara and Megan are sisters. Of course I can't say if she met any of them last night. No, Brand, not now, Di's busy.' She didn't quite push the child away. Her hands on his shoulders, she bent down to him and shook her head several times. 'No, Brand, do you hear me? Play with your dog. Take him for a walk round the room.' Her tone was cool, more the primary schoolteacher of Wexford's own youth than the nursery nurse of today. 'I don't know how I'm going to manage,' she said to the policemen. 'It's been hard enough with Amber here for part of every day. It's not even as if she was my daughter. It's not fair on me, is it?'

Wexford was seldom lost for words but he was then. He got up. Burden got up. Brand was walking round the room, pulling the dog on wheels behind him. Instead of 'Mama' this time, he said, 'Di,' and then, 'Di, Di, Di.'

Probably it wasn't a first time but still Wexford expected delight to show in Diana Marshalson's face. Unsmiling, she heard the little boy repeat the diminutive of her name, looked at him briefly and turned away.

'I've had most of the care of this child since he was born,' she said. 'It's not really fair, is it? Amber hated me from the start. She'd have hated anyone who married her father. Oh, I'm not saying she kept up a vendetta, she got used to me, she more or less accepted, but she always disliked me. Yet when he was born I was the one left to look after him when she was at school. After a while I left my job. I was in partnership with George but I had to give up. She never asked me, she took it for granted. Because I'd no children of my own, I must want to look after hers. When she went out in the evening and half the night I was the one who had to get up to him when he cried. Still, it's no good going on about it, is it? Worse than useless. Is there anything more you want to know?'

After a glance at Wexford, Burden said, 'Not now, thank you, Mrs Marshalson. We shall certainly want to see you again, though.'

In silence, they went out from a warm closeness into punishing heat, an August fast becoming the hottest on record. For

29

a few moments, before it became stifling, Wexford felt the heat like comfort. He put up his face to the sun as Burden exploded.

'God help me, but I'll have sleepless nights over that child. Poor little boy! His grandfather can't bear to look at him because he reminds him of his dead daughter. His step-grandmother makes no bones about finding him a nuisance. His mother is dead and by the sound of it she wasn't winning any prizes for nurturing. And they're not poor, they could afford a decent nanny, someone who might love him. It makes me sick to my stomach.'

'Calm down, Mike. I'm the emotional one, remember? We've got a reversal of roles here.'

They got into the car. Standing so long, it had warmed up inside. Donaldson started up and switched on the air-conditioning. The searchers were still scouring the meadow.

'I'd go over and see if they've found anything,' Wexford said, 'only I've got a press conference at six thirty. And by the way, I entirely agree with you about those Marshalsons and the little boy.'

'Why did the girl keep him? If she doesn't care for him she could have had him adopted. Plenty of people would – would treasure him. It's so wrong. The whole thing is. The girl's only just left school and she's out clubbing till all hours. I don't know what's happened to people, and so fast. Twenty years and their whole attitude to life has changed.'

'Perhaps we need to know them a little better before we're so judgemental.' Wexford felt sweat running down his chest and he wished he had a clean shirt to change into before the journalists came. 'They've had about the worst shock they could have had. D'you know what affected me most? Brand calling for his mother.'

'It didn't even seem to touch that Diana. It's enough to break your heart, yet it didn't even seem to touch her.' He looked at Wexford almost suspiciously. 'What are you thinking now?'

Not often inclined to lie, Wexford saw no need to be truthful about his thoughts. 'Just that I'd rather face the London papers any time than that new guy on the *Courier*.'

He returned to what truly occupied his mind, his own daughter.

Chapter 5

The conference lasted only a short time. There was little for Wexford and Sergeant Vine to tell the press and for once Darren Lovelace, the new man on the *Courier*, failed to make a nuisance of himself. Wexford spoke for two minutes on BBC 1's regional evening news and for three on Mid-Sussex Radio, and then it was over.

'Are you going to put Marshalson on to make an appeal?' Burden asked him.

'You know, I don't think I'm ever going to do that with anyone again. For one thing, it happens so often these days, it's so much routine, the public have got blasé about it. They probably switch off when the parent or lover or wife comes on, begging for the person who's killed their loved one – as we're supposed to call relatives – to come forward. Then there's the awkward fact that the bereaved one often turns out to be the killer.'

'You don't mean you suspect Marshalson?'

'At this point, Mike, I have no suspects.'

Resisting Burden's urging him to a drink in the Olive and Dove, Wexford went home, thinking how he had said earlier that their roles were reversed that day, for it was usually he who persuaded the inspector to after-hours meals and drinks and seldom the other way about. He wanted very much to hear what his wife had to say about Sylvia.

That she was pregnant and without husband or partner he already knew, and that there was something wrong. Dora had told him that, had told him what she knew, which wasn't much. Wrong with her or with the baby, neither knew, but Sylvia had promised to see her mother that day and tell her 'the whole thing'.

'What does that mean?' he had asked.

'I don't know, Reg. I wish she hadn't told me that much. I keep thinking she's found out the baby's got one chromosome too many or not enough. I just wish we'd been left in ignorance.'

'So do I.'

Like all his neighbours', and almost every private house in Kingsmarkham except those in Ploughman's Lane, Wexford's house was without air-conditioning but all the windows were open, including the french windows in the living room. Since the garden outside had lain in shadow for some hours, the room was a lot less hot than it might have been. A breeze had risen and fluttered the heavy-hanging leaves of lilacs.

'I'm going to have a drink,' Wexford said.

His wife's reply he had never heard on her lips before. 'Yes, I think you should. And get me one, would you? There's Sauvignon in the fridge and it should be icy cold by now.'

A fertile imagination is more trouble than it's worth. So he often thought and did now as he poured the wine into two large glasses, envisaging a handicapped child, more painfully beloved than its brothers, a beautiful brain-damaged child, a child doomed to die at birth but never to be forgotten . . . He shook his head as if to negate these thoughts. A handful of fattening calorie-filled cashew nuts went into a bowl. He loved cashew nuts with what he sometimes thought was an unhealthy fixation. Now was no time for what his old dad had called 'banting'.

'There's nothing wrong with it,' Dora said as he went back into the room. 'If that's what you've been thinking. I know I have. It's fine. Sylvia's four months pregnant and Neil's the father.'

'*What?*'

'Yes, you did hear me. That's what I said. Neil's the father. There's more to come, though. A lot more.'

Dora took an unladylike swig of her wine and sighed. 'I hoped they'd get back together, she and Neil. I always hoped that, as you know. But that's not it. He's apparently very happy with his girlfriend – what's she called?'

'Naomi.'

'He and Naomi are happy but for one thing. She can't have children and it's not a simple case of trying and failing. She'll never be able to have any.'

'I see what's coming,' said Wexford. 'I see it in all its horror. She's having this baby for them, she's going to give it to them.' Suddenly the room was hot, the shade outside made no difference. It was hot and close and oppressive, and he was sweating again, beads of sweat breaking out on his face. 'She's got Neil on her conscience because she thinks, or both of them think, that she left him for no reason. Just because she got fed up or bored. So she's making it up to him by having his baby as a present for him and his girlfriend. I know her. I know the way her mind works. Why can't she confine her social-worker do-gooding to her clients?'

'Every digit of your blood pressure is showing in your face,' said Dora. 'You want to calm down. You're even worse than I am.'

Hannah Goldsmith was writing her report. Or her new computer measuring twenty centimetres by twelve was writing it while she did the thinking, remembering and transcribing of her notes. Jewel Terrace, Brimhurst was her subject. She and Baljinder Bhattacharya had spent a large part of the day there and been back in the late afternoon. It was a piece of luck that of all the four occupants of the terrace, while two of them were in full-time employment, only one was out at work. Only John Brooks had left his house that morning, at the early hour of six thirty, to drive to the Stowerton Industrial Estate where he was security officer at a large manufacturing complex.

The occupant of number one was a horror. Hannah knew she shouldn't be ageist but really there were limits. She realised she had an irrational dislike of old men. Not old people, only men. This prejudice shouldn't be allowed to go on and perhaps she should think about having counselling for her problem. Briefly, she lifted her fingers from the computer, thinking about whether to go back to her old counsellor or find one special-ising in relations with the elderly. Still, for now she must get on with this report.

The horror's name was Henry Nash. His living room was hot and stuffy with a nasty chemical stench overlaying cooking smells, which Wexford would have known but which Hannah was too young to recognise as camphor. Henry himself wore a pair of striped trousers, evidently part of a suit, fraying blue braces and a collarless striped shirt done up tightly at the neck. Hannah, who found stubble on a man's chin attractive, particu-larly on Bal Bhattacharya's, was repelled by the half-inch growth of white beard on Henry Nash's.

All this would have mattered little in comparison with Henry's attitude towards herself, the senior officer. He addressed all his replies to DC Bhattacharya, irrespective of who had made the enquiry. She could see quite clearly that he was torn between racism and male chauvinism but finally decided that talking to an Asian man was preferable to talking to a white woman. When she asked him what time he had gone to bed the previous night he treated her question as if it had sexual undertones, made a sour face and spoke to Bal. 'You want to know what time I went to bed?'

'That's right, Mr Nash.'

'I don't know what it's got to do with you but it was ten o'clock. I always go to bed at ten. On the dot.'

Bal said that the elderly were well known to be light sleepers ('Who are you calling elderly?') and asked him if he had heard anything in the night. Though looking at least eighty, Mr Nash said he wasn't old enough to have broken nights. His neighbour John Brooks sometimes disturbed him, slamming his car door and starting the engine at six thirty, but not this morning. He had slept, had heard nothing and seen nothing until he looked out of the window just before eight and saw 'a crowd of folks trampling down' the grass verge opposite. He didn't know Amber Marshalson to speak to or her parents and didn't want to.

'She's that little chit who had an illegitimate baby. She wouldn't have dared show her face outside in my young days. And is anyone saying that was worse than what we've got now?'

Hannah was but she knew better than to say it out loud. She, who could hear of any perversion, incest, bestiality, extreme sadism, with equanimity, was deeply shocked by hearing the word 'illegitimate' on anyone's lips. Even more, perhaps, on these wrinkled lips, surrounded by white stubble. Illegitimate! It was unbelievable.

Bal's telling this appalling old man Amber had been murdered seemed to cause him no shame or embarrassment at what he had said. He merely nodded, as if the slaughter of a young girl was commonplace or only what should be expected by someone who sinned as she had done. Hannah put very little in her report about him and not much more about John and Gwenda Brooks at number two.

Gwenda was a young woman of about Hannah's own age but otherwise very different. Her mid-calf-length skirt was a brown and beige check and her blouse beige with a brooch at the neck. Hannah thought she had seen the last of permed hair when her grandmother died but Gwenda Brooks had a perm and one that was 'growing out'. In her rather querulous voice, she said how she had seen her husband off in his car at six thirty. Apparently, she had no job herself and she had no children. It mystified Hannah what she did all day. But that was far from the matter in hand. Mrs Brooks had slept all night until her alarm sounded at six a.m. She announced with pride that she was a very sound sleeper, nothing woke her. One piece of information interested Hannah because it was unexpected and would need further looking into.

'My husband was sleeping in the spare room,' Gwenda Brooks said. 'It's – well, it's on account of his snoring. He's not yet thirty but he snores like a . . .' She was unable to find any animal whose vocal emissions were comparable to John Brooks's snoring. 'Well, I don't know, but I can't sleep through it.'

'We'd like to speak to your husband,' Bal said. 'When does he get home?'

Not till seven thirty, it seemed. John Brooks's days were long. His wife knew the Marshalsons only 'to pass the time of day'. She had once spoken to Amber when she was out with the baby because Brand was 'so sweet, always smiling and happy'. She loved babies and longed to have one of her own. Her husband had once or twice been to Clifton to teach Amber something to do with a computer. Gwenda didn't quite know what. She had never been able to get the hang of computers herself.

'All butter-fingers,' she said to Hannah's disgust. 'I expect I'm dyslexic. That's always the excuse, isn't it?'

Hannah put it in her report. If the Marshalsons had a computer why did Amber want to know how to use it? Couldn't her stepmother have taught her? Anyway, it was inconceivable that someone of eighteen had no computer skills. They all did, from the age of five at least. Maybe John Brooks was having a secret relationship with Amber. This would be worth looking into.

Lydia Burton at number three was altogether better and more rewarding, though when Hannah thought about it she realised she might only be thinking this way because Ms Burton was her kind of woman, single, independent and with a highly responsible job. Amber Marshalson had attended the school, of which she was head teacher, for several years after her father and by then seriously ill mother had moved to Mill Lane. The first Mrs Marshalson had died when Amber was seven and her father had married a fellow director of his interior decorating company a year afterwards.

'Poor Amber became very difficult. She never really became reconciled to her stepmother, and that's a shame because Diana is a very nice woman. She's been wonderful with the baby.'

A small West Highland dog came into the room and jumped into Ms Burton's lap. Bal asked her again about walking her dog at half past midnight and she repeated her story of seeing the man in the hooded jacket standing among the trees. No, she didn't think he was holding anything, though perhaps he had a backpack. Yes, she was sure he had a backpack. If she closed her eyes she could see the bulge on his back.

'It might have been a sack or a bag slung over his shoulder. I was a bit frightened, you see. It was getting on for one by then and I was out alone with my dog. He obviously isn't much of a guard dog, as you can see, poor little chap. I crossed the road and let myself in here as fast as I could. I should have called the police, shouldn't I? One always thinks of these things when it's too late . . .'

In the great heat that continued next day they went on search-ing for the weapon, knowing only that they were looking for a lump of concrete, a breeze block, a brick or even an iron bar. Though he knew not to expect it yet, Wexford grew impatient waiting for the plinthologist's verdict.

Leaving her report on his desk, Hannah told him why she thought they hadn't found the weapon. By then they knew that Carina Laxton had fixed the time of death as nearer to two a.m. than one.

'Because whatever it was was inside his backpack, guv. The guy Lydia Burton saw had a backpack. What else could he have had in it but the brick or concrete block he used to kill Amber?'

'Maybe. I'm not calling off the search until the brick man comes up with something definite. He has a specimen from the wound to examine – poor devil.'

Hannah thought it unbecoming in someone of Wexford's rank – or indeed any rank – to make remarks with such an undercurrent of emotion running through them. This was the brick person's *job*. She was used to it, for God's sake. It was her career. Hannah deplored Wexford's use of the word 'man'. How did he know this expert wasn't a woman? The pathologist was, after all, as was the coroner who would open the inquest on Amber's body tomorrow.

'He brought the brick or whatever with him, guv,' she said, 'and when he'd . . . used it, he took it away with him.'

'Or maybe "she", Sergeant,' said Wexford in a neutral tone.

Chapter 6

Gated estates were not common in this part of Sussex but it seemed to Wexford that each time a new enclave of middle- to high-income houses was built, living there wasn't considered secure without gates at its entrance, a key-operated barrier and an English version of a concierge in the gate-house. The one on duty at Riverbank Close, Sewingbury, was a six-foot-five African in black jeans and T-shirt with 'Riverbank' in yellow letters on the front. The driver of the car which preceded Wexford's through the gateway received a hearty 'Good morning, sir' and a smile of radiant amiability, while Donaldson was greeted with cool contempt and a demand for identification from all of them.

'I suppose', said Burden when they were in, 'that if I lived here, if I were the kind of person who'd want to live here, I'd love that guy and feel really safe when he was on duty. As it is, however . . .'

Wexford nodded. 'I first saw this kind of set-up in California and hoped it wouldn't have to happen here.'

'Does it have to happen here?'

'I don't know, Mike. Where's the river bank, anyway?'

'About half a mile away and the river's what you might call

a tributary of the Kingsbrook if it hasn't dried up altogether by now.'

Some sort of building work was evidently going on at number four. A board in the front garden proclaimed the construction workers to be Surrage-Samphire, Specialist Decorators and Restorers, but as is the well-known way of builders, no decorator or restorer was in the house at present, though the hall, which seemed to be in the process of being panelled, was a chaos of wood strips, glue pots, brushes, sheets of paper and dust sheets. 'But no bricks,' as Wexford remarked to Burden later.

Though expected, they had to ring twice before someone came. She was a teenage girl in a denim miniskirt of extravagant shortness and a bustier so revealing that, much to Wexford's amusement, Burden turned away his eyes, though whether in prudery or suppressed lust was unclear.

'Yes?'

'We have an appointment with Mrs Hilland,' said Wexford, stepping in among the building materials without waiting to be invited. 'And you are?'

For a moment he thought she would tell him it was no business of his but she relented a little and said, 'Cosima Hilland.'

'Daniel is your brother?'

Everyone knew that, her look seemed to say. The question was unworthy of reply. Picking her way over pots and a stack of wood strips, she led them to a pair of double doors and said, 'In there,' as if she had only just thought better of giving the two of them a push.

The mother was about the same age as Diana Marshalson, a thin tired-looking woman of faded blonde prettiness. She got up from the chair in which she had been sitting, writing something at a desk. Wexford had noticed, from the moment they entered the house, that this was one of the few in the neighbourhood with efficient air-conditioning but perhaps only one among many in Riverbank Close. With not a window open, the room was as cool as on an autumn day. Outside the sun glared over parched lawns and distressed trees with drooping leaves.

The woman said nothing, neither smiled nor held out her hand, but raised her eyebrows to an alarming extent so that the pencilled ellipses vanished into her fringe. Wexford took this as an enquiry as to their business in her house rather like her daughter's 'Yes?'. Not invited to sit down, Burden sat in spite of this omission and Wexford, once she had returned to her chair, did so too. A phone call had been made before their visit but she gave no sign that she knew of it. She sat in silence, first gazing out of the window, then turning her eyes on Wexford.

He responded by asking her if he was right in thinking she was Mrs Hilland.

'Vivien Hilland, yes,' she said, her voice several degrees higher up the class scale than the home she lived in. A small manor house would have been more appropriate.

'You will have heard of Amber Marshalson's death.'

'I suppose that's why you're here.'

'Your son is the father of Amber's child, I believe.'

'I believe so too,' she said. 'From what I hear and read, about a third of all men who think they are their child's father are wrong. It may be so in this case but my husband and I prefer to think Daniel is Brand's father.'

'Quite so,' said Wexford, sighing inwardly. 'Where is your son now?'

'He's an undergraduate at the University of Edinburgh.' She paused as if expecting one of the policemen to ask her what an undergraduate was. 'At the moment, however,' she went on, 'he's in Finland with friends. By some lake or other.'

'Does he know of Amber's death?' Burden asked.

'My husband left a message on his mobile. He hasn't yet

responded. He and Amber were no longer . . . er, together. They hadn't been since six months before the child was born.'

'We'd like the number of his mobile, please, Mrs Hilland.'

She looked as if about to protest but shrugged instead and wrote it down on a piece of paper she tore from a block on the desk. The girl Cosima came in, drinking Coke out of a can. She passed them without a glance, opened one of the french doors and, leaving it open, wandered into the garden where she lay face-down on the lawn. Mrs Hilland's eyebrows went up again.

Footsteps sounded in the hall and a man put his head round the door. 'Just to let you know I'm going into town for that beading,' he said. 'I won't be long.'

He was handsome, blue-eyed and smiling. Her face softened. She almost simpered. 'All right, Ross. That's fine.'

'When did you last see Amber?' Wexford asked when the man had gone and Vivien Hilland's flush had faded.

'Oh, two or three weeks ago. She used to bring Brand quite often. After all, he's my grandson.'

'Yes.'

'The last time, if that's what you want to know, would have been – let me see – July the twentieth. I know the date because it was when the builders started. It was Diana Marshalson who recommended Ross Samphire. He'd done some work through their studio. I remember I was talking to him when she and Brand arrived.' There was nothing granny-like about Vivien Hilland but now she was talking about Brand a degree of animation had crept into her voice. She had even moved on to answering when no question had been asked. 'He's very like Daniel to look at and that's as it should be.' She didn't explain this rather cryptic remark. 'My husband and I would have preferred it if he and Amber could settle their differences and he live with her during his university holidays. That's why we were letting her have the flat. You do know about the flat?'

'No, we don't.'

43

'I thought Diana Marshalson would have told you. Of course you're aware that my husband, Stuart Hilland, that is, used to represent the parliamentary constituency of South Crenge in the House of Commons for the Conservative Party.' That had to be the most circumlocutory way possible of saying the man was a Tory MP, Wexford thought. 'When he went into the Commons we bought a flat in Crenthorne Heath but unfortunately he lost his seat when this terrible Labour government came in in nineteen-ninety-seven. We've had tenants in the flat since then, but the present lease comes to an end in November and we offered it to Amber.'

'She and Brand were going to move to London?'

'Well, very suburban London. She didn't object. She was thrilled at the prospect of having a place of her own. Kingsmarkham Council wouldn't do anything for her. Well, what can you expect?'

'This offer', said Burden, 'was conditional on Daniel also living there when he could?'

'Frankly, I thought it should have been but my husband wouldn't have it. No, it was just for her. I really don't understand why you're asking all these irrelevant questions. It was surely some paedophile or psychotic who killed her, wasn't it?'

'I don't think so,' said Wexford. 'I'd like to ask another question you may think irrelevant, Mrs Hilland. Where were you on Wednesday morning between, say, one and three a.m.?'

'I?' As if the room were full of people. 'I? In bed, of course.' Almost before the words were out second thoughts seemed to dawn on her. 'No, I wasn't. Of course I wasn't.' She had become almost human. 'My husband and I had been to this very long play in town – London, that is – and we had supper afterwards and he drove us home. We got in about half past two.'

'I see. Thank you. Your daughter was alone in this house?'

She took it for criticism. 'Cosima is a very responsible sixteen, she's quite old for her actual years.' As if on cue, the girl got up from her prone position on the grass and sauntered in, dropping her Coke can as she came.

'Daddy and I got in about half past two yesterday morning, didn't we?'

'I don't know,' Cosima said. 'I sleep at night.'

'You heard us. I know you did. You called out something to us.'

'"Fuck off," I expect it was. '

Vivien Hilland began to scream at her. 'How dare you use that language, you foul-mouthed little slut! And pick up that Coke can. Pick it up, go on.'

Shaking her head slowly from side to side so that briefly she looked like the mature person her mother had optimistically said she was, Cosima passed through the room and, once outside it, crashed up the stairs, as heavy-footed as someone three times her weight. Mrs Hilland turned on them a forced smile. 'Now, is that all?'

'For now,' said Wexford.

Outside, Burden wiped his forehead on an immaculate handkerchief, though it had been cool inside the house. 'She'll be picking up that can now.'

'Pity she wasted her energy on screaming reproaches when it's ten years too late. Why didn't Diana Marshalson tell us about the flat?'

'Thought it wasn't relevant, I dare say. Is it?'

'Don't know,' said Wexford. He withdrew his hand from the car door with a sharp exclamation; the metal was burning hot. 'God, that hurt. Diana, if not her husband, will have been overjoyed at the prospect of seeing the back of Amber whom she had never really got on with and the baby she obviously sees as a nuisance.'

'You're saying this takes away from her any motive for killing Amber. Not that I for one suspected her but she did dislike the girl and she has no alibi.'

'Her husband would have noticed if she'd left the house, surely. Anyway, she didn't. She had every reason for keeping Amber alive. Let her go to Crenthorne Heath and take Brand with her and maybe they'd hardly see her in the future.

'I wonder', he said as they got into the car, 'if there was some amount of jealous rivalry between the families. The Marshalsons, presumably since Diana left the company, don't seem to have been too flush with cash. They don't own a London flat. If they had, Amber and Brand would have been settled in it for a year by now.'

'And she'd be still alive.'

'Maybe. But "what ifs" are useless, aren't they? We can't read the book of fate and thank God for it. Chance and contingency rule all. For instance, Donaldson could take us back to Kingsmarkham via the Stowerton bypass or take the B road through Framhurst. If it was the latter we might pass under that bridge where there was the crash back in June and someone might drop a lump of concrete on us. If we take the bypass a truck might come off the slip road without looking and send us all to kingdom come. Who knows?'

'I always take the bypass, sir,' said Donaldson seriously. 'But if you'd rather it was Framhurst . . . ?'

'Oh, no, no,' said Wexford, laughing. 'We'll take your way.'

Ben Miller was a tall handsome boy, fair-haired and thin. Hannah and Baljinder had found him alone in his mother's little end-of-a-terrace house in Myfleet. She was at work, as was his sister, who also lived at home. Ben had been working at his computer, not as Hannah had at first thought playing some game on-line, but writing a dissertation for his return to university in six weeks' time.

'You seem to have been the last person to see Amber Marshalson alive,' Hannah said to him after they were all supplied with glasses of water, a necessary prerequisite for any

46

sort of conversation in the heat, which today was climbing to thirty-three. 'Can you tell us about that? In as much detail as you can manage, please.'

'I was at school with Amber,' Ben Miller said. 'We'd known each other for years and years. It's terrible, this thing that's happened to her. I can still hardly believe it.' He looked genuinely distressed. 'What happened that night? Well, I went to the Bling-Bling Club at around nine with my girlfriend. She lives in Kingsmarkham. She's called Samantha Collins.' Ah, the 'Sam' one, a woman after all, thought Hannah. 'And after a bit some other people we know joined us. There was Lara, Lara Bartlow. And Chris Williamson came with his girl-friend – what's she called? – oh, yes, Charlotte, Charlotte Probyn, and then two more girls came, Veryan and Liz, I've no idea what their other names are.

'I don't drink and Amber doesn't – didn't, I mean. Horrendous, isn't it, when you're talking about someone and you have to change the tense because they're dead? I was going to drive Sam home and then take Amber on to Brimhurst. God, I wish I'd taken her all the way to her house. It's just that we often all met in Kingsmarkham and I nearly always took her home – well, I did since her accident. She'd never driven since that happened. But I always dropped her at the end of Mill Lane. I never thought and I don't think she did . . .'

'What accident would that be, Ben?' Bal asked.

'When she went into the back of that car in Brimhurst Lane.'

'She drove into the back of a car?'

'You must know about it.' Ben Miller revealed himself to be one of the many who took it for granted that CID knew the details of every traffic accident. 'It was when some bastard dropped a lump of concrete off the Yorstone Bridge. It didn't hit Amber, it hit the car in front of her and she went into the back of it. Well, anyone would have. It shook her up and she

47

wouldn't drive again. I mean, I expect she would have eventually, but it was early days, the crash only happened in June.'

'And that's why you drove her home?'

'Did you think it was because she'd been drinking? She never touched alcohol. Or I never saw her. She used to but she said she gave up before Brand was born, just like she gave up cigarettes.'

Hannah knew that Bal's nod and slight smile indicated approval. He was well known for his almost pathological hatred of smoking. 'Can you remember what time you dropped Amber off?' he asked.

'To the minute. As we were coming along the Myfleet road Amber noticed I'd never put my car clock forward. You know, what we're supposed to do in March and October. "It's not twelve forty," she said. "It's got to be later than that," and I said, "It's one forty, I keep forgetting to put the clock on and I'm not going to bother now. It'll only have to go back again in a couple of months." That was just when I pulled up at the Mill Lane turning.'

'Did she stop in the car for a chat or anything?'

Ben Miller looked annoyed. 'No, she didn't. And there wasn't any "anything". There never was. I've got a girlfriend. She got out, said she'd see me later and that was the last I saw of her. The last for ever, my God.'

'She'd see you later?' said Hannah, failing to understand contemporary usage of the word. She was young but just too old for that.

'Next week, she meant.'

'And you drove straight home?'

'It took me maybe ten minutes.'

'Is there anyone who could confirm that?'

'I wouldn't think so for a moment.'

Back in Kingsmarkham Hannah found Wexford in his office with Burden. 'Miller's sister came home from work as we were leaving. She's a hairdresser. Pathetic that, isn't it? The boy's at university while she's a hairdresser.'

'You're a snob, Hannah,' said Burden.

'If you can be an education snob, I expect I am. I'm not a class snob. This woman couldn't confirm the time Ben got home. She was asleep. She says she never heard him come in. I spoke on the phone to the mother and she said the same. I can't think why he'd have hit her over the head with a brick, though, guv.'

'No, but we don't know much about him yet, do we?' said Burden.

'We're starting to know a good bit about her, though. She was driving one of the cars involved in that crash in Brimhurst Lane when some villain dropped a concrete block off the bridge.'

'Amber Marshalson was?' Wexford got up from his chair and came round the desk. 'I was talking about it this morning, Mike, d'you remember? See if you can get something up on the computer, will you, Hannah?'

As usual, Wexford admired the facility with which she did this. He would have got into a mess. He would have got into a hyperlink or inadvertently sent an e-mail attachment. Hannah described what she had found, reading parts of it from the site.

'There were two vehicles involved. A silver Honda and a grey Honda, both the same model. The silver Honda was driven by Amber Marshalson, aged seventeen, the grey Honda by James Andrew Ambrose, aged sixty-two, and his wife Mavis, sixty, was in the passenger seat.

'The grey Honda was being driven in the direction of Myfleet, as was the silver Honda, which was behind it. A concrete block weighing approximately twenty-two kilos was dropped from the bridge as the two Hondas passed beneath, striking Ambrose's car on the windscreen and bonnet, and causing the driver to lose control and collide with a tree. The silver Honda went into the back of the grey one. Amber Marshalson wasn't hurt but Ambrose sustained serious injuries – of what kind not specified here – and so did Mavis Ambrose, including a number of broken bones and a punctured lung.'

'And Mavis Ambrose has since died,' said Burden gloomily. 'We never got anyone for it. All we managed to find where the concrete block came from. Probably came from, I should say. Off a building site in Stowerton. But we couldn't trace it after that.'

'At the time,' Wexford said thoughtfully, 'we took it that this was just a random piece of violence, what we're supposed to believe is some deprived person taking revenge on society for his sufferings.' Hannah's opening her mouth to protest he ignored. 'But it wasn't, was it? It wasn't random and it wasn't aimed at James Ambrose. It was aimed at Amber Marshalson, only he confused the two Hondas, one following close upon the other. It was getting dark, too dark to read number plates, and he got the grey when he meant to get the silver.'

'He caused that woman's death,' said Hannah.

'She died in Amber's stead. He failed with Amber in June, so he tried again in August and this time', said Wexford grimly, 'he got it right.'

Chapter 7

When they were children, she and her sister, their father had taught them how to convert one temperature scale into another, a useful formula no one had ever mentioned at school. In those days it was always Fahrenheit you wanted to convert into Celsius – or Centigrade as they called it then. Something about multiplying by nine, dividing by five and subtracting thirty-two. Sylvia thought she ought to teach her boys. But not now. She wanted no encounters with Robin and Ben for at least an hour after what they had put her through. They had gone into the garden where they were playing in an inflatable pool, a grandparent's gift, and she hoped they would stay there until teatime.

She had told them about the baby. She was showing now and very soon they would notice. So she told them, remembering all those years ago when her mother had told her she was pregnant with Sheila. What had she said in reply? She had a vague idea it was something like, 'Will you love me best?' Like a policeman, Robin had said, 'Who's the father?'

No child would have said that when she was his age. She had blushed to hear it. 'Dad is.' And when she was Robin's age no child would have had to hear that either. Of course they wanted her and Neil to get back together. Never mind the two lovers she herself had had, never mind Naomi. They wanted their mother and their father living together again with them. All children wanted that.

'So Dad will be back here with us,' said Ben, a statement of fact, not a question.

'No,' she said. 'No.'

This was too much for them. They looked at her. Then Ben got out his Gameboy and held it, staring at it. And now, when it had come to the crunch, she funked it, she chickened out. She couldn't tell them – not *now* – that the baby wouldn't be 'theirs' but would go to Neil and Naomi, be put into Naomi's arms before she could make herself miserable by bonding with it.

'Well, that's it,' she said. 'That's my news. Now you know.'

They said nothing. What had she meant by saying to herself that they had put her through it? They had hardly said a word. It was her own deepening guilt that put her through it. Every day, nearly every hour. And this evening her parents were coming. She didn't know what her father would say. She never did know with him.

The young people Barry Vine and Lynn Fancourt interviewed all told much the same story. Amber had come alone to the Bling-Bling Club 'some time around ten' and stayed until a bit after one. Chris Williamson said he didn't notice the time and Charlotte Probyn said it was later because she and Chris left when Amber, Samantha and Ben Miller did. Lara Bartlow had already gone with James Sothern. She wasn't his girlfriend but they lived near each other on the Muriel Campden Estate. It was a puzzle to Sergeant Vine what they went to the club *for*: Ben, Amber and Veryan Colgate didn't drink, Liz Bellamy drank one glass of wine and the others beer. None of them danced because, it appeared, the boys wouldn't. Lynn Fancourt couldn't understand Vine's attitude but then she was much nearer their age.

'They're with their mates, aren't they? They talk, have a bit of a laugh. Then there's the music.'

'*Music*,' said Barry who was well-known for his preference for the operas of Bellini.

Samantha Collins was more interesting. Her dislike – jealousy? – of Amber was plain from the start of the interview. Unasked, she took a high moral tone. 'I always thought it was wrong her going clubbing. I said so often enough to Ben but he wouldn't see it my way. She had a year-old baby at home, for God's sake. I mean, never mind the ins and outs of whether anyone *ought* to get pregnant at just seventeen, she did and she'd got the baby and she ought to have got a better sense of responsibility, don't you think?'

Neither Barry nor Lynn had the least intention of saying what they thought and Barry believed in never stopping a possible witness when in full flood.

'I know you shouldn't speak ill of the dead but there's nothing I'm saying I hadn't said to her face. I believe in speaking my mind. Those parents of hers – well, her dad. He acted like he was broken-hearted when she told them she was pregnant. He didn't even like Brand. I'm not saying her and him'd have been unkind to him but would you leave your baby boy with people who didn't care for him? To go clubbing? And it wasn't just once in a blue moon, it was every week. But everything goes right for some people, doesn't it? You have to admit. I mean, getting the offer of a flat to live in! In London! I should be so lucky. I'd just love to live away from home. Me and Ben'd move in together if we could get a place but not a hope. Not for years and years with prices the way they are.'

Finding a brief second or two of silence in which to intervene, Lynn asked her to tell them about the evening in question.

'What's to tell? Ben picked me up and we went to Bling-Bling. She came after around half an hour or a bit after that.

She was later than normal, I don't know why. We all three left together, which actually I never liked. I mean, Ben might have been her friend but he's my *boy*friend and you don't want a third person there with her ears on stalks when you're saying goodnight, do you?'

'What time was that?'

'Maybe one fifteen, one twenty. It's no distance – well, you can see. I'd walk it but not at that hour, no thanks. Besides, why leave those two together? I had to for the drive to Brimhurst but I didn't like it, I can tell you. Actually, I may as well be honest with you, I couldn't wait for her to move into that place of the Hillands.'

'She died before she could do that,' said Barry and if there was admonition in his tone he didn't care. The interview left him with a strong feeling that the motive for Amber Marshalson's murder had something to do with the Crenthorne Heath flat.

Wexford, alone in his office, was having much the same idea. He had phoned Vivien Hilland and in the light of what he had learnt of the road crash on 24 June, asked her when the offer of the flat was first made.

'I don't know exactly when. But wait a minute – yes, I do. It was some time in June, two or three weeks before Amber's birthday. Amber was going to be eighteen in July. You know how these days they must have a party when they're eighteen and probably another when they're twenty-one. We'd been talking about it and then my husband came in and whispered something. I went out of the room with him and he said to me, why not offer her the flat when Mr and Mrs Klein go in October. Well, I went straight back in there and made the offer and she was absolutely ecstatic, said I couldn't have given her a better birthday present.'

'When was her birthday, Mrs Hilland?'

'Let me see. July the first, I think. No, July the second.'

'So your conversation about the flat was mid June?'

'It must have been.'

'Before the car accident Amber was involved in?'

Light dawned. 'Oh, yes, of course! It was about a week before.'

So was the attempt to kill her on 24 June made to prevent her having the flat or to make sure she never reached the age of eighteen? It failed. He must find out what happened when Amber was eighteen. Did she inherit money and in the event of her death, would someone else inherit it? Unlikely, for if she were financially sound she would hardly have needed to avail herself of the Hillands' offer. Another visit to the Marshalsons shouldn't be put off for too long. Meanwhile he must scrutinise the file on the concrete block dropped from the bridge and the death of Mrs Ambrose.

A dearth of witnesses was one of the first things he noticed. James Ambrose remembered hardly anything of what had happened. Mavis Ambrose was dead and so was Amber Marshalson by this time. Approaching the dip under Yorstone Bridge, Ambrose remembered only seeing a figure on the bridge, a vague shape, but man or woman he couldn't say. He thought the figure, of which he could only see the outline, was wearing a jacket with a hood. Wexford looked up from the file. At first it seemed too good to be true. A man in a hood had been on Yorstone Bridge before the attempt to kill Amber Marshalson and a man in a hood had been seen among the trees in Mill Lane before the successful attempt. Almost certainly the same man? He read on.

The woodland was dense on both sides of the bridge. On the southern side the track through the woods was a short cut to avoid the wide loop in Yorstone Lane, meeting the lane again just before the bridge, ran from the Kingsmarkham road to the bridge, a distance of rather less than a mile. In the days when you could build a house more or less where you liked, a cottage for woodman or gamekeeper had been put up at about the middle point of the track. Its occupant was a woman called Grace Morgan and she was ninety-three. It was coming up to dusk but not yet dark and she was looking out of her front-room window in the hope of seeing a pair of badgers, which sometimes appeared at this time, but she saw nothing that night.

The lump of concrete looked like other blocks on a building site in Stowerton and they seemed to be getting somewhere until similar blocks were found on sites in Kingsmarkham, Sewingbury and Pomfret, not to mention the villages. It seemed, as Burden remarked, as if the whole of mid Sussex was constantly being demolished and rebuilt and, of the ancient thoroughfares, no sooner was one street or half-street refurbished than work began on the next. Breeze blocks, concrete blocks, lumps of broken masonry abounded. Even if they were able to identify the particular site they wouldn't be able to infer that the block was taken by someone who lived nearby. Almost everyone had a car these days. It would have been a simple matter to drive after dark into Stowerton or York Street, Kingsmarkham or the old cheese market in Pomfret or the precincts of Sewingbury Minster, pick up the concrete block and drive home.

As to the weapon used on Amber Marshalson in the second and successful attempt, a call came to Wexford announcing the arrival of a Dr Clansfield who was asking to see him. 'Who is he?' he said to the duty sergeant who made the call.

'He says he's a plinthologist, sir, whatever that may be.'

'Send him up, will you?'

Wexford already had the plinthologist's report on his desk, though he hadn't yet even glanced at it, as he hastened to explain to the man who came into the room.

'No real point in your doing so,' said Dr Clansfield. 'I'm on my way home and I popped in to do it by word of mouth. Just in case you thought I hadn't done a thorough job.'

'Sit down.'

'Just for a moment. I can't stop. I've promised to take my daughter to the county tennis finals . . .'

And I have promised to take mine to task, thought Wexford. Or said to my wife I would.

'I don't know how much you know about bricks . . .'

'You build houses with them,' said Wexford, 'and that's about all.'

'Yes, well, I don't want to go into too much technical stuff but there are all sorts of bricks and they've changed over the years. Once there were Roman bricks. More like tiles, we'd say, and there are Tudor bricks which are bigger but still quite small and flat. Mostly in the eastern counties you'll find white bricks. They're actually yellow but the substance they're made from is that colour because there's sandstone – that is, no iron – in that part of the world.'

'I see.'

'Well, there are thousands of types of bricks these days. Extruded perforated wire-cut bricks come in smooth, sand-faced, drag-faced, rolled, rusticated. Then there's the smooth sanded type and the repressed.'

'A repressed brick?' said Wexford.

'It's just a term,' said the plinthologist without a smile. 'Like the waterstruck and the frogged, just terms.'

'I fancy the repressed ones. Can't I have one of those?'

This time Clansfield's mouth did stretch a little. 'That's the commonest type and as a matter of fact that's what you've got. There are literally millions in this country. Millions, if not billions.'

No one could live in Great Thatto without a car. There was no public transport. The lane which approached it from Myland was so narrow that for quite long stretches cars were unable to pass each other. There was no shop. The church was unlocked only on the first Sunday in the month when the vicar of St Mary, Myland, came over to take morning service. Sometimes not one inhabitant of Great Thatto – there were only sixty-one – attended that service, so the vicar locked up and went home again.

The remoteness of the place was redeemed by the scenery. Along the road you had the South Downs always on your right, Clusterwell Ring, a cone-shaped tree-crowned hill, on your left, and everywhere huge beeches spreading their green branches almost to meet above the narrow lane. At night it was as dark as the inside of a black velvet bag but when the stars appeared you could see them better here than anywhere else in Sussex.

Leaving Kingsmarkham very late with a feeling that he should have stayed behind and gone on studying that brick report, Wexford drove over to Great Thatto, wearily pulling into the lay-bys whenever another car approached him. They were all big cars too, those four-by-four people carriers, high up off the ground and with grinning bonnets like primitive masks.

'I'm tired,' he said to Dora. 'I shan't want anything to eat.'

She shook her head. 'I'm too cross to eat.'

Not for the first time Wexford wondered as he turned the car into the Old Rectory's drive what had possessed Sylvia and Neil to buy this place. It was big, true, it was in the depths of the country and paradise for children, but he had never seen an uglier house. Its mix of neo-Gothic and Arts and Crafts affronted his eyes. As for its surroundings, no one had done any gardening at Thatto Old Rectory for several years and the grounds had long returned to wilderness.

Warning of trouble ahead came when Dora stood aside and refused with a shake of her head to kiss her daughter. He kissed her. Why not? It wasn't his baby. He wasn't going to have to fight for it, argue over it, threaten a Judgement of Solomon division of it. Sylvia was very nervous, he could tell. If Dora was going to be difficult she could be the one to drive them home and he would have a glass of wine.

They went to sit by the wide-open french windows, Dora adamantly refusing to go outside on account of the mosquitoes. Swarms of them had gathered in the shady spots and begun their strange dance. They talked about Sylvia's mother's violent reaction to mosquito bites and her and her father's imperviousness. They talked about her sleeping sons and whether or not they would be going away on holiday. And then, because she could stand it no longer, Sylvia said, 'Well, you may as well tell me what you think about me having a baby for Naomi.'

'What I think will make no difference,' said Wexford.

'Perhaps not but I'd like to know what it is. OK, it's not your business but I can't bear this terribly important thing not even mentioned.'

Wexford waited a few seconds. 'You're wrong there. If you're part of a family what you do is bound to some extent to be the business of the others.'

'So what do you think? That I'm crazy, no doubt.'

'I think you will make yourself very unhappy.'

'So do I,' said Dora in a voice very unlike her usual low and gentle tones, 'and probably the boys too. All this stuff that happens now, IVF and cloning and women of sixty having babies, it's all wrong. It leads to misery and confusion.'

'I thought you might at least be pleased Neil's the father. I don't think Dad cares but I know you don't approve of me having . . . well, relationships with people.'

'No, I don't. Not while you have children living with you. And if you want to know, I don't approve of you. Not at present, I don't.'

Wexford asked her when the baby was due.

'December the fifth.'

'Before you started this,' said Dora bitterly, 'you might have thought it wasn't only your child you'd be giving away but our grandchild.'

'Look at it like this.' Sylvia's voice rose. 'If I wasn't going to hand it over to Neil and Naomi I wouldn't be having it at all. I've got a new job. I wouldn't have the time to look after a baby. You have to think of it as already theirs. I do.'

Wexford looked at her in an assessing way, without sympathy. 'I wish I believed you. You're not tough enough for this, Sylvia. Someone being "in denial" is a favourite phrase of yours. Well, I think you're in denial. You're hiding your true feelings under a bunch of social-worker gobbledegook.'

He saw the tears come into her eyes and overflow. Not he but her mother said in a tone he had never before heard from her, 'All right, that's better, cry. That's how you really feel, like having a good cry. Have a cry for the lot of us. In case you don't know it, you're wrecking this family.'

He said nothing but he took his wife's hand and held it. 'If you're ready we'll go home.'

Wexford kissed his daughter. Dora didn't kiss her. Her mother standing there, just standing, with her car keys in her hand, Sylvia turned her tearful face away. Wexford felt an angry longing to take her in his arms and hug her but he did nothing, only following Dora out of the house and thinking of a young mother, half Sylvia's age, who had died horribly and left her small boy motherless.

Chapter 8

Even seeing the child this morning brought Wexford such distress that he had to turn his attention immediately to George Marshalson. He wanted the child not to be there, out on the grass on a blanket, watched over by his indifferent step-grandmother. He wanted not to be exposed to the sight of innocence and obliviousness to what had happened, in case he inadvertently looked out of that window again. For sooner or later Brand must be told, the true explanation must be given to him of why his mother was no longer there and never coming back.

Burden, smart casual in linen trousers and jacket of fine striped cotton, had asked Marshalson about the events of 24 June. 'You didn't mention the accident in which Amber was involved.'

'Is it important?' His surprise seemed genuine. Wexford waited a few seconds, allowing him to think a little. Or not think, it appeared. 'Is there something I should be seeing here and don't?'

'Mr Marshalson, the concrete block which was dropped from the bridge hit the car in front of Amber's, a *grey* Honda as against a *silver* one, the two of them almost identical at dusk. I don't wish to cause you more pain than you're already suffering, but doesn't this suggest to you that this was an earlier attempt on her life?'

'My God. Oh, my God.' Marshalson seemed genuinely shocked and astonished.

'Yes, it's not pleasant to think of but I'm quite sure that what I've told you is the case. Was it Amber's own car?'

In a dazed tone, Marshalson said slowly, 'I gave it to her for her seventeenth birthday. That was before the child was born. Then, after that' – his voice faltered – 'she took lessons, passed her test. . . . Are you *sure*?'

'Yes, Mr Marshalson, I'm sure. Whoever aimed that concrete block at Amber's car meant to hit Amber's but hit Mr and Mrs Ambrose's in error. Mrs Ambrose died as a result. One thing all this shows us is that your daughter's murderer knew her and purposely set out with her death in view. I'm sorry to put it in these crude terms but at the same time I don't want to leave you in ignorance.'

'No, no. Thank you. It's a great shock, though, a great shock. Why should anyone make an enemy of Amber? She was only a young girl. She'd never harmed anyone, she was innocent.' His voice wavered and cracked. 'What's she supposed to have done? Nothing, I'm sure, it must be nothing.'

'We don't know, Mr Marshalson,' said Burden. 'You can be sure, though, that your daughter was in no way to blame.' He glanced at Wexford. 'There is one other thing.'

'Amber was carrying a thousand pounds in notes in the pocket of her jacket,' said Wexford.

Not even a great actor with years of stage experience could have produced such incredulity. First Marshalson said, 'Are you certain of that?' And when they assured him they were, 'I am absolutely dumbfounded. Amber hadn't any money except for the allowance – the very small allowance, I must say – I was able to give her. She couldn't even have saved up that sum, and she wasn't a saver. Where did it come from?'

'Again I have to say we don't know.'

'Why didn't . . . I mean, why didn't the person who did this take it?' It was plain that he shied away from such words as 'killer' or 'murderer'. 'Surely they must have done what they did for the money?'

'But they didn't take it, Mr Marshalson,' Wexford said gently. 'Did Amber have a bank account?'

'Yes, she did, but there was never anything much in it.'

'One more thing, Mr Marshalson,' said Burden, 'and then we'll leave you in peace. Did Amber inherit anything when she became eighteen?'

Again his incredulity seemed genuine. 'Amber, poor child? No, nothing.' In spite of his gift of a car, he seemed to need to justify the small allowance he gave his daughter. 'I'm not a rich man, Chief Inspector. I'll admit the company hasn't been doing well lately. My wife has money but that is hers.'

In the garden the little boy was awake. As children his age often do, he awoke with a cry that sounded more frustrated or petulant than distressed. The woman he called Di got up from her chair and lifted him in her arms – as someone might lift a shopping bag too heavy for its handles, Wexford thought. When they came close to the window on their way to some rear door he heard Brand say in wistful tones, 'Mama, Mama.'

As time passed he would come to accept Diana as his mother. No doubt the Social Services would intervene but it was almost beyond doubt that Brand would remain with his grandfather and a step-grandmother young and vigorous enough to have charge of his upbringing, one who would do her duty, be an efficient carer, see that he ate healthily and watched only a modicum of television. Many a natural mother does less, he thought.

She, he found, seemed to have no more idea of where the thousand pounds came from than her husband had. Brand now in a high chair, sucking orange juice out of a bottle and eating a sliced banana, Diana Marshalson showed nearly the same degree of surprise.

'What became of the car Amber was driving when the concrete block was dropped from the bridge in June?'

'It was a write-off.'

'I see. Mrs Marshalson, I should like to have a look at Amber's bedroom. There's no need for a thorough search as there would be if this were a case of a missing person but I should like to cast my eye over it. Inspector Burden will come with me.'

Apart from the bed which was neatly made, everything in the room was in chaos, exactly the way you would expect to find the bedroom of a teenage girl whose motherhood seemed extraneous and no natural part of her character. Clothes lay about. The two chairs were covered, enveloped, lost, in the piles of clothes and more hung from cupboard door handles on cleaners' wire hangers. When Wexford opened one of these doors it was hard to see how they could have been put away, so crammed was the interior with miniskirts, long skirts, jeans, trousers, tops, jackets, dresses and coats. The number of garments was matched by the quantity of cosmetics that stood about on every available surface. One drawer in the dresser refused to close, it was so stuffed full with bottles and jars, make-up brushes and tissues. From another trailed the end of a pink chiffon scarf and one leg of a pair of fishnet tights.

'Imagine the mayhem when Brand came in here,' said Wexford.

Burden shrugged. 'If he ever did. The child doesn't seem to have figured large in her life.'

'Well, we don't know that yet. Maybe we don't need to.' Wexford meant, let it stay that way so that I don't have to wake up in the night and worry about it. Sylvia's predicament is bad enough to be going on with. Let me have an ostrich side to my life.

Burden was opening those drawers, one after another. No

order was to be found anywhere. One, scattered with drifts of a white substance Burden said was talcum powder, also held screwed-up used tissues, balls of cotton wool and half-used jars of cosmetics. Others were crammed with a heterogeneous mix of things to wear, things to read, cuttings (or, rather, tearings) from magazines, ballpoint pens, single socks, sunglasses, curling tongs, a hairdryer and several hairbrushes and combs. Mixed up with them was a passport. Opening it, he looked first at Amber's photograph, for once a passport photograph that showed its subject as beautiful, then at an inside page on which were stamps for entry to Thailand on 7 December and exit on 21 December of the previous year. He passed it to Wexford and turned his attention to those of the garments that had pockets, and after a search which revealed two squashed cigarettes, several coins of small denomination, more used tissues and another condom, pulled out with something like triumph an envelope stuffed full of notes.

'I'll count them,' he said, 'but there's at least another thousand there, don't you think?'

'Probably. I'm mystified. Did she steal it or earn it?'

'If she earned it,' said Burden, pulling a long face, 'she must have been on the game. There's no other way she could have got that much.'

'For such a puritan,' said Wexford, 'your mind steams along lurid channels.'

In Kingsmarkham High Street the digital clock outside the Kingsbrook Shopping Centre showed the time as eleven fifteen and the temperature at thirty-three degrees.

'That's ninety to you,' said Burden kindly.

'All right, I can work it out. I taught my daughters how to do it. It's just that the mental arithmetic takes time.'

A good-looking young man with longish fair hair was leaning against the boot of a car in the police station parking area. He had positioned his Audi in the bay marked 'Reserved for the Chief Constable'. Wexford went over to him and, meeting his eyes, dark blue with very clear whites, said sharply, 'What can I do for you?'

'It's really what I can do for you. Or can't do, come to that.' A long brown hand was extended. 'Daniel Hilland. How do you do?'

There is really no answer to this and Wexford made none. Nor did he shake hands. 'You can't leave your car there. Whatever they do out there, in here we clamp.'

'I thought you wanted to see me. Can't we go inside?'

'Not leaving your car there, we can't. It won't take long and then you can remove it. You're aware of what has happened to your former girlfriend?'

Hilland nodded. 'Of course.'

'I believe you've been on holiday in Finland?'

Another nod.

'I'd like to see your passport, Mr Hilland, and any other documentation you may have to prove you were there at the relevant time.'

Hilland stared. 'What do you mean by documentation?'

'You might, for instance have the receipt for your air fare, the bit that looks almost identical to your ticket but isn't valid for transport.'

Feeling the heat, Hilland looked peevishly at him and then at Burden. 'No one keeps those things.'

'It's unwise not to. Perhaps you've kept your receipted hotel bill?'

'I might have done if I'd stayed in a hotel. We were camping. Look, you can't seriously think I had anything to do with Amber's murder. That's surreal. I mean, why would I?'

'It's not the business of the law to look for motives, Mr Hilland. But at the moment we are just trying to eliminate people from our enquiries. It's not possible for me to exclude you if you can't show me any evidence that you were where you say you were. No doubt one of the friends you were with can tell me.'

'I suppose I'll have to ask them.' Hilland spoke in an even more ungracious tone than he had up till then. 'It's a bore but I suppose they will. They don't like this sort of thing.'

'What sort of thing would that be?'

'Oh, well, the police and murder and suspects and all that sort of thing, especially when everyone knows it's some psychopath who's addicted to porn on the Web that goes for these girls.'

Wexford didn't have to remind himself that among 'these girls' was the mother of Hilland's child. He had seldom if ever met a more objectionable young man. A yob from one of the estates, until now categorised at Kingsmarkham police station as 'lowlife', was preferable. 'Right,' he said. 'I'd like the name and home address of one of these friends of yours and I'd like it now.'

Surprised by Wexford's change of tone, Hilland looked sulky but he gave the Chief Inspector two names, one with an address in Wales, the other nearer home in Lewes.

'When her body was found, a thousand pounds was in her jacket pocket. Have you any idea how she came by such a large sum?'

Hilland managed to look as if it wasn't a large sum to him by raising his eyebrows and setting his head on one side. 'No idea. I never saw her, you know. We split up before the child was born. Not that there was ever much to split.'

Reminding himself to keep his temper at all costs, Wexford tried asking why she needed money, though he knew very well that need is not a motive relevant to stealing or any other ways, allowed or illicit, of acquiring it.

'She was going to live in my dad's flat,' Hilland said. 'She'd need something to live *on*. It'd be different from home with

67

her dad and what's-her-name? – Diana. Amber hadn't anything of her own. And before you ask, with censoriousness in every syllable, no, I don't give her anything. I haven't anything to give. I'm a student, OK?'

'Right. That's all,' said Wexford shortly, glad that the man was feeling the heat, sweat pouring down his face and soaking his armpits. 'I'd like you to bring your passport and whatever other documentation you have back here tomorrow morning. You can go now and please don't park your car in here again.'

Chapter 9

Global warming had compelled the management of the Olive and Dove Hotel to install air-conditioning, a rarity in Kingsmarkham. On the grounds that the doors kept opening and shutting, it had not been extended to the public and saloon bars, only to the lounge bar. There Wexford and Burden sat, the television on, the early evening news telling them that the temperature had been thirty-two degrees.

'It's actually cold in here,' Burden said, pressing the 'off' button on the remote. 'They can never get it right, can they?'

'It's OK for an hour or so.' Wexford took their two drinks proffered by the barman and passed one to Burden. Paying for them, he said, 'Have one yourself. These glasses are quite cold enough. The day you start putting ice in beer I stop coming in here.'

'Excellent,' said the barman, 'as that will never be.'

When he had gone, Wexford said, 'That Hilland is a complete little shit. I know you don't like that word but nothing else quite expresses him. He never once mentioned his child and he talks about Amber as if she were a one-night stand.'

Burden shrugged. He wasn't surprised. 'The mother and the sister gave us a foretaste of how he'd be. An idea has occurred to me that I think we should do something about. That money that was in Amber's pocket, it must have got there after she went out, right? She wasn't so butterfly-minded that she went around with a thousand quid on her for days and days.'

'I suppose not. I mean, you're right.'

'So someone gave it to her that night. Not after she got to the Bling-Bling Club they didn't. She was with the others all the time and one of them would have noticed. I mean, it's not like handing someone a couple of pound coins, is it? Well, we know what time she left home to go to the club but we don't know what time she got there. No one said, though Samantha Collins said she got there later than usual.'

'You mean, however she'd earned the money, someone gave it to her between the time she left her home and went to the club. There can't have been much time, Mike.'

'Why can't there? Diana Marshalson said she left between half-eight and nine. It's five minutes, if that, to the bus stop and the bus takes twenty minutes to Kingsmarkham. Even allowing for the bus being late and her taking ten minutes to get to the stop and not leaving till ten to nine, she'd still be in Kingsmarkham by nine thirty. With a half-hour for her transaction she could get to the club at ten.'

'Bit late, isn't it?'

'To you and me, Reg,' said Burden, 'it's very late to go anywhere. It's more like the time to leave and get home. But not to the young. These places don't really get going till nearer midnight.'

'OK, we must find out the bus times, whether the bus ran on time, and see if we can get a more precise time of her leaving from George Marshalson. I'm afraid I'd taken it for granted young Hilland was paying her child support. With that and Jobseekers' Allowance, which she'd presumably take, and child benefit, she'd have been just about all right. Now I'm beginning to see why she needed money.'

'I thought she wanted to go on to higher education?'

'Mike, I'm starting to believe that was George Marshalson's wishful thinking. How could she have? What would she do with Brand?'

'Come to that,' said Burden, 'what did she do with him when she went to Thailand?'

'Left him with Dad and Diana, I suppose. But we must find out more about Thailand. It's possible, of course, that they all went. A family holiday. And we need to have a look at Amber's bank account, if she had one. The two thousand we've found may not be all she had. Shall we have another?'

'Why not?' said Burden.

He sat where he was while Wexford went off to fetch their drinks. An idea had come to him. A pretty obvious idea, he thought, wondering why he hadn't seized upon it in the girl's bedroom. Could she have taken such a risk? Could she have been such a fool? Coming back with a glass in each hand, Wexford said, 'You look as if you've had a shock.'

'If I have I've given it to myself. Reg, I think we have to go back to Brimhurst and the Marshalsons and we have to go soon. What time is it?'

'Twenty past eight. What's come up?'

'When we were going through those drawers in Amber's bedroom,' Burden said, 'we found something we said was spilt talcum powder. I didn't think anything of it at the time, I just accepted it, and then in conjunction with the other stuff we've found out, I understood something. Girls her age don't use talcum powder, they've never heard of it, they don't know what it's for. It's as out of date as – as – pound notes and phone boxes and gramophone records.'

'So what was it? Oh, yes, I see . . . I'm going to call Marshalson and then get Donaldson to pick us up here in ten minutes.'

* * *

'I very much doubt if there was more than, say, fifty pounds in Amber's account,' George Marshalson said. 'I opened it for her' – he sighed heavily – 'when she was sixteen. For her sixteenth birthday. With a hundred pounds. I doubt if she added to it. If they make any difficulties at the bank about letting you have access, I'll willingly give my permission.'

Wexford thanked him. The house seemed oppressively silent. At nine o'clock Brand had long been in bed. The temperature, though not to be described as 'the cool of the evening', had fallen a long way below the un-English heat of noon. Although all the windows were still wide open, a large bumble bee crept up one pane, hopelessly seeking a way of escape. Gnats danced in shadows on the lawn.

Diana Marshalson was walking about in the garden, watering dying plants from a can. She shook her head at a shrub whose leaves had turned yellow and came towards the house, dropping the empty can and stepping inside by way of the open french window. 'It's hopeless,' she said, sinking into a chair. 'Everything needs a downpour going on all night, not half a can of water. Still' – she looked at her husband – 'what does it matter? What does anything really matter now?'

No one had an answer for that. 'I see from her passport', Wexford said, 'that Amber went to Thailand last December?'

'We all went,' Diana said. 'Well, not Brand. We left him with my sister.'

A three-month-old baby, Wexford thought indignantly, left with a comparative stranger. Then he told himself sternly to leave it, it wasn't his business. He was becoming obsessed about this child, sensitive to every possible hint of neglect or indifference. He must stop himself, get a grip. 'That is, you, your husband and Amber?'

'It was arranged a month before Brand was born,' Amber's father said. 'Amber was all for taking him too but of course she felt differently when the time came. Diana's sister Laura offered to have him and Amber jumped at the chance.'

'I'd like to have another look at Amber's bedroom,' Wexford said.

Just as they were going, Diana said, for no obvious reason, 'If you're interested in Amber's lifestyle, you may care to know she went on a trip to Frankfurt in May.'

'Did she go alone?' Burden asked.

'A friend went with her. A girl – I don't remember her name.'

Annoyed with himself for asking, Wexford said, 'Who looked after Brand? Your sister?'

'She wasn't going to take that on so soon after the first time, was she? I did, of course. The twenty-second of May it was and never mind that I had an important engagement. I'm actually surprised I was excused nursemaid duties and allowed to go to Thailand.'

'Diana,' said George Marshalson. 'Please.' He sounded broken. 'Poor Amber's dead.'

'I know, George. I'm sorry. We're all on edge.'

A curious way of defining bereavement, as Wexford remarked to Burden when they were upstairs.

'She hated that girl,' Burden said.

'Yes, but I'm wondering if what she felt for her when she was alive wasn't nearer indifference and maybe impatience. It was her *dying* which brought out the hatred because, by dying, she encumbered her with the child.'

Burden scraped a little of the white powder into a plastic envelope and sealed it. Then, moistening his forefinger, he ran it lightly across the remaining drift and sniffed it. 'It's not what you thought and I thought,' he said. 'It's not talcum either. I've smelt that smell before, years ago when my son John was at school but God knows what it is.'

Downstairs they were together in the living room, George

lying back in his armchair, his eyes shut, Diana with a laptop on her knees. The screen was filled with the largely turquoise-blue page, bidding users to search the Web. She turned round as they came in.

Burden said, 'Mrs Marshalson, perhaps you can tell us. Did Amber have athlete's foot?'

'How on earth did you know? She thought she picked it up at the new Kingsmarkham swimming pool and she found it humiliating.'

'And I was sure it was cocaine,' Burden said when they were outside once more. 'But, of course, our failure so far to discover any evidence of drugs doesn't mean she wasn't trafficking. Maybe she was. Maybe that's where the money came from. By the way, who was the other girl?'

'One of the crowd at the Bling-Bling, I expect, but we shall have to find out.'

Chapter 10

The bank in Kingsmarkham High Street made no difficulties about granting access to Amber Marshalson's bank account. 'The poor girl's dead, after all,' as the manager said. George Marshalson had been wrong but not far wrong. The sum in Amber's account had swollen to seventy-five pounds. Nothing had been paid in for over two years and nothing had been drawn out.

'Either she didn't trust banks,' said Wexford, 'or, more likely, she hadn't yet got around to paying that two thousand in. It must all have come to her very recently.'

'She went to Thailand but if she was trafficking she wasn't paid, so it was probably an innocent holiday.'

'You mean, she didn't pay whatever she was paid into her bank account. She may have had payment in cash and just spent it. It looks as if she and possibly the friend carried something to Frankfurt – one of the main European hubs, is Frankfurt – and met someone there who carried whatever it was on to its ultimate destination. When she came home she got paid.'

Wexford knew no more about drugs than any police officer in his position who hadn't specialised in them but Burden had become an expert, largely through masterminding the big substance abuse purge carried out in Kingsmarkham and the surrounding villages the year before. 'She carried it?' he now said. 'Do we mean carried in her luggage or was she a body packer?'

The idea of someone swallowing a package of hard drugs and then excreting it at the journey's end always turned Wexford queasy. 'God, I hope not.'

'We've got a lot of work to do in this area. Find who the other girl was. Maybe get a sniffer dog into Clifton. Question all those pals of hers again.'

In his hot and stuffy little living room, Hannah and Bal were having what Bal cosily called 'a little chat' with Henry Nash. In her eyes, the room was just like a section of a museum of bygones. Everything in it, including its owner, was close on a century old and a lot of it much older. The few books, which included a Bible and a *Hymns Ancient and Modern*, were bound in scuffed black leather and their fellows, with indecipherable titles, in dark green and dark red. Two tinted lithographs on the wall above Mr Nash's head were of plump maidens in a Victorian idea of Grecian dress, drooping over draped urns. The carpet was the Turkey kind, very worn, and the chairs of the 'fireside' type. One corner was filled by an upright piano, on whose stand rested the music for 'The Bluebells of Scotland'.

The telephone was, naturally, nowhere near as old as the piano or the Grecian maidens but it looked to Hannah to date back to the fifties. It was black with, instead of a keypad, a dial of a kind she had never seen before. On this instrument Mr Nash had phoned Kingsmarkham CID to tell them he had important information. But now Hannah and Baljinder were here, he seemed to have no intention of imparting it until he had delivered a diatribe against a number of aspects of modern life. Single parents, fertility treatment, calling the unemployed 'jobseekers', benefit fraud, foreigners, particularly those of a different physical appearance and colouring from his own, all came in for vituperation. As Hannah's resentment mounted, she felt particularly for Bal, though he seemed impervious to such expressions as 'blackie' and 'slant-eyed', listening with calm patience and smiling slightly.

Her indignation made her hotter than ever. She felt sweat pricking the skin of her face and a drop actually trickle down, warm and salty, on to her lips. As a post-feminist, she knew very well that she ought to take this in her stride. Hadn't she as much right to sweat as a man? But she knew, too, that a great gulf is fixed between what we think and what we feel. She had a right as a human being to sweat but she *felt* Bal would notice and how dreadful it would be if damp patches appeared on her crisp snowy white shirt. Suddenly angry, she cut short Mr Nash on the subject of television after the nine-o'clock watershed. 'You have some information for us.'

Disgruntled, he frowned at her. 'I was talking to this young man,' he said to her fury. 'You people don't know the meaning of patience.'

Bal said, 'Patience is a luxury, Mr Nash. We haven't a lot of time.'

In spite of having insulted his ethnic group five minutes before and suggested that everyone of his origins should go back to 'them temples and elephants and suchlike where they belong', Henry Nash now looked at him with new respect. 'All right,' he said. 'You have to do your job. I know what work is, unlike some I could name.' He kept his eyes carefully averted from Hannah, as if he were some kind of ascetic and she a belly dancer. 'It's the chap next door. Brooks, he's called. John Brooks. Must be hundreds of folks called John Brooks but there it is.'

Because he had fallen silent, Hannah said, 'What about him, Mr Nash?'

He answered her but he looked at Bal while he was speaking as if it was the man rather than the woman who had asked the question. 'He goes out in the night-time,' he said on a note of triumph.

'Goes out?' Bal said. 'What do you mean, "goes out"? What sort of time? You've seen him?'

'I've heard his car. He keeps it in the road. Why, you may well ask, when he's got a bit of concrete at the side. I'll tell you. *Because his wife sleeps in the back.* They have separate rooms if you've ever heard of such a thing. I sleep in the front and when he starts the car it wakes me up.'

'What time, Mr Nash?'

'Any time it is, one, two, three, but it's mostly around one. She won't hear him in the back. She won't know he's gone. That's what comes of separate rooms. No wonder she don't have no babies. He snores, she says. Yes, I bet he snores. Does it on purpose to get himself in another room.'

'Did he go out on the night Amber Marshalson was killed?'

'Don't know. I don't always wake up, not if I've got nothing on my mind. Not if I'm not tossing and turning, thinking about the state of the world.'

The thought of tossing and turning, as against remaining perfectly still, brought a fresh flow of sweat to Hannah's face. She could feel it on her body now, a stream of it running down between her breasts. She got up, feeling she might faint if she stayed another minute in that hot and airless room. Outside, in the shade, it was cooler and at least the air felt fresher.

'We'll have to talk to this Brooks,' she said, 'and he won't be home till the evening. If he was out that night he may have seen something but I can't see him as the perpetrator. If he wanted to kill Amber he'd hardly have got into his car and driven off somewhere.'

'No,' said Bal, 'but driving off would give him an alibi and he could sneak back on foot to do the deed.'

78

'I suppose he could.'

He was looking hard at her and suddenly she thought how people of what she called 'Asian subcontinental origin' – she wouldn't have objected to being described as of 'Caucasian-Celtic origin' herself – were so often as immaculate as if all their clothes were new. A damp patch had definitely appeared across her midriff.

'You look so hot, Hannah.' It was the first time he had called her by her given name as against 'sarge'. 'Come on, I've got sparkling water in a refrigerated bag in the car. That'll set you up.'

Daniel Hilland's friends with whom he had spent his Finland holiday had not yet been run to earth. It seemed that they had gone, in Daniel's own words, on to 'Iceland or Latvia or some-where like that' and the hunt for them was so far unsuccess-ful. Ben Miller's alibi, resting solely on his word that he had dropped Amber off on the Myfleet road at twenty minutes to two and reached home ten minutes later, couldn't be substan-tiated. Neither his mother nor his sister had heard him come in. He often came home late and had learnt to be silent about it, even taking off his shoes at the foot of the stairs. Mrs Miller's 'But I know he came in – what else would he have done?' was worse than useless.

George and Diana Marshalson alibied each other, an unsat-isfactory state of affairs, but in the absence of motive, seeing that Diana, at least, had the best of reasons for wanting to keep Amber alive, this was no line to pursue. Besides, Wexford was sure that George's love for his daughter was far stronger than what he felt for his wife and if it came to Amber's murder, he would never consider shielding his wife. That marriage, and what the Marshalsons felt for each other, interested Wexford. He had begun to believe there was some reason for the fading of the love George had once felt, something Diana had done.

But that something was certainly not the murder of his only child.

The scrapings from the drawer in Amber's bedroom were analysed and it was as Burden had thought. This was the usual widely used remedy for athlete's foot. Did he have to abandon his theory of why Amber had been twice out of the country this year? Not yet. The fashion for drinking bottled water had largely passed Wexford by but now, with the temperature once again moving up through the thirties, he was gulping down glass after glass of it. Sitting opposite Hannah Goldsmith, a bottle of the sparkling kind and a pile of paperwork on the desk between them, he listened while she told him about John Brooks and Henry Nash's malice.

'I'm going back,' she said, 'when he's likely to get home.'

'Be careful what you say if the wife's there.'

'Surely it's best if she knows, guv. A relationship is no more than a sham if the partners aren't honest with each other.'

'"Each other" are the operative words there,' said Wexford. 'It's not for you to be honest with them and they won't thank you if you are.'

His advice had less than the effect he desired on DS Goldsmith who was planning the direct and brusque words she would use on that womaniser, that two-timing Brooks, in his wife's presence, when she encountered Bal Bhattacharya downstairs, cool and sweat-free from a thorough though fruitless attempt with Ben Miller's mother's neighbours to establish his alibi. Could there be something in that old reactionary belief that people with dark skins were less affected by heat than the fair? She felt a rush of blood to her face, making her even hotter. That had probably been the most racist thought she had ever had!

'Back to Mill Lane, then, DC Bhattacharya,' she said sharply, forgetting how he'd called her Hannah so caringly that morning.

'Yes, I've been thinking about how to ask the guy without arousing his wife's suspicions.'

Hannah's retort that Mrs Brooks's suspicions should be aroused and soon, faded on her lips. 'That's your feeling too, is it? That we should tread a bit softly?'

'Well, it is. What did you mean by "too"? Did someone else take the same line?'

'The guv,' said Hannah.

Sure enough, John Brooks's red VW was parked in the roadway, just where Henry Nash said it would be. But repeated ringing at the doorbell and rapping on the knocker fetched no one. It was Lydia Burton, her front door wide open to cool the house, who came out to tell them no one was at home. The Brookses were out celebrating their wedding anniversary. A taxi had come to pick them up ten minutes before and take them to a restaurant in Myringham.

'So John can have a drink, you know,' said Lydia Burton.

'It's really appalling,' said Hannah when she was out of earshot, 'how two-faced some people can be. Celebrating your wedding anniversary in the evening and shagging another woman by night, because that's what he must be doing.'

'Not so bad as murdering,' said Baljinder, and then, as if he were the superior officer, '"Shagging" is not an attractive word for a beautiful woman to use.'

If anyone else in Bal's position had reprimanded her, DS Goldsmith would have rounded on him with a sharp scathing phrase, but whether it was being called beautiful that mollified her or simply Bal's own undeniable beauty and style, she couldn't tell but she said nothing, only looked at him, hoping he would smile, which suddenly he did.

'Come along, Sarge,' he said. 'There's a pub down the road called the Lamb and Flag. I'm going to take you in there and buy you a drink.'

* * *

He was thinking about going home. Sylvia was coming over, leaving the boys with a sitter. His conscience troubled him over their last meeting. He had been unkind to her (though not as unkind as her mother) and nothing she had done or meant to do excused that. When he saw her he meant to make it up to her, not changing his point of view, of course, but being gentler and more sympathetic. He should be flattered, he should be proud, he told himself, that his daughters actually took notice of what he said. Other people's daughters, as far as he could see, paid no attention whatever to their fathers' views.

The temperature was falling. He went to the window and looked down across Kingsmarkham to the west where the drooping sun was sinking through narrow bands of cloud that were almost black. A flock of starlings rose from the water meadows by the Kingsbrook and sailed in perfect formation across the treetops. He heard the door behind him open and turned to see Burden.

'I was thinking of going home,' he said.

'You may think again when I tell you. A girl's gone missing. She's twenty-one, works in that souvenir shop in the High Street – Gew-Gaws is it called? – lives with her boyfriend in a flat over the shop. She's called Megan Bartlow.'

'Bartlow, Bartlow . . . Where have I heard that name before? It was somewhere quite recently . . .'

Burden ignored him. 'We've no reason to think there's any connection between her and Amber Marshalson. This Bartlow girl may just turn up unharmed. It's a dodgy sort of set-up, no one knowing exactly when she went missing or where she might have gone or even if she's just run off with another chap. The boyfriend and the mother are downstairs. They came in to report her missing. I don't know if you'll want to . . .'

'I've remembered,' Wexford interrupted him. 'Bartlow –

it's not a common name. You were wrong about our having no reason to connect her with Amber Marshalson. She had two friends who were sisters. Lara and Megan Bartlow.'

Chapter 11

Rather than one of the bleak interview rooms, Sergeant Camb had put them into Kingsmarkham police station's newly set-up 'family room'. This offspring of the caring society, to use Wexford's own words for it, had been born of an idea of Hannah Goldsmith's and enthusiastically taken up by the Chief Constable. A former repository of lost property, it measured no more than twelve feet by ten and had only one small case-ment window, but it made up for what it lacked in space and ventilation by its cheerful furnishings. The hard-wearing cord carpet was a rich emerald green, each of the three small armchairs was a different primary colour and the fourth striped blue and yellow. A painting large enough to cover one wall almost entirely was a coral and crimson medley Wexford described as looking like a butcher's block at closing time on a Saturday night. He had suggested to the Chief Constable that the council-tax payers of Kingsmarkham should be offered a tour of the place, seeing that they had paid for it. For a moment he thought he had been taken seriously.

He found Megan Bartlow's boyfriend and her mother sitting side by side, he in the yellow chair, she in the red one, facing the picture across a white plastic table, laden with very old colour supplements from Sunday newspapers. Neither of them had disturbed the neat stack, which still looked the way it had when the family room was opened by a celebrity (a local man who now played for Manchester City) eleven weeks before. The two appeared to be much the same age, late forties. Megan's mother was a thin haggard woman with dyed blonde hair hanging well below her shoulders and a face coloured as brightly as the furniture and in much the same shades. The boyfriend – a 'kind of common-law son-in-law', as Wexford told Burden later – looked as if he had dressed himself up for a fancy dress party as a twenty-first-century villain. His grey hair was long and tied back in a ponytail. He wore half a dozen rings studded through the outer curve of one ear and a silver or white metal cross hanging against the triangle of grey furry chest which his dirty white vest exposed. Ferocious tattoos, red, black and broccoli green, covered his arms. His jeans were skintight with frayed hems and ragged holes on each knee.

Wexford said a courteous 'Good evening' to both of them and asked their names.

Megan's mother seemed to have left Bartlow behind long before and gave hers in some confusion. 'Lapper, Sandra Lapper,' she said, and then, 'Oh God, no, it's not. I've got a memory like a sieve. It's Warner now on account of I got married last week. What a fool!'

'Keith's my name. Keith Prinsip.'

The man had a deeply lined dark face with a wide but thin mouth and narrow eyes under hood-like lids the colour of black grapes. He lounged in his chair, one leg crossed over the other knee and, lips pursed, appeared to be whistling silently to himself. Mrs Warner rummaged in a black handbag heavily decorated with straps and gilt buckles, and produced a photograph wrapped in cling film. Burden took it from her, studied it and passed it to Wexford. Megan's looks were the prettiness of youth, her nose large and her chin small. She had the requisite long and straight blonde hair and had followed her mother's example in the application of make-up.

'Do you have another daughter called Lara, Mrs Warner?' Wexford asked.

'How did you know?'

Police officers never answer that question. 'Tell me what happened.' Wexford looked from one to the other, having no preference as to which of them should be the narrator. Sandra Warner looked at Keith Prinsip and Prinsip continued with his soundless whistling but neither said a word. 'All right,' Wexford said. 'Since you and Miss Bartlow live together, Mr Prinsip, perhaps you'd begin.'

'My dad died,' Prinsip began. 'I had to get up there for the funeral and once I was there, see, I stopped over with my sister as my dad lived with, right?'

Restraining an impulse to say it was far from right, Wexford asked him where 'up there' was and which day and night he was talking about.

Like many people of his kind, Prinsip seemed to find it incomprehensible that the circumstances of his family and details of his daily life should be unknown to the world at large. Incredulously, he said, 'Brum, innit? Birmingham, right? Where I come from, where me dad lived. Not yesterday. The day before and the night before yesterday I'm like talking about.' Desperately, he made a mammoth effort. 'Like Saturday it was me dad died. I went up there like Monday and the funeral was Tuesday. I come back Wednesday. Yesterday, that is. Yesterday, innit, Sand?'

'You're upset, Keithie, and no wonder.' Sandra Warner said to Wexford, 'He went up there August thirty-first and he come back yesterday.'

'Miss Bartlow wasn't with you?'

'Meg never got on with my family. Her and my sister, they fought like two cats.'

'So you left home at what time on Monday? And where was Megan?' said Burden. This was very hard work. If they relied on this man they would be here all night. 'Mrs Warner?' he said.

'Half-nine you left, Keithie, that's right, innit? So Megan'd have been at the shop. They open nine. Is that right, Keithie?'

Wexford saw that words had to be put into Prinsip's mouth or they would get nowhere. He waited while Mrs Warner prompted him again.

'You'd said goodbye to her and said if Kath wanted you to stop over you'd give her a bell and then she went down to the shop.'

'Megan works at Gew-Gaws?'

'Yeah, right,' said Prinsip, relieved. He made another effort. 'She works for Jimmy Gawson. I give her a phone around six like on the Tuesday but she got her mobile switched off.'

'Did you make any more attempts to phone her? I mean,' said Burden, realising the limitations of his listener, 'did you try again?'

'Yeah, but it wasn't no use.'

'You give me a ring, Keithie. Ever so late it was Tuesday night, like midnight. You know what Lee said? "That Keith wants to remember we're newly-weds," he said. "For all he knows I might have been on the job."' Sandra Warner let out a screech of laughter. 'Hark at me. I'd better get a hold of myself. God knows what may have happened to Megan and there's me laughing like a drain.'

'I give Sand a ring like I say and I done it again next day on account of I was getting worried.' This time Keith Prinsip needed no prompting. 'I mean, where'd she got to? I got back from Brum round dinnertime yesterday, like twelve-ish, and there wasn't no sign of her.'

'There wouldn't be, though, Keithie. She'd have been at the shop.'

'She wasn't, Sand.' The interview was turning into a conversation between the two of them. 'First thing I done was go down there. Jimmy as owns the place, he said, "Where's that Megan, then?" First thing he said to me. "Where's that Megan, then?"'

'Keithie come round to ours and had a bit of dinner with Lee. We said, I mean we all said, Lee as well, we'll give it twenty-four hours, we said, and if she don't show up, we'll . . . well, we didn't know what but we reckoned we'd have to do something.'

Wexford and Burden looked at each other, both bludgeoned into silence by these repetitive and largely useless accounts. Still, Sandra Warner remained the better source of information. It was her Wexford asked if her other daughter, Lara, lived at home with her and if the sisters were close. Meanwhile Burden went to get a missing persons form.

'What you want to know about my other daughter for? Lara's not missing, thank God.'

'She was a friend of the dead girl, Amber Marshalson,' said Wexford, unable this time to avoid all explanation.

'Not to say a friend. Not a friend.' Mrs Warner looked affronted. '*Friendly*, I'll grant you that.'

Wexford had not the least idea whether what he said was true but he said it just the same. 'She and Amber went to Frankfurt together.'

Guesswork or inspiration, he was nearly right and thereby absolutely wrong. 'Not Lara. Megan, and what if she did?' Sandra Warner was quick to take offence. 'That's not a crime, is it? I don't even know where the bloody place is. Somewhere they use them Euros.'

It may well be a crime, Wexford said to himself. 'I'd like to talk to Lara tomorrow. What time does she go to work?'

'She don't work. She's in like higher education. Stowerton Business School, only it's not a school, it's a college.'

'I'll see you and her tomorrow. By then we may have news of Megan.'

Burden came back with the form and stood looking from one to the other, uncertain as to who would claim it.

'Give it here,' said Sandra. 'No good leaving it to Keithie. He's forgot his glasses.' She winked ferociously at Burden who interpreted this signal as indicating Keith's inability to read. Keith himself showed none of the shame typical of the illiterate but resumed his whistling, not silently this time but a vague and soft rendering of 'Can't Buy Me Love'.

It was late. Wexford said goodnight to Burden and walked quite slowly home. The girl was dead, he was sure of it, and this knowledge made looking back on the interview with anything like the amusement he would otherwise have felt impossible. She was dead because she had known Amber Marshalson, more specifically because she had been involved in the same traffic as Amber and both of them, somewhere along the line, had talked of exposing those who paid them. Or, he corrected this account, Megan had threatened to tell on those who had been responsible for Amber's murder. That was most likely. No one went to Frankfurt on holiday. You went there for a conference or a business meeting or to change planes. Amber and Megan had gone there in order to hand over what they, or one of them, was smuggling out of this country and into Germany on its way, probably, to the Far East.

Nothing, it seemed to him, would have much effect on the bovine stupidity of Keith Prinsip – it was a Serbian name, the name of the assassin of the Archduke Ferdinand – but he thought with a kind of dread of its impact on the jolly Sandra Warner, so obviously happy in her new marriage, to whom the worst appeared not to have occurred. It would hit her all the more resoundingly.

He came to his house and saw that Sylvia's car was still outside. Glad – he couldn't help that – yet dismayed too, he told himself to go easy with her, be kind, hand out no more reproaches. What, after all, was the use? He let himself into the hall and heard the unwelcome sound of a voice which was neither Sylvia's nor his wife's. For a moment he couldn't place it but he opened the door, went in and found himself shaking hands with Naomi Wyndham whom he had met maybe once before. She was a small slender woman of about thirty-five with the kind of long red hair that would have sent Rossetti into ecstasies. There was something distasteful to Wexford in this present-day matiness of ex-wives with current girlfriends and ex-husbands with their one-time wives' lovers, yet when he examined what he felt, he had to confess that discord and spite would be far worse.

Dora felt much more strongly about it than he did. It seemed that she disapproved of her daughter and everyone associated with her daughter. When Wexford walked in she was telling Sylvia in a cold voice that she had better get back and relieve the woman who was sitting with Ben and Robin. She could hardly understand, she said, why Sylvia had come over when it involved the trouble and expense of a sitter. With him she became scathing. 'Naomi's so involved with the infant already, Reg, that she's keeping a proprietory eye on Sylvia. Checking she doesn't drink any alcohol and takes all her vitamins, aren't you?'

Sylvia looked displeased, almost stormy.

'You see, I can't help imagining it's me carrying our baby,' said Naomi. 'I mean, I know it's not but I kind of pretend it is. Sylvia's felt it move – well, him or her move, she won't find out its gender, I don't know why not – and I imagine it's me feeling it. Well, it's more than imagination, actually. I really felt a flutter this morning. It was just like a little foot giving me a gentle kick.'

Sylvia said in an unpleasant tone, 'Imagination is right. You can't feel it. You don't know what it's like.'

'I know that only too well, Sylvia, and that's my tragedy. But I make up for it by trying to feel what you feel. When you go into labour I bet I'll have the pains.'

'Husbands in the South Seas do that,' said Wexford. 'They go off into a hut and simulate their wives' pains. The couvade, it's called.'

'How lovely,' gushed Naomi. 'I shall do a couvade when the time comes.'

'Why don't we all have a drink,' said Wexford hastily, expecting Sylvia to say no.

She surprised him with a mutinous, 'I'll have a large glass of white wine, please, Dad. Naomi will abstain for me, so she can drive me home.'

After they had gone, he lay back in his armchair by the wide-open french windows. A little breeze had risen, the first for weeks. 'Perhaps the weather's changing,' he said. The ice-cold beer glass in his hand reminded him, oddly, of the pleasure of clutching a radiator on a snowy day in January. 'That girl would drive me mad if I were Sylvia.'

'She'll go about telling everyone she's doing a couvade now you've put that into her head,' said Dora.

'Where was Neil?'

'Keeping well out of it if he's got any sense.'

Later he lay in bed beside her, covered by no more than a sheet, thinking of the girl who was dead and the girl who was probably dead and the money for which they had paid so much higher a price.

Early morning is a beautiful time when the weather is fine but the heat is still hours away. Hannah had been told at school why dew settles on grass on such mornings but she had forgotten what she had learnt. In such a long-drawn-out drought, it seemed strange to her that this abundant water should be there sprinkling the grass verges with gleaming drops and lying like rows of pearls along the crossbar of the Brookses' gate.

John Brooks's car was parked against the kerb and there was a mist of dew on its windscreen. It was not quite seven o'clock.

She had come alone, having a very unfeminist idea – a very incongruous idea for an ambitious detective sergeant – that she couldn't fetch Bal out at this hour when he had bought her two Camparis and soda the evening before, abstained from alcohol himself to drive her home and, parting from her, given her a gentle kiss on the cheek. She could have phoned Brooks but, having done so several times in the past days, she was sure an answering machine would be on and no one would return calls made to it. She rang the doorbell but no one came. She rapped the knocker, rang again and this time a young man with wet dark curly hair and a boyish face came to the door.

He held a towel in his hand and was rubbing his hair with it as he spoke. 'Who are you, at this hour?'

'Detective Sergeant Goldsmith, Mr Brooks.' Hannah produced her warrant card and set one foot over the threshold. 'I'd like to speak to you and you're a difficult man to catch.'

'You want to speak to me *now*? I'm just leaving for work.'

'I need to speak to you as a matter of urgency.' She could hear her voice growing cold and sharp. 'Preferably now but if that's impossible I'd like to make an appointment to do so as soon as possible. I'll leave you with one point to consider until we meet again. Information has reached us that you're in the habit of going out in your car by night – in the middle of the night or before dawn, that is.'

'It's a lie.'

'Very well, but we need to talk about it. I suggest this evening at seven thirty.'

He said nothing, nodded, then shrugged.

'Mr Brooks?'

'Oh, all right. It's not really convenient, though.'

'It's convenient for me,' said Hannah and went back to her car. She drove to the corner and waited, pretending to be reading her notebook. Within five minutes Brooks passed her in his car, heading for Kingsmarkham.

Her business skills course, at a breakaway department of the old Stowerton polytechnic, Lara Bartlow took very seriously. In the living room of the housing association flat she had shared with Sandra alone until Lee Warner moved in, she was putting folders and books into a new briefcase when Wexford and DS Goldsmith arrived. Warner was nowhere to be seen, was probably still in bed. A strong smell of frying bacon pervaded the place. Lara's clothes were businesslike, a black trouser suit with white shirt and 'sensible' flat-heeled shoes. Instead of the voice he had anticipated came a sixth-form-waiting-for-A-levels accent. If it had been her Amber had gone on holiday with he would have been less surprised but it had been the sister, girl-friend of Keith Prinsip . . . Still, it hadn't been a holiday, had it? More in the nature of a business trip.

'I don't want to be late,' were her first words.

'We'll drive you to your college, Ms Bartlow,' Hannah hastened to reassure her. 'It's not a police car.'

No strangers to the police, he was sure, the Bartlow–Lapper–Warner family would have lived on the fringes of petty crime for the girls' lifetimes and more: a little shoplifting, a good deal of expert benefit fraud, driving without insurance, that sort of thing. Respectability for Lara probably consisted in not being seen anywhere in the vicinity of one of the Mid-Sussex Constabulary's turquoise-blue and flamingo-red chequered vehicles. Yet perhaps he was being unfair. This girl was plainly, to use an old-fashioned term, pulling herself up by her bootstraps. He asked her how she came to know Amber Marshalson.

'We were at school together.'

'Ben Miller was there too?'

'That's right. They're a bunch of snobs round here but Amber had no side to her. If it didn't sound daft in this day and age, she's what my nan calls a real lady. It broke my heart when I'd heard what happened to her.'

'It was through you', said Wexford, 'that she met your sister Megan?'

'Yeah, that's right. She came to the Bling-Bling Club with me one night and Amber was there. Just her, not that Keith.' She hesitated, said, 'Look, Megan'd be OK once she got away from him.'

She's got away from him now, Wexford thought sadly. 'You don't care for him?'

'Layabout scumbag,' said Lara savagely. 'He's dragged her down. He's got her doing things she'd not have dreamt of when she was with Mum and me.'

'What kind of things?'

'You want to know, you ask her. I'm not telling on my sister. And I've got to get to college – like now.'

As they went down to the car, he reflected that asking her was the one thing he couldn't do. Already the heat was beginning, the temperature palpably rising, the air calm and still, the leaves on the pavement trees hanging limp. The night hadn't been long enough or damp enough to revive them.

It was Hannah who asked, 'Why did she and Amber go to Frankfurt?'

'Don't ask me. Maybe there was a cut-price flight or something.'

'Where do you think your sister is now, Lara?'

'Gone off with someone she's met and left that Keith, I hope.'

'If you're serious,' said Wexford, 'would she do that and not get in touch with you or your mother?'

'We're here. This is my college.' Lara got out of the car,

Wexford noticed, in a way women rarely do today, but the most elegant way. Her knees pressed together, she swung both legs off the seat, put her feet to the ground and stood up, all in one graceful movement. 'Look, she just might. I mean, she's not said anything to me about another bloke but that's how she got together with Keith. She was seeing this really nice guy, and good-looking too, wow, like Jude Law, and then one day she just . . . well, disappeared. Turned up, oh, four or five days later with that Keith in tow. She'd got a week off work and she'd gone to Brighton on her own and she found him – in the gutter, I reckon – and brought him back. That was three years ago.'

They watched her walk into the building up a flight of steps, a tall assured sort of girl who knew where she was going and how she meant to get there.

'Now we have to start the search for her sister,' said Wexford.

Chapter 12

Bal was more than willing to come with her. Of course, strictly speaking, he had to come if she told him to, but she knew real enthusiasm when she saw it. He wasn't accompanying her because it was his duty but because he liked her company and – she was pretty sure – found her sexually attractive. Well, she *was*, she had no difficulty in telling herself, as she went into the women officers' washroom, combed her long hair, sprayed on a little Chanel Chance and applied lip gloss. As a large number of men had told her, she was extremely good-looking. Moreover, she belonged to a type Bal might be expected specially to admire. With her olive skin, dark-brown eyes and dark-chestnut hair, she could be taken for a woman of Indian origin – well, very far north Indian. Now, Hannah, she murmured to herself, that's close to racist.

She passed on tiptoe through the conference room as Wexford was addressing the media. There was no other way out. His appeal was going out live on the six-thirty regional news. She heard him say, 'Megan Bartlow has now been missing for more than forty-eight hours. We have serious fears for her safety. If anyone has . . .'

Closing the door silently behind her, Hannah went out into the still brilliant, still dazzling light of another hot evening to find Baljinder Bhattacharya waiting for her at the wheel of his car. As soon as he saw her he was out of the driver's seat and over on her side to open the passenger door. If we hadn't got to do this, she thought, we could go somewhere nice to drink and eat, not bloody Brimhurst Prideaux, maybe sit out in the moonlight – not that I'd need moonlight – and I bet we'd be in bed in my flat by ten. Oh, I do like a thin man with a concave belly and a profile like a hawk winging its way across the plains of the Punjab. . . . Come on, Hannah, get yourself together. She got into the car.

John Brooks's red VW was nowhere to be seen but there was nothing surprising in that. It was still only ten to seven. Hannah rang the bell and Gwenda Brooks came to the door. She had a what-is-it-now look on her face.

'It's your husband we want to speak to.'

'He'll be a good half-hour yet.'

'We'll come in and wait,' said Hannah in her sharp tone. 'He expects us. I made an appointment with him' – she looked at her watch – 'twelve hours ago.'

It seemed to be the first Gwenda Brooks had heard of it but she stood back to let Hannah and Bal pass through and showed them into a living room they had been in before. Mrs Brooks was one of those women who dislike ornaments and pictures because they need dusting and was fond of beige as a furnishing colour. It was the shade of carpet, three-piece suite, woodwork and wallpaper, its tone slightly varying between shortbread and caffè latte.

The windows were wide open on to a small garden, which had once had a lawn. This had been recently covered by a wooden deck, more suited to a Malibu beach house than a Sussex cottage. In the very narrow borders surrounding it grew a few dispirited, flowerless evergreens. Hannah, who was usually less aware of beautiful scenery than beautiful men, found herself thinking that, no matter what they had done to house and garden, the Brookses hadn't been able to lay a chilling beige hand on the splendid landscape of wooded hills beyond their back fence.

Gwenda Brooks didn't offer them anything. Somewhere a radio was playing very softly, not music but a male voice apparently giving a lecture. Perhaps Gwenda couldn't bear silence. Any background noise was better than none. She had been reading, or looking at, a glossy magazine before they arrived and now returned to her perusal of a double-page spread of photographs of a house, rooms and garden.

Perhaps it struck her that this was impolite, for she suddenly thrust the magazine at Hannah, saying, 'That's Mr Arlen's house in Pomfret. Isn't it lovely?'

Having no idea who Mr Arlen was, Hannah took the magazine and had barely glanced at it when Bal, obviously deciding that being nice to Gwenda might be no bad thing, reached for it and cast the kind of appreciative gaze at the pictures she must have hoped for.

'A beautiful house,' he said. 'Where exactly is it?'

'Just outside Pomfret. I've been there.' Gwenda sounded immensely proud. 'It was such a surprise opening that book and finding those lovely pictures of those rooms and that beautiful garden.'

As a scream rose in Hannah's throat that she fought successfully to control, the phone rang. Mrs Brooks went out of the room to answer it. Bal raised his eyebrows and smiled at Hannah. Hannah smiled back. She looked at her watch and saw that it was twenty past seven. Gwenda Brooks came back, said, 'That was my husband. He's working late. He won't be back till eleven, if then.'

It was at this point that Hannah thought of asking her about the night drives and she would have done so but for a glance from Bal. It wasn't admonitory, as the 'shagging' reproof had been, or even cautionary, but just a glance beyond interpretation.

Still, it stopped her. 'I must speak to your husband, Mrs Brooks. He works in Kingsmarkham, doesn't he?'

'You can't go to the factory!'

'I may have to. What does the factory . . . er, manufacture?'

'They make electrical equipment. Pallant Smith Hussein, they're called. And it's not Kingsmarkham, it's Stowerton.'

The two towns were only about a mile apart and growing ever closer. 'Will you tell him that I'll see him here at eight thirty tomorrow morning or at Pallant Smith Hussein at ten? Get him to give me a call on this number.' Mrs Brooks looked apprehensively at the mobile number on the card Hannah passed her. 'Any time between now and eight tomorrow morning. He can leave me a message.'

Outside, one house along, Lydia Burton in a green and white sundress was watering her parched front garden from a can. She smiled and lifted her hand in a wave, the gesture of the innocent who have nothing to hide from the police. Now John Brooks was inaccessible until tomorrow, it occurred to Hannah that she and Bal had a free evening after all. There is nothing like a fine summer evening to put one in a mood for romantic sex. The air is warm and soft, punishing heat fading. The sky is still blue but the light is beginning to dim as the sun starts its progress to the dark horizon. (Well, it doesn't, thought Hannah, but that's how it *seems*). Day is past and a lassitude settles on the limbs. It's the time for wine, for looking into another's eyes, for flowers closing their petals, for hands meeting across a table, for the decision, mutually taken, to leave and go where two can be alone.

Bal opened the car door for her. Was she going to have to ask him? And ask him exactly what? He started the car, looked at the clock on the dashboard and said, 'Good, I won't have to miss my Hindi class after all.'

'Hindi?' she said faintly.

'It was my first language till I was about three. We were

99

living here – I mean, in Lancashire – but my parents were studying English and they decided it would be best always to speak it at home for my sake and my sisters'. They didn't want us growing up with that sing-song accent.'

If she had said that it would have been the most politically incorrect thing . . . !

'So the result was that I've forgotten most of my Hindi but I really feel it would be sensible to get fluent in it again. With such a large Indian community in Britain, you see.'

'Oh, yes, I see. Of course I do.'

Nothing more was said. He took her to where she lived, the flat in a block called Drayton Court in Orchard Road.

'Well, goodnight,' she said.

'Sarge. I mean Hannah?'

'What?'

'I don't know if it's OK for a DC to ask a DS this but will you have dinner with me? Friday or Saturday? Is it OK? I'm not sure about the what-d'you-call-it? – etiquette'

'It's quite OK, Detective Constable,' said Hannah, laughing, 'and yes, I'd love to.'

After the briefing, the press conference and the news appeal, Wexford sat at the desk which had been provided for him and looked at the list DS Vine had given him of suspected users and dealers in Kingsmarkham and outlying districts. It was formidably long. Some of these people had been prosecuted, some charged but no crime found and some simply looked on with suspicion. He couldn't help harking back to the past, when he was young, and in the whole of the British Isles there were something like 600 registered drug users. Two years ago that had been the number of dealers calculated to live in these three towns and the surrounding villages, and even after the concerted purge he and his team had carried out reasonably successfully, he was sure over a hundred remained and more were creeping back. Useless to think like that, useless to reflect that in his childhood a man or woman living in Pomfret or Myfleet thought heroin was a girl in a romantic novel and cocaine the anaesthetic given you by the dentist.

Barry Vine was at this moment searching the flat over the souvenir shop occupied by Keith Prinsip and Megan Bartlow with PC Overton to help him. DS Goldsmith and DC Bhattacharya were pursuing enquiries in Brimhurst. Burden had gone to talk to the Marshalsons in an effort to find out more about the curious friendship between Amber and Megan. Karen Malahyde had just returned from visiting the souvenir shop. She said to Wexford, 'The chap who runs it is called Jimmy Gawson – hence the name Gew-Gaws. Ghastly, isn't it?'

'I know him,' said Wexford. 'I've known him for years. Rehabilitated drunk.'

'Right. That figures. He says he came in as usual at ten on the second and Megan wasn't there but there was this note on the door which just said "Back soon". He says now he had a feeling all wasn't well but I think that's hindsight.'

'He'd better not have too many feelings like that if this is murder.'

'No, sir. Gawson says after he'd been there a few minutes a woman came in and said she'd tried to get into the shop about nine fifteen but it was locked up and that notice on the door. He hasn't seen Megan since.'

Wexford put Vine's list into his pocket and went out into the comparative cool of the evening. One car still remained on the forecourt, as much an interloper's as Daniel Hilland's had been. But Wexford said nothing to Darren Lovelace about towing or clamping. He said nothing at all. Well named, Lovelace had a pink baby face with soft red lips, blue eyes, fair but thinning curly hair and the perpetually surprised expression of a fruit bat.

'Reggie, babes!'

It was worse than being called 'guv', far worse. But every-one got it: 'Mikey, babes' and 'Barry, babes' and, if he encoun-tered the Deputy Chief Constable, probably 'Sammy, babes'. Wexford said, 'What?'

'Just a couple of questions.'

'I've given you everything you're getting. You were there just now and that's your lot.'

'Oh, dear,' said Lovelace, 'I hope you won't regret it. No, don't look like that, not that naughty face. Did you think I was threatening you?'

'I came out for some fresh air and what I found was you.'

'Some people love me. Well, my mother does. You aren't exactly whizzing through this Marshalson business, are you? You haven't got anywhere at all as far as I can see.' Sorrowfully, Lovelace continued, 'I don't want to do this, it hurts me more than it hurts you, as they used to say in my distant schooldays, all changed now thanks to the Charter of Human Rights, but I'm going to have to do a piece about your lack of progress. I really am, Reggie, babes.'

Usually skilful at repartee, Wexford always found himself bereft of wit and innocent of innuendo in the face of Lovelace's onslaughts. 'I can't stop you.'

'You may not be right in other respects but you're right there, ducks.'

Sylvia couldn't remember when she had last been so angry. She had just got home from work, having picked up the boys from school, and had made herself a pot of tea. It is a pecu-liarity of the British, and probably the British alone, that to cool down on a very hot day they drink very hot tea. Sylvia really believed it was more efficacious than iced water or orange juice and she was drinking her first cup when the doorbell rang. She dragged herself to the front door, noticing that her ankles were swollen, which hadn't happened in her first two pregnancies. It was hotter and she was older, she thought despondently, and opened the door to Naomi and a woman she vaguely remembered seeing somewhere before.

That had been at five thirty. It was nine now and her fury was fading. Robin and Ben had finally gone to bed after the usual complaints that it was too hot to sleep, they could hear a dog barking, a bee was buzzing against the window and it was mean not letting them play video games in their bedrooms. The night was a purple sort of colour and she could see what whoever it was meant when he called this 'the violet hour'. A bird was singing somewhere among the weary leaves. A nightingale, she'd have thought, only nightingales don't sing in September. What the hell was Naomi playing at?

She had said, 'May we come in, dear?' in that sweet little winsome voice. Sylvia sometimes wondered how Neil could stand it. 'This is Mary, Mary Beaumont. She's come to live next door. Now you didn't know that, did you?'

Sylvia had no option but to say hello to this Mary, a rotund black woman with a friendly smile, and invite them both in. As for 'next door', the Old Rectory had no immediate neighbours. 'You mean the cottages at the end of the lane,' she said in a cold tone, recalling where she had seen Mary, and at once despised herself for being an unjustified snob.

They went into the rectory's cavernous and little-used drawing room, which was bitterly cold in winter and cool in summer, even on the hottest day.

Mary sat down with a sigh of pleasure. 'It's lovely in here. Like air-conditioning.'

So long as you don't think you can settle there for the rest of the evening, thought Sylvia nastily. Naomi, who had legs like sticks and ankles the span of a child's wrists, was staring at her feet.

'Your ankles are a bit puffy, Sylvia. I expect Mary will have something to say about that. Now I'll fetch the drinks, shall I? I'm sure you've got sparkling water in your fridge.'

Though fairly watchful of her alcohol intake, Sylvia had been looking forward to a large glass of Sauvignon. She turned to Mary. 'What does she mean, you'll have something to say?'

A ready laugher, Mary burst into a merry peal. She shook with laughter, her cushiony breasts and plump shoulders wobbling. 'I'm a midwife, darling. Get it? The idea of bringing me here is I keep an eye on you.' The rectory was a big house and the kitchen a long way away. Naomi wouldn't be back yet. 'Don't you worry. You've got no pre-eclampsia coming.'

'Keep an eye on me?'

'I don't know why, darling, but don't you worry. I won't be always in and out, seeing how you are. Too busy myself, for one thing. But with that Naomi, you got to humour her, get it?' Mary didn't explain how she came to know Naomi. 'We'll drink our water – not that I wouldn't rather have something a bit stronger – and then we'll be going,' she said. 'See the back of us, darling, and you can put those feet up. Them your boys out there? Lovely boys, I must say.'

True to her word, Mary drank down her water in two gulps, got up with surprising agility for one so large and said her husband would be waiting for his tea. The idea that any female should provide sustenance for any male shocked Naomi as much as it would have appalled Detective Sergeant Goldsmith. She was silenced and by the time she began protesting that they had only just come, Mary was out in the hall. Still, she managed to have the last word.

'Mary lives in Gamekeeper's Cottage, Sylvia. I've written down her phone number for you but you probably won't need it as Mary has promised me to pop in *very frequently*.' Behind her back, Mary winked. 'Of course I'll still often be around myself to give you moral support but do watch those ankles, won't you?'

To Sylvia, who had a lot of her father in her, this suggested her spreading her legs and feet out in front of her and staring at them for half an hour at a time, as in some yogic or meditative exercise. She had saved her glass of wine until this violet hour and the quiet. The mosquitoes that attacked her mother left her alone. She watched a moth alight on a mossy stone and spread flat its Persian-carpet wings. The wine was reducing her bad temper to a minor irritation. Mary had been so funny that she began to feel she wouldn't have minded all that much if she *had* 'popped in very frequently'. How had Naomi come across her? And what on earth did she think Mary could do if Sylvia smoked cannabis, drank brandy, ate soft cheeses, threw away her vitamins or, come to that, had an abortion? Well, no, not this last. It was too late for that.

When she had finished her wine she went upstairs to check on her sleeping sons and then she walked up the lane in the cool, as cool as it would get all night. A little wood separated the rectory from the two cottages, Gamekeeper's Cottage and Shepherd's Cottage, that faced the church. The latter was in darkness but in Gamekeeper's lights were on and a bright television screen could be seen through the front window but neither of the occupants. I don't suppose I'll ever see her again, thought Sylvia as she walked back. Why would she bother with me?

Prinsip's home had surprised him. Barry Vine had expected a tip, old clothes stuffing carrier bags, car and bike magazines in stacks, broken furniture which would never be repaired and plates, cups and glasses waiting not to be washed but rinsed under a cold tap. The flat over the souvenir shop wasn't like that. Knowing that Prinsip lived on the benefit, DS Vine wondered where all the electronic equipment had come from, a new desktop computer, very state-of-the-art, a CD player with huge speakers and a portable CD player lying alongside it, a DVD player as well as a video under the TV and a brand-new drum kit which made Barry's soul shrink as he thought of the noise this couple must make.

He hadn't come alone. With him was a drug-dog handler, PC Overton, and the dog himself, last of the drug-dog team, useful in the purge of two years before. All the others had gone back to the forces they came from but this dog remained, semi-retired and now the household pet of the Overton family. His name was Drusus, not because PC Overton was a student of Roman history but on account of its being the only name anyone could think of which began with 'dr' for 'drugs'. No one had ever called him by that name. A docile but enthusiastic golden spaniel, he was known to everyone as Buster.

A reluctant and puzzled permission to allow the dog on his premises was extracted from Keith Prinsip. He asked rather pathetically if it would help to find Megan and when told it very likely might, nodded his head. Buster galloped up the stairs to the three rooms at the top which were Prinsip and Megan's home but his excitement was short-lived. Obviously losing confidence in the revitalising of his career, he grew more and more despondent as, sniffing expertly in corners, under furniture and inside drawers, he could only draw his nose away unsatisfied.

Prinsip gave him a surreptitious chocolate which Buster was chewing with gusto when PC Overton spotted him. Apparently, no chocolate had ever before passed Buster's lips and an argument broke out between the two men, Overton telling Prinsip roughly that he ought to know better than to give harmful substances to a working animal and Prinsip answering that Overton was a cruel master. The fracas was put an end to by Barry Vine, who declared that his own search was being seriously interrupted by 'a lot of nonsense'. It was he who finally found the drug, in the pocket of another pair of Prinsip's ragged jeans. The paper screw of cannabis, maybe ten grammes,

Prinsip indignantly defended as being for his own use and no longer illegal. Vine said nastily that it was amazing how well informed ignorant illiterates could sometimes be on matters of law when it came to their own interests.

'Who are you calling ignorant?' said Prinsip.

'I was merely making a general observation.'

No longer fighting Buster's corner, Prinsip said he didn't think much of the dog as a sniffer when he couldn't even find a spot of weed.

'He's trained to find only class A substances,' said PC Overton loftily.

Chapter 13

It was too hot to sleep and when Wexford heard the paper come just after six he got up, went downstairs and picked up his copy of the *Kingsmarkham Courier* from his doormat. There was Lovelace's story with that old photograph of himself, taken years before, drinking a half of bitter in the Olive and Dove's garden. He made tea, took it up to his wife and, passing her the paper, said, 'It ought to be easier the second time but it's not.'

'I don't know why it should be.'

'I suppose I thought it wouldn't happen again.'

'Shall I read the story and tell you if it's safe for you to read?'

Her tone had been impatient. 'You know me better than that,' he said. 'If it's there I have to read it.'

Hannah bought her *Courier* from the paper shop in Brimhurst St John, which opened at eight. The lead story said Wexford was getting nowhere with his investigation of Amber Marshalson's murder and a photograph of him drinking beer carried the caption, 'DCI Loses the Plot'. She threw it into the back of the car, supposing the guv was impervious to this sort of thing by now. Within five minutes she was in Brimhurst

Prideaux, parking the car a few feet from where Mill Lane joined the Myfleet road. She had twenty minutes before her meeting with John Brooks and she picked up the paper.

All the faults and intrusions of the media stemmed from male journalists, in Hannah's opinion. Therefore she wasn't much surprised to see Darren Lovelace's byline above this one or to read a series of inaccurate statements and wild exaggerations. The job was getting on top of Wexford and he was ageing fast. As could be seen from the picture, he was subject to inexplicable violent rages and paranoia. No progress had been made towards finding Amber Marshalson's killer and now another girl, a friend of hers, was missing. Did anyone 'not living in cloud-cuckoo-land' have doubts that she too would be found murdered? The Chief Constable was on the point of taking Wexford off the case and replacing him with someone younger. As for the 'loved ones' of the missing girl, left in the hands of such an inept investigator, they had the *Courier's* deepest sympathy.

Much as Hannah liked and admired 'the guv' and knew all Lovelace's stuff was ill-informed slander, she had to admit that Wexford was a *man* and she couldn't help feeling that a woman would in the nature of things do the job better. Someone like herself, for instance, in, say, ten years' time . . .

It was twenty-eight minutes past eight. She got out, locked the car and walked up to where John Brooks's VW was parked as usual – but not usually at this hour – outside number two Jewel Terrace. She had been looking at his car, for no particular reason except to use up the remaining minute, but when she turned round she saw him in his front garden, standing just inside the gate.

'Well, Mr Brooks, at last . . .'

She had hardly got the words out when he said in a low voice, 'Can we do this in my car?'

There was no need to ask him why. The front door was

ajar, his wife was inside and might hear anything that was said. 'As you like,' she said.

The sky was overcast this morning but the heat had already begun. It had scarcely diminished during the night. As John Brooks's car was parked, the passenger window was on the offside. He wound it down about two inches but left his own closed. Hannah glanced at him. Some would have called him good-looking. He had the face of a minor celebrity, a pop singer or a TV presenter, bland, soft and mobile, with unremarkable features but for his eyes, which seemed to have more whites round the irises than most have. He was thin and dark, and those eyes were a dark blue-grey.

'What's the problem?' he said in the minor celebrity's voice, which is far from that of the Keith Prinsips of this world but not too 'posh' either.

Hannah was going to take a great leap here. It was not what Henry Nash had said but Brooks could always deny it if it wasn't true. 'The problem, Mr Brooks, is that you're in the habit of going out for drives in the middle of the night and you went out on the night Amber Marshalson was killed.'

'What if I did?' Her calculated guess had paid off. 'I wasn't killing her.'

'Did you know her?'

Perhaps he thought the original 'problem' wouldn't be pursued, for he looked relieved. 'Of course. Everyone knows everyone in a place like this. She was a nice kid. Actually, I helped her find something on her laptop when she was having problems.'

'I thought you were a health and safety officer.'

'OK, I am, but I know about computers and she knew I did. She came round and asked me for help.' He glanced at his house and the half-open front door. 'My wife didn't like it but there was nothing, less than nothing, between me and Amber. I mean, I thought of her as a child.'

A child who'd had a child, Hannah thought. 'What was wrong with her computer?'

'Nothing, really. These kids are usually brilliant at technology but she wasn't. She couldn't get the hang of it. She wanted me to help her find some website and I did. Easy-peasy, actually.'

'And what website would that be?'

'I mean I showed her how. I don't know what it was.' She could tell he was lying. 'Is there anything else? Only I do have to get to work.'

Hannah said smoothly, 'Oh, dear, yes, Mr Brooks. There is quite a lot else. If you have to get to work I can always see you there. Say in half an hour?'

He sighed. 'Ask what you have to ask now and get it over.'

'I simply want to know where you go in the night-time. Easy-peasy, as you say.'

'I can't sleep. I just drive around and sometimes I can get to sleep when I get back.'

'You drive around for *two hours*? Where do you go?'

Brooks was growing angry. His pupils seemed to shrink and the whites round them to grow. 'I'm not obliged to tell you that. I've done nothing wrong. I'm an innocent man and I very much resent being interrogated like this.'

'Yes, well, I'm afraid you are obliged to tell me. I don't have to remind you that this is a murder case. Failure to tell me will be obstructing the police in their enquiries.' Hannah had always wanted to say that and up till now had never had the opportunity. 'I'll come to see you at work in your lunch hour. When is that? One till two?'

A terrible feeling came over Hannah that he might prefer her to come back this evening and be once more closeted in this car with him. She was dining with Bal at seven thirty . . .

Duty came first, of course. 'If you'd prefer to see me here again this evening . . . ?'

She was glad she had made the offer. 'All right. Come to the works if you must. One thirty?'

'One thirty it is, Mr Brooks.'

They had begun searching the towns and the surrounding countryside. Prinsip was asked to furnish them with the names of everyone Megan knew and struggled to do so. In the end, it was Sandra Warner and her daughter Lara who had to do the job for him. The lead the police wanted would come when they found someone known to both Megan and Amber. Ben Miller, Chris Williamson and James Sothern came, of course, into this category, but all of them said they had only once met Megan and that was on the single occasion when Lara brought her sister to Bling-Bling. It was much the same for the girls, Samantha Collins, Charlotte Probyn and Veryan Colgate. Samantha alone had encountered Megan on more than one occasion and she had disliked Amber but it took a wilder stretch of the imagination than anyone in Wexford's team possessed to see plump little Samantha in the role of a concrete block dropper and brick-wielding assassin.

Wexford took Sergeant Vine and PC Overton with him to the Marshalsons. George appeared horribly shocked when asked if his daughter could have been involved in drug trafficking. 'She has a baby while she's still at school, she stays out half the night at clubs and now you tell me she carried drugs to Thailand and into Europe. Where did I go wrong? Is all this because her mother died when she was still a child? I did my best. I thought I'd found her another mother . . .'

'Mr Marshalson,' Wexford said, 'we aren't saying Amber was involved in this trade, only that she could have been. It may be that with your co-operation we can establish that she was not.'

'My co-operation?'

'We would like to search this house with the help of a . . . a sniffer dog. Would you object?'

George said he didn't like it but as for objecting, no, he wouldn't do that. It seemed to bring him no pleasure, though it brought a lot to Wexford, to see Brand's delight at the appearance on the scene of Buster. Whether a sniffer dog of Buster's eminence should be permitted, on grounds of *noblesse oblige* and hygiene, to lick enthusiastically the face of a one-year-old client he hardly knew, but Brand loved it and for the first time Wexford heard the little boy laugh. His peals of laughter echoed through that sad house as he put up his arms to hug the golden spaniel.

But Buster had work to do. He concentrated mainly on Amber's bedroom, covering every inch of floor, the insides of drawers and the inner recesses of cupboards, like the expert he was. His search was in vain and if an animal could look disappointed, Buster did. He had found nothing.

'I suppose the time will come when I'll have to get the child a dog,' said George, his voice empty of all enthusiasm. 'I don't suppose you're interested, this is something I have to teach myself to come to terms with, but I can't contemplate the future with this child growing up in my house and Diana and I having to look after him. Get him a dog, like I said, or a cat maybe. Find a school for him. Get him to the doctor for all those injections they have to have. Find friends for him to play with. I can hardly contemplate it. I seem to have made a mess of it last time. Why should I be better now? I've lost my beloved daughter. I'm older and I'm tired and, well, broken-hearted. I'm an old man. Is that how I'm to spend my retirement, bringing up another child?'

Maybe they'll take him away from you, Wexford thought, and someone will adopt him, someone who desperately wants a child. 'This missing girl,' he said, 'Megan Bartlow. She and

Amber went to Frankfurt together. Now, Mr Marshalson, you know as well as I do that a couple of young British girls don't go to Frankfurt on holiday, any more than a couple of young German girls would come to Birmingham. So why did they go there?'

'You think they were carrying . . . well, hard drugs?'

'It's a possibility.' Wexford avoided looking at George's stricken face. 'Megan Bartlow doesn't appear to have been a close friend. Not before that weekend, at any rate.'

'A lot of girls came here. She may have been one of them. I'd never heard her name till Amber said they were going to Frankfurt together. I answered the phone to her around that time and I must say she hadn't the sort of accent I'd like to think of my daughter's friends having.'

'It wasn't a friendship, was it? It was a business arrangement.'

'What did Amber know about business?'

People pick up that sort of knowledge very fast when there's money to be made, thought Wexford, but he didn't say it aloud.

No sooner had Hannah parked her car on an area restricted to 'Staff and Bona Fide Visitors' than John Brooks came down a flight of concrete steps from a green-painted door on the end of the block. He came towards her, smiling and holding out his hand, so that she wondered what he had told colleagues as to her identity. Certainly he wouldn't have revealed that she was a police officer. A prospective client perhaps? Some sort of health and safety inspector? He opened the green door and ushered her into a small office full of filing cabinets. John Brooks evidently made his own tea and coffee and now, plugging in the electric kettle, he offered her a choice.

'Nothing, thank you.' She wasn't going to turn this into a social occasion, a cosy chat over the teacups.

'Pity. Are you sure? Well, if you won't you won't.'

'Mr Brooks, let's get down to why I'm here. I want to know where you go on these night drives of yours. Is that why your wife sleeps in one bedroom and you sleep in the other? It's not really to do with your snoring, is it? You fake the snoring so you've an excuse for sleeping elsewhere, which makes it easier to get out for a drive.'

'I don't know what you want me to tell you.'

'Where you go. Please don't say you just drive around.'

Brooks put a teabag into one of the mugs and poured boiling water on to it. He opened a drawer and took out a packet of chocolate chip cookies. 'Biscuit?'

'No, thank you. Do you visit a woman?'

'If I said yes and told you who, would it go any further?'

'If you mean would we tell your wife, no, I shouldn't think so.' Her contempt had crept into her voice and she saw him shrink. 'If this woman confirms that you visit her by night and that you did so on the night of Amber's death, no one else need know. A name and address, please, Mr Brooks.'

He wrote down a name and an address in Pomfret on a piece of scrap paper. After that, he escorted her down the flight of steps to her car. Anxious to get her off the premises, she thought as she drove away. Once he knew she was out of the way he'd be on the phone to this woman, this Paula Vincent of Foster Way, Pomfret.

Brooks's girlfriend was not at all as she had expected. Someone a few years younger than Gwenda was most likely and a glamorous contrast to her, a sort of bimbo in a miniskirt. The woman who opened the door to her, saying nothing but slightly raising her eyebrows, was forty at least, her short hair lank and dark, her face free of make-up and her figure far from what beauty editors in magazines call 'toned'. The only name for her trousers, Hannah thought, was one her own mother used, 'slacks'. She had on a dirty whitish jumper and quilted slippers.

Hannah was not to be invited further in than the narrow hallway. In answer to her questions, Paula Vincent said, yes, she and John Brooks were 'in a relationship'. They would marry when he was divorced. She, Paula, was a widow. He sometimes visited her in the night. It was the only time he could get away. Hannah merely noted all this down, saying nothing, but thinking what fools these women were. If he was going to get divorced, what stopped him telling his wife he'd got a girlfriend? Because he wasn't going to get divorced, of course, he was a deceiver as so many of them were. Briefly, she thought of Bal with whom she'd be dining five hours from now. Was he different?

On her way back to Kingsmarkham she passed the searchers, most of them a group of a dozen or so public-spirited volunteers under the direction of a single police officer. She waved to Lynn Fancourt and half a mile further on to Karen Malahyde. Burden she didn't see but he was there with DC Damon Coleman and four members of the public, exploring the streets, lanes and open spaces of Pomfret. While Hannah went back to the murder room in Brimhurst village hall, Lynn and Karen and their teams moved up to Sewingbury, and Burden took his group to the larger and more formidable Stowerton.

Darkness would fall at about nine after a prolonged twilight, so the searching of unlit places could continue well into the late evening. Burden went home for his dinner at six thirty and was back in Stowerton by seven fifteen, at which time Damon Coleman was released to eat pizza with Lynn Fancourt in a Sewingbury café. He returned as the evening began to darken.

Stowerton, with a huge industrial estate on its outskirts and an inner-town network of streets criss-crossing each other and lined with terraces of small houses, originally built to accommodate chalk quarry workers, was not an attractive place. Residents of Kingsmarkham and Pomfret, especially, regarded it as an eyesore, though most admitted that its appearance was much improved by the little houses in Oval, Rectangle and Pyramid Roads being bought and refurbished by upwardly mobile couples. They found the freshly painted front doors pleasing – Wexford called the occupants the Rainbow Nation – the window boxes artistic and the flowering trees and trimmed box hedges a mark of civilisation. Stowerton was within commuting distance of London if you didn't mind spending two hours of every day five days a week sitting, or more likely standing, in a train.

Burden, with Lynn Fancourt, Damon Coleman and a team of uniformed men and women, had searched the open spaces and those of the gardens which were wild or overgrown. But the town wasn't entirely composed of a sprawl of factories and £150,000 two-up, two-down cottages. In its centre, dating from when it had been a place of nineteenth-century elegance, were streets of houses built in the 1840s. The long walled gardens of Victoria Terrace backed on to the tiny fenced gardens of Oval Road. Frontages had long sash windows, elegant lacework balconies and steps up to a front door, flanked by pillars. They might have been in Cheltenham or Bath and they had once been as pretty as anything comparable in Kingsmarkham. For years now they had been divided into flats and single rooms or occupied by small struggling businesses and were sadly in need of refurbishment. These houses had recently been bought en bloc by a property developer who was about to have them renovated. Scaffolding had been mounted against their façades, the whole covered in green netting. No builders had yet started work, though front gardens were stacked with bricks, breeze blocks and new window frames.

The back gardens of Victoria Terrace looked like a meadow

that is fast becoming a wood, the walls between them over-grown and obscured by brambles, wild roses, ivy and the clematis which at this time of year was covered with the fluffy seedheads of Old Man's Beard. Burden and his team searched this wilderness from end to end, beating down nettles and lifting matted webs of brambles in the warm sultry glow of the setting sun. They found empty cans, chip papers, condoms, ice-cream wrappers, beer bottles, a single high-heeled shoe, an ice tray from a fridge, a syringe, a Lotto ticket and a DVD of *Apocalypse Now*. The shoe caused some excitement until Lynn pointed out that it was a size 41 while Megan wore a size 38.

Dusk came slowly but they would soon need lights to help them.

'We'll call it a day,' Burden said.

A woman should never dress up for a man. Hannah firmly believed this. It was one of her rules of life. For one thing, men never noticed what a woman wore, only that she looked good or not, and for another, why pander to men in this way when it wouldn't cross a man's mind to buy something new to wear when out on a date? She believed in this principle and had usually adhered to it. Today was different, though of course it should make no difference to abiding by her rule. But it did. She admitted to herself as she took her third shower of that hot day that she really fancied Bal, quite uncomfort-ably so, and the best thing would be to get things on a clear footing from the start. Like tonight. So, rule or no rule, she was going to wear the sexiest stuff she had, take a long time over her face and leave this new conditioner on her hair for an extra five minutes.

Very tall, she was anxious not to wear shoes that would raise her head above Bal's but as soon as that thought formed she castigated herself for even thinking it. Why fall into that trap?

What authority or power or arbiter decreed that a man must be taller than a woman? And even if such a power had done so once, it was outdated now and of no account. She slipped her feet into the highest-heeled shoes she had; black patent and backless, they were very hard to walk in but she didn't intend to walk much. Scented with Donna Karan's Cashmere Mist and lightly made up, she was ready to meet Bal. Not, of course, at seven thirty precisely but, as was more suitable for a woman not wanting to look too keen, at twenty-five minutes to eight.

Halfway through dinner Hannah steered the conversation away from shop. It was only natural that at first this was what they talked about for this was what they had in common. From crime and crime management it was a swift step to the personalities of their fellow officers and Hannah had no qualms about discussing Wexford's character with someone who was her subordinate. After all, she had nothing but praise for him. There was no need to mention his outdated attitude to certain things, language mostly, and his peculiar preference for books over videos, DVDs and CDs, which after all wasn't surprising.

But after half an hour of this she felt, in a favourite phrase of hers, that it was time to move on. She had drunk a good deal of wine but it wasn't the wine that was making her feel amorous. One look at Bal was enough to do that. He, of course, was driving so had confined himself to one half-glass of Chablis and had been drinking mineral water ever since. But why should it be 'of course'? They didn't live very far from each other. She had come to the restaurant in a taxi and they could have shared one going home. She felt unreasonably annoyed because Bal, though smiling at her in a rather sweet way across the table, hadn't moved to lay his hand upon hers, which she had rested rather obviously on the cloth. Nor had his eyes once met hers. Not surprising, perhaps, while he was talking so enthusiastically about Inspector Burden's pleasant manner with the team and had Hannah ever noticed that he was the complete reverse of rude abrupt DIs on television?

She guided the talk on to their own personal lives and learnt that Bal's parents lived in Somerset. His father was an accountant, his mother – well, she had never worked but was just mother to him, his brother and two sisters, and wife to his father. Hannah disapproved, of course, but now wasn't the time to say so. She was even more appalled to hear that his elder sister had had an arranged marriage. The shock she felt was impossible to conceal.

Bal laughed. 'I said "arranged", not "forced".'

'Just the same . . .'

'The point is, Hannah, that it's not just the same. Lamila's husband was a sort of cousin, second or third cousin. They didn't know each other but they were introduced and as a matter of fact they fancied each other from the start. If she hadn't liked him or he hadn't liked her that would have been that. There was no coercion. I can't see that it's so different from meeting someone through a dating agency except that our way is safer and, well, more decorous. Lamila and Kanti are very happy, and Lamila's going to have a baby. It'll be my parents' first grandchild. You can imagine how excited they are.'

'Would you do that? Have an arranged marriage?'

'We're not talking about me,' he said and she thought, no, we haven't been. Not at all. Just about your family. Not a word about what you want and aim for and dream of. Nothing about girlfriends and there must have been lots. With those looks he'd have had to fight them off. 'Now you can tell me the story of your life,' he said, pouring more wine for her.

She was less discreet than he had been. The last thing she wanted was for him to have the impression that she had led his sisters' kind of life, surely one of unblemished chastity until that arranged marriage was signed and sealed. She talked of the 'relationships' she had been in, those to which she had made a 'commitment' and those far more numerous encounters that had been casual. It would be disastrous were he to get the idea that she was interested only in serious long-term partnerships. The notion of the light-hearted but passionate affair was what she hoped to plant in his mind. As she spoke she watched his face but his expression was unchangingly pleasant and friendly. He seemed interested but not involved.

Dessert wine was offered her with her panna cotta but she refused it, taking caffeine-free coffee instead. To be sexy is one thing, unsteady on one's feet and – awful thought! – hiccuping, quite another. It was such a warm evening that she had no coat to be helped into, so no opportunity for Bal to lay his arm round her shoulders. Outside the restaurant it was brightly lit, but darkish in the car park. Town car parks are no places for dalliance but those in the country may be quite different, enclosed by hedges, overhung by foliage swaying from heavy branches, not even packed with cars except on Saturday nights. Walking across lawns and under a yew arch, Bal might have taken her hand or hooked her arm in his but he didn't. He even managed to open the car door for her without touching her shoulder.

The first thought of a woman in Hannah's situation is that the chosen man may be gay. She knew Bal wasn't without being able to say precisely how she knew. If anyone else had said to her, about knowing some fact, that she 'just had a feeling' she would have despised this answer but that was how it was for her. She had a feeling; she knew. Once they were back at her flat, of course, things would be easier. She had put a bottle of champagne in the fridge that afternoon. Although they had been changed just two days before, she had put fresh sheets on the bed. He lived only about a quarter of a mile away and in any case it wouldn't matter how much he drank since he'd be spending the night with her.

'You'll come in, Bal?'

He had pulled up outside Drayton Court and made her heart leap when he took the key out of the ignition. All the way home a voice had been whispering, but suppose he says no? He said yes, opened the car door for her and then the gate to the flats' garden. Her heart gave another little blip when he turned and pressed the remote that locked the car doors. He wouldn't have done that if he meant no more than to see her up the stairs and into her own domain.

But not far in and not for long. He refused a drink.

'You know how it is, Hannah. When one of us is over the limit it's the end. It's not like a member of the public who can weather it.'

'Half a glass wouldn't put you over the limit.'

They were sitting side by side on her sofa. At her pleading look, he laid one hand on her knee, leant towards her, smilingly shaking his head. She felt rather faint and it wasn't the drink but that long slender hand on her leg.

'You don't have to go home.' She would never have believed she'd feel so diffident, so bashful, making a remark she'd made, in various versions, so many times before. 'You could stay here.' He listened, one eybrow raised. 'With me,' she said.

It was suddenly as if he were very much older than she was instead of a year or two younger. With the hand that had rested on her knee he lifted her hand and brought it to his lips. Then he was on his feet, his face humiliatingly kind. 'I'm enormously flattered. You're just about the most beautiful woman I know, Sergeant Goldsmith. And nice with it.' He kissed her cheek. 'I'm going now but some time soon I'll tell you why I won't stay the night with you.'

Speechless, she nodded.

'I'm not gay and I'm not involved with anyone else. Goodnight.'

They had come out into Victoria Terrace and were making for car and van when an elderly woman came up to them, not to Burden but to PS Peach. Later on Burden was to be thankful for 'uniform'. If his team had all been in plainclothes their discovery might have been delayed for weeks. For the woman who was plaintively imploring a rescue operation be mounted for her lost cat would never, he was sure, have approached them if she hadn't seen the reassuring and comforting dark-blue jacket, trousers and cap of four of their number.

She gave her name as Mrs Lyall, Pauline Lyall. 'I'm not asking you to look for him,' she was saying. 'I know where he's got to. I can see him. Look up there.'

Burden looked. It was still light enough to make out, in a gap between the sheets of green netting, the orange and white shape of a large cat at an upstairs window. The cat's mouth was stretched wide open in what seemed a continuous wail. The last thing he wanted to do at this hour was somehow find a way into that house and catch, possibly with difficulty, this stupid animal. Burden disliked cats. But of course they had to go in, there was no choice about it.

'What's the best way to get in there, Sergeant?' he said to Peach.

'Back door, sir. It didn't look too secure. I noticed it when we were in the back.'

The cat's owner asked if she could come too. She would be a nuisance, he thought, but on the other hand the creature was more likely to go to her than to any of them. 'All right,' he said. 'Let's have a look.'

Lynn Fancourt, Damon Coleman and the rest were sent home. Burden, Peach and Pauline Lyall went round the back through waist-high weeds, snagging brambles and nettles which disobeyed the rule about not stinging when an R was in the month. Four steps led up to the back door of number four. Battens had been nailed diagonally across the door in which was a pane of glass. Burden didn't want to have to break that glass and there was no need, for when the battens were off the door came open easily, its lock being broken. They stepped into a large kitchen, fitted up in the style fashionable in 1950. Once they were out into the hallway, from which an elegant curved staircase wound, the cat's yowls could be plainly heard.

'Oh, poor Ginger,' cried Mrs Lyall. She was more agile than she looked and had begun running up the stairs.

Burden was no student of early Victorian elegance or he would have eyed the ceiling mouldings, the arched alcoves and the curving balusters, all scuffed and crazed and dilapidated as they were, with more interest. The house smelt of rotting wood and urine, and something else Peach said was mice. 'Which might account for that Ginger finding his way in here, sir,' Peach added.

Burden didn't care about Ginger's motivation, nor did he think the smell was mice. He had smelt it before and had hoped never to smell it again. Dreading what might be at the top, he followed Peach up the stairs. But there was nothing – except the smell. All the doors to the three rooms on this floor were wide open and Mrs Lyall stood just inside the largest one, holding a cat the size of a lynx in her arms and crooning softly to it.

'I can't tell you how grateful I am.'

He wanted her out of there. Of course, if it was what he thought it was . . . 'I'll just have your home address, madam, if you please.'

'Oh, yes, with pleasure. It's fifty-two Oval Road.'

'Right, then. If you'll just take – er, Ginger, is it? – home we'll do our best to lock up here.'

Calling back more thanks, she went downstairs carrying the cat. Burden heard her feet on the steps outside the back door.

'It's somewhere,' he said to Peach. 'I don't suppose the lights in this place work, do they?'

'No, sir. I tried.'

'I'll call in for back-up. And lights.'

When Burden had made his call they explored the rooms on this floor. There was a cupboard in each, one a large walk-in place, almost a room in itself, but nothing in any of them but rolls of carpet, rolls of wallpaper and a dead mouse. Peach seemed to think this mouse vindicated him but he admitted it wasn't what they were looking for. By now it was dark, the only light that which came from street lamps on stilts but was muted by the sheets of netting, an unearthly yellowish-green light that lay like a gilt varnish across floors and up walls. They went on up to the next floor, their footfalls noisy on the uncarpeted stairs, the smell growing stronger as they mounted. The stuffy heat was almost intolerable and Burden, a fastidious man, felt sweat roll down his sides, staining his oyster-coloured shirt. Fortunately, it was too dark for the wet patches to show. He thought that for ever after when he saw that sour lime-green colour he would associate it with the smell of death.

At the top of the stairs was a landing from which three doors opened. Here, when he opened the first door, he experienced a revulsion so strong that he almost gagged. The room was bare, a rectangle of sulphurous chrome light lying across the wooden floor, the colour of jaundice. In the far corner, beyond the yellow glaze and in deep shadow, he could just make out a door with a round knob and a keyhole.

'He'll have locked it and taken the key.'

'A cupboard, is it, sir? You want me to break the door down?'

'Check that it's locked first.'

Of course it was. A heavy muscular man, Peach put his

shoulder to it and at the second attempt the door gave way and burst open. Burden would have said the smell couldn't have been worse but it was. His eyes accustomed now to the darkness, he could just make out its source. He could see the bilious sheen of lamplight on long blonde hair and, with his handkerchief held against his nose, was stepping forward to take a closer look when the footfalls of those coming to help them sounded on the stairs.

The lights they brought showed, slumped against the rear wall of the cupboard, the body of a girl. The hair, which in the near-dark had looked glossy, even dazzling, now appeared as it truly was, streaked and matted with dried blood. Dark-red brick dust was on her face and marking the black T-shirt she wore. Her high-heeled white sandals were still on her feet and her white handbag was still hooked over one arm.

Burden had seen a version of that handbag before but of black leather, as ornamented with gilt buckles and studs and as heavily embellished with small buckled purses, on the arm of Sandra Warner, Megan Bartlow's mother.

Chapter 14

There was never any doubt that the dead girl was Megan Bartlow. The handbag which had been with Megan's body contained her credit card but nothing like the sum of money that had been found on Amber's and no banned substances. Unless the murderer had ransacked the bag, it confirmed Wexford's opinion that some women carry handbags simply as an attractive accessory and may keep nothing much in them. Megan's wallet had a ten-pound note and a fiver in it, several pound coins and a fifty-pence piece, no make-up, no tissues, no mobile phone, no cigarettes, nothing else but a pair of sunglasses with one lens missing.

Wexford and Burden sat in Wexford's office, leaving the team to a house-to-house enquiry in the Victoria Terrace–Oval Road area and a search for the owners of the house in the terrace.

'It has to be drugs,' Burden said. 'Where else would Amber Marshalson have got that kind of money? How else would Megan and Prinsip have got all that equipment except by dealing or trafficking?'

'We've no evidence that Megan used drugs or sold them or trafficked in them,' said Wexford. 'All we have to link the girls is the fact that they met, they made phone calls to each other and went to Germany together. And when you come to think of it, this is odd in itself. The class thing has changed enormously since I was young but some things about human nature never change. Amber came from a well-off if not rich background. She didn't go to a private school, true, but to a state school with a very high profile and then to a reputable sixth form college. She herself went back there after her child was born to do her A levels. She intended to go to a university. Her boyfriend and the father of her child comes from a similar background. His father is an ex-Member of Parliament and the son is at Edinburgh University.

'But take poor little Megan. Brought up in various dumps by a mother generally called a single parent in spite of the stepfathers she has given her daughters. Left school, I've no doubt, at sixteen. Shop assistant. Lives with Keith Prinsip who is one of these people who probably have never worked and, unless things change very much in this country, will take damn good care he never does work. What could have brought those girls together except some sort of business partnership, to put it grandiosely?'

'Drugs, like I said,' said Burden. 'As to what brought them together, Megan's sister Lara did. *She* was Amber's friend originally.'

'Yes, but though she came out of the same nest, Lara is a very different creature altogether. A cuckoo, maybe. She was at a different school from her sister, Amber's school, or at any rate she stayed on longer. She means to get on in life. Look how she dresses, how she's put some upward mobility into her accent. When she introduced Amber to her sister I don't think it was with a view to their becoming friends. I think it was because they were out together somewhere, happened to meet her sister and introductions were inevitable.'

'But it wasn't a one-off, was it? They must have got in touch without Lara's knowledge. One of them, Megan probably, recognised something in Amber, something in her appearance or what she said, maybe the words she used, that told her she'd be a suitable, well, business partner.'

'I can see all that. You're almost certainly right. But was it drugs she saw there? That which "defeats the steady habit of exertion but creates spasms of irregular exertion. It ruins the natural power of life, but it develops preternatural paroxysms of intermitting power"?'

'*What?*'

'De Quincey. I've been reading his *Confessions of an English Opium Eater.*' Getting up, Wexford almost laughed at his friend's bemused, slightly aghast, face. Adding to his consternation, he said, 'Not for work. For fun.'

'Oh.' Burden put on his polite face that was so uncomprehending it made Wexford smile.

'Anyway, if they were trafficking it wasn't opium. And traffickers don't use – usually. But I don't think it was drugs they were in partnership about.'

All of them, not just Wexford and Burden, knew the danger of holding a preconceived theory, yet each of them was doing this. The idea of the man in the hood was imprinted in their minds. A man in a hood had been seen on Yorstone Bridge at the time of the car crash; a man in a hood had been seen among the trees on 11 August when Amber was killed. And Amber and Megan were connected. Their deaths were connected, one surely consequent upon the other. So all of them, beginning their house-to-house investigation, were waiting to hear that a man in a hood had been seen in the vicinity of Victoria Terrace. But none of the people they talked to gave them the information they expected.

Mrs Lyall's house was furnished as a cat's abode. A kind of climbing frame the size of a small tree and composed of posts and bars and platforms, all covered in felt or bound with cords, dominated the living room. A scratching post and claw-exercising tray occupied another corner. Ginger's water bowl, feeding bowl and dish of snacks took up the area beneath the bay while the symmetry of the french windows had been ruined (in Burden's view) by the insertion of a cat flap of what looked like advanced design. Abandoned beside it, like a child's cast-off toy, lay a much-chewed cloth rabbit. The possessor of all this largesse lay asleep in the middle of a three-seater sofa, the length of its outstretched body making it impossible for anyone else to sit alongside it.

Burden took a small upright chair and, while Mrs Lyall went to make tea, directed at Ginger in a sibilant whisper a few well-thought-out insults. Tea and cakes were brought. Ginger slept on, snoring lightly and twitching as he dreamt. Burden asked about number four Victoria Terrace. Mrs Lyall's garden backed on to the garden of number four. What had she seen from these french windows in the past week? Had she seen anyone go in by the back door or come out? Or go in by the elegant if dilapidated french windows of number four with their panels of stained glass and their bars in art nouveau curves?

'If only Ginger could talk,' said Mrs Lyall, 'he'd have some tales to tell. He spends so much time in that garden, it's like a little woodland to him. Of course, he understands every word that's said to him, he's a particularly intelligent cat. It's just that he doesn't talk.' Anxious to justify this deficiency on the part of her pet, she added, 'It's not that cats aren't bright enough. It's something to do with the shape of their throats. I read that in my cat magazine.'

'But what have *you* seen, Mrs Lyall?'

'I sometimes think it's wrong of me to let him go out there. Go outside at all, I mean. My friends tell me I shouldn't and it's true I do worry when he's missing. I mean, anything might have happened to him when he was in that house. Whoever killed that girl wouldn't hesitate to kill an animal, would he?'

'Probably not.'

Burden told himself that, come what might, come what further ghastly anthropomorphic tributes to Ginger and admissions of exaggerated fears for his safety, he must maintain his politeness and pursue these enquiries with tact and consideration. Perhaps he should even take a tack more congenial to this household and gear his questions from Ginger's point of view. Swallowing hard and taking a deep breath, he began again.

'Do you think Ginger saw anyone behaving suspiciously around the back of number four Victoria Terrace? Would he be nervous, for instance, if he encountered a strange man in his, er, his haunts?'

Thank God he had come here alone! Imagine Barry Vine or Karen Malahyde hearing him talk this crass nonsense. It was clearly the right line to take. Laying a caressing hand on Ginger's large pointed head, Mrs Lyall hastened to assure Burden that her cat was afraid of nothing and no one. He was as brave as a lion. Just the same, about a week ago, the Saturday evening, as it was beginning to get dark, he had come through his cat flap from outside at tremendous speed and with a crash that set the flap swinging. She had looked out, naturally she had, and seen a man looking through one of the glass panels in the french windows of number four.

Burden was too old a hand at this to ask her if the man had worn a hood. The question was there, though, in his mind. 'What did he look like?'

He had his back to her, Pauline Lyall said. He wasn't doing anything, just staring in, but she hadn't liked him being there and had seriously considered calling the police, but suddenly the man had turned away and made his way across the gardens to where a portion of the wall was crumbling, giving access to Pyramid Road.

'Perhaps I should have called them. It's not right a man going about frightening an animal like that, is it?'

'Would you know this man again? Can you describe him?'

Pauline Lyall poured Burden another cup of tea. He thought he detected disappointment in her face that she couldn't pour one for Ginger.

'All I know is he was thin and tallish. It was getting dark, you see.'

'Did he have a hood?' Now he had to ask.

'A hood? Oh, no. It was so warm. You know how it's been. He was in one of those – what do you call them? – T-shirts.'

Burden thanked her for the tea and left, cursing under his breath and picking ginger hairs off his charcoal linen trousers. At least ten of the little houses in this street backed on to the gardens of Victoria Terrace. Karen Malahyde came out of number forty-eight as he walked past its gate.

'The old man who lives there says his sight isn't good enough to see to the end of his garden, let alone to that back door, but there's a woman at forty-seven who's positive those battens weren't nailed across the door until this week.'

'Have you been to forty-six?'

'Not yet, sir.'

'We'll both go,' said Burden.

Mrs Spear, catless but with a small suspicious-looking pug at her heels, had an invalid husband in a wheelchair and a blue budgerigar in a cage. John Spear's chair was positioned immediately in front of the french windows and, as his garden sloped a little towards its rear wall, the whole panorama of the Victoria Terrace land lay in his view. On the table beside him sat a small pair of binoculars.

'Nothing very exciting to see most of the time,' he said to Burden, 'but I get some surprises. There was a fox made her home down there in the spring – well, nest, I should say. She had her cubs there and I sat here and watched them playing for hours, didn't I, Eileen?'

The residents of Oval Road were animal-obsessed, Burden

thought, but Mr Spear might be a godsend just the same. He wasn't likely to find anyone else rooted to the spot, so to speak, and the spot the best vantage point in all the ten houses.

'Get a lot of birds too. They wake me up in the small hours with their singing. Still, better them than the courting couples. If courting's what they're doing. We had a different word for it when I was young and we thought you ought to get married first.'

'Did you notice the battens on the back door over there, Mr Spear?'

'I noticed *when* they were there. One day they weren't, they never had been, not in all the twenty-five years we've lived here, and the next they were. Eileen wheeled me over here eight o'clock in the morning, the way she always does, and I took one look out here and said to her, "Them bits of wood are new," and she said, "What bits of wood?" and I said, "On that back door at number four in the terrace."'

'And he was right,' said Mrs Spear. 'I looked and then I said, "You're right, Jack. Them bits of wood are new. I wonder why they put them there," I said and he said, "Somebody'll have broken in there and that's why they've done that."'

'Can you remember which day it was that you saw the battens for the first time?' Karen asked.

'Let me think.'

The budgerigar began twittering while John Spear thought. Outside, in the wilderness, a gust of wind blew through the bushes and set the leaves fluttering. No foxes, no human beings, no birds to be seen, but the hot strong sun blazing down.

'Got it,' said John Spear suddenly. 'It wasn't the day after we saw the young lady out there but the day after that. The day we saw her, like early evening it was, maybe sixish, it had clouded over and I said to Eileen, "The weather's breaking at last." But it didn't and the heat come back next day and the day after that them bits of wood went up.'

'What young lady would that be, Mr Spear?'

'Well, I say "young lady" but I don't call them ladies when they wear them miniskirts. She had one of them on and she was walking about in them bushes. I reckon she came in where they all do, through Pyramid Road where the wall's falling down. She went up to that door and looked at it. Didn't try it nor nothing like that, just looked and went away.'

Karen produced the photograph of Megan Bartlow and both Spears looked at it.

'Couldn't be sure but it looks a lot like her. Like her hair, isn't it, Eileen?'

'That's definitely her,' said Mrs Spear.

'Are you quite sure this was two days before the battens went up? Megan was murdered some time on September the first. The battens would have gone up to secure the door that same evening or night, and you saw them in the morning. She was here on the first, not August the thirty-first.'

'It was the thirty-first I saw her,' Mr Spear persisted. 'It was the day when the sky clouded over and I reckon it was a Monday. It was a Monday, wasn't it, Eileen?'

'Definitely,' said Eileen. 'We couldn't have seen her on the Tuesday because that was the day the ambulance came to pick up Jack and take him to his physio. Well, not an ambulance, they've got some other fancy name for it now. Incapacitated people carrier or some such. Well, that was supposed to come at nine and it didn't come till twenty to ten but you have to be out in the front ready for it, don't you? And then you're there all day.'

'I couldn't have seen her on the Tuesday because I was all day till four at the hospital like Eileen says.'

'It's the wrong day,' Burden said as he and Wexford walked across to the mortuary. 'But he insists he saw the girl on the Monday and not Tuesday when she was killed. A man was seen looking in at the windows of number four but not our perpetrator in a hood.'

'Our perpetrator without a hood, then? It was hot, as your Mrs Lyall said.'

'It was hot on August the eleventh but he was wearing a hood then. Is there any significance in the fact that both girls died on a Tuesday?'

'We don't know for sure if Megan did.'

But Carina Laxton confirmed the day. 'She died on Tuesday the first,' she said an hour later. 'She'd been dead four days when the body was found and I'd say early on that day, not after four in the afternoon. Certainly not. It would have been mid-morning.'

'Can't you be a bit more precise?' Burden sounded querulous.

'Not with this heat, I can't, and the body shut up in a cupboard. I suppose you know she was pregnant?'

'*I* didn't,' said Wexford.

'She was well advanced in pregnancy. About fourteen weeks, I'd say.'

Wexford and Hannah found Prinsip at the home of Sandra and Lee Warner. In the absence of Lara, the place seemed strangely to take on an untidy, even squalid, look. It was as if, while the girl was there, her surroundings picked up something of her neatness and order but once she was gone it reverted to its normal state with a sigh of relief. This flat on the Muriel Campden Estate was a house of mourning, but grief hadn't extended to Lee Warner's appetite. He was sitting in front of the television on a sagging sofa eating a burger with a fried egg on top of it, a double portion of chips and a thick slice of fried bread, the lot doused in tomato ketchup. His wife, who had let them in, wore a soiled whitish dressing gown hanging open over a T-shirt and sweat pants. She excused herself briefly and came back carrying a box of tissues with which she began wiping her dry eyes. Prinsip had a similar plate to Warner's on his lap, the food on it congealed as it lay there untouched. Laying a hand on his slumped shoulders, Sandra said, 'Have you got the animal who did this, then?'

'You didn't tell us Megan was pregnant,' said Hannah.

'You what?'

'Megan was pregnant, Mrs Warner. I assume you didn't know.'

'Too bloody right I didn't and nor did Keithie. What d'you mean, pregnant? There's got to be a mistake.'

'On account of I've had the chop.' Prinsip lifted his grey face to them, his mouth hanging open.

The plate would have slid off his lap if Sandra hadn't fielded it with considerable dexterity. 'He means he's had his tubes tied,' she said.

'A vasectomy – oh, I see.' Hannah was quite unperturbed by this revelation, Wexford not surprised. 'Nevertheless, she was pregnant.'

'Keithie', said Sandra Warner, sitting down and lighting a cigarette, 'has got six kids. Or is it seven, Keithie? No, six. From a' – she paused, racked her brains and came out with it – 'a previous relationship. It stands to reason he didn't want no more. Megan's got a kid, of course. I mean, it's adopted, best thing for it when all's said and done. Megan wanted it to have the best start in life, which she wasn't in no position to give it, though giving it up was a wrench.' She tapped the ash off her cigarette into the coagulated egg, burger and chips on Prinsip's plate.

'It doesn't tie up,' Burden said as they sat in Wexford's office, eating the sandwiches brought in by Lynn Fancourt. 'What was Megan doing in Victoria Terrace on the Monday? It was Tuesday she was there. And what was our perpetrator doing there on the previous Saturday evening?'

'You can make all those things fit', said Wexford, 'if you look at it this way. Our perpetrator, or OP, made a date with Megan and this meeting had some connection with the trade she and Amber were in and which he, presumably, was organising. Number four Victoria Terrace would have been his choice for a venue. Why, we don't yet know. Possibly he'd once worked there or had even lived there. On the Saturday he went there to check up on it and find the easiest way to get in.

'He arranged with Megan to meet her there at, say, nine thirty on the morning of Tuesday, the first of September. He would have told her the houses were empty, about to be converted, and with neglected gardens at the back. She was to come through those gardens from Pyramid Road, recognise number four by some sign, the colour of the paint on the door or the stained glass in the french window, something like that. Go up the four steps and she would find the door unlocked at the top.'

'Yes, all right.' Burden lifted the top slice of bread from his sandwich and contemplated the salt beef, potato salad and half-tomato underneath. 'Margarine,' he said. 'But what can you expect? All you've said is fine. I see all that. Only she was supposed to do that on the Tuesday, not the Monday.'

'No, but suppose she was a bit nervous about going there. OP may have been a frightening figure in her life – and with good reason, as we now know. What could be more natural than that she should try out his instructions and go over to Pyramid Road after she'd finished work on the Monday? Go into those gardens, have a look round, try the door – or just look at the door. If everything was the way he said it was she'd be reassured up to a point.

'She went back on the Tuesday morning. She left the note on the door at Gew-Gaws, got the bus to Stowerton, went into the gardens via Pyramid Road and found the back door to number four unlocked. Your Jack Spear didn't see her because he was in the front of his house, waiting for the ambulance to take him to hospital for his physiotherapy. How's that?'

'OK. It probably was like that. How's your sandwich?'

'It'd be all right without the mayonnaise, only the filling's nearly all mayonnaise and I hate the stuff. Hannah found the owners of Victoria Terrace, by the way. They're called Iannoides PLC. There are two of them, cousins, living in Cyprus. As you might expect, they're totally uninterested in poor Megan except insofar as her being killed on their property may affect sales of the flats when they've been done.'

'Have they got builders on contract yet?'

'Fish and Son of Stowerton to do the major work and Surrage-Samphire for the decorating. Apparently, these flats or "apartments", as the developers call them, I quote from their prospectus, are to be "recreated" in a very classy way. Victorian mouldings on the ceilings, panelling, carved woodwork, antique doorknobs and fingerplates, all that sort of thing. Surrage-Samphire are specialists in wood and plasterwork, restoration techniques, and so forth.'

'Funny name, isn't it?' said Burden. 'Not a name you'd forget. Have any of these people been into number four yet?'

'I imagine they all have. To take a look and give an estimate. Work's not due to start till the end of next month.'

As he walked home in the warm glowing dusk, Wexford thought about Megan Bartlow. She already had one child and had been pregnant again. What would have been that child's destiny? Children appeared to be treated in a very cavalier fashion by some of these people, easily conceived, no doubt, but easily disposed of once born, yet this in a time when 'the family' was spoken of with more weight and reverence than had perhaps ever been accorded it before. Keith Prinsip had six children, abandoned to their mother or mothers, no doubt. Then there was Brand – his thoughts often returned to Brand.

The little boy had another grandmother. If Vivien Hilland hadn't seemed a very maternal sort of woman to him, Wexford, that impression he had of her had nothing to do with the way she might be with Brand or the way Brand might see her. He recalled his visit to the house on the gated estate, trying to remember any sign of tenderness or sensitivity in Mrs Hilland, but finding none he did, at least, recover something else. That was where he had seen the name Samphire, on the sign in the Hillands' front garden: Surrage-Samphire, Specialist Decorators and Restorers. One of them, the man she called Ross, had put his head round the living-room door while they were questioning her and she had said Diana Marshalson had recommended him. Was this connection of any significance?

His daughter's car was parked at the kerbside. He told himself he was always happy to see his children but just at this moment, this evening, he would have preferred to be alone with his wife without Sylvia. Not that Dora had been her usual self recently. When they were alone together she never ceased to bemoan Sylvia's behaviour and constantly took him to task for being 'too lenient' with her.

Still, here was Sylvia now, inside and weathering her mother's scolding. He saw his grandsons first. Unaware of his arrival, they were at the bottom of the garden playing in the fountain made by the hose. Sylvia was sitting in an armchair she had turned round to face the wide-open french windows beside her mother who was in another, and this time it was his daughter who was holding forth, his footsteps unheard as he came into the room.

'It isn't that I mind Mary, she's a perfectly nice woman, but I do mind the fact that Naomi's set her to spy on me and she's happy to go along with it. She's taken to dropping in. She always wants to know how I'm feeling and if she can do any shopping for me or sit with the kids while I go out.'

'Some would call that very kind,' said Dora in her new scathing tones.

He made his presence known. 'Just in case you think I'm spying on you.'

'Oh, Dad.'

He went up to her and kissed her. 'Where does Naomi come into all this?'

'I was just telling Mother that Naomi's friendly with this woman who lives on the corner of my road and I *know* she's fixed up with her to sort of keep an eye on me. She's a midwife, you see.'

'Who, Naomi?'

'No, Dad, this Mary. Naomi doesn't trust me to look after myself properly while I'm pregnant. Oh, it's not me she cares about. It's the baby, *her* baby. Mary came in yesterday evening – without being asked of course – and said would I like her to check on the vitamins and supplements I'm taking to see if they're all right. And then she asked if was I eating properly. I'm not very big, was what she said, and she hoped I wasn't on a diet to keep my baby small. Mind you, she was laughing when she said it. She's always laughing even when things aren't in the least funny. And the awful thing is the boys adore her. She never gets cross, Ben says. Of course she doesn't, I said, she's not your mother. And then he said, and this really hurt, "I wish she was. I wish she was my mother."'

'Children', said Wexford, 'do say that sort of thing. I don't suppose there's a child who hasn't said it some time or other to a mother or a father. You said it to me once when I wouldn't let you go swimming on an icy day in May. It was an outdoor pool and your best friend Louise Cole was going. "I wish Mr Cole was my father," you said and it was like a slap in the face. But I came to learn that while you meant it at the time you didn't mean it for long and that's how it is with Ben. You'll see.'

Apparently touched by this story, Sylvia reached for his hand and held it. 'Mary's the real problem. I don't want her interfering in this. It's not that I don't like her. Actually, I don't think anyone could help liking her. It's knowing she only comes round because Naomi's sent her.'

'As far as you know,' said Wexford. 'Maybe she's been sent once and goes on coming of her own accord. If you like her you haven't a problem. Can't you just relax and enjoy her? And now I'm going down the garden to see my grandsons and after that I want a drink and my supper. I'm starving.'

Dora said nothing, watching him with cold eyes.

'I really hate that Naomi,' said Sylvia in the manner of a teenager. 'Sometimes I think I'd like to kill her.'

Wexford laughed. 'You're not supposed to say things like that to me. I'm a police officer – remember?'

Chapter 15

It was a Sunday. Thinking how pleasant it would have been to be meeting Bal for coffee or a drink and then how embarrassing and awful any encounter with him must now be, Hannah phoned Karen Malahyde and asked her if she were free.

They met at the Parasol Café recently opened by the Olive and Dove Hotel on the west bank of the Kingsbrook. Wooden tables and chairs were arranged under red and yellow striped umbrellas. The umbrellas were all unfurled this morning, as they had been every morning for months, keeping off the South of France-style sun.

'This is nice,' Karen said. 'The Costa del Kingsmarkham. Do you mind if I smoke?'

'Not in the least. Make the most of it. I'm sure they'll soon ban it in public places.'

They ordered caffè lattes and because it was close on midday and a Sunday, glasses of wine. The tables began to fill up, mostly with couples, as the Parasol Café offered a bistro lunch.

'Sundays are no good if you're single, are they?' Karen was expressing Hannah's own, highly unwelcome, thoughts. 'I don't know why they should be so different from Saturdays. Most of the shops are open. No one goes to church any more. The cinema's got the same programme as it's had all week. They shouldn't be different from Saturdays but they are.'

'Yes, you're right.' Hannah didn't want to agree with her. She wanted to be able to say it didn't apply to her, she had a boyfriend. Only she hadn't. And if she had Bal in mind, she never would have. 'But . . . if, for instance, we were married we might be expected to be home now cooking roast beef for a spouse. Oh, don't look like that, we wouldn't, not you and I, but we'd probably give in when it came to watching rugby all the afternoon and having tea with his old mum. As it is, we're free and' – she broke off, her attention caught by two women who had come to sit at a table nearer to the river bank.

'What's the matter?'

'I don't know. I think my eyes must be deceiving me. You see those two women at the table over by the tree, the copper beech? The one in the pink skirt and beads is Gwenda Brooks of Jewel Terrace and the other one is her husband's girlfriend.'

'You have to be joking.'

'I know, but I'm not. That is Gwenda Brooks and that is Paula Vincent. When I interviewed John Brooks he told me he was having an affair with that woman and sent me to her address in Pomfret to check out he'd spent the night with her.'

'And here she is about to have lunch with the wife. What d'you think it means?'

'I don't know, Karen, but I'm going to find out. No, wait . . .' Hannah clutched her friend's arm. 'That's him. That's the husband!'

John Brooks was approaching the table by the copper beech tree. Instead of kisses, he gave both women a little pat on their shoulders and sat down.

'Finding somewhere to park the car,' Hannah whispered. She got up and walked over to the Brookses' table, Karen behind her. Afterwards, she thought how with people more used to keeping cool heads, it might have been possible to bluff it out. Some kind of *ménage à trois* scenario might have been suggested by Brooks and Gwenda might just have confirmed it to maintain the respectability she was so fond of. But their reactions to the sight of her were very different, or those of Brooks and Paula Vincent were. He went white and she crimson. He stood up so abruptly that he knocked over a glass, which fell and rolled across the grass. Gwenda plainly had no idea what was happening. She stared.

'Perhaps you'd like to explain, Mr Brooks,' Hannah said, and suddenly she knew. She needed no explanation. Seeing John Brooks and Paula Vincent together she saw how marked was the resemblance. They might have been twins. Perhaps they were. 'Ms Vincent is your sister, isn't she?'

It was Gwenda who answered her. 'Of course she is. Why shouldn't she be? What do you want?'

'At present, Mrs Brooks, nothing from you.' Hannah turned to Paula Vincent whose colour had subsided and who was looking defiant. 'Would you care to explain, Ms Vincent?'

'There's nothing to explain. I did what John wanted, that's all.'

'I don't think so. You lied to the police.'

'What is all this?' Gwenda Brooks was shouting now. 'What's going on? I want to know. I've a right to know.'

Ignoring her, Hannah said, 'Lying to the police is an offence, Ms Vincent. The same applies to you, Mr Brooks. Whatever else may come of this I can't tell. For the present, however . . .'

Karen intervened at a nod from Hannah. 'You'll both be charged with wasting police time.'

Back at her flat where Hannah set out smoked salmon and salad on the table on her little balcony, Karen pointed out drily that since Brooks had obviously not been committing incest in Pomfret, he must have been up to some other illicit, if not illegal, activity.

'Yes, but what?' Hannah poured orange juice into two ice-filled glasses.

'At the moment, without having given it much thought, I can't see why if he was visiting some woman he couldn't give you her name instead of the one he did. After all, until you spotted the sister with Gwenda, you and the DCI believed he was committing adultery. So what difference does it make who it was?'

'It does make a difference,' Hannah said. 'Come and eat. Of course it makes a difference. For one thing, the real woman might not have been quite so willing to tell us he was with her. She may have a husband or live-in boyfriend. I realise that's unlikely seeing that Brooks visited her by night but it's possible if, for instance, husband or boyfriend worked nights. Also, you've got to remember that if his sister's name got back to his wife all she's going to do is enjoy the joke. It's quite another thing if the real woman's name gets back to her.'

Karen laughed. 'He was taking quite a risk having that little lunch party with both wife and sister.'

'Oh, I don't know. The public don't believe we have private lives. When we're not on duty or in uniform, as the case may be, they think we get into our boxes and pull down the lids till our next shift starts.'

'Then what about all those cop sitcoms they see on TV?'

'They know that's not real,' said Hannah, 'and they're right.'

After Karen had gone Hannah found her sunglasses, rather a nice Armani pair, lying on the arm of her sofa, and when the phone rang an hour later she was so sure of who it was that as she lifted the receiver she said, 'Hi, Karen. They're here.'

Bal's voice said, 'Who are there? Are you having a party?'

Blushing when one is alone is so absurd as to make one blush again. This was what happened to Hannah as she struggled to find a voice, her cheeks burning and the sun pouring in at the open balcony doors. 'I thought you were a pair of sunglasses. I mean I thought you'd lost a pair of sunglasses.'

'Never wear the things. If you're not having a party will you come out and have a drink with me?'

She was astounded. After last time, what did he want of her? She couldn't ask. 'All right,' she said.

'I've had more enthusiastic responses to my invitations. But no matter. Shall I come round in about an hour?'

Friday might never have happened. He was nice, warm, with plenty to talk about. Except that he obviously wasn't gay, he behaved rather like her gay friends did when she was out with them. She could be relaxed with them, free and easy, because she knew they would never make a pass. Yet, what was she thinking of? The other night Bal making a pass was what she had passionately wanted . . .

She hadn't dressed up like last time. If she changed the white trousers for a black pair it was only because on a hot day white doesn't look fresh after a few hours. They sat in the garden of the Olive and Dove and after a time, after they had talked about everything under the sun but their work and his private life, she started thinking, but he's not gay, he's not. The appreciative look he'd given her when they met confirmed that. On an impulse she said, 'Bal, have you got a girlfriend? Is that what it is?'

He laughed. 'Is that what what is?'

Usually so open, she couldn't put it into words and she fell back on the feeble, 'Oh, *you* know. You know what I mean.'

His smile was that of a man who is going to let someone off the hook or just give up teasing. 'Right, I suppose I do. No, I haven't got a girlfriend. If it's possible, I hope – no, I won't say that. Not yet.'

She laid her hand on his and he let it lie. It was a nice hand, she thought narcissistically, long and smooth and slender, the nails longish but unpolished. She hated nail varnish and by the way he looked at her hand, so did he.

'If you mean', she said, 'what I think you mean – no, I can't ask. I'm not as uninhibited as I thought.'

'Hannah.' He leant towards her across the table, said, 'Come on, let's walk. It's a lovely night. I can't say what I have to say with all these people around.'

She was going to walk beside him but without touching him. As they went down the flight of stone steps that led to the footpath across the meadows, he took her hand and hooked it over his arm. The air was still and quite cool by now, and from a dark horizon a red harvest moon was rising.

'If I know my Kingsmarkham as well as I think I do, I can walk you home across these fields and call in at that little pub on the Kingsbrook on the way. Meanwhile, I'll try to explain.'

In the little pub on the Kingsbrook, once called the Anchor, now renamed the Gooseberry Bush, Wexford and Burden and their wives were having a last drink. Neither man would have dreamt of dividing the party into two groups, the men to talk shop and the women left to domestic issues, but Jenny had divided it herself, wanting only Dora's ears for her diatribe on the horrors of fitting twenty-first-century teenagers for their A levels. Snatches of the conversation reached Wexford, expressions such as 'national curriculum', 'dysfunctional families' and 'parental responsibility', but when he attempted a remark he was too forcibly squashed by Dora to try again.

'Why the Gooseberry Bush?' he said, changing the subject.

The barman didn't know.

'I suppose they just liked the sound of it,' said Burden. 'No one eats gooseberries any more, though.'

'I made gooseberry jam two years ago,' Jenny said, 'but no one wanted to eat it.'

Wexford laughed. 'A gooseberry bush is what you find babies

under. That's what my grandmother told me. Even then it was an out-of-date version of the facts of life. When she was a child she'd been told it was the stork brought babies. That was the favourite explanation, which is odd when you consider there have never been storks in England.'

Dora cast up her eyes, he didn't know why. The break in the conversation this scorn of hers caused Burden rushed in to fill with his continuing certainty that drug smuggling was at the bottom of the two girls' deaths. If only they could find a witness, if only there were a shred of evidence. But he, Burden, would find it, he would never give up.

'A kind of human Buster, are you?'

'If you like to put it like that,' Burden said rather stiffly.

'I think it's something else. The trouble is I don't know what else. It's a matter of finding what could have brought them that kind of money and I don't know.' He saw Dora move her chair and turn her back on him. Waiting for Burden to argue and realising he wasn't going to, he said, 'I've got two things on my mind that on the face of it don't seem important yet I feel they are. Very.'

'Oh, yes?' Burden was smarting a little from the comparison with Drusus, the drugs-busting dog. 'Like what?'

'I'd very much like to know what the website was Amber tried to get access to but couldn't and wanted it so much she asked for John Brooks's help.'

'Probably some company putting out cheap pop CDs or the sort of things teenage girls want. You know, you've had two. Fancy face creams or stuff for waxing their legs.'

'I expect you're right. No doubt you'll dismiss the other thing with equal facility.'

'Try me.'

Wexford thought, Dora said when we first knew about this baby that Sylvia's behaviour would wreck our family. Is it starting to wreck my marriage? Aloud he said, 'The Hillands offered

Amber their flat in mid June, to have possession in November. What they never said to us and we didn't ask about was the rent. Was it to be rent free?'

'Surely.'

'You really think that? I'd say surely not. Crenthorne Heath isn't a very upmarket suburb but it's nearer to London than Croydon and it's on a tube line. If they let the flat they could get two or three hundred pounds a week at present prices. Are they so well off they could afford to miss out on that for what might be years?'

'You're saying', said Burden slowly, 'that they offered the flat to Amber but probably at a reduced rent. Of course she accepted but she knew she had to start making money. Old Marshalson wouldn't pay it.'

'No. He'd have wanted to avoid losing his daughter even if that also meant keeping Brand.' Wexford's eye caught his sergeant and one of his DCs entering the bar together. Well, it was as he had thought. . . . 'Tomorrow, we'll find out,' he said.

The giant in the 'Riverbank' T-shirt was again on duty at the Hillands' gates but more affable this morning. He let their car in with a smile and a cheerful 'Good morning, gentlemen'. Wexford was surprised to see Surrage-Samphire's board still up in the Hillands' front garden. The work seemed to be completed and very stylish it was, if somewhat over the top. The hallway of this house was just a little too small and its ceiling a little too low to carry such grand linenfold panelling, such ornately carved shields and elaborate Tudor roses. But Surrage-Samphire certainly knew their business.

Vivien Hilland seemed rather taken aback by his praise of the workmanship as if she expected policemen to confine their comments entirely to forensic matters. Neither Cosima nor Daniel was anywhere to be seen this morning. With both her children absent, Mrs Hilland seemed calmer and under less strain. But when Wexford told her that Daniel's friends had provided him with satisfactory alibis for the night of 10 August, instead of relief she showed indignation: 'Well, of course. What else would one expect?'

He asked her about the rent of the Crenthorne Heath flat.

'We were charging her a token rent.' She sounded defensive and he understood why when, asking her to be more specific, she said, 'Well, actually, a hundred a week.'

'Where was she going to find a hundred a week, Mrs Hilland?'

No doubt she hadn't much cared for Burden's tone. Her defensiveness was even more marked when she said, 'That really wasn't our concern. It was actually about a third of what she would have had to pay for the flat if she'd been let it by anyone else. As a matter of fact her father phoned me to say paying rent meant she couldn't take the flat but that was all nonsense, that was just him saying anything to stop her going, he was so besotted with her. As for Diana, she's got plenty of money and I think she'd have paid the rent herself just to get rid of the girl. Let me tell you something. I think girls like her need to be taught responsibility and the value of money, and that's exactly what our offer would have done.'

There seemed no more to be said. As both got up to leave, the front-door bell rang. 'That will be the men coming back for their tools,' said Mrs Hilland.

Someone else's footsteps crossed the hall to answer the bell and when Wexford and Burden came out of the room they found Cosima there with a fair ruddy man of about thirty. Wexford, who had expected to see the man called Ross who had been there on a previous occasion, introduced himself and asked him who he was.

'Colin Fry's my name,' said the rugby player, his eyes following Cosima's long legs moving up the stairs.

'You work for Surrage-Samphire?'

'Got it in one,' said Fry.

'Who else does?'

'There's me and Rick and Mr Samphire. That Megan something, that's what all this is about, is it? If you want to know about that place and the work and all, you want Mr Samphire. Mr Ross Samphire. He'll know all about it.'

Chapter 16

Leaving the inquest on Megan Bartlow, Wexford walked down towards Gew-Gaws, the shop where she had worked. When he pushed open the door Jimmy Gawson's bell rang, summoning him from the back regions. Wexford had known Gawson slightly for years, long before the opening of the shop, and rather liked talking to him for the pleasure of hearing an accent so Etonian – or ham actor outrageously overplaying Etonian – that it strained credulity yet never lapsed.

'Ah, good morning, Chief Inspector,' he now said, extending a pale and rather damp hand. 'I've told your good people absolutely everything I can about that fateful morning, you know. Which, actually, amounts to very little. I wasn't here and by the time I was here poor little Megan had vanished and her note was on the door.'

'I know. I don't want to talk about that. I want to talk about *her*. What you know of her.'

Gawson waved his hand at a seat for Wexford and sat down himself behind a counter laden with plastic models of Big Ben, miniature London buses, stick-on Union flags, photographs of Princess Diana and nodding-head bulldogs. He took an inhaler off a shelf, inserted a nicotine cartridge and drew heavily on it.

'Just as good as a cig,' he said, 'but cheaper and good for you. Marvellous, isn't it? I've been on them for three years now.'

Doubting that Gawson was using his device for quite the purpose it was designed for, Wexford made no comment. 'You were going to tell me about Megan.'

'You mean you thought I was going to tell you about Megan. The question is, do I know anything about her? She was most awfully common, you know. The sort of person this government calls socially excluded. Nice expression, that, don't you think? She would certainly have been excluded from any society of mine.'

Wexford knew that if he was rude to the man he ran the risk of getting no more out of him but he couldn't help himself. 'I don't know that I'm much interested in your views on the class system, Jimmy. Apart from being several miles beneath the likes of a purveyor of tourist trash, what sort of a girl was she? Did you like her? Silly question, I suppose. You're too grand for likings.'

'Now come on, my dear. You know all I said was my little joke. Where's your sense of humour? There was no harm in Megan, I suppose. Her accent hurt my ears. I actually believe one of my tympanic membranes was permanently damaged by her assaults on it.'

Wexford watched him take his third or fourth draw on the nicotine inhaler. 'Did you ever see her, well, engage in any transactions in here that weren't strictly a matter of flogging mini-Buckingham Palaces to unsuspecting visitors?'

'You mean drugs, don't you? Oh, I know all about it. Who doesn't? You've not exactly made a secret of the great drugs bust you mounted in this burg. But no, I didn't. Frankly, I don't think she'd have had the nous.'

Wexford shook his head. 'You'd make me wonder why you employed her, Jimmy, if I didn't know. You were paying her below the minimum wage, weren't you? You needn't answer that. It's too late. But if you take on another assistant, I should watch it. That's all. The boyfriend in here much?'

A rapid succession of puffs had exhausted the cartridge and Jimmy Gawson inserted another. 'As I've said, Megan wasn't too bright but she was Einstein compared with him. I wouldn't have him in here. He tried it on once or twice but I told Megan no way. Her mama would have fancied dropping in for a chat but I squashed that too. In fact, my dear, the only one of that family I wouldn't have objected to was Grandma.'

'Grandma?'

'Old Gracie Morgan, that is. Years and years ago when all the world was young, lad, and all the leaves were green, and we Gawsons were Kingsmarkham gentlefolks, and that *meant* something, Gracie used to do for us. She must be over ninety now, as I know from Megan who used to go and see her some-times. You might say a fondness for old Gracie was the only thing poor little Megan and I had in common.'

'Those things you're sucking on', said Wexford distantly, 'are designed to wean you off smoking, not to supply you with alternative dope.'

He left, his dignified exit slightly marred by bending down to pick up a London Eye, re-created in silver plastic, the hem of his raincoat had swept off a low table. To Burden later he said, 'Jimmy mentioned a woman called Grace Morgan to me. I know I've heard the name and not long ago but I can't for the life of me think when or where.'

'I can,' said Burden. 'She's one of our witnesses, or would be if she'd seen anything. She's ninety-three and she lives in that cottage in the woods where we think whoever chucked the concrete at Amber's car must have passed by.'

'She's also Megan Bartlow's grandmother.'

'You mean . . . ? Wait a minute.'

'We didn't know that when Hannah and Lynn went to see

her. Jimmy wasn't interested in Megan's private life but her grandmother may have been.'

'Yes. Well, we talk to Grace Morgan.'

'We will. As soon as possible. I don't want to sound callous but when you're ninety-three death is an existential hazard, so it really is urgent.'

A soft mist hung low over the fields. Because it had been dry for so long and the trees starved of water, their leaves were turning early. The woods were yellowing before autumn had come and while the sun was still hot. It blazed through the veil of mist, burning it off from everywhere but the shady places and the deep hollows. Wexford and Burden left the car at the top of Yorstone Lane and walked along the footpath that led into the woods. The berries on the Wayfarer's Tree which grew here in great profusion had turned from green to gold, from gold to red and now were almost black. In the distance a woodpecker could be heard, its beak drilling into a tree trunk.

'I wonder how long she's lived here,' Wexford said. 'Years, of course. Maybe all her life. And every time she went out and came home she had to walk this path, carrying whatever she had to carry, her children at one time, I expect.'

'Mm.' Burden wasn't much interested.

'You could bring a car across here. You can see by the ruts that people have. Possibly our man did. And you could take it into the wood – just.' They were among the trees now and the path had narrowed. 'The tree trunks are too close together to bring it much farther than this. He could have left it over there.' Wexford pointed to a grassy space, almost a lawn, over-hung with hawthorn and a canopy of brambles. 'Under that lot it would be almost concealed.'

'Especially if he wasn't fussy about his bodywork. Those branches would cover a vehicle with scratches.'

Wexford nodded. 'The pity is that we didn't know about this – that is, we had no reason to suspect that the concrete block off the bridge business was an attempt on Amber's life until her death six weeks later. We thought it was a simple act of vandalism. "Taking revenge on society", as some people call it, not directed at a specific target.'

It is not uncommon for the homes of very old people to look, to the careless eye, as if they are uninhabited. Their own eyes are no longer able to see dirt and untidiness. Decorating is expensive and DIY is now beyond them. The curtains at their windows, often lace or net and once pristine white, collect dust and hang limp inside fly-spotted glass, and these windows are seldom opened, if by now they can be, for the elderly feel the cold. Mostly, too, they are poor and often proud so that their relatives think this is their chosen way to live, not what it really is, a precarious hanging on to life at whatever cost.

These thoughts passed through Wexford's mind as Grace Morgan's house came in sight, a squat, brownish, part-tiled, part-thatched cottage surrounded by a dilapidated picket fence. The front gate had come off its hinges and lay across a slight hollow in the path, placed there evidently to serve as a bridge or ford in wet weather. It was so long since there had been any wet weather that the path itself had dried to dust and the once-green grass of the clearing in which the cottage stood turned yellow like hay.

It was unlikely that any house in the villages from Framhurst to Forby had all its windows closed today. Except Grace Morgan's. Their frames looked rotted, as if you could poke your forefinger through the woodwork, as if any attempt to open them would cause the whole window to collapse.

'I suppose she's out,' said Burden in a gloomy voice. 'That comes of having no phone. Everyone', he added illogically, 'has a phone.'

'She's not out.' Wexford banged the door knocker hard.

'If you do that you'll frighten her to death.'

'If I don't,' said Wexford, 'she won't hear.'

They were on the point of giving up when the door was at last answered. Grace Morgan was a tiny woman, shrunk to several inches under five feet, thin, spare and shrivelled. Her face was a mass of wrinkles, cobwebbed and grey as a cobweb is. What remained of her hair was a white wisp screwed up on the top of her head with two long black pins. She looked not in the least disconcerted by the arrival of two tall men she had never seen before. 'You look like policemen,' she said.

'That's so, Mrs Morgan.'

Burden showed her his warrant card, then Wexford showed his.

'It's no good, I can't see. It's all a blur. Might be James Mason and Michael Redgrave for all I know.'

After offering this evidence of a distant cinema-going past, Grace Morgan opened the door wider and stepped back to let them in. 'It was two girls as came last time. DS this and DC that, whatever it means. I don't hold with girls being policemen. What happens if they get hit or shot?'

Wexford said he hoped that wouldn't happen and that DS Goldsmith and DC Fancourt were very good officers.

'That may be but girls do get killed. Look at my granddaughter Megan. She got shot.'

Believing it unnecessary to correct her, Wexford said that was what they had come to talk to her about. They were very sorry about it, it must have been a great shock to Mrs Morgan and a blow. He understood her granddaughter was a frequent visitor to the cottage.

'Frequent, did you say? Depends what you mean by frequent. I reckon I'd seen her three times since Christmas and Christmas I was at my daughter Sandra's. Reckon I was bound to see her there. When she came here it was on the scrounge.'

'The scrounge?'

'That's what I said. She knew I never spent all my pension, not living here and having the meals on wheels. There's a girl comes with it on a bike. If Megan came it was to borrow my pension. Well, "borrow" is what she called it. I never saw it back, that's for sure. I will say for Sandra, she never knew.'

She had brought them into a dark-brown living room crowded with dark-brown furniture, and smelling of boiled greens and reused fat and camphor, and clothes worn year in and year out without being washed or cleaned. The only thing in the room that looked less than a century old was the television set. Burden said afterwards that he couldn't understand anyone who had television not also being on the phone but Wexford disagreed. You got entertainment and companionship out of the telly while all you got out of the phone was complaints and nagging.

'Mrs Morgan,' he began, 'I've been wondering if Megan came to see you the evening you were watching for the badgers?'

It was a long shot but when she asked 'Did she what?' he repeated it and reminded her that on the evening she had seen the hooded figure in the wood she had only done so because she had been watching for badgers.

'Better than the telly, they are, if only you can get to see them. If nobody comes along and makes them all skedaddle.'

'Did Megan do that, Mrs Morgan?'

'She was upstairs. She wanted fifty pounds off me and I sent her upstairs to fetch it. Get her out of my way while I watched the badgers but they never came that evening.'

'The man with the hood, Mrs Morgan' – Wexford felt his heart begin to sink. Had he been wrong again? 'Could Megan have seen him from upstairs? Did she mention seeing a man?'

'Not her. There's two rooms up there. I sent her up to the back. That's where I keep my pension money, see? I said to fetch it all down and I'd give her fifty out of it. So she did, after that fellow in the hood had been and gone. She came down with the tin it was in, there was a hundred and thirty-five pounds in there. I give her fifty in five ten-pound notes and she had the nerve to ask for more. Well, mustn't speak ill of the dead.'

'How long after that did Megan stay with you?' Burden asked. He was wearing a new lightweight jacket of light tan seersucker and was beginning to wonder if the smell would adhere to its fibres. More dry-cleaning, he thought. 'Five minutes? Ten? Longer?'

'About twenty, I reckon. It was dark. I said, have you got a torch, going back through that wood and she said she'd got the lamp on her bike.'

'She came on a bicycle?'

'That's what I said. She went off. I said to her, don't you bother coming again if all you want is cash. Mustn't speak ill of the dead, eh?'

The air in the wood smelt wonderful. Like flowers and new-mown hay and ripe apples, said Burden, uncharacteristically lyrical. They walked back along the path, inhaling the scented air with deep pleasure.

'What d'you think?' Burden said, sniffing his jacket as he did after he'd been in a smoke-filled pub.

'What do I think? I think Grace is right when she says Megan couldn't have seen Hood from upstairs when he was on his way to the bridge but she saw him on his way back. She left her grandmother just about the time he too would have been returning.'

'If he returned. If he didn't go on over the bridge.'

'I think he returned, Mike. He'd have wanted to go back the way he came because going on over the bridge would mean that (a) his vehicle, whatever it was, was parked on the other side and (b) by going on he'd have a detour of at least six miles before finding his way back to his vehicle. No, Megan saw him. That's what I think. Whether he saw her we don't know. She saw him and knew him.'

'How d'you make that out?'

'Because she found him again. She knew where to look. I'm not saying she knew him better than just knowing him by sight. And then . . .'

'You think she blackmailed him?' said Burden.

'I think she tried. As Mrs Morgan said, mustn't speak ill of the dead, but Megan Bartlow wasn't exactly a nice girl, was she? She borrowed money off her grandmother who seems to have lived on nothing but the state pension, and never gave it back. It may be politically incorrect to say so but I don't think much of a girl who's living with a man and gets herself pregnant by someone else. Though we don't yet know what it was, she was carrying on some illegal trade.'

'Drug trafficking,' said Burden.

'You remind me of that guy in the Roman Senate who used to get on to his feet every day and say "Carthage must be destroyed". *Delenda est Carthago*.'

'And?'

'Well, it was destroyed finally. End of story.'

Getting into the car where Donaldson sat waiting for them, Burden said triumphantly, 'There you are, then. That proves my point. It's drugs.'

Wexford ignored him. 'I've no difficulty in believing she was blackmailing OP.' The car started and gradually cool air began to pour in. 'That's better,' he said. 'The forecast is there's going to be a storm later. I think she saw him coming back from the bridge, probably saw him getting into his car which he'd very likely left where we thought he had and probably thought no more about it until the crash was in the *Courier* and Lara told her or Amber told her herself she'd been involved in it. Even then she wouldn't have thought OP was a murderer, only a normal sort of vandal, the kind of person she'd no doubt associated with all her life.'

'But when Amber was killed she'd look at it differently.'

'Exactly. In spite of what Jimmy Gawson says, we've no reason to think Megan was a fool. She'd have put two and two together and what she came up with was that Hood had made his first murder attempt with the concrete block off the bridge and that his second was successful.'

'Does Prinsip know any of this?'

'I doubt it but we'll try him. Try Lara and the mother too but blackmailers don't often confide in what these days we have to call their loved ones or anyone else, come to that. Funny, isn't it, "loved ones" are usually talked about in connection with families where there's no love lost. No, Megan knew OP's identity and she kept it to herself. When the time was ripe she went to see him and demanded payment for silence. A very risky thing to do, as we know. She made an arrangement to meet him that Tuesday morning. Now we know that she died on site and on that Tuesday morning. She went into Gew-Gaws at nine, put that notice on the door and, knowing Jimmy Gawson never came in before ten, went off to Stowerton on the bus, hoping to be done and back again before ten.'

'OK. That's good. I see all that. But that means he could be anyone. Almost anyone could have gone into that house in Victoria Terrace.'

'Give me a break, Mike,' said Wexford. 'Unlike the White Queen, I can't think of six impossible things before breakfast.'

'Which reminds me, I got to that inquest so early I never had any.'

'Nor me. I think we should. Vice has changed, hasn't it. It's no longer adultery that's the crime, let alone fornication. Beat someone up and no matter if he never walks again, you're out after two years inside. Drunk driving and killing a couple of kids disqualifies you for a bit and sentences you to what amounts to nine months. Smoking dope is "what everybody does" but have a cigarette and you're a pariah, though that's nothing to eating a fry-up in a greasy spoon. That's the ultimate sin. Shall we?'

'Why not?' said Burden.

Trying to concentrate on all the paperwork which must be completed before charging John Brooks and his sister with conspiring to pervert the course of justice, Hannah let her thoughts drift back to the previous evening. At the entrance to the Gooseberry Bush she and Bal had almost bumped into the guv, his wife, DI Burden and *his* wife, an encounter which vaguely embarrassed her. Still, it would have been worse if they had all been there at the same time. Bal had bought drinks and then, touching her hand but not holding it, he'd said, 'I haven't taken a vow of celibacy. I'm not "saving myself for marriage", the way this new virginity cult recommends, though I expect my parents would like it if I did. This is nothing to do with them. This is – well, if and when I get into a relationship, I want it to be serious. I don't want a one-night stand, I don't want a drifting into something, I don't want an affair with someone because I'm here and she's here and we might as well. Do you understand?'

'I don't know,' Hannah had said.

'I wish there weren't so much jargon in use. I'm using it myself, I know I am. I mean, I wish I didn't have to talk about "commitment" but that does express what I'm on about. What I'm saying is, if I'm going to start seeing someone – you, for instance – I want to get to know you first. I want to know what you like and don't like, and I want you to know what I like and don't like. I'd like us to know about each other's families, what we believe and don't believe, what we're aiming at and what we want to avoid. All that sort of thing.'

Hannah said, bracing herself, 'You mean you don't want to

make love to me till you've known me for ages? That way you might never do it.'

He laughed. 'Not ages. A few weeks, maybe. Is that so terrible?'

'I suppose not,' she said. 'This, actually, is a bit embarrassing.'

'Only because you're not used to it. I'm not used to it. We're used to making love to someone the first time we go out if we fancy them. Make love first and talk afterwards. I've reached a point where I want it to be the other way round. I want it the other way round with you, dear Sarge, because I've got a feeling this may be serious. So will you come to the cinema with me one evening this week?'

Of course she had said she would. He took her home and kissed her but didn't come in. She went to bed to think about it all but fell asleep before she could. And now she had these forms to do . . .

Bacon and eggs (which the proprietor of the Queen's Café described, American fashion, as 'sunny side up'), fried potatoes, fried bread, fried tomatoes (the 'healthy option') and fried mushrooms. Wexford hadn't enjoyed a meal so much for a long time. The only thing that marred it was the possibility of Darren Lovelace coming in for a cappuccino and witnessing his indulgence. Encountering his daughter Sylvia as soon as he and Burden came out into the bright sunshine of Queen Street was far less alarming, though she did immediately remark on the nature of the place he had come out of.

'Listening to you,' he said, 'anyone would think I'd been in a brothel.'

'Which would probably do less harm to your heart.' She introduced him to her companion. 'This is Mary Beaumont. Mary, this is my father and this is Mike Burden.'

'I've heard a lot about you,' Mary said, apparently

including both of them. 'Policemen, aren't you? I don't care what others say, I think you're doing a grand job. Grand. It wouldn't suit me. You could get a knife in you or a bullet through you at any minute.'

'We're not used to so much praise,' Wexford said. 'Stick is what we usually get but not bullets. Not often, anyway.'

She laid her hand on his arm and smiled broadly up into his face. She was a very plump black woman in her forties in a scarlet dress with large black-and-white flowers all over it and her smile was like an advertisement for cosmetic dentistry. 'I'm just giving Sylv a hand with her shopping. "I don't need you, Mary. I've got the car," she said but I said, "So you can take the car into the supermarket? You can take it up the escalator at Marks & Sparks?"'

In a frosty tone, Sylvia (who was never called Sylv) said, 'Mary has been very kind.'

'And don't think it's just because Naomi asked me. It's my pleasure, you have to know that.'

Wexford and Burden said goodbye and it was nice meeting her. 'Sandra Warner now, I suppose?' said Burden.

'Mike, I think we'll have her and Prinsip over at the station. I can't stomach that place of hers and that husband of hers. Not after eating that fry-up I can't.'

Chapter 17

Prinsip, sitting under the butcher's block painting, from the way he ground his heavily studded boots back and forth across the carpet, seemed determined to gouge a trough out of it. This behaviour irritated Sandra Warner who told him to stop it.

'I can't. It's my nerves,' he said. 'It's what I've been through.'

'I've been through it too,' said Sandra.

Since Wexford last saw her she had had her hair dyed jet-black. It couldn't be for mourning, the idea was too bizarre, but it seemed to him an unfortunate coincidence. Huge rings in gold metal, each the size of a bangle, hung from her ears. She wore a very short red skirt and tight T-shirt. Both she and Prinsip chain-smoked. Suggestions were frequently made that Kingsmarkham police station should become a smoke-free zone but opposition from the Chief Constable, himself a smoker, and from Wexford who considered it a bit mean-spirited, had delayed this move indefinitely. Now, he thought, he was paying the price of his tolerance with what felt like the onset of asthma.

He tried not to cough, which made his coughing worse. Naturally, Prinsip and Sandra thought he was putting it on and Prinsip lit another cigarette from the stub of the last one, continuing to grind his right boot into the carpet.

Seeing Wexford temporarily incapacitated, Burden took up the questioning: 'You've no idea who this man might be?'

'Me, I've got my own ideas,' said Prinsip.

'OK. Can we hear them?'

'He's like the father, innit?'

'The father?'

Flicking back a long lock of black hair, Sandra answered for him. 'You don't want to listen to him. He's like obsessed. He's got this obsession there's a chap Meg was meeting that's the father of the kid she was carrying. Well, you can't blame him, can you? There must have been someone. You don't get that way selling Union Jacks in souvenir shops.'

'So your opinion, Mrs Warner, is that this man' – Burden hesitated while he decided how best to put this – 'was in an . . . er, a relationship with Megan?' He looked away from Wexford's wince. 'Mr Prinsip?'

'Course it was,' said Prinsip. 'What else? If he'd of come near me I'd of killed him.' Slow though he was, Keith Prinsip seemed to realise in a dim way that it is unwise to say this sort of thing to two policemen. He amended this remark. 'I'd of made him sorry.' With no idea of what he was implying, he added, 'He wouldn't of done it twice.'

Believing she should defend her daughter's virtue, Sandra said, 'It wasn't nothing like that. This bloke was maybe a customer in the shop she met once. My belief is that this kid she was carrying was Keithie's. It's a well-known fact them vasectomies aren't a hundred per cent.' She smiled fondly at Prinsip. 'Not when a bloke's young and fit like Keithie.'

The young and fit Prinsip sighed heavily, his face grey and sagging, his chest concave and his hands trembling. 'Do leave off what you're doing to that carpet, Keithie,' Sandra said, 'and have another fag. And you can give me one.'

Finding a presentable voice, Wexford said, 'We believe this man was Megan's killer. I realise all this is very distressing for you both but I think it necessary to explain. We believe Megan saw him coming away from Yorstone Bridge through the woods where your mother lives, Mrs Warner. The probability is that she threatened to come to us unless he paid her to keep quiet. I am sorry to have to tell you this.'

Regret was unnecessary for Sandra had failed to understand him. 'Yeah, well, I don't know what you're on about. Who is this bloke?'

Burden sighed, but with his inner voice. His face remained calm and patient. 'We hoped you could tell us that, Mrs Warner.' He looked from her to Prinsip and back at her. 'Did Megan mention any of this to you – either of you? Did she ever say she'd seen a man she suspected might be involved in causing the road crash under Yorstone Bridge? She said nothing about seeing a man in the woods on the evening she had been to Mrs Morgan's? Nothing about recognising him when she saw him again?'

'It don't mean a thing to me,' said Prinsip.

'Nor me, Keithie.'

A concrete block, a brick, maybe two kinds of bricks . . . 'Do you know anyone in the building trade, Mrs Warner?' Wexford asked. 'Did Megan? Do you, Mr Prinsip?'

'Only my Lee,' said Sandra, 'and he's been out of it ever since he put his back out in ninety-six.'

'I think she just saw him in the street,' said Burden after they had gone. 'Saw him and recognised him as the man she'd seen in the wood.'

Wexford took up the reconstruction. 'We have to remember that the first time she saw OP she probably didn't know him. He was just a man walking through a wood at night. It was dark and she'd have been, if not frightened, a bit alarmed, aware of his presence. That's going to be *why* she noticed him. I dare say she wouldn't have remembered him later if she'd seen him in broad daylight in the High Street but she saw him after dark in the wood. Saw him, no doubt, by the light of her bicycle lamp.'

'Where did she see him again, then?'

'If we knew that we'd be close to answering the whole thing.'

They went up to Wexford's office, a room where the slatted blinds had been kept half closed for weeks to keep out the brilliant light. This morning that unseasonable sun had been veiled first in thin cloud and was covered by now in piling cumulus. Wexford opened the blinds, then raised them on to a sky panorama of clouds like mountain ranges, like the view from an aircraft where white and grey and purple vapour has tumbled and swelled into a fantastic landscape.

'It's still hot,' he said, then, 'We've never done a, well, a character analysis of the man we're looking for. It is a man, isn't it?'

'I think so. We ought to assume it's a man while leaving the possibility open that it could be a very strong woman.'

'He's young middle-aged, I'd say. Forty or a little more. The district is well known to him. He has a car or a van. Possibly unemployed. On the side, somehow or other, he's engaged in some illegal trade.'

'Drug trafficking,' said Burden.

'*Delenda est Carthago*. He's engaged in some illegal trade. Something involving that trade was his motive for attempting to kill Amber in June. That was his motive for killing her in August.'

'But not his motive for killing Megan?'

'We've already settled for that motive being to silence a blackmailer.'

'But that doesn't work,' Burden objected. 'The two girls knew each other. They went to Frankfurt together carrying drugs. Please don't say that "*delenda*" stuff. They went to Frankfurt together *for business reasons*. Not because they were friends but they did know each other, through, no doubt,

Megan's sister Lara. They also, both of them, knew OP. OP knew them. He got them to go on the trip. That means when Megan saw him in the wood she already knew him. He was, in a manner of speaking, her employer.'

'So?'

'Would she have dared blackmail him? She'd know him for a ruthless dealer. She'd have had a good idea what he was capable of. In fact, she'd *know*. She knew he'd first attempted to kill Amber, then succeeded in doing so.'

Wexford sat down behind his desk. The air felt heavy. He was beginning to get that feeling some people suffer from when the air pressure suddenly falls, a tiredness, a throbbing in the head. 'It doesn't work, Mike,' he said, 'because of your insistence on drugs, because you're determined that OP employed those girls to do his drug running for him. Oh, I know the two of them were up to something they shouldn't have been, that's for sure, but there was no dealer involved, no ruthless character paying them to carry class A substances to Germany. How many of your old drugs contacts have you questioned about this?'

'Twenty-nine,' said Burden promptly.

'And have you got a word out of any of them implicating Amber and Megan? You haven't, have you?'

'Since you put it like that, no.'

'Those girls didn't know OP, neither of them knew him until Megan saw him in the wood. She didn't recognise him then, she'd never seen him before. Some time later – probably weeks later – she read or someone told her about the concrete block dropped from the bridge and Amber's involvement in the crash. It came to her then that the man she'd seen might be the perpetrator. Time went by, weeks went by, and during that time maybe the two girls met for whatever purpose they had previously travelled to Frankfurt together. Then Amber was killed. In the days that followed or the weeks that followed,

Megan saw OP – in the street, in the shop, driving a car – and recognised him. She found out where he lived and they met. Maybe he paid her once but OP doesn't waste time. When she demanded money the second time he killed her. Right?'

Burden nodded, unconvinced. He turned to look at the window as, far away, like gunfire in the siege of a distant city, thunder rolled. 'What now?' he said, walking to the door and leaving the question unanswered. Wexford stood where he had left him, looking from the darkening cloud-piled sky down to the yellowed grass, the dry rattling leaves and the dusty roadway, when he saw Lara Bartlow cross the High Street and enter the police station forecourt. He hadn't asked her to come. No one had. She was coming of her own accord. A small surge of excitement made him pick up the phone and ask the duty sergeant to send Miss Bartlow straight up here.

She was in the same black trouser suit. Her white T-shirt was very white and her face was free of make-up. She took the place in her stride, not fazed, scarcely hesitant. 'All right if I sit down?'

'Why don't you take that chair?' Wexford went behind his desk. 'I'll sit here. What did you want to say to me?'

'There's things I should have said and I didn't. That day in your car, I mean. When you gave me a lift to college.' She paused, looked steadily at him. 'Meg wasn't dead then.' She corrected herself. 'Well, she was but I didn't know it. I didn't want to tell on my sister. But you can't – well, betray, that's what I mean – you can't sort of betray someone that's dead, can you? I wish she'd not been with that Prinsip, though. I wish she'd got shot of him first.'

'You know Megan was pregnant, Miss Bartlow?'

'Call me Lara, please. Oh, I know. Not that Meg told me. It was Mum that said. It wasn't that Keith's, I'm glad of that, though I don't know why I say it. The poor baby's dead too, isn't it?'

'What did you mean about betrayal, Miss . . . er, Lara?'

She looked up at him, a steady gaze. She was no prettier than her sister, though Megan's had been a face he wanted to call unfinished, as if it were made from clay and the potter had got bored and knocked off early. The nose had been spread and too long, the eyes small, the mouth wide and uneven. Lara's skin was equally fair, would be ruddy in middle age, and her hair equally straw-like, but there was character in those features, astuteness, determination and perhaps some quality of soldiering on against the odds.

'I'd better tell you for a start that I don't know what they were up to, her and Amber. "In business together", that's what Meg called it. Of course I said what business and she said she'd only tell someone if they were in it too, if they had what she called "the qualification".'

'The qualification?' said Wexford.

'I hadn't got it, she said, so it was useless thinking I could come in on it. If I didn't know, she said, I couldn't tell anyone. I didn't like that much because it was through me she met Amber. I mean, Amber was *my* friend. I said I could still go to the police. It's not against the law, she said, and then she sort of thought and said, well, maybe it could be if it goes the way I reckon it will.'

'This wasn't drugs, was it, Lara?'

She shook her head vigorously. 'I know it wasn't. Meg wouldn't touch drugs. That Keith uses grass and I've known him use speed and E. Meg tried E once. It was after her baby was born – you know she had a baby when she was fifteen? – and it made her so sick. They took her into the hospital but she never said what was wrong – well, Mum told them it was food poisoning. Meg never touched the stuff after that and she wouldn't have been dealing, I know that.'

It looked as if Carthage had finally been destroyed . . . 'This business, as you call it, Lara – presumably the aim was to make money?'

'I asked her. She said you couldn't make mega-bucks but it was a nice little earner. When they went to Frankfurt, that was really Meg like introducing Amber to the business. They were going to meet some people there and there'd be what Meg called a "transaction". Amber told her the word, she said.'

'But what was it?' Wexford said.

'Look, I really wanted to know. I said, you've got to tell me. Well, you'll get to know in time, she said. Mind you, I think she liked making a mystery out of it. One thing I do know. It started with the Net. She hadn't got access then but Amber had. Later on, when she'd made a bit of money, her and Keith bought a computer and all the accessories and CD players and a digital camera, the lot. But not then. That's how I think it started with the two of them, I mean their sort of partnership. Meg came to Bling-Bling with me one night. Prinsip was up in Brum seeing his old dad. I reckon he'd got money to leave. Nothing else'd have fetched him up there so often. Anyway, Meg came to the club. That'd have been . . . oh, wintertime. February, I reckon. Amber was there with Ben Miller and Samantha and – I don't remember how it came up – Amber said she'd been looking something up on the Net and Meg said, oh, you're lucky, or something like that. You see, I think that up to then she'd been doing the best she could in the Internet Café. I know she went to Amber's place in Brimhurst because she told me what a great place it was. She called it a mansion. That was her word, a mansion.'

February, he thought. 'Exactly when was the Frankfurt trip?' he asked. 'Refresh my memory.'

'She'd never been to Europe before,' said Lara. 'Well, only over to France, picking up cheap booze and fags with that Keith. She sent me a postcard with a picture of the hotel her and Amber stayed at.'

Again that quickening of the blood, that jump of the heart. 'Have you still got it?'

'No. I never kept it.'

'Pity.'

'Mum got one too. I remember the date. It was May the twenty-second.'

A month later, Amber had been in the car crash. The offer of the Hillands' flat had already been made to her and in early July she had become eighteen. She never went away again and nor, apparently, did Megan. On 11 August Amber was killed and Megan killed exactly three weeks later, on 1 September.

'Do you often go and see your grandmother, Lara?'

It was a surprise question and he could see she didn't like it. 'Not as often as I ought. It must be a couple of months.' She levelled at him once more that direct gaze. 'To be honest, I don't want to go through the woods. The woods are scary.'

'Are they? Why?'

'There's been two girls murdered here since August. I don't want to be the third one. The man who was trying to kill Amber with that rock, he could have gone through there.'

'Megan never mentioned to you who he might be? I think it was someone she knew.'

'She didn't know anyone but us, Mum and Lee and me, oh, and Nana, and Keith's people and she really hated them.'

'The baby that was adopted – did she ever see him? Him or her?'

'It was a little girl. No, she never did. She was my sister and I loved her and I don't want you thinking I didn't, but she could be quite cold-hearted when it came to kids. She never wanted any, she said, and she was glad to see the back of Kili – that was her baby – never had a moment's regret about having her adopted. I suppose she'd have done the same with this one.'

Chapter 18

He asked Burden and Hannah. 'What qualification could Amber and Megan have had in common?' he asked them. 'Nothing academic, I don't mean that. Some physical peculiarity?'

'Both young,' said Burden. 'Both female white Caucasians. Much the same sort of height and figure.'

Hannah was shaking her head. 'They had much more not in common. One woman was good-looking, the other not. One was blonde, the other dark. One was living with a partner, the other living at home with her family. One left school at sixteen, the other was going on to higher education.'

'None of that gets us very far, does it?' Burden shrugged. Everyone who came into this room gravitated to the window to contemplate the sky, the gathering clouds, ink-coloured and snowy. 'I've seen the builders who'll do the work on Victoria Terrace. They're William Fish and Son of Stowerton and they tell me they don't have keys to any of the houses. They've been in to look the place over, of course they have, but they've no keys. Fish says no one would need a key if they were prepared to do a little breaking and entering. None of the back entrances was securely fastened. A child could have forced the back door of number four.

'As we know, Surrage-Samphire are doing the decorative work.' Burden perched himself on his favourite corner of Wexford's desk. 'Ross Samphire is the dominant one in that partnership and the one with the cabinet-making skills. He's been to Victoria Terrace and been inside all the houses, assessing what has to be done on the decorative side. On the face of it, he seems a respectable sort of bloke . . .'

'But yet,' said Wexford, quoting from his favourite play. '"I do not like but yet." What's wrong with him, Mike?'

'It has to be prejudice,' Burden said. 'He's a very good-looking man and he knows it. On his living-room wall he's got a huge nude. I don't know anything about art but could tell this wasn't a reproduction of something you'd see in a gallery. More like the sort of stuff you used to see for sale in DIY places in the nineties. I don't mean it was indecent. There were too many wispy bits of scarf floating about on it for that. But Ross Samphire is married with kids and it wasn't the sort of thing a woman would fancy up on her walls.'

Wexford burst out laughing while Hannah fixed on the inspector a stony gaze. It was a glare, Wexford thought, which encompassed disgust with Ross Samphire, distaste for that sort of picture, militant feminism and impatient contempt at Burden's whole philosophy of life.

'It has to be prejudice, as you say,' he said. 'Who's Surrage?'

'His wife's maiden name. I suppose it's some tax dodge. She doesn't take an active part in things. The brother is called Rick. He lives in Pomfret and his job description is "company secretary". But these people only have a tenuous connection with the house where Megan's body was found.'

'Maybe,' Wexford said, 'but they have a rather complex connection with several aspects of the case. Look at it this way. They were contracted to do the interiors of the houses in Victoria Terrace. They were used by the Marshalsons in jobs done according to their interior designs and they were recommended by the Marshalsons to the Hillands. Now there's nothing sinister in any of this on the face of it but it is a three-fold connection.'

The pressure in Wexford's head seemed to slacken a little as the sky darkened. He crossed to the gauge on the wall, turned off the air-conditioning and flung open two of the casements. Hannah looked shocked. Burden went to the window and took a deep breath. Above the skyline, the outline of the downs, a tree of lighting, thick twisted trunk and flaring branches, reared up in a brilliant dazzlement.

'Storm's coming at last,' Wexford said.

'Surrage-Samphire, guv,' said Hannah at his computer, 'have a website. Here it is.' Burden was looking at the screen over her shoulder. 'Ross is very proud of all his qualifications, diplomas and whatever. A lot of City and Guilds stuff, training at the William Morris School and a year spent in Florence studying.

'Rick is hardly mentioned here. Lots of illustrations of wood carving and plaster moulding and statuary and . . .'

Thunder cracking, then rolling and reverberating, cut off the end of her sentence. The sound it made was like barrels rolled off the back of a truck into the cellars of a pub. He stood at the window as the wind began to rise, increasing in seconds from a gentle breeze to a tearing gale that ripped leaves from the trees.

'Anything known about where these people were on June the twenty-fourth?'

'Ross was away on holiday in the south of Spain with his wife and kids,' Burden said. 'I don't know about Rick. I haven't talked to him yet.'

'It must have been bloody hot,' said Wexford as branched lightning suddenly sprang from the dark curves of the downs. The thick clouds, purple, deep grey and a livid-edged white, began to drop rain in great globules that made coin spots on the car park tarmac. Suddenly the cloud canopy seemed to split and spill rain which in seconds poured in sheets. Wexford closed the casements as water splashed against them inside and out. 'Alibis for the relevant times will have to be checked. It probably really is a matter of eliminating people from our enquiries.'

'Yes, apart from your threefold connection, which is pretty tenuous, we've no reason to suspect them. You might as well suspect Jimmy Gawson for having a threefold connection with the Bartlow family, employing Megan, having her live above his shop and knowing her grandmother.'

'Maybe I do,' said Wexford.

Burden ignored him. 'I asked Ross about September the first. He says he, Rick and a man who works for him called Colin Fry were all in the old Westminster Bank Building in the High Street here – you can just see it from this window – from eight a.m. till four p.m.'

They were all at the window but the sheets of rain made it impossible to see the old bank building on the corner of Queen Street.

'All of them would have had easy access to bricks and concrete blocks. We ought to know more about this Rick before we go searching for more people with a knowledge of Victoria Terrace.'

'Did Megan herself have any connection with it?' Hannah asked.

'It might be a good idea', said Wexford, 'to ask Sandra Warner about that. And perhaps Lara Bartlow. Incidentally, is there a Mr Bartlow about?'

'He lives in Pauceley, guv. He's remarried and got more children. I think he's worth a visit.'

When they reached the foot of the staircase it was impossible to get out of the double doors, the rain was so torrential. It was the kind of rain that falls in the tropics, straight down, taps turned on to full capacity. If a dark translucent curtain had been hung between the doors and the forecourt it could not have obscured more densely the parked cars, the walls and the street beyond. All that could be seen were black shapes and a curious kind of glitter as the torrent streamed on to the tarmac, plummeted and splashed. Everything had become black but shiny, colour banished, wet beyond belief as puddles grew into lakes and a million points of rain struck and bounced off sheets of water. And all the time lightning, the zigzag variety now, split the sky, growing closer and closer, moving overhead as the thunder came a nanosecond after its visible sign.

Donaldson was stuck outside in the car. A twenty-yard dash to the doors would have half drowned him. The duty sergeant, Campbell, came out from behind the desk and two women PCs emerged from an office, to stand at the big windows and watch the storm. When Bal Bhattacharya came out of the lift and crossed the black-and-white floor to join them, Wexford saw Hannah turn her head and their eyes meet and knew at once in that glance. So long as whatever was going on didn't disrupt his team . . .

Off to pick up her sons from school, Sylvia had given a lift to Mary Beaumont, whom she found waiting for a bus.

'My husband's got the car today,' Mary said and, with a burst of laughter, 'Naomi'd call that domestic violence.'

'I expect she would' and Sylvia laughed too, feeling even more drawn to Mary when the other woman said she hoped Sylvia had noticed she hadn't been dropping in. 'How did you and Naomi meet?'

'Oh, didn't you know? At SOCC.'

'What's SOCC, Mary?'

'The Sussex Overcoming Childlessness Circle. I do a bit for them. A bit of counselling. To get back to me and you. You know you can drop in on me any time. If you need anything, that is, or there's something troubling you. I'll give you my mobile number.'

'Well, thanks, but they do keep an eye on me at the ante-natal centre, you know.' Once the words were out Sylvia thought they sounded cold. 'I don't want you to think I'm not grateful.'

'Nothing to be grateful for. Would you drop me at the next corner?'

But by the next corner the rain had begun, in half a minute had reached torrent proportions and Sylvia had to park the car. On a double yellow line. It was no use, she couldn't have driven on. The windscreen wipers were unable to cope, in minutes the roadway would be under water. Leaning back against the driver's seat, Sylvia felt the baby move more strongly than had yet happened. For the first time she could see the movement. Mary saw it too and announced the sight with a peal of laughter.

'He's a big strong boy, Sylvia.'

'He's a girl.'

'That'd please Naomi. They'll have to keep your two at the school till this stops.'

'If it ever does, even if it doesn't, would you and your husband like to come round for a drink about six?'

The stereotypical middle-class family was how Hannah saw the Bartlows – and therefore looked on them with a distaste she was careful not to show. Their home, in a Pauceley close, was a three-bedroomed semi-detached house with a Norway spruce (discard from Christmas past) in the front garden and a doorbell which rang like a peal of church bells.

Almost certainly in expectation of this visit, the living room – three-piece suite, television, a small terrier and a boy and girl sitting at the table doing homework – was exquisitely tidy,

Gary Bartlow's wife in afternoon frock and make-up, Gary himself looking sheepish in the suit he had worn to work. He had come a long way since his marriage to Sandra Warner but probably as far as he would get. Hannah thought it sad that a man, in bettering himself, should take this route to this goal – another dreary marriage (as she saw it), another dull family, no doubt a crippling mortgage when he could have been free, adventurous, ambitious. Bourgeois was the word and she often thought it a shame that it had gone so utterly out of date.

Having assembled the family for Hannah's edification, Mrs Bartlow swept children, homework and dog out of the room to leave her husband alone with the policewoman, as she would no doubt have called her. Gary started to talk about Megan.

'I've always seen my girls,' he said. 'My big girls, I called them. Poor Megan – it was terrible, wasn't it?'

'Yes, it was. Very terrible, Mr Bartlow.'

'She was over here just a while before, you know. On the Saturday. Let's see, it would have been August the twenty-second. It was the day of the Pauceley Summer Fair. They have it on the water meadows down by the river. Meg came over for that. Keith was up in Birmingham with his sister, I think. She had a bit of lunch with us and then we all went down to the fair. I didn't think I'd never see her again.'

'I don't want to cause you any more distress than you must be feeling already, but did Meg say anything to you about her pregnancy? You did know she was pregnant?'

He made a face, a kind of wince, rueful and resigned. 'After she was dead I did. Her mother and me, we talked. It's not something we often do but we did after Meg was . . . was killed.'

'Did Meg say anything to you at lunch or at the fair? I mean, anything unusual, anything apart from ordinary family things?'

'Nothing I can recall.'

'Well, if you do, Mr Bartlow, if you remember anything, you will let us know, won't you?'

Hannah went back into the torrential rain she had come from. The car was parked no more than a dozen feet away but by the time she had unlocked the driver's door and flung herself inside her clothes and hair were dripping with water. She was supposed to be going out with Bal this evening. Going out with, not staying in with. Wherever they went they'd get soaked again – with no warm comforting bed at the end of it.

Across the valley of the Kingsbrook the storm swept on. A man on Sewingbury golf course was struck by lightning and died at the fourteenth hole. The River Brim burst its banks where it ran beside Mill Lane but no water reached the kitchens and living rooms of the three houses in Jewel Terrace. Those of the overhead electricity cables in the Brimhursts, Myfleet and west Kingsmarkham that were not damaged by lightning were beaten to the ground by wind and rain. The light went out in Dora Wexford's fridge, the ice began to melt in her freezer, her oven ceased to function but her gas hob still worked. Sylvia had no ice for drinks when the Beaumonts scuttled round under umbrellas at six.

Chapter 19

The morning was dark, so dark as to need lights on – only there were no lights. He had forgotten about the power failure when he got out of bed and even then didn't connect it with the hot water. But there was no hot water either. He hadn't had a cold shower since a holiday in Spain and that had been years ago. The cold shower was welcome then but very different now. When the first jet struck his shoulders he thought it would kill him.

Dora was still asleep but stirring. He asked himself why he should make tea and bring it up to her when she treated him as if he had betrayed her. Because he refused to put on a solid front with her against their daughter? He wouldn't. Let her see what it was like to be cold-shouldered. Then he told himself not to be a fool. That was the way marriages started to break up. Those were the opening moves. He went downstairs, put a saucepan of water on the gas hob, two teabags in cups and lit the gas. 'I just hope there's enough bottled gas,' he said aloud.

The saucepan seemed to take ages to boil. He took the cup up to her. She was sitting up on the side of the bed and she had been crying.

'What is it?'

'The baby,' she said. 'I can't bear it. I can't bear the thought of never seeing our grandchild. Not because it's died – that would be appalling, I know – and not because its mother can't afford to bring it up, but just through a stupid whim. One of the worst things ever thought up in the world we have to live in.'

He put his arms round her but she stiffened and pulled away.

'We'll never see it – him or her. Yet we'll know he's nearby, a few miles away. In time to come I could be out shopping and see him and not know it's him. I could keep looking for his features in the children I see. Why can't you see it my way? Why do you have to see her point of view?'

'Because I'm a different person, I dare say.'

'People who are married are supposed to be one.'

'I'm afraid that's too idealistic. We have to agree to differ. Can't we do that? I don't like it any more than you do, you know. I just don't see the point in doing anything now. We can't cut ourselves off from our child and think, well, we'll send her to Coventry for a while and then we'll all be close again. Because it's never going to go away. It's as you say, he or she will be living quite near us. Sylvia herself will be affected by it too, whatever she says. She'll need us because, if you come to think of it, she won't really have anyone else.'

The same type of brick, possibly even the same brick, had been used to kill Megan as had been the murder weapon in Amber's case. One, as the plinthologist said, of a million like it. None of them, as it happened, in the vicinity of Victoria Terrace because none would be used in its reconstruction and refurbishment. But they could be found, Wexford reflected bitterly, on almost every other building site in the county; in the country, come to that. William Fish or one of the two men working for him, or Ross Samphire or his brother or the assistant who had been at work with him at the Hillands' house, any of them could have picked up a brick probably within yards of their homes.

On the side of the hill behind the town, lights were coming on in houses where before all had been dark since the previous afternoon. Theirs would be on too and he'd be able to have a hot shower in the morning. He had called the Samphire link with this case threefold but wouldn't it really be fourfold? Surrage-Samphire worked for Marshalsons' Studio. They had done decorating work for the Hillands. They were about to start work on the house where Megan's body had been found. *And* Ross Samphire had met Amber. He had done more than just seen her, for the last time she had come to the Hillands' home he had been in conversation with Vivien Hilland. He had been talking to her when Amber and Brand arrived. So four connections, though all of them tenuous.

He rang for Hannah and when she came said, 'I'm getting over to Sandra Warner's and I want you with me.'

'Right, guv.'

'We'll walk.'

No doubt she would have much preferred Baljinder's company to his. That was natural. They walked in silence and he thought about his daughter and her sons. Like Dora, he was beginning to wonder if things could ever be right again in a family of which one member had been taken away, if the others, mother, grandparents, even sister and cousins, could ever quite forget, could ever forgive. For the first time he asked himself what it had been like in Sandra Warner's family when Megan had given her baby up for adoption. According to Lara, she spoke of it robustly, as if this relinquishment of the child was so obviously wise and prudent that there was barely any question about it. Did she really feel that way or was she merely putting a brave face on it? And what about Megan herself? How had she really been? How would his Sylvia really be when she had given birth and handed the baby into Naomi Wyndham's arms?

He didn't speak at all for nearly ten minutes and then it was Hannah who spoke first, asking him in a small voice unlike her usual tones what they were to see Mrs Warner about.

'Samphire,' he said. 'Does she know him? Megan's pregnancy. Can she throw any light on that? I'm doing it', he added rather bitterly, 'because, frankly, Sergeant, I don't know what else to do. We have nothing to go on except the fact that Ross Samphire was contracted to work on Victoria Terrace and Ross Samphire had once seen Amber. That's all.'

They went up the concrete staircase of the flats on the Muriel Campden Estate and took the walkway five doors along to Sandra Warner's. Lara had already left for her business college. Lee Warner was close in front of the television set, his shoulders hunched and his head thrust forward like a turtle's from its shell. Breakfast things, however, had been cleared away, and Sandra divested of her dressing gown and wearing a mauve tracksuit. Lee took no notice of the two officers. As far as he was concerned, they might not have come in, but, rather to Wexford's surprise, Sandra was pleased to see them and gratified by their visit, which she seemed to take as a kind of condolence call.

'It *is* good of you. We appreciate it, don't we, Lee?' No answer from the television watcher. 'It's true like my Lara says about the police being more community-friendly.'

'Then perhaps you'll give us a few moments of your time, Mrs Warner,' Wexford said. 'I have some questions for you.'

'I don't mind,' said Sandra graciously. 'What was you wanting to know?'

'Number four Victoria Terrace,' Hannah began. 'I'm sorry to have to remind you of the place where your daughter was found.'

Sandra made her reply quite cheerfully. 'That's all right.'

'Did she know the house? Did she ever talk of it? Say she'd been there?'

'She never did to me. It's funny you ask because my Lara said to me only yesterday, "Meg never mentioned that place, did she?" she said. "Whatever made her go there?"'

'At the time of her death,' Hannah said, 'Megan was approximately fourteen weeks pregnant.'

'As long as that, was it?'

'About fourteen weeks, yes. That takes us back to conception having taken place about the last week of May.'

'Right,' said Sandra uncertainly.

Wexford said, 'Megan was in Frankfurt in Germany from the twenty-second to the twenty-fifth of May. Have you any idea if she might have met the father of her child during that weekend?'

'Well, she never said. Mind you, she wouldn't. Not with her being with Keith. I mean, like being married really, isn't it?'

'Did she ever mention the name Samphire to you?'

Before Sandra could reply, Lee turned his head and said irritably, 'Can't you go in the other room? It's not some film I'm watching, it's the Cup.'

'We'll go in the kitchen, love.' Sandra turned to Wexford. 'I'll make you a cup of tea. I'm sure it's the least I can do.'

The kitchen was barely big enough to contain three people. Wexford was crammed up against a fridge whose door was stuck all over with postcards attached to it with magnets of teddy bears and ducks. Hannah had to sit on a stool and Sandra, waiting for her kettle to boil, propped herself up on one corner of a washing machine.

'Samphire,' Wexford said, trying to jog her memory.

'I've never heard that name.'

'Did she ever speak of someone called Ross?'

'Not to me she didn't.'

His teacup was passed to Wexford. Reaching to take it from Sandra's hand, he brushed his arm against the fridge door and dislodged one of the cards and its teddy bear magnet. Getting down on his hands and knees in that none-too-clean place wasn't much to his taste but he did it, picked up the fallen card and in doing so spotted another one a little way underneath the fridge. This had perhaps been dislodged in the same way weeks before.

At once he knew what it was. The card showed a house with steep red roofs, green shutters, a sign that said, Hotel Die Vier Pferde above a picture of four brown horses with blond manes pulling a carriage. The date on the postmark was 22 May. That was before Sandra's recent marriage and Megan had addressed it to Mrs Sandra Lapper. In an unformed, rather shaky hand she had written, *Wish you were hear. The sunshine is nise. Luv Meg.*

'This is the card Megan sent you from Germany, Mrs Warner.'

'Ooh, let's have a look. So it is. I wondered where that had got to. Funny writing, innit?' She scrutinised the Gothic script in which the name of the hotel was lettered on the old-fashioned inn sign. 'More like Chinese. However do they read that?'

'May I have it?'

'Ooh, I don't know. It's like the last thing of hers I've got. I'd best hang on to it. I'd feel funny if I let you have that.'

They left soon afterwards. Wexford went up to his office and noting that the time in countries on the continent of Europe was eleven a.m., one hour ahead of here, asked International Directory Inquiries for the number of the Hotel Die Vier Pferde in Frankfurt.

The building in Kingsmarkham High Street which had once housed the Westminster Bank had been put up at the time when banks were grand edifices, red brick or white stucco with porticoes and double oak doors, long stately windows and, inside, high decorated ceilings, panelling made from tropical hardwoods and marble floors. Like Victoria Terrace in Stowerton, it was to be transformed into luxury apartments and the work of conversion had already been done. Burden found Ross Samphire there on his own. Ross was putting the finishing touches to panelling in the hallway of the penthouse flat, much the same kind of design as that fitted into the Hillands' house.

Wexford had noticed when encountering him in the Hillands' house that he was a handsome man with blue eyes and classical features. Had he been there, it would have struck him now that this face was very like that of Michelangelo's David, only a David approaching middle age. Such comparisons were never apparent to Burden. Ross put down the tool he was holding, came over to him and shook hands. They had met before at Ross's home and there was nothing wrong in this; no doubt he was merely being friendly and co-operative. But to Burden it nevertheless seemed as if the man wanted to put himself on the same level as a fairly high-ranking police officer, show himself as being on that police officer's side, rather, as Wexford might have said – Burden had often heard him say it – himself and Samphire *contra mundum*.

'I honestly can't tell you if I ever met Amber Marshalson, Inspector Burden,' Ross said, using style and surname like an equal, almost like a friend. 'I may have done. I simply don't remember.'

'She was a very good-looking girl.'

'Ah, now, Inspector, I'm a happily married man. An eye for the girls is something I haven't had since I married. Do you know what I say to myself? I say, what would my children think of me if they saw me looking at girls?'

Burden thought of the nude on the man's living-room wall. 'Let me refresh your memory. I think you met Amber at Mrs Hilland's in July. She came over with her little boy.'

The gesture Ross made was theatrical, a throwing back of

his head, a striking of his forehead with his hand and a punch-ing of the air with that hand. 'So I did, so I did,' he cried. 'My God, I'd forgotten all about it.'

Quite a performance, Burden thought.

'Where do you live, Mr Samphire?'

The question surprised him. 'Pauceley Avenue. Why?'

'Perhaps you can also remember seeing Megan Bartlow. When she'd been to visit her father in Pauceley she was in the habit of walking back to the bus stop along Pauceley Avenue.'

Ross made no reply to this, merely shaking his head. Perhaps he thought he couldn't be responsible for everyone who walked past his house over the years. Burden asked him if Colin Fry was in the building, to be told he wasn't. He had other jobs apart from helping Ross out. Footsteps sounded on the stairs. It was the bank's grand staircase, of marble with wrought-iron banisters, which now served all the flats and the footfalls sounded unmuffled on the stone. A strange expression showed on Ross's face. If he had had to define it – and Wexford would have been better at this – he would have called it 'caring'. Perhaps 'considerate' would have been better or even 'protec-tive'. But Ross didn't express his feelings in words. A man came into the room, carrying a large looseleaf book.

Almost unbelievable as it was, this man was Ross's twin. This was Rick Samphire, precisely Ross's own age, to the same hour. Superficially, he wasn't at all like Ross, but he looked as Ross might have done if he had been confined for a couple of years in a brutal prison camp. He looked worn out, a shadow man, his hair thinning and grey-streaked, his face lined and hollow-cheeked, his eyes faded. Only the profile he turned to Burden when speaking to Ross was identical to his brother's.

Ross said gently, putting his hand on the other man's shoul-der, 'Everything's quite OK, Rick. Nothing to be worried about but this gentleman is a police officer, Inspector Burden.'

Rick Samphire looked at Burden with the kind of horror

dawning on his face that is seen in film characters when confronted by the beast from ten thousand fathoms. He shook off Ross's hand, leapt for the door and pounded down the stairs. Not waiting to hear Ross's explanations or apologies, Burden went after him.

Chapter 20

The manager came on the line. And there Wexford's excitement took a dive, his high dropped and he knew that somehow, somewhere, the postcard had led him astray. For Frau Stadler, rapidly checking guest lists on a computer, checking them again when he asked her to do so, could find no record of a Miss Megan Bartlow and a Miss Amber Marshalson having stayed there in May or at any other time, separately or together. He asked her if it would be possible to stay in her hotel under a false name. Frau Stadler seemed shocked at the suggestion. 'We ask for our visitors' passports and keep these for twelve hours. If a visitor had a false passport . . .' She left the monstrous suggestion hanging in the air.

'A postcard was sent from your hotel to England on the twenty-second of May,' Wexford said. 'Would a visitor staying somewhere else go into your hotel and buy a postcard at reception? Does that happen?'

'We don't like this. We – what is the word? – discourage this. But naturally it happens. It happens especially when there are many at the reception and the staff are busy. It is possible one of the ladies you mention came into the hotel, perhaps took tea there or met a friend in the bar and then buy a postcard. That we cannot stop.'

He could imagine it only too easily. His Internet skills were still in their infancy – they might never progress beyond a second childhood – and his first attempt at summoning up a catalogue of hotels in Frankfurt somehow managed to land him in a list of Frankenstein films. But at last he got what he wanted. Die Vier Pferde (apparently named for the Four Horsemen of the Apocalypse when it or its forerunner was an inn in the Middle Ages) had been accorded four stars, was described as 'comfortable with some luxurious suites, excellent cuisine awarded a star in the Michelin Guide and pleasant inner-city garden'. Plainly, it had not been the kind of hotel Megan and Amber would have used. Probably they had stayed at the German equivalent of a B and B and had gone to Die Vier Pferde, just as Ingrid Stadler suggested, and bought the card or cards after having a drink in the bar. It was the kind of thing which appealed to the young, to pretend 'for a laugh' that they were staying in a four-star hotel while in reality sharing a room in a poky boarding house with a bathroom at the end of the passage. None of this came near explaining why they had gone to Frankfurt in the first place.

Chasing after a man who ran away when he discovered you were a policeman was something you did as a matter of course. Burden had been doing it since he was eighteen. Sometimes he had caught his quarry and sometimes not. Today was going to be one of the second sort. Rick Samphire had had a good start on him and though appearing unfit, had contrived to vanish somewhere outside the makeshift doors put up on the old bank building. Burden toiled back up the marble stairs to where Ross had calmly returned to whatever he was doing to the panelling.

'What was that about?' Burden asked.

Favouring him with the charming smile that appeared to be his stock-in-trade, Ross laid down his tools. He spoke patiently.

'You have to understand that my brother's . . . well, not disturbed, I wouldn't say disturbed. He's not mentally ill but he's very nervous. He's had a lot to bear.'

'Oh, yes?'

'People have treated him badly. Losing his children is very hard on a man, especially when he thinks he's done nothing to deserve it.'

'So he runs away at the sight of a police officer?'

'Well, actually, yes. That's what he would do. You'll find out so I may as well tell you. He's got a couple of convictions. He's been in prison. But he's completely harmless. I don't mind telling you I see it as my mission in life to look after him. My twin brother and all that, you know. To be frank, he's not capable of a company secretary's job, he's not a real accountant, but . . . well, like I said, I look after him. I suppose you'd think me a fool if I said I love him.'

Taking in the sweet sad smile, the corners of those blue eyes crinkled, the well-marked black brows lifted, Burden had no intention of saying what he thought about fraternal love or anything else. 'Twins, are you? You don't even look like brothers. You're not much alike.'

'We were once.'

Ross's tone was rueful, yet it seemed to Burden that he rather liked being told he and his brother didn't resemble each other. To be fair, no one could want to look like Rick Samphire. 'Where does he live?'

'Potter's Lane, Pomfret. Go easy with him. He's harmless.'

But Rick hadn't reached home by the time Wexford and Burden got to Potter's Lane. It was a street of mixed houses running parallel to that in which Paula Vincent lived. Number twenty-six was a bungalow standing between a small red-brick villa and a purpose-built block of nineteen-thirties flats with metal frame windows and a sunray entrance door. Rick's bungalow was so stark and dismal in appearance as to be grim, its paintwork peeling, several tiles missing from its shallow roof, concrete path cracked. No plant or tree grew in its vicinity. The front wall had been removed and the former front garden concreted over as a parking place for Rick's car.

After about ten minutes, they saw a blue Volvo turn the corner out of Pomfret High Road and pull over on to the concrete slab garden. The man Burden had chased down the stairs got out of the car and, without looking in their direction, walked up the path, his shoulders stooped and his head lowered against the rain. He walked as might one who has ceased to resist and who knows when to abandon hope. Once he had let himself in at the front door and closed it behind him without looking back, Wexford and Burden left their car and crossed the road. They were halfway across the pavement when Rick Samphire opened the door and stood waiting for them with bowed head. He might have been waiting to be summoned to his own execution.

Of the interior of this house, Wexford said afterwards that if he had had to live in that he'd have committed suicide. The tiny room at the back into which Rick took them was furnished with a television set and an old sofa, covered in torn and very dirty red velvet, and a kitchen stool with a plastic seat. No curtains hung at the window, no carpet or rug covered the bare board floor. A calendar, depicting gloomy paintings of sailing ships, hung on one wall, no pictures on any.

But it was what they saw outside the room, in the narrow passage that ran from the front door to the back of this small house, which brought to each of them a hope they had come to the right place and to see the right man. At the end of this passage, on one of the curved horns of the coat-stand, hung a grey fleece with a hood.

If Rick Samphire saw them eyeing this garment he gave no sign. His hangdog face showed no change. His eyes looked dead. Wexford and Burden sat down and, after a slight hesitation, Rick sat down too, on the edge of the stool, his hands hanging limply between his knees. Wexford began, asking him if he knew Amber Marshalson and showing him her photograph, then doing the same in respect of Megan Bartlow.

The reply was unusual: 'I don't know.'

'You didn't know them, Mr Samphire, or you don't know if you knew them.'

'I don't know,' Rick said again. 'I don't know if I knew them. I may have seen them. I can't remember. I've got a bad memory. My ex-wife wrecked my memory.'

Deciding not to pursue this, Burden asked him if he knew Yorstone Wood.

'Where?' Rick's sombre mood had changed. He was suddenly a little wary, conscious apparently that he must now take care what he said, be cagey.

'Yorstone Wood. It lies to the south of the Kingsmarkham-to-Lewes road, about halfway between Stringfield and Pomfret Monachorum. Have you ever been there?'

'I don't go in woods,' said Samphire. 'Why would I?'

'I don't know, Mr Samphire. You tell me.'

Wexford asked him, 'Were you in Yorstone Wood on the evening of the twenty-fourth of June? Did you park your car in the wood and walk towards Yorstone Bridge past the woodman's cottage, carrying a backpack with a weapon in it in the shape of a concrete block?'

'In the shape of what?'

'A lump of concrete.'

'I've never been there. Not ever.'

'When you were in Yorstone Wood and again when you were in Mill Lane, Brimhurst, did you wear that grey fleece with the hood?'

Silence. Then Rick said in a slow truculent tone, 'I don't want to talk to you. I've had enough trouble with the law. The law's always had it in for me. It took away my house and my money and my kids.'

'Mr Samphire,' Wexford said, 'we'd like to know where you were on the evening of the twenty-fourth of June, the night of the tenth to eleventh of August and the morning of the first of September. This is very important. Perhaps you'll think about it and tell us when we come back tomorrow.'

'I won't be here. I'll be at the old bank building tomorrow.'

'We'll see you there,' said Burden. 'At nine.'

The blue Volvo on the concrete slab was an old car, perhaps fifteen years old, its paintwork had long lost its gloss and become dull. It was covered with scratches, some old, some not so old, and some apparently new. They walked round it, looking at those scratches, before they left.

His entire team in his office, Wexford addressed them on the subject of Rick Samphire. 'His brother volunteered to us that he has a record. What for we don't yet know. I don't know if he killed those two girls. So far I've no idea where he was at the relevant times. Maybe he can produce satisfactory alibis and maybe he can't. We don't need to find a motive, as you know, but I think all of us would like to establish some reason for such apparently purposeless and mindless murders. What I emphatically don't want to do is get this force the reputation of arresting and bringing to trial people against whom the evidence is dodgy and about whom we only have shaky knowledge. Never mind what the *Courier* says about us. We can shut our eyes and close our ears to that. It's for the reputation of this force that we don't arrest a man whom we only have to let go after thirty-six hours because the evidence is weak and he, with a little help from his friends, can establish rock-solid alibis.'

Burden said, 'His car has scratches on it which may have been made by low branches in Yorstone Wood and he does possess a fleece with a hood. So, probably, do at least a hundred other men in the area.'

Hannah put up her hand. 'We think the motive has something to do with whatever scam Amber and Megan were up to, don't we, guv?'

'I don't know that it was a scam, Hannah. It may not even have been illegal. But, yes, I believe both were killed for a reason to do with that.'

'On the subject of convictions, sir,' Barry Vine said. 'I've done my report, but it may be helpful for everyone here to know what Rick Samphire has a record for. He's got one conviction for assaulting his then wife, Alison. He broke her jaw and kicked in two of her ribs. And he's got another for knocking down a man outside a pub in Myringham.'

Thanking him, Wexford said, 'I'd like you all to investigate the Samphire background. Not just Rick but Ross too. So far all we've got is "golden opinions from all sorts of people" and I don't believe anyone can be that pure and excellent.' He glanced in Burden's direction. 'No, Mike, I can't say I agree with you that having a rather daring nude hanging up in one's living room constitutes an utter breach with virtue.'

Vine and DC Coleman laughed and Burden had the grace to join in.

'And now will someone kindly get me the Surrage-Samphire website up on the computer and all the information from it we can. That's not a bad way to start.'

He stood behind Bal in the open-plan office and when he exited from the programme he had been studying, asked him to summon up the Samphire website on to the screen. Bal had typed in 'www.surrog' when Wexford stopped him with, 'Since when can't you spell, Bal?'

Bal looked up, his hands poised above the keys. 'Where have I gone wrong, sir?'

Wexford didn't answer. He was staring at Bal's mis-spelling.

'I think maybe you've gone very right. Don't change anything but add an A, a C and a Y, will you?'

Mystified, Bal did so.

'Congratulations.' Wexford patted him on the shoulder. 'By being unable to spell you've solved a mystery that's been vexing me for the past two months. Now print out everything you can get under "Surrogacy", will you? Everything that's on offer.'

Chapter 21

'I've been a fool,' Wexford said. 'I should have known weeks ago. My own daughter is doing it and still I didn't see. If it wasn't drugs and it wasn't prostitution, what else could bring in money in thousand-pound tranches but surrogacy?' He tossed a sheaf of printouts across the desk at Burden. '"Intended Parents", "Surrogacy the answer to your dreams", "Host or Gestational Surrogacy", "Straight Surrogacy". Listen to this.

'"Straight surrogacy is when the egg of the surrogate mother and the sperm of the intended father are employed. The process can take place in an IVF clinic but more often the technique of artificial insemination is used at home. The baby is biologically the child of the intended father and the surrogate mother. Host surrogacy uses the eggs of the intended mother combined with the sperm of her husband or donor sperm. A baby conceived by this method has no biological connection to the surrogate . . ." Yes, yes, well, we know that. I may be thick but I've known the facts of life this past half-century. It wasn't that kind of surrogacy that Amber and Megan were doing.'

Burden scanned the sheets of paper, shook his head and put them down. 'It says here, which I think I knew, that it's illegal to advertise for a surrogate in this country. They recommend joining one of the surrogacy agencies.'

'I don't think Megan and Amber did that either, do you?'

'Are you saying they were doing nothing illegal?'

'I'm sure they were doing plenty that was illegal. Sit down and I will a tale unfold. Some of this will be my own invention but not much. It started – probably – with Megan reading a story in a tabloid, one of those stories about a surrogate mother refusing to give up the child she'd given birth to. Maybe she also read that this woman's introduction to surrogacy had been via the Internet. But Megan hadn't access to the Internet. All that equipment in the Prinsip–Bartlow menage came later from the ill-gotten gains. The only access to a computer she had was through one of those Internet Cafés – not much use since she'd never in her life used a computer. Her sister Lara had, but to ask her would mean taking her into her confidence.'

'Then she met Amber,' Burden said.

'Then she met Amber. In the Bling-Bling Club, where Lara took her one evening. I don't know when or how the subject came up but I can see that those two girls had one thing in common. They were both very young, Megan nineteen then and Amber seventeen, but they'd each had a baby. That was the "qualification" Megan told Lara she'd need to have. What more likely than, sitting at a table next to each other, Megan and Amber talked about what they had in common? Now I'm not suggesting that these two girls talked about surrogacy at their first meeting but I believe they made a date at the Bling-Bling to meet again, perhaps at a café somewhere and then at Amber's home where Amber had access to a computer.'

'You're saying that at the café meeting, say, Megan outlined a plan she had for the pair of them to set up as surrogate mothers? Not "host" but "straight" mothers?'

'That's right. Megan hadn't got it in mind to go near any IVF clinics or surrogacy agencies. First they had to find out what they could about it from the Internet, which Megan couldn't use and Amber couldn't use with much expertise, though they had one in the house. Her stepmother could use it but asking her stepmother obviously wasn't on. John Brooks, on the other hand, knew about computers; he would help her. We know she asked him because he told us so.'

'What, asked him to get a surrogacy website up for her?'

'Maybe she asked him to find the website for her and what he found put the idea into his head and he told his wife, his wife who very much wants a baby. He didn't want that known, that's why he lied to Hannah. But back to Amber and Megan.

'They could do no more without joining a surrogacy agency because it's illegal in this country to advertise for a surrogate or for a surrogate to advertise. But it's not illegal to join an agency and be introduced to couples who need a surrogate mother to bear a child for them. I think I know someone who'll know all about surrogacy agencies . . .'

The scent from Sylvia's stove was one of the most glorious Wexford had ever smelt. That it contained meat of various kinds was unmistakable even if Naomi Wyndham had not already condemned it as unsuitable for a pregnant woman, children and indeed anybody except perhaps himself whom she considered too far gone in culinary vice to be salvaged. He was sitting in his daughter's kitchen with Dora, Naomi and Mary Beaumont, creator of what she told him was a cassoulet, its ingredients goose, pork, bacon, beans and herbs.

'I shall just have vegetables,' said Naomi with a stagy shudder. 'If I ate that I should be thinking all the time of what it was doing to my aorta.'

Mary laughed. 'I've seen a few aortas, darling, inside and out,' she said, 'and it's my belief people are better off if they don't know they've got one.'

'Have some more wine, Dad,' said Sylvia. 'Mum can drive.'

'Just one of the claret, then,' said Wexford. 'Naomi won't

object to red wine. Even Dr Atkins isn't against that.' Naomi was beginning on a fierce denunciation of the Atkins Diet when he interrupted her. 'Naomi, as a sensible woman' – God forgive him! – 'you won't mind my asking you this. When you and Neil decided you wanted to find a surrogate mother were you members of an organisation combating . . . er, infertility?'

'We were members of two. Babies for All and SOCC.'

'SOCC?'

It was Mary who answered. 'The Sussex Overcoming Childlessness Circle. They're based here. I work for them.'

'You're a nurse, aren't you?'

'Midwife, darling. My work for SOCC is voluntary.'

Naomi gave a tinkling laugh. 'Advertising for a surrogate and advertising yourself as a surrogate is against the law but there's nothing to stop you meeting and talking about the great tragedy in your lives. Nothing to stop you bringing someone who might think of becoming a surrogate so long as you are *punctilious* in referring her to Babies for All.'

'Or, I suppose, if she offered her services privately to a couple among your membership.'

'That too, of course.'

'They'd be fools if they didn't check her out thoroughly before having anything to do with her,' said Mary robustly.

Thoughtfully, Wexford said, 'But people often *are* fools or they can be very reckless if they're desperate. And it's hard to think of anything a woman especially can be more desperate for than a child of her own.'

To his astonishment, Naomi took his hand and squeezed it. He looked at her, scarcely able to believe that this woman he had thought superficial and shallow was capable of such deep feeling. Tears had come into her eyes and glittered there, unshed.

Dora drew a sharp hard breath, 'What do you want to know for, anyway? You're so accustomed to interrogation you take it with you wherever you go.'

He managed to laugh. 'I'm sorry. I'll shut up. Can we eat now, Sylvia? That beautiful smell is almost too much for me.'

When they came into the old bank building at nine next morning, Ross Samphire was again there on his own.

'Rick'll be along any minute,' Ross said.

He was halfway up a pair of aluminium steps, attaching fruit and flower mouldings to the centre rose of a ceiling.

'He won't run away when he sees me, will he?' Burden spoke drily. 'I don't want to go chasing him down the High Street again.'

'I can guarantee he won't. You leave it to me. Here he is now.'

A night's sleep had done nothing to improve Rick Samphire's appearance. Seeing them together for the first time, Wexford marvelled that these two men could be twins. Seen side by side – Ross had come down the ladder to smile and say, 'Hi, Rick. How're you doing?' – they looked like the characters in one of those 'before' and 'after' advertisements.

He spoke the longest sentence they had yet heard from him. 'If I've got to talk to you I want to do so in the presence of my brother and I don't want to go somewhere else where my brother can't hear what I say and what you lot say.'

The expression of gratification on Ross's face was almost funny. He smiled and gave Rick's shoulder a squeeze.

'I've no objection to your brother being here,' Wexford said. 'First, I want to know where you were on the evening of June the twenty-fourth between eight and ten p.m.'

'Ross was away on his holidays,' he said as if his brother's whereabouts must be his first concern. 'Me, I was in the Mermaid with Norman.'

He had no need to think about it, Wexford noted, had no hesitation in supplying a name and a place from four months in the past.

'Who's Norman?'

'Norman Arlen,' Rick muttered.

'Right. Mr Arlen's home address, please.'

Wexford had known Ross would intervene sooner or later. It turned out to be sooner. 'You can't be serious. Everyone knows where Norman lives. His home is famous.'

'Not in the circles where we move,' said Burden.

'Well, then. It's Pomfret Hall.'

No alibi at all would have made a better impression on Wexford than the elaborate one constructed for the night of the tenth to eleventh of August. It had the air, as Burden said afterwards, of being the work of a committee, as perhaps it was. His head bowed, mumbling, Rick said he had been at his ex-wife's, looking after his children.

'It's the only way I get to see my kids. Looking after them. Her and the bloke she's with, they went out. It's my house she lives in with him. She got that just through being divorced. Sitting's the only chance I get to see my kids. The dad counts for nothing these days. I'm joining Fathers4Justice.'

His hand back on his brother's shoulder, Ross cut in with, 'Alison lives in Myringham. Rick does a bit of sitting for her. It's not an ideal situation but what can you do?'

'Nothing at all in your case,' Burden snapped, 'I didn't ask you. If you want to stay while we talk to your brother, please keep quiet.' Ross looked hurt rather than offended. 'You weren't looking after your kids at two o'clock in the morning,' Burden said to Rick. 'When did you leave your ex-wife's place?'

'Not her place, mine,' said Rick, making it plain that he never intended to give his unjust treatment a rest but would worry at it whenever the subject arose, however remotely. 'It's my house I bought on a mortgage with money I earned.'

'What time did you leave?' said Wexford roughly.

Ross raised his eyebrows and said like a solicitor called to protect a suspect, 'Now surely there's no need to take that tone?'

'I shall take what tone I like. Let's get on with this. What time did you leave?'

Ross contented himself with casting up his eyes. Still mumbling, Rick said, 'About eleven it was. They came back and I went. The kids were asleep. I don't say more than I have to to her and her bloke. I went off and my poxy car broke down.'

'You know I'm going to get you a new car, Rick,' said Ross.

Losing his temper but not showing it, Wexford said with controlled venom, 'Please don't interrupt again, Mr Samphire. If you do I shall have to ask your brother to come down to the police station.'

Suddenly Rick began to talk without being questioned or prompted. It sounded as if what he said he had learnt by heart or had it thoroughly dinned into him. If I wasn't convinced before that this guy is our man, Wexford thought, I'm coming close to it now.

'I was on the road out past Pauceley. It's the A3923. The motor stalled and it wouldn't start again. I looked but I couldn't find what it was. I was a good eight miles from home. I knew I'd have to leave the car and walk it.'

'Are you a member of the AA or RAC?'

'Do I look as if I am? I haven't got a phone anyway. I can't afford a mobile. She's skinned me alive so I can't afford things like that. Everything I've got she takes off me.'

Deciding that he could only proceed by putting words into the man's mouth, Wexford asked if he would agree it was now midnight. Rick nodded. 'Did anyone pass you? You must have seen other cars? Did anyone stop?'

'Permission to speak, sir,' said Ross.

'All right. What is it?'

'There was one driver stopped. He offered Rick the chance to make a phone call. I said to him next day, why didn't you call me and he said he didn't want to disturb me at that hour.'

'Your brother could have told me that,' said Wexford. 'What was this driver called?'

By another feat of recall, possibly of a learnt piece of fiction, Rick said, stumbling over the name, 'Steve – well, Stephen Lawson. He'd come from the Cheriton Forest Hotel, he said. He offered me a lift but that wasn't no use to me. He was going in the opposite direction. He'd come from where I was going.'

Here at last was something that could be checked. If there really was a Stephen Lawson who had been staying at the Cheriton Forest Hotel on the night of the tenth of August, he should be easy enough to find. 'So you walked home to Pomfret?'

'Took me three hours. I'm not fit like I used to be.'

'All right,' Burden said. 'What became of your car? Was it collected next day?'

'Rick phoned me and I had a recovery service bring it to my place.'

'All right, Mr Samphire. That's enough,' said Wexford. 'Since you can't keep quiet, we'll go to the station.' Seeing that Ross intended to come with them, 'Not you. If I need to talk to you I'll do so alone.'

Rick Samphire shuffled into Kingsmarkham police station like one entering the ante-room to hell. *Abandon Hope All Ye who Enter Here* might as well have been written above its newly installed automatic doors. Wexford took him into the less pleasing of the interview rooms with its whitewashed brick walls, vinyl-tiled floor and the kind of furnishings you might have found in a nineteen-fifties kitchen.

Here they resumed the interrogation.

'Why was the car taken to your brother's house? Why not a repair shop?'

'We used our own mechanic, if you want to know,' said Rick.

'Of course we want to know. That's why you're here. What were you doing on the morning of the first of September?'

Rick didn't seem surprised by the question. If this date meant nothing to him, wouldn't he have come back to them with a 'When?' or a 'Say again?' not kept to his morose expression and said, 'I was in the old bank building. Along with Ross and Col.'

'That would be Mr Colin Fry?'

'Right.'

'When did you get there and when did you leave?'

'Eight I got there. Eight a.m. and I left at four p.m. Colin will tell you. He's a good bloke, is Colin.'

'Now, Mr Samphire,' said Wexford, 'tell us about the Sussex Overcoming Childlessness Circle and surrogate mothers, will you?'

'I haven't a clue what you're talking about,' said Rick. 'Overcoming what?'

'The Sussex Overcoming Childlessness Circle or SOCC.'

Suddenly red in the face, his dull eyes narrowed, Rick burst out, 'If you want to know what I think about childlessness, I'll tell you. It's a bloody good idea. I wish to fuck I was childless. I wish mine had never been born.' Suddenly articulate, even voluble, he came out with it almost triumphantly. 'I didn't want them. She wanted them. But when they're born you like love them, you can't help it, and it's you that have to pay the price of them for the rest of your bloody life.'

It wasn't the sort of day for going to the Gooseberry Bush for lunch. Sunlight should have been sparkling on the waters of the Kingsbrook, a Michaelmas mildness in the air and no wind to blow away the table napkins. All that could be said for this day was that it had stopped raining. A whitish mist, cold to the feel, hung above the river.

'Apart from that fry-up,' said Burden, 'this is the first time you and I have had a proper midday meal since the beginning of August.'

Wexford passed him the menu. 'And it isn't as if we had anything to celebrate.'

Wexford took a draught of his sparkling water. 'I wonder if there's a restaurant worth its salt that isn't serving sea bass now while we speak. Thousands of them must be consumed every day. When I'm feeling hard-done-by or things at home get rough, I thank God I'm not a sea bass.'

A waitress closed and locked the glass doors which led on to the river terrace, giving the day up as a bad job. Wexford ordered for both of them, looked longingly at the wine list and pushed it away.

'What I'd like to do this afternoon, Mike, is talk to the chap Ross Samphire employs, Colin Fry. See if he really was there with those two on the first of September, see if we can find out more about the brothers from him.'

'OK, we will.' Burden said it absently. He was staring across the restaurant at a table where a man of about thirty and a younger man were sitting. He looked away. 'You know who that is, the guy in the leather jacket?'

'Should I?'

'Probably not. I don't think you've ever seen him but that's John Brooks. Jewel Terrace, right?'

'If you say so. What of it?'

'I can see them from here without staring. I wish you could. There's no doubt the chap with him is his boyfriend. It's not that they're touching – though Brooks did put his hand on his shoulder when they came to the table – but the way they look at each other. It's unmistakable.'

Wexford sighed. 'I may be losing my grip but enlighten me, Mike. Why shouldn't he be his boyfriend? Practising homosexuality's been legal for nearly forty years.'

'I don't mean that,' said Burden impatiently. 'Brooks is the fellow who accounted for his going out at night by telling Hannah he was visiting his girlfriend and then she turned out to be his sister. Remember?'

'Now you tell me I do.'

'Well, that's why he said it was a woman he visited. Because he's in the closet and he doesn't want his wife to know.'

Wexford's smile became a quiet laugh. 'We're not going to do anything about it, are we?'

'Hannah wants him done for wasting police time – but no,' said Burden. 'I think I'll just say good afternoon.'

And as they passed Brooks's table, he did. Looking back, Wexford saw that Brooks had flushed a mottled red. Outside, the afternoon was grey, foggy as if a cloud had sunk to the ground and settled there, the kind of day when it seems impossible that the sun will ever show itself again.

Burden expected his discovery of John Brooks's secret to amuse Hannah and wondered if 'a generation thing' was responsible for her look of slightly distasteful contempt. Surely she, with her sometimes shockingly progressive outlook, wasn't disgusted? Not Hannah, not she of all people. Baffled, he left her and went back to investigating Ross Samphire's background.

And Hannah, of course, wasn't disgusted in the sense he had meant. Her outrage came from finding that a gay man of mature age – not a teenager – could be so out-of-date, so feeble and pusillanimous, as not only to be in the closet but positively cowering and shivering in its depths under piles of *medieval* blankets, stifling rugs and freedom-crushing pillows. It wasn't that he had lied to his wife – men did lie to their wives and wives to their husbands, and this was one of her many objections to marriage – but that he had lied to *her*, to the police. For such a reason as that! It made you despair of humankind. And just when she was feeling that really people were not so bad, that it was amazing and immensely gratifying just how intelligent and adaptable and altogether remarkable some people were.

Bal had taken her home to meet his parents. Just for the Saturday night. All the way up to Hereford, where they now lived, she had been imagining them, Rajiv, his father, in that long white garment Indian men wore – it was unforgivable of her not to remember the name of it – and his mother, Parvinder, in a sari, her grey hair in a knot on the back of her head, her neck and arms loaded with jewels. And when they got there, and the house turned out to be a stone cottage in a village, his father was in grey flannels and a zipper jacket and his mother in jeans and a sweater. She was a little disappointed and a little more when dinner wasn't chicken vindaloo at home but Italian cuisine in a Hereford restaurant. Total disillusionment would have set in if she and Bal had been shown into the same bedroom but she was sent off to sleep at one end of the house and he took his own room at the other. In this, things were no different from what still prevailed in Kingsmarkham and looked like continuing to do so indefinitely.

Chapter 22

Colin Fry lived with his girlfriend in a flat over the dry-cleaners in Glebe Road but he wasn't at home. The girlfriend said Colin had a number of part-time jobs to 'fill in' when he wasn't working for Ross Samphire. She wasn't sure where he was today but she gave them two addresses in Kingsmarkham. 'You could give them a go,' she said. 'He won't be being a mechanic today. He may be lawnmowing or maybe window cleaning.'

The flat was a surprise. Wexford told himself he must be a middle-class snob because he had expected something like the place Keith Prinsip lived in but without the state-of-the-art equipment. This place reminded him of a suite in a middle-ranking hotel. Not in the Vier Pferde class, a couple of stars lower than that, but very presentable. Pale coffee carpeting covered the floor. The covers and curtains were a darker shade, the furniture well-polished and the pictures on the walls in the Athena Art league. It was tidy and it looked discreet, unlike the girlfriend who, in spite of the temperature, was in red shorts, a white T-shirt with 'This Bitch Bites' printed on it in purple, and high-heeled red sandals.

Showing them out, she said, 'If you can't find him, he'll be back here around six and you could catch him then. Only we've got to go out at seven, leave the place clear.' She caught Burden's eye and winked.

'What was that about?' Burden said, going down the stairs.

'God knows. Surely nothing to do with the matter in hand.'

'Probably not. It's not often young women wink at me.' They got into the car. 'An intelligent guess would be that after all the rain we've had he can't be lawnmowing, so he'll be window cleaning.'

He was. They found him at a house in Ladyhall Road. He was sitting on a windowsill with his back to them three floors up, polishing the sash.

'When you consider', said Wexford, 'the way the health and safety people won't let children go on swings any more, I wonder they haven't banned window cleaning altogether. Mr Fry!'

'That's me.' He didn't turn round.

'Kingsmarkham CID. May we have a word?'

'I'll be down in a minute. I'm just finishing off.'

A weak sun had appeared among the porridge-like clouds. It brought a faint warmth and the mist began to lift. Wexford and Burden sat in the car and presently Colin Fry emerged from the front door, carrying a bucket and a bag of rags. He was a short slight man of about thirty, red-headed and pink-skinned.

'We can talk in here,' Burden called out to him.

This was obviously unacceptable to Fry. The prospect of sitting in a police car to talk perhaps reminded him of similar situations in which his role had been less innocent. Whatever it was, he shook his head, said 'No way' and invited them into his van. This vehicle looked as if it were used as the repository of all the accumulation of litter and refuse not permitted to sully the flat in Glebe Road: empty cans, cigarette packets, magazines, takeaway packaging, plastic bags and various garments of the sweatshirt-fleece-kagool variety.

One of these, Wexford noticed, was a dark-grey fleece with a hood.

'He's a good guy is Ross,' said Colin, echoing Ross's words about himself. 'What you'd call a straight kind of guy. Five years I've worked for him and never a cross word. I mean, the way he's been with his brother, you won't find many guys like that. Bought him his house, you know. Gave him his car. Gave him his mobile and pays for it. There's not many would do that.'

'You'll have followed the two murders, Mr Fry,' said Wexford. 'Amber Marshalson and Megan Bartlow. Did you know either of those girls? Did Ross?'

Colin shook his head. 'Never heard of them before all this.'

'Tell us where you were on the morning of the first of September, between nine and ten, will you?'

Like Rick's, his response was unsurprised and rapid. It wasn't natural to answer so promptly. 'In the old bank building with Ross and Rick.'

'How can you be so sure?'

'Look, I just can,' Colin said. 'We come in at eight, I went upstairs and Ross and Rick was down below doing the ceiling. Me, I was on the top painting the walls.'

'Not the kind of job you could leave halfway through,' said Wexford lightly.

Fry looked at him, puzzled. 'Not if you're doing it right. Was there anything else because I've got my job to do?'

They followed him as far as Glebe Road, parked and watched him let himself in by a red-painted door next to the dry-cleaners' window.

'Did you notice?' Burden said. 'Rick said he hadn't got a mobile but, according to Fry, Ross supplied him with one. It's a small point, of course.'

'It shows Rick up as a liar.'

'Two other things have come out of this that strike me as interesting,' said Burden. 'First of all, Fry's home. Its condition, I mean. That's a mystery. Why does it look as if they're about to show prospective buyers over it? Perhaps they are but I don't think so. For one thing, I don't suppose it belongs to them. They'll rent it. The other is that hooded fleece in the van. Oh, I know the world is full of fleeces with hoods, especially *now*, but I still think it shouldn't be ignored.'

'Certainly not,' said Wexford. 'As to Fry's flat, I think they're running a knocking shop. Of course, it's not an offence unless there's more than one woman on the premises; it's not brothel keeping.'

'What, you mean a couple rent the place for an evening or a night?'

'A long evening, I should think. The girlfriend said they were going out, leaving the place clear, and winked at you. You, not me. Maybe she thought you were a likely customer. What else could that wink mean?'

Like almost everyone else in Kingsmarkham and the villages, Burden had seen the feature on Pomfret Hall in the *Sunday Times* magazine. People in photographs often look worse than reality (fatter, older, shorter) while places look better. Driving up to the front door of this Palladian house, Burden noted that it wasn't true in this case. The photographs had been impressive; the reality was stunning. Unaccountably, the day was bright and sunny, the sky a radiant blue and Norman Arlen's house stood out against it as if it might be a palazzo in Italy or an ante-bellum mansion in the Deep South. Two balustered staircases mounted its façade to meet at its porticoed front doors. Its statuary reminded him of the sight he had once had, while on holiday, of the Parthenon frieze. He told himself that just as a man might smile and smile and be a villain (as Wexford said) so he might possess one of the handsomest houses in England and be a crook.

Having lived in the neighbourhood all his life, he had of

course seen the house before. He had seen it in the days when an old baronet lived there, when it was a shabby grey house in wild untended grounds. According to the article, Norman Arlen had spent a fortune on it and was still spending. Where had the money come from? The journalist who wrote the piece had described him as a travel agent and implied he had other irons in the fire. Burden went up the steps on the left-hand side, DC Bhattacharya following him, and tugged at the bell pull.

He expected a butler, at least a maid, but Norman Arlen came himself. Burden recognised him from the photograph in the feature. Although he had had no warning of their arrival, Arlen was gracious, particularly affable to Bal, believing apparently that patronising politeness, accompanied by smiles frequently flashed in his direction, were less racist than indifference. He led them across an enormous hall with a drum ceiling about thirty feet high into a room Burden recognised, the sort of room you expect to see only in great houses you are being conducted round on tours. Huge portraits of eighteenth-century people, no ancestors of Arlen's he was sure, hung on the walls alongside mirrors in ornate gilt frames. The furniture had a lot of gilt about it and was upholstered mostly in yellow satin. In Burden's opinion, the sort of chairs and sofas you bought at John Lewis's were far more comfortable than this sort of thing. He sat on the edge of his chair. Norman Arlen, a small man with a trim little beard, had apparently just been out riding, for he wore jodhpurs and a hacking jacket. He perched himself on the end of a chaise longue, his feet barely reaching the ground.

To start with, Burden left the questioning to Bal who began by asking him if he knew Rick Samphire. On the face of it, this had seemed unlikely but Arlen nodded and smiled.

'The fact is I've known both brothers practically all my life. We were boys together, went to school together, as a matter of fact, in south London.'

'So it's not unusual for you to meet Rick and the two of you to have a drink together.'

'Not at all unusual.' Arlen paused and seemed to be considering the best way to put this. 'Look, I'll be honest with you. I'll be completely frank. Ross and I have a good deal more in common. In fact I'm godfather to his daughter Laura.'

'So you were having dinner with him at his home on August the tenth?'

'Yes, indeed. Ross and I had a lot to discuss and I stayed rather late. It must have been after midnight before I left.' Arlen got up, crossed to a black and gilt table, opened a drawer in it as if looking for some document and closed it again. He turned round with a smile. 'To get back to Rick. The fact is that, if one has any humanity, one's sorry for Rick. He's had a raw deal, been unlucky and, by God, he's been punished for it. You know what I mean.'

'Not exactly, Mr Arlen,' Burden said. 'If you're referring to his sojourns as a guest of Her Majesty in Myringham and Brixton prisons, I don't quite see where the ill luck comes in.'

Arlen's answer to this was a rueful laugh that managed to contain a good deal of sympathy and fellow feeling. He turned to Bal, said, 'Do go on.'

'Did you meet him,' Bal said briskly, 'in the Mermaid pub in Pomfret on the twenty-fourth of June between eight and nine in the evening?'

'I did indeed. Let me get the facts absolutely right. I called for him at his home in Potter's Lane. It would have been about a quarter to eight. As a matter of fact I wanted to take him out to dinner and I had the Cheriton Forest Hotel in mind. Taking him out for a meal is something I in actual fact do from time to time. But poor Rick was rather frightened off by what he saw as the grandeur of the Cheriton Forest, said he hadn't got the clothes, you can imagine the sort of thing.'

'A grey fleece with a hood wouldn't do, I suppose,' Burden put in.

Arlen smiled uncertainly at this, the first sign he had given of the slightest unease.

'So you went to the Mermaid at about eight?'

'That's exactly right.' Arlen broke off when a middle-aged woman in a dark dress and 'sensible' shoes came into the room. 'Can I offer you gentlemen any refreshment? Tea? Mineral water? Orange juice?' In unison Burden and Bal refused. 'No, thank you, Wendy, not just now. Where was I? Ah, yes, as a matter of fact, I gave the Mermaid a call from Rick's house and asked them for a table for two in the brasserie. Rick and I had a drink in the bar first and then a meal, nearer supper than dinner, I think you'd call it. The fact is that we were in the Mermaid.'

'So he wasn't ten miles away in Yorstone Wood?'

'Yorstone Wood? Yorstone Wood? Ah, you mean where that dangerous bend is. No, indeed, he was with me in the Mermaid until just after ten.'

The time a man – Rick? – was walking through Yorstone Wood and dropping his lump of concrete off the bridge was covered. Burden would check with the pub but he had no doubt Arlen had been in there with someone. The brasserie staff might remember that but after nearly four months not who it was. And Arlen would have taken care to pay in cash. He got up, said, 'I may want to see you again, Mr Arlen,' more in vain threat than hope.

'Always a pleasure, Inspector.'

The feature had mentioned a girlfriend but there was no sign of anyone else in the house beyond Arlen and the woman who was plainly a housekeeper. Arlen conducted them back across the hall.

'Did you notice how often he talked about "facts"?' said Bal in the car. 'We were only there less than ten minutes and he said the word "fact" eight times.'

'I dare say that's because he doesn't know what it means,' said Burden gloomily.

'There was another thing. I can't be sure, it may have been something quite different – but did you notice how he went over to that fancy gilt table and opened the drawer?'

'I believe so.'

'When we went in there was something lying on that table and after he'd opened the drawer there wasn't. He put it away. I could be wrong but it looked like a gun.'

'We'll never get a warrant on that evidence,' said Wexford. 'We can't search a man's house because Bal thinks he may have seen a gun but can't be sure.'

'We can bear in mind that it may be there, though.'

'Yes, we can do that. Of course we will do that. Now the tighter these alibis get and the more unassailable they become, the less anybody can believe them. Yet in court everyone will *have* to believe them, simply because their statements are water-tight, so it's impossible for us to bring charges. We know before we start that any charges will fail. It's not natural to produce mates who'll swear to your being somewhere at a precise time three months ago, yet it's the only thing that will satisfy the court. Anything else will be shot down in flames.'

'Bal's been to the Mermaid,' said Burden. 'They know Arlen and they know Rick Samphire. They've seen them in there together. But of course they can't remember if they were in there together on the twenty-fourth of June and not one of them is going to say they weren't.'

Even more incredible and even less destructible was Rick's alibi for the night between the tenth and eleventh of August. He had left his ex-wife's house in Myringham at about eleven fifteen, a time vouched for by Alison Rowley (as she now called herself) and her partner. Wexford thought them reputable witnesses, while asking himself if the reason for his thinking in this way was partly because Alison had left Rick. Hannah Goldsmith liked them for their lifestyle and this in her eyes vindicated their honesty. It was afterwards that the difficulties arose. Rick had come up with this story of his car breaking down and a subsequent encounter with a motorist. Wexford and his team had gone to a great deal of trouble to find this motorist, were on the point of giving up, when a middle-aged man with a bald forehead and large glasses walked into the police station, announced to the duty sergeant that he had been away on holiday for the past two weeks and had only now heard that the police were looking for him.

He gave his name as Stephen Lawson, his address as Lady Lane, Forby, and his occupation as fund-raiser for a Kingsmarkham-based charity. 'I'd have presented myself a couple of weeks ago if I'd known I was wanted,' he said. 'Any sort of subterfuge is very distasteful to me. I couldn't sleep at night if I thought I was evading my duty.'

'I'm glad to hear that,' Wexford said, 'but what exactly have you come for?'

'I', said Lawson, drawing himself up, 'am Stephen Lawson. I am the driver who stopped and offered a lift to a man whose car broke down. In the night-time. At one a.m., that is, on August the eleventh.'

'All right. DS Goldsmith will take a statement from you if you'd like to follow her.' They were leaving the office when Wexford called after them, 'Know Mr Rick Samphire well, do you?'

'Who?' Lawson turned his head, his face wearing a puzzled look.

'I was returning to my home in Forby on the A3923 from Myfleet,' Lawson's statement ran, 'where I had been spending the evening with friends at the Cheriton Forest Hotel, when I passed a stationary car which had evidently broken down. Its driver had lifted up the bonnet and was looking inside. The clock on my dashboard gave the time as twelve thirty-two. I pulled into the grass verge and asked the driver if I could help. He appeared to have no phone in his car, which was a blue Volvo, about fifteen years old. I cannot remember the index number but it had the letters VY in it and the number 7.

'The driver said he had been trying to restart the car for the past twenty minutes. Two cars had passed him but neither had stopped. I asked him if I could phone one of the motoring organisations for him, the AA or RAC, but he said he was not a member of either. I then took a look at the car myself and could tell the battery was flat but not being a motor mechanic could not help. I asked if there was anyone I could phone for help and he said, "My brother, but not at this time of night. I wouldn't disturb him at this hour."

'I did not ask him for his brother's name or phone mumber. He said his own name was Richard but did not give a surname. I offered him a lift but as he was heading for Pomfret and I was going in the opposite direction he refused. It would have been about eight miles to Pomfret from where we were and he said there was nothing for it but to start walking. I watched him set off and then I drove on home. I looked at my car clock again when I started and saw that the time was twelve fifty-two.'

The 'friends at the Cheriton Forest Hotel' turned out to be a couple and a single woman friend from Birmingham spending a week's holiday there. Their story had some interesting aspects. DS Vine spoke to them, first on the phone, then to their woman companion at her office in London. It was true that they had spent a few days at Cheriton Forest but Stephen Lawson was unknown to them before they went there.

'He picked me up,' the woman said. 'I may as well be honest about it. I was waiting for my friends in the bar and he came over and asked if he could buy me a drink. This was at about eight on the Tuesday evening. I didn't see why not. My friends didn't come down for about half an hour. We had a chat and then when my friends came we all went in to dinner.'

'Mr Lawson joined you?'

'Not then. We had a table for three and he was alone. About halfway through the meal I said to my friends, should we invite him to have coffee with us and we did. Well, I did. We all had coffee brought into the lounge.'

Vine asked her what they had talked about.

'The Forest, I suppose, and the countryside. It's very pretty around there. He said he lived in a place called Forby which had been called the fifth prettiest village in Britain and I said how awful to be only the fifth and then he told us he was a fund-raiser for a society giving aid to Uganda – no, Kenya. He went on and on about poverty and disease, and how the women had dozens of babies and left them on rubbish dumps because they couldn't afford to bring them up. I don't think my friends liked any of this much. They told me afterwards they hadn't liked him and when it got to about half past ten they said they were going to bed. I thought he'd go then but he didn't. He asked me to come into the bar with him while he had one for the road.

'Anyway, I did. There wasn't anything – well, I mean, he never made a pass or anything. We sat at a table in the bar and I had a glass of wine and he had a tomato juice he called a Virgin Mary because it hadn't got any vodka in it. He went on talking about the Kenyan women and how tragic it was, and at about half-eleven he said he'd soon have to go. He asked me for my phone number and I . . . well, I gave him one I made up because I really didn't want to see him again.

'After that I said goodnight and went to bed. He was still in the bar but they closed at midnight so I suppose that was when he left.'

And drove the three miles along the little unclassified road through Cheriton Forest, Wexford calculated, joined the A3923 at Myfleet and went northwards. He must have taken things at a leisurely pace because it was just after half past midnight when he reached the point where Rick Samphire claimed his car had broken down. Wexford had no doubt he had driven that route at that time. The organisers of this alibi did their work thoroughly. Rick's car contained the letters X and Y and the number 7. The doubt came when he was asked to believe that Rick Samphire's car or Rick Samphire were there. It was a job for Hannah and Bal to find out if that car had been in for repairs next day.

'It was taken to my brother's house and he had Col pick it up,' said Rick to Hannah. 'Got a towbar on the van and he's a good little mechanic.'

No one was going to be able to prove that Colin Fry had towed Rick's broken-down Volvo from Pauceley to Kingsmarkham or, come to that, that he had not. 'Of course he'll say he did,' Hannah said as they drove along Glebe Road. 'He'll say he had to repair the big end or the distributor or whatever goes wrong in cars.'

'You don't know?' Bal smiled the smile that induced in her something near enslavement. 'I thought you'd be an expert. I think of you as being good at everything you do, Hannah.'

'You thought wrong,' she said sharply. Enslaving smile or not, she was getting angrier with him by the day. 'Nobody's perfect.'

Colin Fry's white van was parked outside the dry-cleaners in Glebe Road and Colin and his girlfriend Emma were both at home, eating cold Thai takeaway leftovers for their lunch. The weather having turned rather cold, Emma was in combat trousers and a skintight white sweater. Hannah thought Bal looked at her rather longer than he need have. I bet he'd do it with her at the drop of a hat, she said to herself. He wouldn't respect her or need to be serious about her the way he is with me. She asked Colin about Rick's car in a voice so gruff that Bal gave her a glance of surprise.

'Yeah, I fetched that old jalopy of his from Ross's place. What day? I can tell you that straight off. It was the hottest day since records began. They said that on the telly, the hottest day since records began.'

'Were you able to repair it, Mr Fry?'

'Needed a new battery. I went down to the Volvo shop in Kingsmarkham and got one for him. It was in by midday, wasn't it, Em?'

'What did all that set him back?' Bal asked.

'Not him. Ross paid. He always does. They think the world of each other, Ross and Rick. There's nothing Ross wouldn't do for Rick and Rick's grateful, isn't he, Em? I'll say that for him. He knows the meaning of gratitude.'

Two other police officers called on Colin Fry and Emma Sams that day. They were DS Vine and DC Fancourt and they presented themselves as Barry and Lynn, enquiring if they could book the flat from seven p.m. till eleven p.m. that evening. Or any evening that week.

'I don't know what you're talking about,' said Colin Fry.

'We got your name from Mr Robinson,' said Barry. 'He recommended you.'

'No, he didn't. I don't know any Mr Robinson.' Fry slammed the door so violently that Lynn had to jump backwards. But his shocked reaction and aggressive antagonism did as much for Wexford as a willing response and he put DC Coleman on to watch the place.

Chapter 23

Letters were unusual these days. Wexford regretted this, though he admitted to himself that e-mails were quicker and easier, and phone calls even better. If the post brought anything any more it was bills and fliers and catalogues. So the letter in a cream laid envelope addressed to 'The Officer-in-charge', with the direction in a large forward-sloping hand and with a German stamp, came as a surprise. It began 'Dear Sir' and the written English was as impeccable as Ingrid Stadler's spoken English.

> *Dear Sir,*
>
> *As you see from the heading on this paper, I live just outside the German city of Frankfurt. I shall be in your country on business on Monday, 10 October, and would like to come to see you and discuss a serious matter. If you will excuse me, I prefer not to enter into details in a letter. Would Tuesday 11 October, or Wednesday 12 October be a suitable date at 3 or 4 p.m.?*
>
> *I enclose my e-mail address and phone number.*
>
> *Yours truly,*
>
> *Rainer König-Hensel*

'Unless I'm much mistaken,' said Wexford, 'this chap is one

of those unfortunates who used Megan or Amber as surrogate mothers. Megan, probably. He may even be the father of the child she was carrying when she was killed.'

Burden took the letter from him and read it again. 'One of the possible fathers, you mean.'

'At least he'll tell us what the arrangements were and what he paid the girl, and I suppose there's a chance he'll tell us where those Samphires and their henchmen came in. It may be that Ross organised the whole thing. They've got to have been involved somewhere and so far we've found nothing.'

Being black made shadowing someone or watching a property more difficult than it would have been for DS Vine, for instance, or DC Archbold. In Kingsmarkham, at any rate, Damon Coleman thought, where only a very few years back anyone of African descent stood out like a single kidney bean in a packet of haricots. Now their numbers had quadrupled, someone as dark as he was no longer a freak to be stared at in the street. But he was still noticed more than a young white man would have been and the irony was that he, a black officer of the law, was looked on with greater suspicion than a white thug. A good many people, especially the elderly, concluded that his standing about, looking in shop windows, taking a walk round the block or sitting at the wheel of his car, was loitering with intent to commit a felony. Possessed of a sense of humour, Damon got considerable amusement out of their disapproving glances but was still often apprehensive that one of them might summon a policeman.

He had been watching the dry-cleaners above which Colin Fry lived for several evenings in succession. The clocks had still not been put back and darkness didn't start to fall before six. After that the street lamps showed him up even more. Sitting in his car was probably the most secure option but the very presence of his car there evening after evening was suspicious. Colin Fry and that piece of jailbait, his girlfriend, had stared through the passenger window as they passed two nights ago, and after that he had borrowed Bal's car and left him his. That particular evening, the first he had seen Colin and Emma go out, though he had seen no one go in since his arrival at five forty-five, he had had high hopes of a couple emerging at eleven. But Colin and the girl had returned long before that hour in an unsteady and amorous condition, and he had abandoned his watch until next day.

No one had gone in that evening, nor had the tenants gone out. As far as he knew, that is. But at seven, after he had seen a man of about thirty-five let himself in at the red front door and a woman rather younger admitted by this same man ten minutes later, he left Bal's car where he had parked it and went to investigate the back of the building. From the parallel road, the rear of the little row of shops was hidden by tall trees still in leaf but Damon discovered an alley which led, not into Glebe Road itself but, by describing a wide curve, into Glebe Lane. Halfway along, he could see the back of the dry-cleaners and the flat above it, and make out in the lamplit dark an iron fire escape running in zigzag flights from the upper floor to the backyard and a path to this very alley.

So Colin and Emma had spotted him the night before, prob-ably without absolutely identifying who and what he was, and prudently made their escape this way rather than coming out into the street. He couldn't be in two places at once but he could station himself in the alley and, once he had seen Colin's and Emma's departure, be back in Glebe Road in two minutes, plenty of time to see a couple arrive. Or would the pair 'borrow-ing' the flat also use the fire escape?

Apparently they would. Or else no one had gone out and no one had come in on the following night. After a fruitless hour in the alley, Damon went back to his car at seven thirty and, glancing up at a lighted window in the flat above, saw

Colin Fry looking down. But not at Bal's car. He was scrutinising the street for Damon's own car, whose make, colour and index number he had no doubt memorised, or for Damon himself lurking in a doorway. Though he must have satisfied himself that Damon wasn't there and the coast was clear, he seemed to have no intention of leaving the flat that night. Damon stayed there for another hour, finally going home just before nine.

Tomorrow, he thought, he would park Bal's car as far away as he dared while still keeping the flat under surveillance.

'First it was drugs, now it's having a baby for someone else,' said George Marshalson. 'To me she was an innocent child and you're making her into a monster.'

He was in sole charge of Brand this evening. Diana, he said, had gone to see her sister in Myfleet. She had put the little boy to bed before she left and said he was asleep but George was sure he had heard him cry out and had been on the point of going upstairs to investigate when Wexford and DS Goldsmith had arrived. As he spoke, a loud wail came from upstairs and George got reluctantly to his feet. He went to the door and listened, the expression on his face exasperated, but when the cry wasn't repeated he returned to the ornate oriental chair he had been sitting in.

'I asked you if your daughter ever mentioned surrogacy to you, Mr Marshalson,' Hannah said. 'As a concept, I mean. Not as something she intended to take on herself.'

'Not that I remember,' said George. 'Well, I would remember. I certainly would remember any proposal she might have had to bring *another* child into this house.'

'The idea wouldn't have been to keep the child herself, Mr Marshalson,' said Wexford, trying to keep his voice neutral.

'The idea, as you call it, is preposterous.'

Wexford turned his attention to the Samphire brothers. 'You

told me last time we talked about this, sir, that you doubted if these people had ever come in contact with Amber. Can you be absolutely sure of that?'

'I can't account for what she did and whom she met when she wasn't at home here, can I? Pretty obviously I can't. If I'd had any control over that none of these appalling things would have happened. Maybe she knew Ross Samphire or the other one – what's he called? Rick, is it? – maybe she knew them. I wouldn't know. She didn't meet them in my presence.'

'I'll tell you what I'm thinking, Mr Marshalson, and what I hope may be confirmed later this week.' When König-Hensel comes and reveals everything? 'Your daughter and Megan Bartlow were concerned together in some kind of, er, business of being surrogate mothers. It may have been perfectly legal.' He was certain it wasn't.

'Legal,' said George, 'but hardly moral.'

'That's a matter of opinion. They may have started this on their own but it seems likely they got into the hands of someone – let's call him their organiser.'

'You make him sound like a pimp.'

'We think this may have been one of the Samphire brothers or both of them,' said Hannah, getting a frown from Wexford, 'but as Chief Inspector Wexford says, we hope soon to get more evidence of that. Meanwhile, do you have any views?'

'All I know of Surrage-Samphire is that they did some interior decoration work for us, it was perfectly satisfactory and I'd have no hesitation in employing them again. My wife will say the same. She probably saw more of them than I did.'

He jumped to his feet, slapping his hand into the small of his back with a soft groan as renewed cries came from upstairs, insistent this time.

'I'll have to see to him,' he said. 'I don't suppose I'll know what's wrong. But it's no use leaving him to cry. That's just storing up trouble for later on and we don't want to be up half the night.'

Dining with friends in Savesbury the following evening, Hannah sat next to the only man she had found really attractive since she met Bal. She knew he was going to ask her out and he did. Of course she said no – and regretted it all the way home, thinking what utter nonsense this was, being constant to a man who in anyone else's eyes was no more than a friend.

Then, as autumn came, brown and tired and sunless, he asked her to come away for the weekend with him, to a hotel in a village in Somerset. Which weekend? The first they both had off at the same time from the Friday evening till the Monday morning.

So it was to be the weekend after next. For the first time in months they would both be off duty from the Friday till the Monday morning. They could drive down in time for dinner on the Friday. He made this suggestion while they were dining at the Cheriton Forest Hotel, having had a pre-dinner drink in the bar where Stephen Lawson had ingratiated himself with the visitor from Birmingham.

Hannah was sick and tired (as she put it to herself) of sitting up at bars with Bal and facing him across dinner tables. It was extremely expensive and she insisted on paying her way. Only one of them was able to drink more than a small glass of wine. By this time they had been to every half-decent restaurant in Kingsmarkham, Pomfret and Myfleet, and to the few grand ones as well. If only they could have stayed at home and done their own cooking, played their own music, poured their own drinks and had as much as they liked – but then the inevitable would have happened and Bal's aim was to avoid the inevitable until the time was ripe. Until they really knew each other.

Hannah felt she knew everything about Bal from his infancy, childhood, teenage years, school, university, recruitment into the police, his family, his siblings, his parents. His tastes, his inclinations, his favourite music, his reading matter. And he knew all that about her.

'That sounds nice,' she said in response to his invitation for the weekend after next. But his conduct of their relationship – if that was the word – had so inhibited her that she couldn't ask outright if these days were calculated to see its consummation. She could only manage, 'You do mean to stay the nights?' and like some maiden in times gone by, blush when he laughed and said of course, that was the idea.

Soon after that he drove her home, gave her one of his chaste kisses and didn't even come up to the flat.

He was not at all the idea of a German even intelligent Englishmen hold in their minds to this day, the large burly blond with a shaven bullet head. Rainer König-Hensel was of medium height, thin, with austere regular features, grey eyes and olive skin. He wore the kind of beautiful suit Burden favoured (but wasn't wearing today) in a fine charcoal-grey tweed. Wexford noticed these things while confessing sadly to himself that if he possessed such a suit it would have become a wrinkled wreck within days.

They shook hands and König-Hensel took the chair on the other side of the desk to Wexford. If he was embarrassed, his face showed nothing of it but remained set, almost rigid. He was the kind of man whose face would show nothing, Wexford thought, no matter what he was feeling. If it were possible to say such a thing, his speech was more accented than his handwriting and perhaps a little too correct and with far too many insertions of 'you know'.

'My wife and I', he began, 'are unable to have children. That is to say, my wife is unable. Treatment for cancer when she was still not twenty years of age left her infertile. She knew this and I knew it when we married ten years ago.' He paused and turned his calm blank gaze on Wexford.

'Please go on, Mr König-Hensel.'

'This did not worry me, you know. It was not a problem. Often it is not, you know, with men. But Sabine starts to long for a child and we explore the possibility of in vitro fertilisation but in our case this too is not possible. Then we hear of surrogacy. The child would be mine but not my wife's, you know. To cut a long story short, Chief Inspector, we join a group we hear about in Frankfurt and talk to others in a like situation to ours. We also consult the Web and there we find the website of Babies for All. We sign up and after a time names of suitable surrogates are sent to us. Are you following me?'

'I am,' said Wexford.

'But none is to our taste, you know, nor do we care for the counselling which is offered to us. I must explain here that my wife has a horror of discussing these things with so-called experts, of speaking of her private life and other personal matters. Also, Babies for All warns those who sign up to it that to find a surrogate that suits one may take months or even years. My wife is now forty-two and I am six years older. We feel we cannot wait so long, you know. Still, we have given our name to Babies for All, you know, since there seems no harm in doing so and one day last April we receive an e-mail from a Miss Megan Bartlow.'

'Ah,' said Wexford.

'You say that, Chief Inspector, as if you know what I am about to say.'

'I have an idea. But go on.'

König-Hensel hadn't moved in his chair since he had first sat down but now he shifted a little and leant forward. 'This e-mail told us that Miss Bartlow was not herself on the books, you know, of Babies for All but that she had access to their list of intended parents. She and her friend, a Miss Amber Marshalson, were anxious to be surrogates . . .'

'Excuse me, Mr König-Hensel, but do you happen to have a copy of that e-mail?'

'I have taken it with me.'

It was the first mistake in his perfect English. From his brief-case he handed Wexford a single sheet of printout. It may be in Megan's name, Wexford thought, but Amber wrote it and in text message style without benefit of capital letters.

my friend miss amber marshalson and i are anxious to become surrogates. we want to do this for couples who cannot have children of their own. if you take advantage of our offer you will not have to wait or be vetted or counselled and the process will not take months. we could be with you in frankfurt within weeks. we are young, fit and healthy and each of us has had a child before. please reply by mail as we have no internet access of our own. megan bartlow, 235 high street, kingsmarkham, e.sussex km1 3dl.

And they fell for this? König-Hensel seemed to read his thoughts. 'I was suspicious from the start, you know, but my wife was made so happy by it. "What do we have to lose?" she kept saying. Our group in Frankfurt has already told us that many surrogacies are privately arranged. "They have had children," she kept saying to me. "We know they can do it," and then she said, very sadly, "They are not like me, they can do it."'

'You wrote back?'

'Oh, yes. After about a week. I asked for more information. Miss Bartlow sent me copies of their children's birth documents – certificates, that is. She sent me a photo of herself and of Miss Marshalson, both lovely girls. "What have we to

232

lose?" my wife said. So I did as she asked and suggested they come to Frankfurt, all expenses paid of course.'

'What fee were you to pay Megan Bartlow?'

'Two thousand pounds in advance and another two thousand when we . . . when we received the child.'

'She came at the end of May and Amber Marshalson with her?'

'Before that I had discussed this matter with the group I told you about and a couple said they also were interested, you know, and would like to meet the young ladies.'

Wexford sighed, but inaudibly. 'Let me guess,' he said. 'They came. You paid for them to stay in a moderately priced hotel. Not, I think, at the Hotel Die Vier Pferde?'

'No, indeed. At the Hotel Jägerhof. Not at a four-star hotel. That was not necessary. Beyond – as I believe you say – the call of duty. I did take a suite in the Hotel Die Vier Pferde for just one night.' He hesitated and a slight flush coloured his pale skin. 'For the, er, transaction to take place, you know. After Ms Bartlow and Ms Marshalson had left, my wife and I remained for dinner and the night.'

He could imagine. For this uxorious man, having his wife there, staying in some luxury, spending the night there together, would partially remove something of the squalor and absurdity that must attach to these things. And also a way of celebrating conception? It might even help to give her the illusion the child would be hers as well as his. 'By the "transaction" you mean you provided a sperm sample?'

'Yes. My friend Mr Dieter Weinstock provided a sample to Miss Marshalson at the Hotel Jägerhof.'

'And you never heard from either of them again?'

'Not at all. We heard. E-mails came, to tell us conception had taken place in each case and then again in July came word that both were well and the pregnancies proceeding normally. My wife was so happy. Miss Bartlow wrote again on the first of September to say she was well and would be in touch again in one month's time. She promised to send a photo of herself when her pregnancy, er, was visible. After the month we heard no more, we heard nothing until my friend Mr Weinstock was over here in the UK three weeks ago, you know. On the flight he received a copy of an English newspaper and in it was an article, only a few lines, saying police had not yet found the killer of Miss Amber Marshalson.'

'I don't think I have ever felt so hostile to murder victims as I do to those two,' Wexford said as he and Burden sat over a beer in the snug of their old haunt, the Olive and Dove. 'I feel vindictive and I know I shouldn't. But if you'd heard that man . . .'

Burden shrugged. 'I hope you told him he'd been very foolish.'

'Of course I did – but gently. He seemed to think the whole business was far less important to the Weinstocks than it was to him and his wife, and it comforted him to know that at least Megan had become pregnant. Amber, of course, was not. Whether she actually tried to impregnate herself with the gullible Weinstock's sperm or threw it down the pan no one will ever know. I didn't tell König-Hensel that it was very likely the child Megan was carrying wasn't his. Why make it worse for him? Megan's child may have been Prinsip's or that of one of the members of SOCC. I'm sure those two contacted them. Remember that thousand pounds she had in her jacket pocket. Before Amber went to the Bling-Bling I think it's practically a certainty she'd popped along to some hotel room – maybe even in here – and taken delivery of another phial of the magic fluid.'

Burden made a face. 'When you come to think of it, they could have hoaxed dozens of couples like this.'

'Hardly dozens, Mike. Let's hope there aren't too many

desperate people who'd fall for this scam of theirs. Maybe three or four.'

'What I want to know is where does Rick Samphire come into all this?'

'George Marshalson said he sounded like a pimp and there may be something in that. Whenever silly ignorant girls get on to making what looks like easy money, there'll always be some unscrupulous man ready to take them over and organise them.'

'Except that it looks as if Megan and Amber did their own organising.'

'He may have put the idea into Megan's head in the first place. Or more likely Ross did. He may have found out all this background stuff for them. The existence of the Sussex Overcoming Childlessness Circle, for instance. We don't know how Megan first got on to the surrogacy thing. My suggestion that she read about a case in the newspaper was only an idea. He may have put it to her.'

Burden went up to the little snug bar and asked for two more lagers. The barman insisted on bringing them to their table, perhaps to have the chance of also offering a big bowl full of exceptionally large and succulent-looking cashew nuts. Wexford groaned when he saw them and sat on his hands.

'You'll have to bring them out again unless you're going to lap your drink.'

'I know. Could you eat what you want of those things and then put them somewhere out of sight?'

Burden ate a single nut, then carried the bowl to the windowsill where he hid it behind the curtain hem. 'There. Out of temptation's way. That theory of yours doesn't work, Reg. It presupposes that Megan knew Rick Samphire, knew him well enough to enter into a conspiracy with him. But we've already established that he killed her because she recognised him *some weeks later* as the man she'd seen in Yorstone Wood.

If he was her fellow conspirator and, in Marshalson's words, her pimp, she'd have known him immediately she saw him in the wood.'

'Perhaps she did,' said Wexford.

'What, she saw him and knew him, and he of course knew her and he just let her go, knowing the connection she'd make between him and Amber's accident?'

'Remember, Amber hadn't been killed. She hadn't even been injured. When the accident was reported in the paper there was nothing about Amber's involvement. Only the Ambroses were mentioned. Why should Megan have suspected Rick Samphire of dropping that lump of concrete off the bridge just because she'd once seen him in Yorstone Wood? Probably she'd no idea of the date when she saw him or when the accident happened. But when Amber was killed and the story of her involvement in the concrete-block-dropping business came out, then it was worth making the connection. She *knew* Rick. It was easy for her to approach him, a simple matter to meet him at an agreed venue, that is number four Victoria Terrace. Very likely she'd met him there before to discuss details of their next surrogacy con or to hand over his cut of the money they took from the unfortunate "intended parents".'

'So you're saying', said Burden, 'that Rick killed Megan because she was blackmailing him. But why did he kill Amber? I'm sorry if this is an unfortunate comparison, but wasn't she the goose that laid the golden eggs?'

Wexford looked for SOCC in the phone book but they weren't there. In spite of the help it had been to him, the Internet was always the last source to come to mind. Half-heartedly, he entered SOCC and, to his surprise, a display headed 'The Stork Can Come To You Too' appeared on the screen. For the first time he had succeeded in conjuring up out of that infernal machine exactly what he wanted. It must have been because he was relaxed about it – or hopeless.

Above the acronym was a picture of a flying stork carrying a shawled baby in its beak. 'The Sussex Overcoming Childlessness Circle', he read,

can really help you become a parent. We offer counselling, group work, psychotherapy and down-to-earth practical help. Not just by putting our members in touch with IVF treatment but by introductions to adoption societies, surrogacy agencies and absolutely new systems of acquiring the child of your dreams. Needless to say, everything is within the law and above board.

You can join today by the simple method of entering your name and e-mail address on page two. No payment is required until you have entered one of our programmes.

Now touch Next.

Wexford touched Next and page two appeared in the shape of an entry form, surrounded by photographs of ecstatic pregnant women and happy mothers with babies.

'I wonder what the "absolutely new systems of acquiring the child of your dreams" are?' said Burden who had come up behind him.

'It can't mean surrogacy because they mention that.'

'Nor IVF because they mention that too.'

'I said the other day that I've known the facts of life for some forty years but now I sometimes wonder. Maybe there's some amazing secret of procreation that's never come my way.' Wexford shook his head, more in incredulity than doubt. 'Their address and phone number are there underneath that touching picture of a fat lady with twins: 167 High Street, Kingsmarkham.'

Walking up and down on the opposite side of the High Street, Wexford decided that the premises of SOCC must be somewhere in the block of shops that included Gew-Gaws at number 163, above which was the flat Megan Bartlow had lived in. But 161 was an off-licence, 165 a hairdresser, 167 – which should have been SOCC – was a pet-food supplies store, 169 a newsagent and 171 an optician. He had already tried phoning the number on the website and after ten rings had an answering service reply.

He crossed the street on the pedestrian crossing and walked along examining all the shopfronts and the doors beside them that led into hallways and upstairs to upper-storey flats. Prinsip and Bartlow was still there, unaltered since Megan's death. Other names were on bell pushes beside other doors, some no longer decipherable. He pushed open the door of Gew-Gaws and Jimmy Gawson's bell jangled. Jimmy was standing in the middle of the shop beside a table, arranging on top of it a pyramid of chocolate bars in Union flag wrappings surrounded by four-inch-high models of the London Eye. On the edge of an ashtray, probably designed to look like the Diana Fountain in Hyde Park, rested his current inhalator.

When he saw Wexford he put it into his mouth and sucked noisily on it. 'Well, my dear,' he said, 'if these things had been invented when I was young I'd have got hooked on them instead of those damned fags. What can I do for you, Reggie?'

'Have you ever heard of something called SOCC? The Sussex Overcoming Childlessness Circle, to give it its full title.'

'Next door but one,' said Jimmy. 'They never bothered to cover up the card with what-d'you-call-it, so the letters got washed off in the rain. The second floor. They've got two rooms at the back.'

'Thanks. That's a great help.'

'I'm not so sure about that, my dear.' Jimmy inserted a fresh cartridge in the inhalator, shifted the topmost chocolate bar infinitesimally to the left and turned round. 'There's never anyone there till the evening and not often then. I should phone and leave a message.'

'I have.'

'They'll get back to you. Just give them time. Have you heard poor old Grace Morgan is no more? Gone to the wood-cutter's cottage in the sky. Keithie himself came in and told me. Not that he or any of them ever went near her.'

In spite of what Jimmy Gawson had said, Wexford tried ringing the bell for the second floor at number 167. No one answered and when he got back to the police station no message from SOCC awaited him. It had begun to rain. So Grace Morgan was dead. No one would live in the cottage now and watch the badgers come out into the wood at dusk. Her remaining granddaughter wouldn't have to brave the terrors of the wood to visit her, or her daughter need to invite her once a year.

Granddaughters and daughters . . . They made him think of his own. The two of each he had and the possible one of the former to come. The associative process was a funny thing, he thought, as his mind drifted from daughters in general to Sylvia in particular, from Sylvia to her child due now in less than two months, from childbirth to those who deliver babies, to midwives – Mary Beaumont was a midwife. Hadn't she once told him she worked for SOCC? He hadn't taken much notice at the time . . . Might she know?

He picked up the phone and dialled Sylvia's number.

'Mary?' she said. 'She's here now. Why don't you come over and talk to her?'

Chapter 24

At first the heavy rain, falling as straight as water from a tap turned full on, seemed against Damon. Even his heavy rubberised raincoat wouldn't stand up to more than ten minutes of it. Waders would have helped, or at least wellies. His private view was that whereas black people looked much better than white in sunshine, the hotter the better, rain didn't suit them. Rain made him look grey and miserable. Damon was vain of his appearance – but so, he'd noticed, was Inspector Burden of his – and he thought it mattered very little so long as he didn't show it.

He was only twenty-five but even he could remember a time when black people, however accepted, were never considered good-looking in the eyes of whites. Then came the years when black men and women were attractive enough when they had Caucasian features. That was gone now and West Africans of pure lineage found favour in whites' eyes – unless the white was a member of the BNP or extremely right-wing. Damon thought about this as he hung about Glebe Alley and thought too that Kingsmarkham wasn't too bad a place to be in, especially when he remembered what it had been like being a child in Deptford.

All the time he kept his eyes on those zigzag white-painted

steps on the rear of the black-painted building in Glebe Road. When he closed his eyes he saw them as black on white. He saw them in dreams at night, black on white or white on black. It seemed like a symbol or an omen but he couldn't for the life of him think what it could mean. Nothing, probably. That made him laugh to himself as he walked down to Glebe Lane and back again. He knew the water would come through the soles of his shoes and it had. Between his toes he could feel it squelch. He had taken off his right shoe and was pouring the water out of it when two figures appeared on the zigzag steps. The sight of Colin Fry's girlfriend made him laugh afresh. She wore a glossy white mac, tightly belted and reaching only to about eight inches above her knees. Those saggy boots all the girls were wearing would have been more suitable this evening but Emma was in peep-toe sandals with four-inch heels. From where he stood, a good fifty yards from the fire escape, Damon could hear her squeals of protest at the weather as she descended the steps, clinging on to Colin's anorak.

He was rather sorry he couldn't linger but they mustn't see him. He splashed down the alley, filling his shoes with water once more, reached his car and hurled himself inside. It might have been wiser to strip off his mac first for now the car seemed full of water, soaking the carpet, making the seat slippery and dripping from the steering wheel. There was nothing to be done except take off his sodden shoes and socks, and regret not bringing a towel with him.

For safety's sake he had parked Bal's car almost at the end of Glebe Road, out of sight of Colin Fry's windows. That meant he could barely see the red-painted front door. He started the car and moved it until he was nearly opposite the dry-cleaners. There was no one about. Usually clogged with nose-to-tail parking, Glebe Road was half empty of cars. Damon had begun to shiver. They must go out sometimes, he thought, and no one come to use the flat. Suppose this is one of those evenings. He'd give it an hour – no, maybe an hour and a half. Awful to contemplate but it had to be. Just as he was asking himself if it would be too wasteful and environmentally unfriendly to run the engine in order to have the heater on, a car drew up and parked in the space next to his. A man and a woman got out. Only their slim figures and the speed of their movements told him they were young, for the woman pulled the hood of her padded coat up over her head before she got out of the car and the man, his raincoat covering him from his head to his ankles, put up a big black umbrella the moment his feet were on the pavement. But it was the red door beside the dry-cleaners' window they were making for. Damon saw the man fumble under his raincoat, bring out a key and insert it in the lock. Both of them were quickly inside and the door shut behind them.

This was the second visitor to Colin Fry's flat he had seen let himself in with a key. Wasn't it a bit careless of Colin to give a key to his home to all and sundry? But then perhaps it wasn't all and sundry, Damon thought as he drove home to a hot bath and a chicken tikka masala takeaway. If not his friends, perhaps all the people who used the flat were well-known to him, people he trusted or people recommended by those he trusted. He'd put that in his report and he'd come back on the following night. Now he'd got somewhere it was starting to be quite exciting.

'They're a perfectly legitimate organisation,' Mary began, 'or they used to be. Still are, for all I know. There's a social worker who works for Kingsmarkham Social Services runs it and me and a couple of trained counsellors. We all do the job for free. Our members really organise themselves. What we do is advise. We're an advisory service.'

Sylvia came in with wine on a tray and cashew nuts and crisps bowls. Wexford extended his right hand to the nuts, withdrew it sharply as if it were surrounded by an invisible electrified fence. 'What sort of advice?'

'Well, darling, people are told what their options are. That means how to go about IVF treatment – oh, and one of the counsellors is a herbalist and advises what to take to promote fertility.' She made a face. 'Then there's the metamorphic technique which is based on "cell memory". According to its practitioners, our cells carry past traumas around with them. Imagine a woman who desperately wants to conceive but has already had a difficult birth. She carries the memory of that birth with her and the fear of repeating it may prevent her falling pregnant. Daft, really, darling. There are people who offer lymphatic drainage and hypnotherapy visualisation,' said Mary. 'Some put a fertility crystal under their pillows.'

Wexford's eyebrows went up.

'Yes, I know. I was never keen on that. Then if that fails or it's impossible there's surrogacy which can be like what Sylvia's doing, helping a friend, or we direct them to an agency such as Babies for All. Adoption, of course, and fostering. We advise, tell them who to go to and how, that sort of thing. Oh, and we hold group therapy sessions. That's really couples or single would-be parents sitting around in a circle talking over their particular problem and saying how they feel about it. That can be very sad, you know, darling.'

'Do women come to you offering their services as surrogates?'

'Yes, often,' Mary said. 'We send them on to the agencies. Babies for All or Intended Parents. I think that girl who was murdered came.'

'You mean Megan Bartlow?'

'No, the other one, the good-looking one. When I saw her picture on the TV I thought, I wonder if that's the girl who came in here. I couldn't swear to it but I was pretty sure.'

'You sent her to an agency?'

Mary sighed. 'First of all she said she was an intended parent but when she got in there – the session hadn't started – she announced she wanted to be a surrogate and she was chatting away before anyone could stop her. She'd been talking to a few people before I realised and threw her out.'

One of those people, Wexford thought, or more probably a couple, found her privately, made an arrangement with her and on the evening of August the tenth she went to their home or met the man in an hotel and took a sperm sample from him. He also gave her a thousand pounds which, free and easy girl as she had been, she put into her pocket and went off to the Bling-Bling Club. Intending to give their cut to Ross or Rick Samphire?

He asked Mary.

'I've never heard of them, darling. I'm sure they don't have any connection with SOCC.'

'Why did you say SOCC *used to be legitimate*?'

'I said they still are, for all I know.'

'But what did you mean by "used to be"?'

Mary swallowed her wine as if she needed it. 'I've resigned if you must know . . .'

'I think I must know, Mary.'

'Well, there's something going on I don't like.'

'I've had a look at their website.' Just saying those words, in casual fashion as if he looked at websites every hour, brought Wexford a pride he knew was ridiculous. 'What are "absolutely new systems of acquiring the child of your dreams"? Some method of reproduction I've missed out on?'

'I don't know but that's why I'm resigning. All I know is that one of our counsellors, a man called Quickwood, is sending women would-be parents to a travel agent in London. It may only be an introduction to cross-cultural adoption, it may be no more than that but somehow I don't think it is and that's why I don't want any more to do with SOCC.'

'I don't think I understand.'

'I don't understand myself,' Mary said. 'All I know is that at a group question-and-answer session last week one of our members said she was going out to Africa on what she called a "birth package". Nairobi, I think she said. She would be bringing back a baby with her. Afterwards our social worker asked her if Kingsmarkham Social Services had made an assessment – that is, what they call a home study, see if the would-be adoptive parents' home and circumstances are suitable for a child. It's even more, well, rigorous when it's cross-culture adoption and it's always quite a long process. Anyway, this woman said that wasn't necessary because this would be her own child. She would give birth herself in Africa. I had a good look at her then and she obviously wasn't pregnant, yet she'd said she was going to Africa in two weeks' time.

'Well, Quickwood, who's a social worker, said the woman was obviously very disturbed. Her husband had left her and she was in a bad mental state. It was nothing for us to worry about because she wouldn't be allowed to take the baby out of Africa, still less bring it here. Probably it was all in her head, he said. But I don't know, Reg, I didn't like it. I made a point of talking to her again and she told me she knew it was all right and above board because a woman she knew in Myringham had gone on a "birth package" and come back with a baby which she'd given birth to a week after she arrived in Nairobi. I asked her a question then. I asked her if her friend was white and she said yes, she was, and then I asked if the baby was black and she said yes, of course. Babies born in Africa *were* black. And then she said she thought I was being racist.

'I told Ken Quickwood. He said it was nothing to do with us, but the woman was one of our members and she was telling everyone about this. That's why I resigned.'

'Is this confidential,' Wexford asked, 'or are you going to tell me this woman's name?'

'I'll have to, won't I, Reg? There's no point in telling you all this if I don't. She a Mrs Gwenda Brooks and she lives at two Jewel Terrace, Brimhurst.'

For a moment he didn't know who this was. Then he remembered his and Burden's encounter with John Brooks and his young lover in the restaurant. This was his wife, his childless neglected wife.

'Who was the woman she knew in Myringham?'

'I don't know, Reg. I've told you all I know.'

It was like going away on a honeymoon. Not as it might be now, a pair of newly married lovers who had been together, perhaps living together, for months, but as it once was, in the old days, when a shy but proud husband was going away for the first time with his virgin bride. Ahead of them a wedding night, a real wedding night, on which sex would be taking place between them for the first time.

So it was for her and Bal. They sat silent beside each other in Damon Coleman's car, just as that bride and bridegroom must have felt, but worse than that because society and its requirements had changed. She found herself resenting Bal for it. This was all of his making. What had given him the idea of going away for the weekend in order to make love to her? He was creating an artificial situation, almost a ritual, serious and momentous, out of something which should have been the natural effect of a cause. How much happier would she and he both have felt if they had gone to bed together (a euphemism she usually scorned) two months ago and been going to bed together ever since. For she was sure, from his long silences and apparent abandonment of anything like conversation, that he was as nervous as she. They could be talking now and laughing, reminiscing about the recent past and just a little too excited for comfort at the prospect of checking into the Maid's Head and finding themselves alone in their room.

246

Instead of this sort of thing – 'How far are we from Taunton now, d'you think?'

Hannah was navigating. 'Maybe fifteen miles.'

'We should be there in plenty of time for dinner.'

Dinner! 'Yes,' she said.

He pulled into a service station for petrol. The afternoon had grown gradually greyer and darker and now, the clocks put back an hour the weekend before, night had come. At only six thirty, night had come. Not a romantic kind of evening, with a moon and stars covering a clear sky, but a thick grey darkness where mist was beginning to obscure the road ahead and a damp heaviness in the air. Bal was silent as he drove away. A few more minutes of it and even he – she put it to herself like that, 'even he', as if he had become obtuse, all his sensitivity departed – seemed to notice the awkwardness.

'Is something wrong, Hannah?'

She didn't answer and he repeated the question.

'Intuitive of you to notice,' she said.

A man all over, as her mother might have put it, 'What have I done now?' he said.

She came to a decision. If she did nothing, if she left it and let the evening take its course, she knew it would be far worse. One or both of them would be deeply humiliated and they lacked love for each other to make it right. But as she briefly looked back over their relationship, she couldn't see how she could have acted differently. What move could she have made or step taken which would have brought them to this point, just outside Taunton, in a different frame of mind? There was nothing. Much as she disliked thinking it, the blame was his. He had tried to live according to an outdated morality in an age that neither wanted nor understood it.

'It's no good, Bal,' she said. 'Maybe it's my fault' – she knew it wasn't – 'but this isn't going to work. I'm sorry.'

'What are you talking about, Hannah?'

'We've left it too long. Don't you feel that? Don't you *see*? This sort of thing should be natural and spontaneous. I did tell you only you wouldn't listen. It all had to be serious and getting to know each other and . . . and whatever. And now it's too late.'

He pulled the car into a lay-by. 'What do you want to do? Stay there in separate rooms? We can do that. I've always said delay is the wisest way.'

'Yes, and look where it's got us. You go on. Drop me in Taunton and I'll go back on the train. Taunton's on the main line, isn't it?'

'Don't be stupid,' he said and his face was as dark as the sky outside. 'Of course I'll drive us back.'

And he did. Speechless, controlled, but sometimes making a noiseless sound like a suppressed growl.

'I need to go to the loo,' she said, somewhere in West Sussex. They had a cup of coffee, remembered they had had no dinner and each tried to eat a pork pie and a tomato.

'I think you have lost your mind,' said Bal.

She shrugged.

'This seems to be the end, don't you think?'

'There was never much beginning,' she said.

He was so beautiful to look at, even when he was tired and cross. What a waste. And she did like him, she'd miss him, only the trouble was she wouldn't because he'd always be there. Maybe she should apply for a transfer – but why should she? She wasn't the one in the wrong. He drove on in renewed silence.

The traffic had thinned out, especially in this easterly direction. As always, drivers were tempted to go over the speed limit, past eighty and into the nineties. Bal, of course, kept to an obedient seventy, unworried when the speed camera flashed, aimed at the eighty-seven miler in the fast lane.

They didn't speak again until they had passed the sign which said 'Welcome to Kingsmarkham, An Historic Town'. Bal went on round the roundabout instead of turning left and Hannah said, 'You've gone the wrong way.'

He gave a humourless scathing laugh. 'One of us has, that's for sure.'

Never again would he say 'us' in quite that way, she thought. He turned the car round, took Orchard Road and stopped rather too sharply outside her block. She turned to look at him but he didn't look at her. His hands were still on the wheel, clenched tightly.

As she left the car she said again, 'I'm sorry.'

Damon could never understand what the radio and TV weather forecasters meant when they said that the rain would move away northwards (or southwards or eastwards) to be succeeded by sunshine and showers. Showers were rain, weren't they? When he was a child one of his parents' white neighbours used to shout after him to go back to where he belonged. As he had been born in London he had no idea of where this might be and one day he turned and asked the woman. He asked her very politely.

'A hot place,' she said. 'Hot enough to burn you up, cheeky monkey.'

But she never shouted after him again. Damon thought it would never rain in the hot place and he rather liked the idea of going there. He remembered this when he was back again in Glebe Alley, watching the zigzag fire escape and wondering if one of those showers was due. It was a moonless, starless night. The sky might be clear or covered in cloud, you couldn't tell. He had put on his thick mac again just in case and it felt hot inside it. Hot enough to burn you up, cheeky monkey. Damon smiled to himself. That poor old woman everyone in the neighbourhood knew was half-crazed could have been up in court these days for saying what she had said to him. It was a funny world.

Because he was using Bal's car and, anyway, parking it more or less out of sight, Colin Fry and Emma might have decided to go back to using their front entrance. There was nothing he could do about that. He couldn't be in two places at once. A drop of rain fell on his nose and as he put up his hand to wipe it away they emerged from the door at the top of the fire escape. He didn't wait but ran down the alley, into Glebe Lane and his car. The good clean he had given its inside first thing this morning had smartened it up but it still felt damp. He moved it a dozen yards along Glebe Road and into the one remaining vacant space. If a visitor to the flat arrived now, where would he put his car?

In the next street along, apparently, or else he had come on the bus, for the man who approached the dry-cleaners and put his key in the lock on the red door had come on foot. He was a tall man in an expensive-looking belted Burberry and he had put up his umbrella. But as the door swung open he necessarily had to furl it and when he stepped inside and shook the umbrella on to the doorstep, Damon saw his face in the lamplight. It was a face he recognised. That is, he had seen it somewhere before without being able to recall who it was.

Silently, he cursed. He must be able to remember whose face this was. Where had he seen the man? He'd think of all the places he'd been recently, all the people he'd talked to . . .

The street was no longer empty. A woman was approaching from the High Street end of Glebe Road. The dark glasses she wore were hardly appropriate for this weather, especially as she had on an ankle-length black raincoat and was carrying a man's large umbrella. Was she also making for Colin Fry's flat?

It would seem so. The rain eased up before she got there and she put down the umbrella. Looking about her, to her right and left, she pushed her glasses up on to the scarf she had tied round her head. Damon had never seen her before. All he could say about her was that she was about forty or younger. But then it was hard to tell when they pulled their hair back like that, stretching the skin under the eyes and lifting the cheeks. Back where he came from they had a term for it, the 'Croydon facelift'.

She went up to the door by the dry-cleaners but before she could touch the bell it was opened and she stepped quickly inside.

Chapter 25

The week of fine weather, which usually comes some time in October, arrived at the end of it. This 'little summer' started the day Hannah Goldsmith began a week of her annual leave so that she wished she hadn't been so hasty as to book, only the previous week, a six-day holiday in Crete. She had left it so late because she had naturally expected that by this time she and Bal would be going away together. But Bal hadn't spoken to her since their ill-fated trip to Somerset, except in the line of work, once more calling her 'sarge', and she had spoken to him only when she had to and calling him nothing at all. Now she was going away on her own and she had never looked forward to a holiday less.

Damon had searched his memory to recall who the man was he had seen go into Colin Fry's flat but without success. He saw the white zigzag fire escape in his dreams but he couldn't conjure up that face again. Did it matter? Damon thought it did because Wexford always said that everything, never mind how small, mattered in a murder case.

A double-page spread story appeared in the *Kingsmarkham Courier* in which Darren Lovelace, who appeared to have been promoted to Chief Reporter, lamented the days when Scotland Yard was called in to investigate murders such as had occurred in the area in August and September. The days before murder squads and serious crime squads existed. What was needed, he wrote, was the creation of a British version of the FBI and, simultaneously, the compulsory redundancy of 'back numbers' like Wexford.

Wexford read it and suffered. He knew that things never seem quite as bad the next day and, by two days later, are well on the way to fading altogether. This, of course, is no help at the time of reading. He opened the *Courier* again and looked at the old picture of himself quaffing beer. Time was when local newspapers were bland and inoffensive, afraid of upsetting their on-the-doorstep readership. If Darren Lovelace regretted the somewhat inaccurate past he attributed to the police force, he, Wexford, looked back with nostalgia on those days when the *Courier*'s big stories were meetings of the urban district council, the flower show and the high school's A level results. He crumpled up the paper in his two hands and was thrusting it into the recycling wastepaper basket when a Mr Bartlow was announced. Would Wexford see him?

'Send him up, will you?'

It was Hannah who had interviewed him and this was Wexford's first sight of Megan's father. His first words after he had introduced himself were that he had just been to his ex-mother-in-law's funeral. 'Grace Morgan,' he said. 'Maybe you've talked to her. She was a good old girl, the best of that bunch. Ninety-three is a good age but I'll miss her, though no one else will. I should have come to you before. Being in Kingsmarkham for the funeral fetched me here.'

'What did you come about, Mr Bartlow?'

'Well, my daughter Megan. Of course, my daughter Megan.'

'Yes. I'm sorry,' Wexford said.

'She didn't let me know, you know.' Wexford had no need to ask who 'she' was. 'I had to see it on the TV,' Bartlow said. 'Well, my wife saw it and told me. Broke it to me, I suppose you'd say. Apart from Lara, I've got two more kids with my wife but that doesn't stop you grieving for the one that's gone.'

'I'm sure it doesn't.'

Bartlow shifted in his chair. 'You may think what I'm going to tell you just, well, a load of rubbish. It's nothing, really. The young lady detective who came, I thought of telling her but, well, frankly, I was afraid she'd think it ridiculous. But it's been sort of haunting me. My wife said it was nothing and to forget it but yesterday when I said I thought I'd go to old Gracie's funeral she said to come in here and get it off my chest. If you think it's rubbish, well, you can just say so.'

'Try me,' said Wexford.

'OK, then. Here goes. I told the young lady how Meg came over the day of the Pauceley Fair. Well, we all had a bit of tea at the fair and Megan said she'd like to get home before dark. I was all in favour of that. I didn't care for her and Lara being out alone after dark. God knows, when it happened to her it was in daylight, wasn't it?' When Wexford nodded he went on, 'I walked her to the bus stop in Sewingbury. It's only about half a mile from where the fair was. There's just one bus every two hours and I wanted her to be in good time for it. We walked down this street called Pauceley Avenue. They're big houses and on the front drive of one of them was this chap getting out of his car. I knew him by sight but not his name.

'Megan stared at him. We could really only see him in profile. He looked thirty-five to forty and he had a lot of dark hair. As I say, Megan stared at him. He didn't look at us but went into the house and I said to Megan, like in a joke, "You'll know him again" and she said, "You're not kidding. I *will* know him again." And that's all really. We went on to put her on the bus and that, well, that was the last time I saw her. Now I've told you it seems more like rubbish than ever.'

'I don't think so,' Wexford said, then added, 'Did you happen to get the number of the house?'

'No, I didn't, but I couldn't help noticing the name. It was so . . . well, who does he think he is? It's called The Manor.'

They were looking once more at the Surrage-Samphire website, Wexford, Burden and Damon Coleman; more specifically, at the photographs of the two brothers. Damon said, 'No doubt about it, sir. That's the man I saw go into Colin Fry's place. The one called Ross, with all the dark hair. He's the man. I saw him twice the first time. Once when he let himself in at the door and the second time when he opened the door to the woman. I went back later and saw them both come out.'

'You'd know him again? You could identify him?'

'Yes, I could, sir.'

'And the woman?'

'She might be anyone, sir. I couldn't even estimate her age. All I could say is that she wasn't a teenager. Quite tall – well, five seven or eight – and not overweight. It was raining pretty hard and she had a scarf round her head and her umbrella up.'

'Damon's been very thorough,' Wexford said to Burden when they were alone, 'but so what? OK, so Ross Samphire, who puts across a touching picture of the devoted family man, is in fact a sneaky adulterer, but adultery's not a crime. More to the point is what Gary Bartlow saw, escorting Megan to the bus stop in Sewingbury. Plainly, the man getting out of the car was Ross and Megan recognised him. This, in fact, is proof of what we've always said . . .'

'You've always said,' Burden cut in generously.

'OK, I've always said. Megan recognised the man she'd seen in Yorstone Wood on the twenty-fourth of June. Now she knew where he lived and could find out his name she had no hesitation in trying to blackmail him.'

'Which was a highly dangerous thing to do with a man like Ross Samphire.'

Wexford was silent for a little while. While he was

thinking like this, concentrating, he always remained perfectly still, his hands relaxed on the desk, his eyes gazing at the opposite wall, yet apparently unseeing. Burden had often seen him like this and when he did he always waited, unwilling to interrupt a reverie. Finally, Wexford said, 'So Ross was the man who crossed Yorstone Wood in an attempt to kill Amber by dropping a lump of concrete on her? He can't have been. He was in Spain with his wife and children. Besides, I'd say he was a highly efficient man as well as totally ruthless, wouldn't you?'

'I suppose I would.'

'He wouldn't have tried that concrete-block-over-the-bridge method in the first place. It's too chancy, too hit or miss. If he had killed Megan in Victoria Terrace, why would he put her body in that cupboard in the first place, let alone leave it there for four days?'

'But he must have done the first or Megan wouldn't have recognised him and he killed her *because* she recognised him.'

'I know,' said Wexford, 'but the incompetence of it is what gets me. It's not like Ross. On the other hand, it's a lot like Rick.'

'Brothel keeping?' Colin Fry curled his upper lip and looked at Hannah and Damon in disbelief. 'I don't know what you mean. There's girls kept when you're brothel keeping. You can't tell me lending your place to a friend for an evening's called brothel keeping.'

'Just tell us what you are doing, Mr Fry,' said Hannah. 'Are you taking payment?'

'And don't tell us this was all out of the goodness of your heart,' said Damon. 'You and your girlfriend were out when this couple came. You were out the week before when another couple came.'

'Suppose we were?'

'Mr Fry, if you'd like to tell us who these people were that came here on Thursday evening, the man at' – Damon referred to his notebook – 'seven twelve p.m. and the woman at seven sixteen p.m., we might take a more lenient view of what you've been up to.'

Pretty sure nothing illegal was going on here, Hannah cut in, 'We're not promising anything, mind you. But we just might.'

'It was Ross Samphire, wasn't it, Colin?'

At this point Emma came in, bringing cups of tea no one had been offered or asked for and which, Damon soon found, was made undrinkable by the copious addition of sugar. He tried not to widen his eyes when she bent over to hand Colin his cup and displayed, as her short skirt rode up, stocking tops and black frilly suspenders. The place wasn't all that unlike a brothel . . .

'OK,' Colin said. 'It was Ross. He'd kill me if he knew I'd told you.' Late in the day, he realised what he had said and clapped his hand over his mouth.

'You didn't tell us. We told you. What does he pay you?'

'Twenty quid an hour,' said Colin sulkily.

'And he was here for three hours. Money for old rope, that is. Have you any other clients? Don't lie about it. We know you have.'

'They're all friends,' Emma said, flying to Colin's defence. 'They *want* to pay. We're doing them a favour. Where's the harm if they use our place while we're out? We want to be out. The dosh is like a present.'

'All right. Who was the woman with Ross?'

The self-appointed spokeswoman, Emma, was much better at this than Colin. She would never have admitted that the money they received was payment for anything. It was a present, it was given in gratitude for the service rendered. Hannah knew Emma was lying but now, when she answered the question, she was sure this was the truth.

'I don't know. Colin doesn't know. He wouldn't tell Colin her name. Why would he?'

Indeed, why would he? Hannah, to whom the concept of a married man renting premises in which to sleep with a woman not his wife was so alien as to be almost incomprehensible, tried to imagine herself in such a man's shoes. She pictured herself presenting the set-up to the friend lending the flat and, this more or less accomplished, found that she wouldn't in these circumstances have mentioned the woman's name. What would be the point?

'All right,' she said. 'That's all for now. We'd like to see you later today at the police station. Say three p.m.?'

'I'll be working,' Colin almost wailed. 'I ought to be at work now.'

'Dear, oh, dear,' said Damon. 'Since you're employed by Mr Ross Samphire, I'm sure you'll be able to explain that satisfactorily.'

He was driving. Hannah sat beside him, wishing it were Bal. It didn't help that during the previous week Bal had been using this car while Damon used his and had left a Mars bar and his copy of the *New Statesman* with 'Bhattacharya' written on the front on the back seat. An awful feeling of longing to touch these objects that he had touched came over Hannah, even to press his name on the magazine to her lips. Fool, she told herself. This was what happened when two people gazed into each other's eyes, slopped over each other and parted instead of taking the healthy option of sleeping together and making love.

She marched into the police station in a bad temper.

Chapter 26

The car turning out of Mill Lane was a dark-blue Mercedes and the driver was Ross Samphire. The man must have been at Clifton, making some interior decorating arrangement with the Marshalsons, Wexford thought, when parking opposite Jewel Terrace he saw Lydia Burton standing inside her gate as if she had just been waving someone goodbye. Tallish, he recalled, remembering Damon Coleman's limited description, certainly not overweight, not very young but not exactly middle-aged either. . . . Was this the woman Ross met at Colin Fry's flat? It looked like it. For her part, she would have had no need to use the place. She had a home of her own and she was single. Going to Fry's must be his choice. But why? Was it the distance of Brimhurst from Pauceley? Or did he know someone in the neighbourhood who might recognise him? Well, the Marshalsons . . .

The weather had turned very cold and Lydia, having waved to him and Hannah in a not at all guilty way – but why should she be guilty? she wasn't married – went briskly into the house. Gwenda Brooks came to the door so promptly that he thought she must have been standing inside it. As an experienced nurse and midwife, Mary would easily have been able to tell if a woman was or wasn't pregnant, even if she was in a quite early stage of pregnancy. But what did he know? What did Hannah? Yet both of them could see that there was no possibility of Gwenda giving birth to a baby in two weeks' time or, come to that, six months' time. Since John Brooks's departure, she had lost a considerable amount of weight. The brown check skirt she wore hung on her hips and flat stomach as garments hang fashionably loose on fifteen-year-old models. There was a gauntness about her face. Her throat and neck had those deep hollows in them that used to be called salt cellars.

The living room Hannah had been in before was no less grim than it had been then. Wexford was reminded of rooms in third-grade hotels where everything is the colour of porridge and wholemeal bread, and there are neither ornaments nor pictures. Gwenda sat on the edge of her chair with her knees pressed together. For the second time she said, 'I don't know what it's got to do with the police. It's my private business.'

Much as it went against the grain with her to call anyone 'Mrs', Hannah did so as a concession to Wexford's sensibilities. 'Mrs Brooks, you're going on a package tour to Kenya, is that right?'

'You know it is. I've said so.'

'And the purpose of this trip is for you and the other women in the party to give birth while there?'

'One of the purposes, yes. We're going to do a week's sightseeing. I really don't see why I should have to tell you all this. But if you insist, yes, we have a week's sightseeing and two nights at a safari park, and then we're taken to this nursing home in Nairobi where we give birth. A painless natural birth, I may add.'

'Have you seen a doctor, Mrs Brooks?' Hannah asked. 'Your GP here, I mean.'

The woman was looking more and more affronted. 'I've no need to see a doctor. There's nothing wrong with me.'

Hannah sighed inwardly. Wexford could have told her that

her probing was useless. All they needed now were some concrete facts. She seemed at last to understand this and asked only for the name of the acquaintance in Myringham and the travel agent who had sold Mrs Brooks the 'birth package'.

'I'm not supposed to divulge that,' she said indignantly. 'I've signed a confidentiality agreement.'

I bet you have, Wexford thought. 'Telling the police *is* confidential,' he said, not strictly truthfully.

'Well, then. She's called Sharon Lucas and the travel agent is in London. It's Miracle Tours of Carlos Place, West One.' She enunciated this address with a pride that was almost pathetic. She was no naïve country mouse but a sophisticate who patronised Mayfair travel agents.

'You mean you just went to them,' Hannah said, 'out of the blue?'

'Of course not.' Gwenda Brooks was growing angry. 'Sharon told me and it was the adviser at SOCC who put me on to them. You do know what SOCC is?'

'Oh, yes, we know. Who was this adviser?'

She named him. Ken Quickwood as Mary had said. Wexford, who had hoped to hear it was Ross Samphire, felt a shaft of disappointment stab him. The minute they left Hannah burst out with, 'Can you believe people can be so crazy, guv?'

'Quite easily,' said Wexford. 'Sergeant, I think I'm going to send you "up West", as they used to say. You can have a day out doing some shopping and dropping in on Miracle Tours.'

Sullen and rather late, Colin Fry turned up at the police station wearing a padded jacket with a hood. This made Wexford vow to himself that he would henceforth reject hoods as having any bearing on the case. When asked once more who Ross Samphire's companion was, Fry again said he didn't know.

'Have you ever seen her, Mr Fry?'

Fry was silent, considering, though this was something no honest person would need to think about for long. 'I might have,' he finally said cautiously.

'What does she look like?'

'Late thirties, early forties. Nice figure. Sort of good-looking – I don't know. I'm no good at saying what people look like.'

'Is her name Lydia Burton?'

'It might be.' Fry sounded cautious. 'I reckon.' His eyes met Wexford's, shifted away. 'I don't want Ross knowing I said that,' he said. 'I don't. You got to remember Ross is my . . . well, my livelihood. I depend on him. You people don't care if you put a bloke out of a job. It's all in the day's work to you.'

From the window, Wexford watched him leave, cross the forecourt to where his van was parked, pulling his padded coat round him and hunching his shoulders. It was turning cold. 'Unseasonable' was Burden's word for it, which Wexford said was a misnomer for any weather at any time of year in this country. Because he'd known snow in June and sitting-out-of-doors days in December. Their next call was on Mrs Brooks's Sharon Lucas. The car had been standing out on the police station forecourt for no more than an hour but Donaldson had to de-ice the rear window and windscreen before they set off.

'To think', said Burden, 'that when this case began it was incredibly hot and the day Amber was killed was the hottest since records began.'

'That's the way it goes.' Wexford was in a cross mood. 'As for its being incredible, I have no difficulty in believing it. I wouldn't have', he said, soaring away in flights of fantasy, 'if it snowed tomorrow or the temperature went up forty degrees, or by the time we got to Myringham a thunderstorm had started.'

Burden said no more, recognising the early signs of rage. Calmer after a moment or two, Wexford said, 'I wish I could say all Damon's work hasn't been in vain. I wish we could have shown Fry to be keeping a brothel because that means he's discredited and his status as the provider of alibis comes to nothing. But as he said himself, there's nothing to stop anyone lending their home to friends for an evening. And if he takes payment for it, so what? You can employ housesitters, if you want to, or babysitters or dog- and catsitters, and you pay for that.'

'It's shown us Ross Samphire as an adulterer.'

'I believe adultery's a crime in some of the Emirates and in parts of Africa but it isn't here and I for one hope it never will be.'

'No, but his conduct discredits him. He's no longer whiter than white.'

'Was he ever, Mike? He *looks* pure but we know he isn't. We knew he wasn't before Damon started his surveillance. We know Rick killed those girls and Ross is covering up for him.'

'There's one little problem there, though, isn't there? Colin Fry. Fry's no saint but he wouldn't lie about Rick's whereabouts if he really thought Rick had killed Megan. He says Rick was in the old bank building with him on the first of September. I don't think he'd say that, Reg, if he believed Rick had killed Megan.'

'Then what does he think he's supplying these alibis for?'

'What people have always believed or convinced themselves of. That we've got it in for someone because he's got form. If he can help a friend out of trouble, why not? That's a far cry from trying to save a friend from a murder charge.'

The flat she lived in was very small, not much more than a studio. It consisted of a single room perhaps fifteen feet by twelve and the two open doors in one of the long walls showed a tiny kitchen and tinier shower room. Wexford's first thought was that no Social Services home assessment would have approved this as a fit space for a child to grow up in. It was too small and too much in the nature of a pied-à-terre. Sharon

Lucas's bed was the kind that lifts up and folds away inside the wall but today no one had folded it away, although it was nearly midday. The baby lay in a drawer. Burden cast an inscrutable glance at this subsitute for a cot but Wexford had heard of it before. His grandmother had told him that this was what 'the poor' did rather than acquire what she called a bassinet.

He was a black baby, or rather, a pale coffee colour with the beautiful face and noble head Wexford associated (possibly erroneously) with Somali people. His hair was black and as tightly curled as an astrakhan cap on this shapely skull. Wide awake and quite calm, he had lifted plump brown arms out from under the covers and was waving them in the air, watching the moving shadows they made on the white wall. If this child was born two, or even four, weeks ago, Wexford thought, I'm Sherlock Holmes. I only wish I were.

The rage which had been simmering on the journey here now swelled and threatened to explode. He was glad this character Quickwood wasn't here. Violence done to the man would mean the end of Wexford's career. And he wouldn't have been able to resist striking him. . . . He drew a deep breath, looked properly, almost for the first time, at the woman they had come to see. She was a poor thing, he thought, his anger dying into a kind of despair, a skinny little wizened woman of forty with over-bright eyes and milk-white skin, anaemic, almost albino-white.

'I'd like to ask you a few questions, Mrs Lucas,' he began, introducing Burden and sitting down on the bed.

'Actually, it's Ms,' she said but in a tone so apologetic as to be almost ingratiating.

Not liking to take the only armchair, Burden perched himself on a kitchen stool. He too looked at the baby and his expression became pensive. Wexford's next question surprised him.

'What's the baby's name?'

'Elkanah,' said Sharon Lucas.

'Really? Did you get it from the Bible?'

She shook her head. 'You know Elkanah Jones who's Dr Steadman in *Casualty*? On the TV?'

It was easier to accept and enquire no further.

'He's black, you see, and ever so good-looking.'

'I dare say,' said Wexford. 'Your Elkanah is black too, isn't he? You're not. Is his father?'

'Oh, no. Anyway, I've not seen him for months and months.' She didn't seem to understand that they found this explanation inadequate.

Wexford couldn't remember when he had been so at a loss. For a moment he could think of nothing to say to her. He had no language; they didn't speak the same one. She seemed not to speak any of the languages he could assume for the various strange people he was obliged to interview. She was looking at him with large, blank, simple eyes. There was an artless innocence about her which struck him dumb. While he tried for words, Burden said, 'You went on a tour to Africa, did you, Ms Lucas?'

'A Miracle Tour,' she said.

'And where was this arranged?'

'Pardon?'

Burden tried again. 'Tell us about your trip to Africa, Ms Lucas. You went to Nairobi, is that right? Was this a holiday?'

She surprised him. 'It was fertility treatment.'

'In Africa?'

With an almost indignant shake of the head, she said, 'The treatment was here. We had to eat special things, take vitamins and not have alcohol or coffee. We did that for six months. Then we went to Nairobi for the miracle.'

'What was that?' Wexford asked, grateful to Burden for preparing the ground.

'I don't know about the others. I never saw them again. They didn't come from around here. I went to this nursing home.

It was a house, very nice and clean, with a doctor in a white coat and two nurses. They were black people. The doctor gave me an injection and I went to sleep.'

'This was an anaesthetic?'

'Yes, it was. When I woke up they put my baby in my arms.'

'Just like that?'

'The nurse said it was a very easy birth and I could leave with Elkanah in a couple of hours. We were ten on the flight but they all came from different places. When I went home with Elkanah the man with us – they called him a courier – he brought me Elkanah's passport. It was really sweet him having a passport at his age.'

By this time Elkanah had grown weary of watching the shadows his hands made on the wall and begun a soft grizzling. Sharon picked him up in stick-like white arms which looked too fragile to bear his weight. But as she held him up to her shoulder, his fat brown cheek against her bony jaw, a look of such tender adoration came into her face as to transform her almost into beauty. Wexford was reminded of another woman with a child, a woman whose attitude to that child was the reverse of this, and for a moment he seemed to see Diana Marshalson's patient indifference.

'Ms Lucas, would you mind telling us what you paid for your Miracle Tour?'

'It cost a lot. They explained about that.' She carried Elkanah into the kitchen and took a feeding bottle from the minuscule refrigerator. Juggling then began as she struggled to hold the bottle under the running hot tap while keeping the now screaming baby's clutching hand as far from it as she could. Wexford wondered how old he in fact was. The passport would say – or this false passport would say something. Satisfied that the bottle's contents were now warm enough, Sharon thrust the teat into Elkanah's mouth and sat down with him, smiling happily. 'I had to take out a mortgage on my flat. Ten thousand pounds it was. But that was for everything, the diet treatment, the flight, the birth and Elkanah's passport.'

'Do you have a job, Ms Lucas?'

'I work nights on the checkout at Tesco. Four nights a week. My mum keeps an eye on Elkanah.' She seemed to realise, in a dim puzzled way, that rather more explanation was needed for this expenditure than she had given. 'I did want a baby of my own, you see. I'd tried and tried. I just longed for a baby. I used to look at other women with babies and I don't know why I didn't take one of them, I was that sick about it.' Elkanah was sucking on his bottle with enthusiasm and at great speed. Sharon stroked his head with infinite gentleness. 'But I'm all right now,' she said. 'I've got my own baby.'

'And we've got to take him away from her,' Wexford said. 'We've got to take the babies away from all those women, or someone has. I almost feel I haven't the heart to do it. I haven't the heart to go ahead with this. Why not pretend we never heard any of that from Gwenda Brooks?'

'You're joking, of course.' Burden said it sternly, almost fiercely. 'Of course we have to go ahead with it. Of course we do. What, let these villains go on conning these fool women? Go on raking in ten thousand a time for one of the dirtiest scams I've ever come across?'

'I was joking, Mike, if joking can be the word in this context. He has to be stopped. It's just that I wish . . . well, I wish people weren't so wicked. That sounds daft, doesn't it? An old copper like me. So we send Hannah into Miracle Travel, posing as a baby-hungry would-be mum?'

'I think so. You wouldn't believe it, though, would you? You couldn't invent it. A whole bunch of women who want babies so much they're prepared to think they can go to Africa, give birth without being pregnant and bring back an African baby as their own child?'

'I once learnt by heart something Bertrand Russell said. Let's see if I can remember it. "The fact that an opinion has been widely held is no evidence whatever that it isn't utterly absurd. Indeed, in view of the silliness of the majority of mankind, a widespread belief is more likely to be foolish than sensible."'

'It's not labour, darling,' said Mary. 'You're having Branxton-Hicks contractions. It probably means baby's coming in a week or two. Could be sooner.'

Sylvia heaved her great bulk up off the sofa. 'I had them with Ben but I'd forgotten. I've got to the stage now when I just want it to stop. I mean I just want to get it over with. Have you noticed something? Unless you have and haven't told me, we haven't heard a word from Naomi for two whole days.'

'I have.'

'And something's happened to stop you telling me.'

Mary went out to the kitchen, was gone perhaps two minutes and came back with a bottle of sparkling water flavoured with elderflower and two glasses. She filled the glasses, held one out to Sylvia and said, 'I don't know how you'll feel but somehow I think you won't like it much. Women don't, even if they no longer care for the man.'

'For God's sake, what is it?'

'Naomi and Neil are getting married in two weeks' time.'

Sylvia sipped from her glass. She set it down. 'It's nothing to me, is it? If it weren't her it'd be someone else. I left him, anyway. I've nothing to complain of.' She closed her eyes, said slowly, 'Yes, I suppose I do mind, I don't like it. Oh, what a fool I am, Mary.'

She began to cry, the tears trickling out from under her closed lids. Mary came to sit beside her and took her hand.

Chapter 27

In the fur coat she borrowed from her mother, Hannah set off for London by the ten fifty-one train from Kingsmarkham. She wore grey flannel trousers, ankle boots and, tied round her head, a silk scarf with a pattern on it of harness and horse brasses. Dressing like this depressed her and made her self-conscious. Never, in her real undisguised life, would she have dreamt of wearing ranch mink or a headscarf or trousers with a long coat. At least she was warm. She had no high heels to impede her if she had to run or tights to ladder. She took off the headscarf in the train and felt a little better.

Having been to university in London, Hannah knew it well. She took the tube from Victoria to Green Park and walked up. It was rather less cold than in Sussex – it mostly was – but she had put back the headscarf. They said London was warmer because of all the hot-water pipes. Could that be true? She passed Nicky Clarke, the hairdresser, and had the ridiculous thought that the people inside must all be looking at her, thinking how dowdy she was and that her hair must be horrible if she needed to cover it up.

Miracle Tours was a little way along. The travel agent's wasn't so much a shop as a bow-windowed office squeezed between two tall houses of Georgian elegance. A bell had to be pressed to let you in. She was the last person they'd let in if they knew what she was up to, Hannah thought. She pressed the bell and the door made a little growling sound allowing her to push it open.

Inside the small and cosily warm office a young woman with long blonde hair sat at a desk stacked with the usual brochures. The emerald-green carpet was thick and soft, the furniture of blond wood and steel. On the walls were the usual posters, advertising holidays in Sharm-el-Sheik, Innsbruck, Penang and Rio de Janeiro but all framed in steel.

'How may I help you?'

Hannah wished she could have her nails done like this girl's but she never could. It was out of the question. They were immensely long, obviously with artificial extensions, and on each was a tiny picture of a tropical beach with silver sand, palm trees and iridescent blue sea. She looked longingly at them, averted her eyes and began on what she had come for.

'I hear you arrange, er, miracle tours.' She sounded nervous, she could tell, but all the better. Anyone asking about a thing like that would be nervous.

The girl said cagily, 'We are Miracle Travel. Did someone you know recommend us?'

'Mrs Brooks,' Hannah said and when this seemed to have no effect, was suddenly inspired. 'She sent me to Mr Quickwood.'

'Oh, yes.' Miss Tropical Beach's accent had gradually been growing more refined and from this Hannah took heart. She must be making the right impression. 'Yes, that's excellent. May I know your name?'

'It's Anna Smithson,' said Hannah.

'And your home address?'

Hannah gave her own. Who could prove no Anna Smithson lived there?

'What kind of miracle tour did you have in mind?'

The time had come for a frank avowal, an opening of the heart woman-to-woman. 'I'm desperate to have a baby. I've tried everything. Miracle Travel is my last hope. I'm so depressed, I think I'll do something, well, something awful, put an end to everything if I can't have a child. Do you think I'm a fool?'

It went against the grain with Hannah to talk like this. The words almost stuck in her throat but she realised that this choking awkwardness was all to the good. This was ten times better than a smooth stating of the case. A spark of sympathy had appeared in Miss Tropical Beach's glassy blue eyes.

'It's best if you speak to our managing director but he won't be up till this afternoon. Could you come back at three . . . well, say three thirty?'

Hannah could. Going out into the cold was very unpleasant and there was no car to dive into. What had that girl meant by 'up'? 'He won't be up till this afternoon'? That he wouldn't be up to London, say, or he wouldn't be out of bed? Surely not the latter. Wexford had said to go shopping. Why not? Reappearing with a couple of Bond Street bags could only add verisimilitude to her disguise when she returned and it was ages since she had bought anything new . . .

On the concrete slab outside the bungalow, instead of the aged Volvo stood a new red Toyota. On closer inspection it turned out not to be quite new and, though a gift from Ross, had been given from necessity not simply altruism. Rick had managed to write off the little Volvo, tough car though it was, by reversing it down a one-way street and crashing it – more violently and disastrously than could have been conceived of in those circumstances – into a big four-wheel-drive Land Cruiser parked by the kerb.

'They say I'm accident-prone,' said Rick. He presented a sorry sight, limping from jarring his left knee, his right arm in a sling from a sprained wrist and a plaster half covering his forehead from where he had struck it on the rear mirror. 'I never saw that four-by-four. I told the guy it belongs to I reckon I had a stroke. They said at the Princess Diana I hadn't but that's all that accounts for it.'

Burden shook his head. 'You're lucky to have your brother, aren't you?'

Rick gave him a resentful look. 'Haven't I always said so? I'm sure I know the meaning of gratitude.'

He began rolling himself a cigarette. Burden could have sworn the soup plate in use as an ashtray hadn't been emptied since he was last in this house. He thought he recognised one particular twisted fag end with a grease stain on its tip. There was an art in surprising someone you were questioning and while Barry Vine asked Rick more about his road accident, Burden planned his attack.

Rick uttered his final miserable monosyllable and Burden said, 'How long has Ross been seeing Lydia Burton?'

As a shock tactic, it was disappointingly ineffective. 'With her now, is he?' Rick said, his habitually depressed tone unchanged. 'One woman's enough for any man, if you ask me. You have two on the go and all it means is that they'll both of them get your money off you and if one gets your home off you, the other one'll get your kids.'

Naomi sounded excited. Cold weather suited her, she said. 'Actually I'm on top of the world, Sylvia. All these years I've been against marriage but somehow, when Neil asked me, I went all weak at the knees. It means a man really loves you, doesn't it, when he proposes?'

This served, unexpectedly, to remind Sylvia of when Neil had proposed to her. They had both been very young and very much in love. It hadn't been snowing then but a moonlit midsummer and the way they felt had, of course, been going to last for ever. Sylvia knew she ought to say she hoped Naomi would be very happy. She ought to *feel* happy for her and Neil because she had read in the paper only that morning that the children of couples who are married to each other grow up in a more stable environment than those of people cohabiting. And these two were going to have a child. As if to confirm this, the child they were going to have gave a great lurch and a kick. She could see it, not just feel it.

'I hope you'll be very happy,' she said in the voice of someone breaking bad news.

'I think we will. The wedding's on Saturday week. We'd actually love you to come but I don't suppose . . . ?'

'You don't suppose right,' said Sylvia. 'I'm not as big as a house. I'm as big as a palace.'

'Well, not long now. Bye-bye. I'll call you again tomorrow. And don't worry about the snow. It won't settle.'

Quite alone, the boys at school and Mary at work at the Princess Diana Hospital, Sylvia tried to phone her mother but got the answering service. Her sister was in a place called Bora-Bora. She didn't even know where that was but presumably it was reachable by mobile. The idea of trying the number and failing to get it depressed her. She lay down on the sofa, picked up the book she was reading but read nothing. She looked at the snow powdering the lawn, then covering it so that blades of grass could no longer be seen. Watching paint dry was supposed to be the slowest thing you could do; waiting for a baby to come was slower. And usually you got the reward for your patience of a baby at the end of it. Not this time, though, not this time.

Spending a great deal of money, far more than she could afford, on a party dress for Christmas and a trouser suit, Hannah economised on lunch, eating a sandwich in a café off Oxford Street. As if, as she said to herself afterwards, saving

273

ten pounds would make a difference when you'd spent several hundred. She walked back to Carlos Place carrying her two large glossy bags and thinking about Bal. They barely spoke these days. Still, she thought of wearing the party dress while out with him on, say, Christmas Eve. She thought of him suddenly asking her out in a way she couldn't refuse and making it clear he'd had a change of heart and wanted her, really wanted her and spontaneously.

Miss Tropical Beach let her in, said, 'The managing director will see you now.'

Didn't he have a name? Hannah supposed she would find it out but when she was shown into a room at the back, the man who came to greet her merely held out his hand and said how nice it was to meet her. He reminded her of David Suchet playing Poirot, but minus the moustache. There were no posters here and no brochures but a little drawing room full of eighteenth-century French furniture. Two paintings on the walls looked to Hannah like Gainsboroughs. The one opposite her was of a very young woman in a low-cut white gown and a huge white hat covered with ribbons and feathers. Something strange about the room puzzled her and then she realised it had no windows.

He offered her a cigarette. It wasn't quite the first Hannah had been offered in the past ten years but probably only the third.

'Oh, no, thank you.' She had already slipped into a gushing tone.

'You won't mind if I do?'

'Of *course* not. These are your premises.' She gave him a sad smile. 'I don't know if the young lady told you how, well, how desperate I am for a baby. My husband and I, I mean, well, I'll go anywhere, do anything. . . .'

He smiled, exhaling blue smoke. 'You won't have to do anything much, Mrs Smithson. What you have to do will be,

I hope, a pleasure. A comfortable flight to a beautiful part of Africa, an excellent hotel to stay in, a tour including a two-night safari and – and what you want at the end of it.'

If only she could be recording this but it would hardly be admissible in court . . . 'I shall actually give birth at the end of it.'

He didn't answer. 'You have already talked to Ms Brooks, I believe?'

'That's right.'

'Good. Then you'll know some preparation is necessary. The usual period is six months in which clients build themselves up with a diet and exercise regimen.'

She persisted. 'Will I . . . will I give birth in Nairobi?'

'The fact is the nursing home has excellent facilities and a trained staff including two senior medical practitioners. Sam will give you a brochure on your way out and a diet sheet and so on. But I don't want to rush you into anything. I'd like you to study the brochure and the other information, discuss the matter with your husband and then come and see me again. Now you live in Kingsmarkham, I believe?'

'That's right.'

'The fact is I have a home near Pomfret myself. Perhaps you'd come and see me there when you've made up your mind.'

'I've made it up already,' said Hannah.

He smiled in fatherly fashion. 'No, Mrs Smithson, believe me you haven't. You need to think some more about it and then, if you want to, come and see me again. As a matter of fact, you can give me a ring here and we'll fix a date.'

Again they shook hands. He hadn't told her his name and he had avoided confirming the purpose of the Miracle Tour. She had mentioned birth and babies but he hadn't. She could almost admire his skill in calling the doctors involved 'medical practitioners' instead of obstetricians. Outside, in the office where Sam Tropical Beach presented her with a prettily packaged sheaf of papers, Hannah asked her what the managing director was called.

'Oh, Mr Arlen. Mr Norman Arlen. Didn't I say?'

Chapter 28

You could have gone through those sheets with a fine-tooth comb, as Wexford put it, without reading a word to tell you that the aim of this tour was to acquire a baby and a passport for that baby, and bring him or her home to the United Kingdom. The words 'baby' and 'birth' appeared nowhere. An expert deciphering cryptic notes could have found nothing beyond the advertising of a trip to Africa, the only odd thing about it its high cost for what it appeared to be. The diet sheet that came with it, a small, brightly coloured and glossy booklet, suggested no reason why readers might need to eat sweet potatoes, white radishes, peppers and coconut, swallow multivitamins, gingko and Devil's Claw. Why it recommended bush meat, available in some London markets – Hannah recoiled in horror from this – wasn't explained either.

'What strikes me', said Wexford, 'is that these foodstuffs all have their origins in Africa or are found in Africa. It's as if Arlen or whoever writes this stuff wants to give his gullible clients the idea that eating African vegetables will somehow make them more suitable as the mothers of African babies.'

Hannah turned to the brochure that set out the conditions and amenities of the tour. 'It costs enough,' she said. 'Ten thousand seems to be the basic minimum. A really downmarket hotel, no courtesy car available. A top-grade one can run you into over twenty thousand.'

'What I'm wondering is where these babies come from. Are they kidnapped? Or do their impoverished mothers sell them?' Wexford asked. 'Either way it's grim to think of.'

'But we're there, aren't we?' said Burden. 'We discredit Arlen and Rick's alibi for Midsummer Night falls. Ross's alibi for the night of August the tenth to eleventh falls.'

Wexford looked up from the brochure. 'Aren't you being over-optimistic? Lawson still alibies Rick for the August date but what of Ross who in the absence of Arlen has no alibi? Neither Rick nor Ross is really alibied for the first of September. Colin Fry genuinely believes he was in the old bank building with both of them but they were on the ground floor and he on an upper floor. Either of them could have gone out for an hour without his knowing. And Megan recognised Ross as the man she'd seen in Yorstone Wood while he was in fact absent on holiday in Spain.'

'She made a mistake.'

'What, he let her blackmail him when he *knew* she couldn't have recognised him. He still silenced her? He got Rick to kill her when he could have proved he was absent in Spain? I don't think so. As for the night of the tenth to eleventh of August, we don't like Lawson and his offer of help. We're sure Lawson's whole story is a positive tapestry of lies. But a jury would believe him, particularly when Colin Fry says Rick's car did break down, he did have a flat battery, which Colin replaced himself next day. *After* thoughtful brother Ross had had the car at his place with ample time to tinker with it.

'And you have to remember that, though strictly speaking we don't need to supply a motive, it would be a help to know what it was. We haven't a clue what it was. Rick kills young girls because he's a psychopath? We've no evidence he is. He's capable of violence, we know that. But beating up your wife and knocking a man unconscious outside a pub are not exactly precursors of killing girls you don't know, apparently at random. Rick hates women because of what he sees as the injury his wife has done him? Then why kill two girls who are not wives, two girls he's never seen before? Above all – and we've never yet asked ourselves this – what's in it for him?'

'What d'you mean, guv?'

'I rather think', said Wexford, 'that Rick would do anything for money. He's always moaning about his ex-wife taking his money. What else would he kill for? And he did kill. I'm sure of it. I could almost say I know it. As Sherlock Holmes says, "When all else is impossible that which remains must be so." It's impossible that Rick killed out of simple hatred or for revenge or passion or fear, so what remains is money. He killed but someone else had the motive. He did these crimes for money, which someone else gave him and he was given it through Ross. It's just what Ross would do – do his brother a favour by giving him the job. Rick's being very careful not to spend the money yet. Not perhaps for a long while.'

'What's he done with it, then?' Burden asked.

'Shall I make a guess? Not put it in his own bank account. Not bought ISAs with it or National Savings bonds. He hasn't kept it in his house for fear we might come searching. No, he's handed it to Ross, to dear old lovable brother Ross, for safe keeping.'

'That doesn't explain why whoever paid for this wanted the girls killed,' said Hannah.

Studying the brochure and the diet sheet once more, she realised that there was little point in this scrutiny as she intended to phone Norman Arlen in any case. She intended, as soon as possible, to go and see him at Pomfret Hall. The only decision to be made was whether she dared record their conversation.

Three days had passed since her visit to Miracle Tours in

Carlos Place and it seemed time to phone him. The woman who answered sounded very unlike Miss Tropical Beach. She said Mr Arlen wasn't in but when Hannah introduced herself as Mrs Smithson, gave her the Pomfret Hall number. It wasn't Arlen who answered when she dialled it, yet she thought she recognised the voice. Some time in the past month or so she had heard that voice, the east London suburban accent they called estuary English. He transferred the call to Arlen.

'You've made your mind up very quickly, Mrs Smithson.'

'I told you I wanted to do it when I saw you in London.'

'Well, that's a fact,' he said. 'Why don't you come and see me here – well, shall we say next Tuesday? Tuesday at three in the afternoon? You'll drive, I suppose?'

Hannah said she would, though she immediately realised this wouldn't be wise. She would have a taxi. But whose was that voice?

Summoned to the police station for a second interview, Stephen Lawson repeated almost word for word what he had said last time but with some embellishments. These almost uncannily matched the account given of his meeting with 'the friends in the Cheriton Forest Hotel' by the woman he had picked up in the bar. This recalled to Wexford how the woman in her statement had said Lawson had talked about his fund-raising for a society giving aid to Africa and talked too about babies abandoned like so much rubbish.

Was there any connection between this and Miracle Tours? Asked, Lawson declared he had never heard of Arlen or his travel agency. Wexford took him back to his encounter with Rick and his broken-down car, and Lawson finished his account exactly as he had done on the previous occasion. It was then that Wexford realised he must be telling the truth about every aspect of his evening, from his dinner in the Cheriton Forest Hotel to his drive across the lonely country road to his final arrival at home. The only addition need be his meeting with Rick. But that the story was set up and every detail prearranged, probably by Ross Samphire, he was sure.

When Lawson left the police station to walk to his car, the first flakes of snow began to fall. Wexford watched the snow from his window, turning round to hear Burden say, 'It won't settle. Not at this time of the year it won't.'

As the birth of her third child approached Sylvia was uneasily aware that her older children were rejecting her. That was perhaps putting it too strongly. Better say they had withdrawn that easy confident affection she usually received from them and both looked at her with puzzled resentful eyes. They simply failed to understand what she was doing or why she might want to do it. Young as they were, it was as if in some mysterious way they comprehended that this was not the way things should be. This was not the way things had traditionally and acceptably always been, had been taken for granted. This was an affront to society and custom and families. Did she recognise it herself, then?

No, she told herself, it was only that she realised that her sons, more conventional and conservative then she, the grown-up, wanted the normal and the ordinary to endure. What she was doing was the right thing. Not even, probably, the new thing, for she had no doubt women had done this for other women and their men throughout history, only in more prudish times it had never been talked about. She was right but still their near-ostracism left her feeling very lonely. Her mother, to whom she had always been close, had been cold towards her for months now. It was a long time since they had been in the mutually reassuring habit of phoning each other every day. As for her father, he was fine with her, once, that is, he had got over the initial shock. But she knew he didn't really approve. He didn't like it.

The snow contributed to her feeling of isolation. It had been falling steadily since before lunchtime, not the kind of snow that is blown in on the wind in sharp showers, but straight-down feather-soft snow, a lace curtain of thick flakes. Where it fell on grass and leafless shrubs it lingered, wet and sparkling, but on stone it melted where it touched. Warmth and sunshine are company in themselves but snow, like heavy rain, cuts you off from the world, imprisoning you in loneliness and walling you inside.

Once antagonistic towards her, she now longed for Mary's visits, for her cheerful presence, her brisk optimism. But Mary was on duty at the Princess Diana today, as she had been since Friday. If the snow fell heavily enough, if the roads were blocked, Mary might not be able to get to Stowerton tomorrow . . .

'Don't be ridiculous,' she said aloud. 'It won't settle.'

Already in possession of her fur coat, Hannah borrowed her mother's car for the drive to Pomfret Hall. There were two reasons for this. She had never seriously considered using her own car, which was police property and could possibly be recognised as such. Hannah thought this unlikely, even paranoid on her part, but she wasn't taking any chances. A taxi had been her first choice. The snow was still falling but not settling when she went to bed on Monday and the weather forecast was for a rise in temperature during the night.

She woke up to a white world, heavy driving snow and a high wind blowing. The two taxi firms she called were adamant their drivers refused to negotiate country lanes in this weather. That was when Hannah went over to Myringham and borrowed her mother's four-by-four, a big silver monster, high above the ground and snug inside. With no permit in its windscreen, the monster had no reserved place in the police station car park, so Hannah put it on one of the four-hourly meters in the High Street.

If she and Bal had been on the sort of terms that existed between them before that fateful trip to Taunton, she would have discussed all this with him, but these days they barely spoke. Besides, he was out with Wexford calling on Lydia Burton, whose school was closed due to bad weather. Burden was at the Princess Diana where a 'body-packer', at death's door, was being operated on for injuries from the bag of cocaine that had burst in his stomach. She had already told him and Wexford she would be seeing Norman Arlen again today but she told Damon Coleman before she went out, just to be on the safe side.

Chapter 29

Driving the monster was so enjoyable, so blissfully high up above roadway and hedges, affording such views, that Hannah wished it weren't only a matter of seven miles she had to go. Even the lightly falling snow and the snow-covered fields added to the pleasure, giving her the illusion she was forging through Antarctic wastes, like some latter-day (and better equipped) Scott or Amundsen. She had to remind herself severely that vehicles such as this one had been censured as environmentally unfriendly. To join the fight against global warming and climate change one should have an electric car.

The turning out of Pomfret High Street was wide enough for two cars to pass without difficulty and its surface had been cleared and gritted, but a mile further on she had to take a narrow lane, deep under virgin snow. The monster handled this with ease. She took it slowly, and further on the high wind had blown a good deal of what weather forecasters call 'precipitation' off the road on to the fields. Some minion of Norman Arlen had cleared his long drive and she drove up to the front door over no more than a thin scattering of flakes melting in the weak sunshine.

The place had impressed Burden. It slightly intimidated Hannah. Burden, after all, had seen houses of this grandeur and magnitude before, if only when visiting them on holiday or converted into country hotels. Hannah never had, except in pictures or in the distance, beyond wide rivers and against a background of blue hills. She had expected an aggrandised farmhouse. But she got out of the monster, mounted the left-hand set of steps and, after speculating for a moment or two as to what its purpose was, pulled the sugarstick doorbell.

A woman in black trousers and blouse let her in. She said nothing when Hannah gave the name 'Mrs Smithson' but nodded and led her across a huge hall and along a corridor wider than most normal-size rooms. Burden had said something about meeting Arlen in what he dubbed with irony 'the yellow drawing room'. Therefore Hannah knew, when at last they reached their destination, a book-lined place rich with dark wood and leather upholstery, that Arlen had chosen a different venue for her appointment. 'The library', he probably called it. Had Gwenda Brooks come here? Had Sharon Lucas?

She sat down and waited. Norman Arlen came in after about five minutes, looking very different from his London image, a tweed jacket over his cashmere sweater and cord trousers. He shook hands with her and sat down behind a large mahogany desk. 'As a matter of fact,' he said, 'I wouldn't have been surprised if you hadn't come, Mrs Smithson. You drove here in this weather?'

'My car has four-wheel drive,' she said.

'Well, I congratulate you on managing these treacherous lanes.'

She told him she had thoroughly read every word of his brochure and prospectus and, yes, she was in no doubt she wanted to undertake the project. Not daring to equip herself with a recording device, she knew she must get him to come out with an open and unmistakable statement of what she would receive at the end of it. She must somehow make him say she would return from Africa with a baby and a passport for that baby. Instead, so far, he talked only about her starting on the diet regimen as soon as possible, her consultation with the Miracle Tours medical adviser and the various non-diet treatments she must receive.

'I want to have a baby,' she said firmly, putting all the sincerity and intensity she could muster into her tone. 'I'll do anything for that. There's no problem about me doing this diet and any treatment I have to have so long as I have a baby at the end of it.'

'There has to be some level of trust between us, Mrs Smithson,' he said. He looked hard at her and she had to prevent herself from squirming under this scrutiny. She was confessing to herself that he was a formidable man. 'Unless you can accept that what is stated in the brochure is true or will become true it won't be possible for us to do business. You've met Mrs Brooks. Mr Quickwood has told you what is guaranteed and what to expect.' He hadn't. Should she have gone to him first? 'The fact is, Mrs Smithson, that once you have paid your deposit and embarked on the various schemes, the promises made in the brochure will be carried out.'

She was starting to assure him that she did trust him, she did believe, it was only that it seemed too good to be true, when the door behind her opened and someone came into the room. Arlen looked up and nodded. He seemed to have expected whoever this was. The newcomer came up to the desk and, walking round it to Arlen's side and whispering something to him, looked up at her. With difficulty she restrained herself from gasping.

It was Stephen Lawson, the man who supplied Rick Samphire with an alibi.

The gale, which seemed no more than a brisk wind in Kingsmarkham, blew in gusts of seventy miles an hour out in the remote villages. It blew the snow off the fields and into deep drifts in the narrow roads; it blew down a fifty-foot beech tree across the road between Myland and Thatto, blocking all ingress and egress to Hurst Thatto and its handful of houses.

At two in the afternoon, Sylvia felt the first pain of labour. 'Thank God for that,' she said. The second one was so long in coming that she wondered if she'd been mistaken. But, no. She wouldn't phone Mary yet. No need to bring her out in this weather before she had to. Besides, this ridiculous unseasonable snow, which everyone had said wouldn't settle, might stop. Studying it critically from the dining-room window, she thought she could see it slackening. The flakes were smaller. Then it came to her that a car might have difficulty getting through.

Perhaps she should phone Mary now. Leave it half an hour. The friend who was bringing the boys home from school would keep them with her if she feared getting through. That was another phone call she must make, to this woman's mobile. She was about to give birth. Well, in a few hours, maybe seven or eight. An awesome venture – it always was. I shall go the Princess Diana in labour, she thought, and no one there will know about Neil and Naomi or that the baby won't be mine to keep. They'll congratulate me. They'll say, 'Congratulations, Mrs Fairfax. You have a lovely baby girl or baby boy.' And I shan't dare even to hold it . . .

But they would clear the roads. They had been good about getting the snowploughs out this year. I'd better phone Mother, tell her I shall go to the hospital in an hour or so. She lumbered into the living room and picked up the phone. It was as dead as a toy phone, dead as an unplugged instrument. Could she walk to Mary's? It was only about two hundred yards. In this snow? Not so much the snow which was falling as the snow which lay. She could imagine slipping over and not being able to get up again. As if to teach her a lesson, a pain took hold of her with an increasingly severe disabling thrust. She leant over the table, holding on to it and breathing slowly. It grabbed her, squeezed, wrung her out and let her go. Nice when it stops, she thought, almost worth having it's so nice when it stops. It was getting dark. She tried to switch on a light but there was no power. She stood in the half-dark, feeling fluid flow down her legs. Her waters had broken.

A key was turning in the lock. She drew a deep breath, went out into the hall to Mary.

'I've started.'

'So I see. OK, darling, let's get this cleared up and I'll examine you in a minute. There's no way I'm going to be able to get you to the Princess Di. There's a tree down and the road's blocked.'

Sylvia's eyes grew very wide. 'What shall we do?' Who is more helpless than a woman in labour? 'What shall we do, Mary? The electricity won't work and the phone won't work.'

'No, but your mobile will, my love. Didn't think of that, did you? So there's two things we can do. I can phone the emergency services and see if they can get a helicopter out to you. Or you can have a nice quiet home delivery with a highly qualified midwife in attendance.'

'At least this time we haven't lost the electricity,' Dora said. 'I just hope it doesn't freeze and then maybe I can get over to Thatto. Sylvia's started. She called me on her mobile. Her what-do-you-call-it phone's not working.'

'Landline.' Wexford sighed. 'I can't take much interest in this baby, I'm afraid. I suppose I've schooled myself not to.' He looked out of the window. 'I could take you to the Princess Diana if you like. I've got to go out again. They're gritting the roads.'

'She's not in the Princess Diana. They couldn't get there. A tree's come down across the road. Mary Beaumont's with her.'

'Maybe it's better if you're not there,' he said. 'You don't want to witness the handover of your grandchild to Naomi Wyndham.'

'And you don't care, I suppose.'

He was so much taller and bigger that he towered over her. Standing above her, holding her by the shoulders so that for a moment she was his prisoner, he said, 'Dora, the worst is to come. If we are against each other who will be for us? We must be united, truly together, not putting on a front. I'm going now. Give me a kiss.'

She kissed him. When he moved away from her he saw that she was crying.

Donaldson drove him to Brimhurst Prideaux. The snow had stopped two hours before, the temperature had begun to rise and the four-inch-deep crust had reached the stage of a melting sorbet. Water ran into the gutters and a fine rain began to fall. But there were no longer any blocked roads or impassable lanes. November's freak blizzard had come to a sudden end.

Although Wexford wasn't much concerned about Ross Samphire's love affairs, he intended to call on Lydia Burton for any information she might be prepared to give him on the Samphire brothers. As had been the case at his earlier visit with DC Bhattacharya, no one was at home. Donaldson drove slowly down Mill Lane through ridges of half-melted snow and pools of water. The early dusk had come and he saw that number three Jewel Terrace was in total darkness. Perhaps she had gone to another assignation at Colin Fry's flat. He still had to decide, he reminded himself, what action to take over that. Bring him to court for keeping a disorderly house or simply tell him these activities of his must stop? Something came back to him quite suddenly. On the night Amber was killed Lydia Burton had been out with a man, had been dining with him somewhere. He had brought her home in his car at midnight. Ross or someone else? Now that was something he must find out, for Ross claimed to have entertained Norman Arlen that evening . . .

Candles were lit in the hall and living room. The single oil lamp Sylvia and Mary could muster was in Sylvia's bedroom. Mary had lit two coal fires but there was no means of cooking.

'What are you going to do about boiling water?'

That made Mary laugh. 'Boiling water is only in books, my love.'

The woman who had fetched Sylvia's children from school had phoned her mobile to say she would bring them back if she could or keep them for the night. When the doorbell rang that was who Mary thought it was. It wasn't. It was Naomi.

'You've been very prompt. The baby's not here yet.'

Naomi looked ravaged. To Mary, who had never before seen her less than well-groomed, perfumed and painted, she seemed ill, an unkempt distraught creature, her hair wild, tears on her face, her shoes and trousers soaked. Mary told her to come in and, following her, explained how it had been impossible for Sylvia to get to the maternity home.

'I don't want to see her,' Naomi said. 'I never want to see her again.'

'Why did you come, then?'

'I was determined to come. I saw the tree was down and I left my car on the other side of it and walked. That's why I'm so wet. I had to come. Now you're here I don't have to see her. I can tell you.'

'Naomi,' Mary said, 'you had better take your shoes and socks off. Sylvia can lend you shoes. She's about your size.'

Naomi kicked off her shoes and pulled off her socks. Her long narrow feet were white from the cold and so wet that when she lifted them up water dripped from her toes. The expression in the eyes she lifted to Mary was that of someone who has seen a dreadful sight, a sight so horrible and searing on the vision that it can never be forgotten. But before Mary could enquire, Sylvia's voice from upstairs came calling, 'Mary, Mary . . .'

'I'll be back soon. Sit in front of the fire and warm yourself. I'll make you a hot drink when I come back.'

Mounting the stairs, Mary decided not to tell Sylvia who had come. If Sylvia had heard a voice she wouldn't have been able to tell who it was, this house was so big, so cavernous. Whatever had got Naomi into this state it was better for a woman in labour not to know about it. Mary went into the bedroom and examined Sylvia.

'That's fine, my darling' she said. 'Everything's going excellently but you've a way to go. Yell if you want. No one minds.'

'Who's no one?' said Sylvia on a gasp. 'I heard a woman's voice.'

'Only my next-door neighbour collecting for Save the Children.'

'It sounded like Naomi.'

'Really?' said Mary. 'I suppose some other people do sound like her, my love. I'll get rid of her and I'll be back.'

'I don't want a hot drink,' said Naomi. 'I've come to tell you what's happened. I thought I'd have to tell Sylvia but I'm glad I shan't have to. I never want to see her again.'

'So you said.'

Naomi held out her feet to the fire, leant forward, staring at her knees. 'Neil's gone,' she began. 'I've thrown him out. I don't know where he'll go and I don't care. He told me, Mary. We were going to get married tomorrow and we were, well, sort of confessing our past. I mean, things we'd done and thought it was better for the other one to know.' She gave a racking sob and momentarily put her head in her hands. Mary waited in silence, thinking about the woman upstairs. 'I hadn't much to tell him,' Naomi said in a broken voice. 'I'd told him everything when we were first together.' She lifted her head and looked into Mary's face.

'But he had?'

'You know?'

'I don't know anything, my dear. And I have to get back to Sylvia in one minute.'

'He told me how they got this baby. It wasn't what-do-they-call-it, AI, artificial insemination. They had sex. *They had sex.* Here. The afternoon in February he came to do the AI. And he said that she said, "We may as well do it. It's easier and more sure." That's what he says she said. He was unfaithful to me with her and this is the result. I don't want this baby. I never want to set eyes on it. I couldn't bear to touch it. You tell her that.'

It was clear that Stephen Lawson had recognised her before she recognised him. That was what he must have whispered to Norman Arlen. They would throw her out now and that would be that. She got up. Arlen said, in a voice that varied not at all from the tone he had used previously, 'Sit down, Mrs Smithson. Or should I say Detective Sergeant Goldsmith?'

There was no point in denying it. She nodded, said, 'Very well, I'll leave.'

'I don't think so.'

It wasn't the first time Hannah had seen a man in serious possession of a gun. In those early days when she was on the beat a 'Yardie' had fired a sawn-off shotgun at her and the shot had flashed past her right ear. A drunk involved in a street fight had pulled a heavy army revolver when she and another officer appeared but had been overpowered before he could use it. These two had both been high and maddened, but Norman Arlen was chillingly calm, just sitting there staring at her, holding something in his hand. It seemed like a very small pistol, though his large broad hand concealed most of it. She could see its barrel, pointing straight at her. He slowly got to his feet, told her to stand up, holding the gun almost buried in the palm of that big hand. She got up, aware that in these situations you had better do as you are told.

Stephen Lawson came up to her, slipped the fur coat off her shoulders and pulled her arms together. She had thought him repulsive when first she saw him at the police station. It was something to do with his thick and blubbery lips. And now the touch of his hands on her skin made her shiver. It was a strong convulsive shudder she gave.

'Frightened, are you, Ms Goldsmith? You do well to be.'

She thought Lawson would tie her hands but he had clipped on handcuffs. These frightened her more than the gun.

'I don't know why you're doing this,' she said, angry with herself because her voice sounded cracked and feeble. 'You've told me nothing.'

Arlen smiled.

'They will come and look for me.'

'Perhaps,' he said. 'And they will find you. In your car, which will have skidded on ice and gone over the parapet at Yorstone Bridge. The second dreadful accident to have happened there. No doubt this will prompt some stringent safety measures to be taken to the bridge and Yorstone Lane.'

They took her out of the room, along a different passage and into what seemed to be a servant's room off the kitchen regions. It was furnished with a single bed, a clothes cupboard and a table and chair. The door to a shower room was ajar. At least let them take off the handcuffs, she prayed silently to whoever one does pray to in these situations. They didn't. They manhandled her until she was seated on the bed and then they left her, locking the very solid-looking door behind them.

There was a window but it had shutters and those shutters were closed. The shower room had no window, only a fan which probably came on when you put the light on. She found she could put the light on by pressing her shoulder against the switch. The basin was half full of water. She thought one of them must have filled it from the cold tap so that she wouldn't become dehydrated. This she took as an encouraging sign. If they intended to kill her in an hour or so they wouldn't have bothered to leave water for her.

In books when people like these two took someone prisoner they never killed them at once but kept them locked up somewhere for hours or even days in advance. She had often wondered about this. Did it really happen or was this delay only a device enabling the author to maintain suspense and make a successful rescue possible? Sometimes, of course, it was created for a ransom to be demanded. A ransom wasn't going to be demanded for her. They didn't want money, they had money and wanted to go on making it. They wanted her out of the way. What they were up to in Africa and here must be sufficiently lucrative and appalling to make killing her necessary. Yet Arlen had said very little, just a phrase or two about a clinic and doctors . . .

Damon knew where she was. Hold on to that, she thought, hold on to that.

Now he was at the door Wexford had forgotten what he had come to ask. There was only one answer to find now and he had no reason to think he would find it here. Though he had never found the motive, the elusive why, he had found the perpetrators. Perhaps he had come to this house in an attempt to quieten his perpetual anxiety about the child Brand. To reassure himself that when he left this case behind him he could also leave behind his worries about Amber's little boy. A word of hope from Brand's grandfather, perhaps, a look of love from Brand's step-grandmother, would help do it. Or news from one or other of them that the Hillands or Diana's sister wanted to adopt him . . .

He had been standing on the doorstep in the cold for several minutes, thinking of possibilities, thinking how hope really does spring eternal. At last he rang the bell. George Marshalson came to the door, an old man now, whose back was bent and whose head was thrust forward as if peering out at a wicked world. Wexford thought he had aged twenty years in four months. He no longer walked, he shambled. His voice had cracked and grown higher-pitched. And his first words deadened Wexford's hopes.

'My wife's putting the child to bed, thank God. I can't stand it, you know, not at my age. All that energy, all that noise. He never gets tired. Not that he'll sleep. He'll be yelling as soon as she comes down.'

Wexford shrugged. He had no reply to make to that. He followed Marshalson into the interior designer living room and sat down in the oriental chair. The noses and foreheads and hands of painted gods poked into his back.

'We have almost reached the end of this case, Mr Marshalson.' Perhaps that was what he had come to tell him. He might even have thought the man would be interested. 'I shall be making an arrest very soon.'

'Frankly, I don't care,' Marshalson said. 'Finding the man who killed her won't bring her back. I used to hear people say that on the television and I sneered. I *sneered*, Chief Inspector.' Tears came into his eyes. A frequent occurrence, Wexford thought. Old enfeebled men weep easily and he had much to weep for. 'I know what they meant now. I don't care. I don't care about anything. She wasn't a paragon, you know. Well, of course you know. She was immoral, by my old-fashioned standards. She was greedy and lazy and feckless, but I'd give everything I have to have her back.'

'I'm sure you would.'

'So don't tell me about it. Don't tell me who you're arresting and why. Go up and tell my wife. You'll find her in the boy's bedroom. You can't fail to find her, the noise the two of them make.'

Wexford was glad to leave this unhappy man whose sorrow evoked in him a pity which almost brought tears to his own eyes. What had happened to Marshalson he had seen happening to bereaved parents again and again. Following the initial terrible shock, they seemed to adjust, to resign themselves and to come to terms with their loss. But after a while, weeks or even months, realisation of the full extent of what they had suffered reached and enveloped them. A sorrowful depression, dull, indifferent, bitter and beyond hope of relief, took them in its relentless grip, a hold from which some of them never unloosed themselves their whole life long. People who hadn't cried since they were children broke down in tears at the mention of the lost one's name.

He began to go slowly upstairs. He had been up here before but only to search Amber's room. The door to that room was closed but another at the end of the passage was open, light streaming from inside. There is something curiously warm and hopeful about light pouring from an open door into a dark place. Voices came to him, hers and Brand's, laughing happy voices, the child's gleeful. He stood in the doorway silently, looking at them and, seeing their faces, he knew.

It shocked him so much that for a moment he could hardly speak.

Chapter 30

With the coming of darkness it grew colder and half-melted snow froze. Bal went home to the flat he shared with his solicitor friend, thinking he would do what he had been doubting for weeks he should do: phone Hannah and ask her out for a drink. Soon after that awful escapade, the abortive trip to Taunton, rue had set in. Bal liked that word, which perfectly expressed how he felt. 'Rue' – more than regret and less than remorse. He had behaved like a prig. Not only moralistic and smug, but acting like someone twice his age and with the code and values of someone three times that. And now he could no longer understand why he had done what he had. What had got into him? Daring to tell an intelligent woman that he was saving her up until he knew her properly? Refusing to sleep with the most beautiful woman he knew on the grounds of some teenage virgin's principles of keeping a relationship pure until they were totally acquainted with each other's tastes and needs?

The chances were that she would never speak to him again except in the line of duty. But he could try. He'd be a fool not even to try. His flatmate was out. The living room to himself, he threw himself on to the sofa and dialled her home number, bracing himself for her voice telling him what he could do and where he could go. No answer. Well, it was only seven thirty. He tried her mobile number. She was bound to answer that. They knew they always had to answer that. It rang and rang, and was abruptly cut off. Odd.

He fetched himself a can of Coke from the fridge, came back and phoned the police station. No, DS Goldsmith had gone.

'Gone where?'

'Home, I suppose,' said the duty sergeant. 'I haven't seen her since I came on at four.'

No, of course not, Bal thought. She had gone to see Norman Arlen. Up to London on the train. He had heard Damon telling Wexford when they came back from their abortive attempt to see Lydia Burton. He hesitated for a moment and called Damon on his mobile. What time had it been when Hannah said she was going to London? About eleven, Damon said. Maybe she'd stayed in London for a bit, Bal thought, met a friend or done some shopping. No matter how intelligent, every woman loved shopping. Of course she had probably come home but wasn't at home now because she was out with some other guy. What could be more likely? Did he think she was staying in night after night, pining for him? They would be dining somewhere now, she looking as wonderful as those times when she had dined with him, and when her new man took her home he wouldn't be such a fool as to leave her with a chaste kiss.

Bal went out into the kitchen and gloomily fetched himself a Marks & Spencer's ready meal out of the fridge.

The electricity came on in Pauceley and Thatto at the very moment Mary delivered Sylvia's baby. Sylvia gave an enormous yell and the biggest final push, and the child came out with a whoosh as the room filled with brilliant light.

'A lovely little girl,' said Mary, holding up the baby as she yelled lustily. 'And not so little. I'll be surprised if she weighs less than four kilos.'

'I don't know what that means. What is it in pounds?'

'I'll weigh her in a minute. Here, take her.'

'No, no, I mustn't! She mustn't come any nearer. Take her away. Oh, God, God, take her away.'

Mary hadn't told her. She did so now, quickly, as the tears poured down Sylvia's face and she put up her arms to take her baby. Mary watched them together, then left them together. The electricity was on so she could make tea. She made it, put a cake she had baked herself on a large plate, loaded the tray and went back upstairs. Sylvia was cuddling the baby, a beatific expression on her face, a half-smile, an adoring look.

'Is that true,' Mary said, 'about you and Neil?'

'Give me some of that cake, would you? I'm starving. Of course it's true. After all, he was my husband for years and years. Why did the fool have to tell her? I never would have. Isn't she a gorgeous baby? I would have given her up, you know, and it would have killed me.'

'What are you going to call her?'

'Mary. What else?'

The news of Mary's birth reached Wexford as Donaldson drove him back from Brimhurst. His wife's excited voice poured out developments he could hardly take in and he came off the phone with a confused impression of a split between Neil and Naomi, a candlelight delivery of his nine-and-a-half-pound granddaughter, and the unexplained 'appalling and immoral conduct' of Sylvia.

'I never want to see or hear of any more babies as long as I live,' he said.

'Pardon, sir?' Donaldson sounded quite shocked.

'Nothing. I was thinking aloud.'

Tomorrow he would make arrests and he would tell them

all. No, tell Burden first, then the Chief Constable and the others who had worked so hard to this end. This awful end . . .

In spite of the conclusion he had come to about Hannah's whereabouts, Bal tried to phone her several times more in the course of the evening. He concentrated on her mobile and when he found it was now switched off, began to feel increasingly uneasy. Hannah *never* switched off her mobile. He remembered all those chaste dinners they had shared, all those proper returns home to her flat. Several times her mobile had rung and she had always answered it. He had been annoyed on one occasion and asked her, for God's sake, to turn that thing off, it won't be for work. But she hadn't. She wouldn't. Why, then, was she doing it now?

At ten he phoned her mother in Myringham. Was Hannah with her?

Mrs Goldsmith seemed not to find this question odd. Hannah wasn't with her. She hadn't seen her since the morning when her daughter came in to borrow her car.

'Borrow your car? But she was going by train to London.'

'Pomfret was what she told me,' said Hannah's mother.

She couldn't come to much harm in Pomfret, could she? He'd been right the first time. She was out with someone else. She wouldn't thank him for calling her at home at midnight, especially if this guy was there with her, but to hell with that. He'd do it or he wouldn't sleep.

Her mobile had been in the pocket of her mother's fur coat. That was now in Arlen's possession. They had her bag as well. Hannah would have liked to know the time. Her watch was on her wrist but try as she might, twisting her cuffed hands as far as she could to the left, then to the right, she couldn't see what time it was. She couldn't even see the watch because her sweater sleeve covered it. She lay down on the bed because there was nothing else to do and thought about her plight. The first duty of a prisoner is to escape. She repeated that and said it a third time. What about a handcuffed prisoner?

Would they really kill her, put her in her mother's car, drive it to the Yorstone Bridge and push it over? It would take more than two of them to do that but maybe Arlen could muster more than two. The woman in black trousers, for one. Damon would tell everyone before anything like that could happen. He'd tell Bal or Karen or Wexford himself. Her left arm was going numb. Was that a gun Arlen had pointed at her? It might have been no more than a piece of piping, even a cardboard tube. How could you tell when your judgement was affected by fear?

She went into the bathroom, bent over the basin and lapped up some of the water. Immediately it struck her that it 'tasted funny'. There was a chemical taste about it, something ferrous, metallic, anyway. Her common sense came to her aid, telling her that she would think that way, it was her fear made her think that way. Drinking water often tasted like that. It was something to do with purification. Why hadn't she stuffed her mobile into her cleavage or even into her trouser pocket? They hadn't searched her. She realised they hadn't searched her because they had already felt the mobile through the folds of the fur coat.

How would they kill her? Not by shooting. Not if they wanted her death to look like an accident. Pushing her over the bridge inside the four-by-four would be enough to do it. Maybe they would rely on that. . . . She sat on the bed and listened. These nether regions of Pomfret Hall were utterly silent, not a footfall, not a closing door. She thought, absurdly, I'd like to have had one night with Bal before I died, though when she was dead it would hardly matter . . .

* * *

Before you panic, he told himself, try her mobile again. He tried it at midnight, got no answer, undressed and went to bed. Of course he hadn't been able to sleep. That dream he had had must have come from the time he and Hannah went to interview Gwenda Brooks and that pathetic woman had showed them Norman Arlen's house and garden in a magazine. He and Burden had been there and he had seen an object he was now sure couldn't have been a gun. He dreamt of picking up the thing that wasn't a gun and its going off with a bang, which woke him. Immediately he thought of Hannah and where she might be. Not in London but at Pomfret Hall. That was where she had gone, he was sure of it. She should have taken him with her, Bal thought, and probably would have done but for their ridiculous quarrel. On the other hand she must have been up to something which required her to be alone, a woman on her own, a woman in a fur coat . . .

He wouldn't disturb his flatmate, bring him into this. The guy slept like the dead anyway. Bal dialled Burden's number. Burden took a long time to answer and when he finally did, growled, 'What is it?'

Bal told him. 'I don't believe it,' Burden said. 'Arlen wouldn't. He wouldn't dare.'

'You remember when we went there, sir. He had a gun.'

'You mean you think you saw a gun.'

'OK, that's what I mean but can we dare take a chance?'

'Leave it with me,' said Burden with a low groan, 'but go down to the station and get Damon too.'

'I don't want anyone armed,' Wexford said. 'I don't believe in Arlen's gun. A man like that wouldn't have left a gun lying about in his living room. Not here. Not in this country.'

'We'll be taking a chance.'

'Mike, we take chances every day. Remember, Arlen's a villain but he's not a Yardie, he's not a teenage thug. Now, how many people can we get together at this hour?' Wexford looked at his watch. 'It's half past two.'

'Four from Uniform,' said Damon. 'You, sir, and Mr Burden and me and Karen and Bal.'

'Right. Nine of us in three cars. Make a show. Lights but no sirens.'

There was a small bed lamp in the room but try as she might, Hannah couldn't switch it on. She could just manage to turn on the top light by leaning against the wall and pressing the switch with her elbow. The bed lamp worked from a plug in a socket on the skirting board under the bed. Though she could see it she couldn't reach it except with her feet. Her toes, which might have operated the socket switch, were enclosed inside socks she couldn't remove.

The choice she had was between sitting here in bright light or deep darkness. The light was dazzlingly bright, putting her in mind of what prisoners in certain countries were subjected to, which constituted torture. On the other hand the darkness would be more frightening, would probably add to the panic she was trying so hard to keep at bay, and if she fell asleep – an unlikely happening but possible – when she awoke she might for a second or two think she was at home in her own bed. She kept the light on.

Thinking of the bright-light torture reminded her of how, when reading in the paper or watching on television some poor hostage pleading for his or her life, she had resolved in case she was ever kidnapped never to do that herself. Never mind if they stood over her while she read a written statement. Never mind if they hit and kicked her, she wouldn't humiliate herself by begging the British government or anyone else for her life. Sitting under the hundred-and-fifty-watt unshaded lamp above her head, she said aloud, 'Did I really think that? Did I think I would hold out when those brave people couldn't? Was I mad? I'd go down on my knees and beg for mercy, I know I would. Give me half a chance. I'd offer them anything, anything I could do or give up or promise, in exchange for my life.'

She began to walk up and down the room. How long had she been in here? Five hours? Ten? *Two?* There was no way of knowing in this shuttered place. Damon might know she was here, the guv might know, Barry might, but why would any of them do anything? She had been to see Norman Arlen, here or in London, done what she had to do and gone home to write her report. That's what they would think. They would do nothing. Bal wouldn't even think about where she might be. He probably never thought of her at all any more. She wasn't expecting anyone to phone or come to see her and her mother had said to keep the car until tomorrow. Hannah suddenly thought, how horrendous, her poor mother was so proud of that car and they were going to push it off a bridge . . .

She must be mad, thinking like that. Did she really believe her mother would be upset about a bloody car when her daughter was dead? She sat down again. It must be hours since she had eaten but she wasn't hungry. Once or twice more she had lapped water out of the basin. She got up again and went to the door to listen. It seemed to her that there was no longer absolute silence. In the far distance she could hear a faint echo which might be footsteps. Two sets or three? To her dismay she found she was trembling.

Maybe no one would come to her rescue or come too late. But she must do something to show them she'd been here. Her shaking hands still locked together, she lifted them above her head and forced them down to the back of her neck. Concentrating on the operation stopped the trembling. She closed her fingers over the clasp on the gold chain she wore, undid it and, lifting her hands back to her lap, held the chain tightly in her fist.

They were outside the door now. She heard the key turn in the lock. The chain pressed into the palm of her hand was strangely comforting.

He hadn't been given a chance to tell the guv about the other thing he had remembered. Of course he knew very well why Wexford had stopped him being one of the team going to Hannah's rescue. It was because he thought Bal was having an affair with Hannah. Or a 'relationship', as she would have called it. He thought of her tenderly as he quoted her in his mind, gently and with some amusement. 'Relationship' was the most passion-killing term he could imagine, guaranteed to make you think of an earnest couple in anoraks and walking boots camping in Snowdonia.

Could he really think that what he remembered hearing in that absurd yellow-satin drawing room had any significance? Yet why would Arlen have talked about a road and a bridge unless he saw a dangerous corner as potentially useful to him? Useful one day. You never knew when you'd need it. On the other hand he might be a villain – he was – but he was a citizen as well. He must have the same concerns about safety and the environment as anyone else.

Bal didn't go home. He sat in his car a little way down the High Street and watched the three cars move off. It was very cold and he didn't want to heat the car by running the engine while stationary. Of course, if he went off to Yorstone he could put the heater on. Going there couldn't do any harm. If he went home he wouldn't sleep, he'd lie there wondering if he ought to have insisted on talking to Wexford, shouted above all the talk, followed him out to his car instead of doing what he was told and leaving. He switched on the ignition and the heater. As usual, icy air came out of it before it warmed up, a blast like a force eight gale. Bal wasn't exactly sure where Yorstone was – somewhere west of Cheriton Forest and on the way to Sewingbury? This country was so badly signposted compared with everywhere else. The signs kept saying Sewingbury and Stowerton, Yorstone only when the turn-off was a hundred yards away. Even then it didn't say Yorstone Lane. He knew that was what it had to be because to the left of him loomed the darkness of Yorstone Wood. He turned down the unlit narrow lane. His headlights on full beam created a bluish mist ahead of him and in the mist tree trunks reared up, dark and straight like figures in a fantasy.

The lane turned sharp left, almost at a right angle. But for the black and white arrows on the right-hand side he might have gone straight on and ploughed in among the tall dark shapes. He was beginning to realise that his whole enterprise was stupid, based on nothing but a sort of hunch that had no real foundation. As he pulled up and parked under the trees, he felt for the first time true terror for Hannah, a real dread that something terrible had happened to her.

When they got to Pomfret Hall lights were shining from every window. Wexford got out of the car, went up to the front door and pulled the bell, Burden and Karen behind him, the rest a few yards back. No one came to the door. Wexford rang the bell again, hammered on the panelled wood with his fists. He told Barry and Damon to go round the back. The house was so big that 'round the back' required a walk of several hundred yards. Its rear, as Wexford said, was more in the nature of a 'garden front', with another double flight of stairs ascending to a terrace and another pair of double doors. Lawns, flower beds, shrubberies and outlying meadows lay glittering under frost from the blaze of light that poured from the windows.

Ringing the bell and pounding on the door fetched no one. There was no sound except for the sound they made themselves.

'We have to go in there,' Wexford said. 'Break the door down.'

They couldn't do it. The combined efforts of Burden, Barry Vine and Damon Coleman failed to move those heavy oak doors. Damon went down into an area behind the stairs, which housed two large stone urns and a ladder, and found a humbler door in the wall. This yielded the second time he ran at it, shivering the wood and splitting the lock. They all went in, through rooms full of flowerpots and brooms and garden tools, then a kind of laundry, on to the kitchens, newly refurbished with state-of-the-art equipment.

'One guy lives here on his own?' Damon had never seen anything like it.

Lights seemed to be on in every room. 'Why is that?' Barry asked but no one knew the answer. 'Surely not to make anyone calling think there were people in here.'

'Maybe he's afraid of the dark,' said Burden. 'Come to think of it, it was early afternoon when Bal and I came here but he had a lot of lights on then.'

Just as the place was brightly lit, so it was as warm as a sunny summer's day. Wexford thought briefly of such a day in August when Amber's body had been found. They climbed the stairs to the gallery and the first floor, and as they came to a pair of double doors, Damon said suddenly, 'Where's Hannah's car?'

'She didn't come by car,' Burden said. 'Her car's parked outside the station. But wait a minute, how did she get here?'

'Taxi?' Wexford opened the doors. Revealing a huge bedroom with four-poster bed, the whole place as neat as if no one had ever undressed, slept and dressed in it. 'She must have taken a taxi. Get on to the station, Damon, and have someone start calling taxi firms now.'

If she came here, he thought, if she was ever here. All we know is that she was going to see Arlen. She might have been meeting him somewhere on neutral ground. The others seemed to have the same thought, voicing it as they walked through the bedrooms.

Karen and Barry spoke almost in unison: 'We don't know she came here.'

'No, but we have to search,' said Wexford.

They went up to the third floor, more empty rooms, more light. Down again, across the gallery, down the great wide curving staircase into the hall, the dining room, the yellow drawing room where Bal might or might not have seen a gun. Back into the hall again, having been through an empty silent house that felt as if no one had lived in it for years, as if it were merely a showplace, open for tours and tour guides on certain days of the week.

'What now, sir?' said Barry.

Wexford didn't answer. He bent down and picked up from the floor a thin gold chain, fine as a hair. 'She has been here,' he said. 'I've seen her wearing this.'

'So have I,' said Karen. 'It was a present from Bal.'

Wexford considered. 'It was a mistake sending Bal home. He may know more than we do. I'll call him.'

In the distance he heard the sound of the four-by-four's engine. Its lights showed between the tree trunks and then it appeared, coming slowly and cautiously down Yorstone Lane. His heart had leapt but now he thought, it's just a car. It's someone going home from a party or a long-distance drive. But no, it was a silver car – Hannah's mother had one just like that. There were hundreds like it. It was probably the most popular car in the neighbourhood. They'll go over the bridge and on up the lane on the other side, he thought. But a dozen yards this side of the bridge the car stopped and a man got out. It was Rick Samphire.

He was hooded as usual. He moved on to the bridge and looked down at the road below, every movement shown up clearly in the four-by-four's headlights. If it's just him, Bal thought, I can handle him on my own, no problem. He was

308

asking himself where Arlen was when the man got out of the driver's seat. Were there any more? Shocking him, his phone suddenly rang.

It could only be Wexford or Burden. If he answered it they would tell him . . . what would they tell him? Something unacceptable, he was sure. He let it ring, hating the sound of it. Then he saw Hannah's face. It appeared at the window by the passenger seat. He answered the phone.

Wexford's voice said, 'Where the hell are you?'

'At Yorstone Bridge,' said Bal, 'sir. They've got Hannah here.'

He put the phone down, knowing it might cost him his job.

What were they going to do? A cold shiver like icy water trickling the length of his back ran down his spine. She wouldn't stay there unless they were forcing her to do so. And, co-occurring with the thought, she was staying there no longer. The door opened and she stepped down from the passenger seat, as if of her own volition. Then he saw there was someone behind her and he recognised to his astonishment the man called Lawson who was Rick's alibi for the eleventh of August. He must be holding something pressed to the small of her back – the gun he had seen that day in the yellow drawing room?

Rick had crossed to the other side of the bridge and Norman Arlen with him. They were looking down over the low parapet and as they did so a car passed underneath them. Just as Amber Marshalson's had passed when Rick had dropped that lump of concrete. Hannah was still standing there, almost leaning, it seemed, against the burly thickset figure of Lawson. They'll put her back in the car, he thought, and – throw her over the bridge? Try to do that . . . But they didn't. Rick was still on the far side of the bridge but Arlen was coming back. Whatever means was being used to keep Hannah rigid and leaning backwards, Arlen took it over. Lawson got back into the car, into the driving seat, reversed it with a roar of the engine and drove it forwards down the slope towards the bridge.

It was the sight of the handcuffs that galvanised Bal. He watched Arlen, unmistakably a gun in one hand, unlock the handcuffs with the other and Hannah lift up her hands to cover her face. Bal leapt from his car, without a thought, without the least caution or fear. Later he was to think, so that's how it feels in a battle, how it felt when they used to go 'over the top', when adrenalin surges and puts the frightened mind to sleep.

He leapt upon Arlen like an animal on its prey. His onslaught was so violent that he barely noticed the crash as the four-by-four went over the parapet, Lawson leaping out on to the bridge at the last moment. Arlen sank to his knees, swaying, then falling forwards. In that moment Bal saw what the gun was, a child's toy of lightweight gunmetal plastic. Rick was running back now but Hannah, her hands free, swung round and delivered a high kick which caught him in the crotch. As he doubled up, Lawson came at her, reaching with his hands for her throat. This time it was Bal who kicked out, toppling him and seeing his agonised face in the blazing lights of the police cars coming down the lane.

Rick turned to run the other way as Hannah gave chase. Halfway across the bridge he turned round to face her but pain from Hannah's kick seemed to catch him. He doubled up, clutching the tops of his thighs, as Hannah came at him again. As if he dreaded another onslaught, he first flinched and, as her hands made to seize him, reared backwards like someone in muscle spasm from a poisonous alkaloid. He fell backwards across the parapet, whimpered something, cried out something and struggled to get back on his feet. But his heels slipped on the wet ice, his arms rose and windmilled in the air and he went over with a scream, thirty feet down to the road below.

Chapter 31

'What was it he said before he went over?' Burden asked.

'Something about bloody women,' said Wexford. 'Ironical, wasn't it? He was obsessed with this idea that women meant to destroy him and in the end it was a woman . . .'

'I didn't mean him to die, guv.'

'Everyone knows you didn't, Hannah. He'd happily have destroyed you. You'd better go to hospital, you know. There's an ambulance down there waiting to take you.'

'Do I have to?'

He laughed tiredly just when he was thinking he'd never laugh again. 'No, you don't have to. Bal can take you home.'

By this time it was raining heavily and they were all soaked. Barry Vine and Damon Coleman got Norman Arlen into the car and took him away to the police station, where he would spend what was left of the night in a cell before appearing before the magistrates in the morning.

'What are we going to charge him with?' Burden asked when he and Wexford were under cover. 'Possession of a firearm? Attempted murder? False imprisonment?'

'All that and a good deal more. Deception, for one thing. Perverting the course of justice. There'll be more charges later.'

Donaldson got out and opened the car doors for them.

Getting in, Burden said, 'Were all those women really fools enough to believe they could go to Africa, be given an anaesthetic and wake up with a baby? A *black* baby?'

'I don't think we, as men, will ever quite understand the longing some women, *many* women, have for a child. We hear talk about sex and self-preservation being the strongest of human instincts or urges. Maybe they are in men. In women the strongest can be the passion for a child of their own. Those women Norman Arlen deceived wanted to believe, they psyched themselves up to believe against all reason because each one of them wanted a baby of her own more than anything in the world. Ten thousand pounds apiece? Twenty? A child of one's own would be cheap at the price. Fly to Africa, undergo an anaesthetic, do something with passports you know in your heart must be illegal – all that is nothing as the price for having your own precious baby. By the way, my daughter Sylvia's had a girl and she's keeping it. Bye-bye surrogacy.'

'How did that come about?'

'I'll tell you tomorrow. I'll tell you everything tomorrow. Meanwhile, we have to get some sleep.'

When they got to her flat he meant to carry her upstairs. Vague memories returned to him of once seeing a video of *Gone With the Wind*, of Rhett Butler carrying Scarlett up a great antebellum staircase. He did try but the flights up to Hannah's flat were steeper than those in eighteen-sixties Atlanta and at the sixth tread they both collapsed in a giggling heap and began a passionate kissing. With a muffled 'We can't stay here', Hannah finally got up, pulled him up after her and, clinging to each other, they got inside her flat.

'I feel so dirty,' Hannah said.

'I don't care.'

'We could have a bath.'

'We could have a bath in the morning,' said Bal and his next effort at carrying her he did manage. He carried her to bed. As her clothes were hurled past him, landing on various pieces of furniture, he stripped off his own, leaving jeans and pants and sweater and shirt on the floor. When he had switched off the light and got into bed beside her, she was already fast asleep. He lay close to her, spoons-fashion, his arm round her waist, smiling in the dark. All those weeks he had refused her and now he was willing – more than willing, urgently desirous – she was refusing him. But the morning would come.

After Norman Arlen had been charged on several counts and remanded in custody, Wexford and Burden came away from the court and walked across towards the police station. After snow, rain and finally hail in the small hours, it was a mild clear morning, a pale sun shining, the streets still wet and gleaming.

'What are you going to do about Bhattacharya?' Burden asked.

'I've done it. Nothing. Told him off, that's all. He rescued her. She'd probably be dead now but for him. I hope gratitude won't spoil things for them.'

Burden looked at him enquiringly.

'Well, you know the old joke. Why does he hate me so much? I never did him any good.'

Burden changed the subject. 'D'you remember the day we had that fry-up? I'd like to go back there. Not for egg and chips but a coffee and a huge Danish pastry.'

'I shouldn't,' said Wexford, 'but I will. I was too tired to have breakfast.'

It wasn't that the superior greasy spoon in Queen Street looked more inviting than on the previous occasion but that this time they saw how much more it had on offer. Ten different kinds of coffee seemed impossibly sophisticated and it was hard to choose between Danish pastries and Florentines.

'It's a funny thing', said Wexford when they had sat down at a table in the window, 'that everyone but the Danes call these things Danish pastries.'

'What do they call them, then?'

'Viennese bread.'

'Why?'

'I don't know,' said Wexford. 'There must be a reason but I don't know what it is.'

'Never mind the Danish pastries. You said you were going to tell me everything and so far all you've told me is Arlen's multitude of sins. Did you mean you know it all? The whole thing?'

'Oh, yes. I like coffee with chocolate on the top, though I expect it's very bad for me.' Wexford sipped the chocolatey froth, set his cup down and after a moment's silence, began.

'This all started when George Marshalson's first wife died when Amber was seven,' Wexford said. 'Or, rather, it started when he married again. Diana's first husband left her a house worth two million and assets of another four million. Why she married George is a mystery. I suppose she loved him. Perhaps she thought she would eventually get on with Amber. George certainly thought he'd be giving her a second mother. Neither of these things happened. Amber disliked Diana from the first. What efforts Diana made to get on with her we don't know but they failed. George adored his daughter and this can't have made things easy between him and his wife.

'Amber was very good-looking and bright and lively. Of course, she had a boyfriend and she became pregnant. She was five months pregnant before George and Diana found out. Or, I should say, Diana found out. Diana *saw*. Both of them would have advised her to have an abortion if they had known sooner. She had taken her GCSEs more than a year before, intended to do A levels and eventually go to university. What would happen to all that now?'

Burden interrupted him. 'Amber would have been what? Seventeen by then?'

'Seventeen in the July and Brand was born in September. It soon became clear she had no intention of leaving school. No, she'd go back to school, leaving the baby at home with George and Diana, which in effect meant Diana because in these cases, as you know, the man goes on with his job and the woman . . . makes accommodations.'

'I have good reason to know,' said Burden, whose first wife had died and his children been cared for by her sister in often difficult circumstances.

'All George did was an occasional bit of babysitting,' Wexford went on. 'Amber took driving lessons and passed her test the following February. Her doting father bought her a car. Meanwhile, her less than doting stepmother was left to mind Brand. She did try a nanny – remember she could easily afford it – but for some reason this didn't work and she was obliged to give up her job.

'At about this time, the winter after Brand was born, Amber began going to the Bling-Bling Club – driving herself there, incidentally, up until the end of June. Her friends, Ben Miller and Lara Bartlow, also went to Bling-Bling and one night Lara brought her sister Megan along. This is guesswork but very likely a fact that these two girls talked about their babies, Amber's Brand who lived with her and Megan's child who had been adopted three years before. On that occasion, or possibly later, Megan put forward the surrogacy idea. It wasn't that they were much alike, they hadn't a similar social and educational background, but each of them had what Megan called "the qualification".

'To find out more about surrogacy they had to know more and the best way to do that was to go on-line. Megan hadn't a computer but Amber had or she had access to one. She asked John Brooks to show her how to find a website. My guess is that John Brooks found several surrogacy websites and SOCC's in particular.'

'Surely he enquired what she wanted them for?'

'Why surely? I think he was too much interested from his own point of view and his wife's. Gwenda Brooks wanted a baby. Maybe he did too – then. Remember, this was long before he met his boyfriend or perhaps even knew he was attracted to his own sex. He told his wife, she got in touch with SOCC and hence Norman Arlen and Miracle Tours. The rest, as they say, is history.'

'Amber and Megan went to Frankfurt,' said Burden. 'They carried out their insemination or whatever you call it at the Four Horses Hotel – or they didn't carry it out but said they had – pocketed the "deposit" and came home. Where they may have deceived other people into thinking they were pregnant by them. Megan's pregnancy may even have been due to insemination with König-Hensel's contribution. Only a DNA test could have shown that. But it's more likely to have been the result of normal sex with someone she picked up or even with the gallant Prinsip triumphing over sterilisation.'

Wexford finished his coffee, looking regretfully at the trace of rich dregs in the bottom of his cup. He sighed, said, 'But, you know, Mike, it was all irrelevant. All this surrogacy stuff, the scam, the cruel deceit. We spent weeks on it. No doubt we wasted the public's money on it. You trawled among the lowlife, looking for a drugs link – and finding nothing.'

'I did find cocaine's come down in price so much that these days a line costs no more than a cappuccino.'

'Really?' Wexford was silent for a moment, digesting this. Then he said, 'All that came out of it of use to us was that those two girls knew each other. Nothing else. Amber's and Megan's surrogacy scam I'd call the biggest red herring I've come across in my whole career. Neither of those girls was killed because she'd set herself up as a surrogate mother or taken money under false pretences. That may have been a crime, but it wasn't the crime we were investigating.'

'You could say Megan was killed because she knew Amber but why was Amber killed?'

'Amber was killed because she accepted Vivien Hilland's offer of a flat, a flat in a suburb of London. If she had said no she might be alive today and if she were alive, Megan would be too. But she accepted. Of course she did. What young girl in her position would have refused?'

'What I don't understand', said Burden, 'is why George and Diana Marshalson didn't buy her a place. George is comfortably off and Diana is rich. I should think they have at least what the Hillands have at their disposal.'

'Yes, but though George might have wanted to be rid of Brand, he didn't want to lose his daughter. It wouldn't even have been like her going away to university. If he had bought her a flat he might hardly ever have seen her again. Now the first attempt on her life was made a week after she accepted the Hillands' offer. That was the twenty-fourth of June and about a week after that she became eighteen. That's irrelevant too, though for a long while I thought it couldn't be.'

'That attempt', said Burden, paying the bill, 'was made by Rick Samphire, right?'

'Of course,' said Wexford as they left the café and came out into unexpectedly warm sunshine. 'Of course. But it wasn't his idea or his motive. He was merely a mercenary, put up to it and paid to do it, by someone else. There were three murderers in this case, Mike, apart from those accessories, Arlen, Lawson and the rather naïve Fry. We'll go back now, round up those of the team not out serving a grateful public and tell them the rest of it.'

* * *

They gathered in his office. Damon Coleman was there, looking as if about to fall asleep standing up. He had to ask if he could sit down and that was enough to make Wexford tell everyone to be seated. DS Goldsmith and DC Bhattacharya, though behaving with perfect propriety, had been standing closer together than is usual in social, still less business, circumstances. Sitting down evidently would only have been to their taste if it had been permissible to hold hands. Karen Malahyde kept giving them sentimental glances but Barry Vine ignored them. He probably hadn't noticed, was very likely rendering in his head the mad scene from *Lucia di Lammermoor*. The others sat at the back, looking both hopeful and apprehensive.

'I want to thank you all', Wexford began, 'for the good work you've put in on this case. We haven't been very speedy. It's nearly four months since we began looking for the answer, but after thorough and painstaking work we got there in the end. So thank you very much.'

Afterwards no one could decide who began the clapping. Burden, who clapped half-heartedly along with the rest but looked disapproving, was loud in his denials of having had any part in it. In his opinion, it was all part of this lovey-huggy over-courtesy that masked an inner soullessness. It was the impulse that made people put flowers in cellophane on strangers' death sites. If Wexford was thinking along the same lines he couldn't tell from the Chief Inspector's inscrutable expression.

Wexford waited for silence, then said, 'There were three killers in this case, not the Samphire brothers on their own. Let's get straight on to June the twenty-fourth, Midsummer Day, when Rick Samphire parked his car in Yorstone Wood and walked through the wood to Yorstone Bridge, carrying in a backpack a lump of concrete he picked up off a building site and wearing, over his other clothes, a grey fleece with its hood up. It wasn't cold, so I suppose he wore it for disguise. From a short distance one man in a hood looks much like another.

'Rick's aim was to drop the concrete block off the bridge when Amber Marshalson passed underneath it in her silver Honda car. He had no motive. He was simply doing what he was paid for: to kill Amber. But being an accident-prone and clumsy man, someone who does nothing quite right, he made a mess of it. He blew it. He got the wrong car, catching by one of his typical mistakes the dark-grey Honda driven by James Ambrose. Mavis Ambrose died as a result of her injuries. That was the first murder.

'Slow on the uptake as he is, Rick must have known he'd got the wrong car. Before he fled the scene he'd have caught sight of Amber alive and well if horribly shocked. He went back the way he had come and as he approached the place in a clearing in the wood where his own car was, he was seen by Megan Bartlow cycling home from her grandmother's house. Whether he saw her he hasn't said. Now what I think she saw was a man in a hood and she saw him only in profile in the light from her bicycle lamp.'

Karen had her hand up as if at a press conference. 'What is it, Karen?'

'Surely he'd have seen her light, sir? It would have been quite dark by then in the wood.'

'You mean, having attempted to kill one girl, why not kill the other one who'd seen him? My guess would be that it wasn't in his brief. His brief was to kill Amber Marshalson. Killing someone else as well without sanction might be out of order. Ross wouldn't like it. Rick would think that way. I think the how had been left to him. If it had been down to his brother Ross he would never have come up with such a risky method. It was literally hit-and-miss, wasn't it? He hit all right but he missed his target.

'And yes, Ross Samphire was behind it. He put Rick up to it, though it wasn't he who put up the money. Strange as it

319

sounds, Ross offered the task of killing Amber to his brother out of fraternal love. He was, in fact, as he'd done many times before, *giving him a job*. A well-paid one-off job. The payment was five thousand pounds. But of course, as he'd also done before, Ross miscalculated Rick's efficiency and underestimated his accident-proneness. Love tends to do that in the love object.

'Now Ross has never been in trouble with the law. That is, he has never been prosecuted. He's never been caught. But I suspect that petty crime has been as much a part of his life as it has of his brother's. Certainly he has had a long association with Norman Arlen. Apparently he and Rick were at school with him. So it was Norman Arlen who was roped in to provide Rick with an alibi for the evening of Midsummer Day. He and Rick, we were told, were drinking and later eating in the Mermaid right through the relevant time Rick was dropping concrete blocks off bridges.

'Beyond a doubt, another attempt must be made. The others were squeamish about actually doing the killing. Rick had two convictions for violence. Unlike Ross, he *knew* about violence, so it had to be Rick giving it another go. He did. On the eleventh of August. At some time before two on that morning, Ben Miller dropped Amber on the corner of Mill Lane, Brimhurst Prideaux. Rick, wearing his hooded fleece, had again parked his car in a sheltered place and was waiting for her.'

'How did he know she'd come there at that time, sir?' This was Damon Coleman who knew all about waiting for people in streets and on corners.

'He was told,' said Wexford. 'Told by Ross who made it his business to find out such things, Ross who had told him – because he had expert information – at what time Amber would pass under the bridge. Now he told him what time Amber might be expected home from the Bling-Bling Club. As we know, this time Rick was successful. He had, however, been seen. Lydia Burton saw a man in a hood walking along the grass verge when she went out to walk her dog at midnight. Now you may think it very odd of her, in her peculiar position, to have mentioned this to us unless she had some ulterior motive. We shall see.'

Putting his hand up, Damon asked, 'Was she the third killer in the trio, sir?'

'Ah, you've latched on to that, have you? Let's leave it for now. Let's ask ourselves why Rick didn't take the thousand pounds out of Amber's jacket pocket. The answer probably is that he only did what brother Ross told him to do and his instructions didn't include helping himself to Amber's property. What we also don't know is who gave her the money, only that it was payment for agreeing to be a surrogate parent. Perhaps we need not know beyond realising it was a member of SOCC, the childlessness circle whose moving spirit was Norman Arlen. But Arlen had nothing directly to do with it and nothing directly to do with Amber's murder. This is where Stephen Lawson comes in. And, no, Damon, he's not your third murderer – sounds like something out of *Macbeth*, doesn't it?'

Their blank polite faces showed him that they had no idea whether it sounded like something out of *Macbeth* or not. It was no use lamenting the loss of poetry from the nation's mindset. It was gone, never, he supposed, to return. 'Stephen Lawson may work for a charity as a fund-raiser. He also works or worked for Norman Arlen. He', he went on, 'was paid to invent that story about encountering Rick with a broken-down car on the Sewingbury-to-Pomfret road. Meeting Rick was a lie, though all the rest was true.

'We must suppose Ross was gratified by his beloved brother's success. Next time he took his paramour round to Colin Fry's knocking shop, he was no doubt able to outline his achievement. Value for money, I expect he called it. All should have been well now, all four of them having got what they wanted

– if he got nothing else out of it, Arlen had the satisfaction of doing ill, of perpetrating evil, a favourite occupation with him. All should have been well but for Megan Bartlow.'

Wexford gave the others – Burden had to listen to it again – an outline of the scam carried on by Amber and Megan. He went on, 'Megan hadn't realised just what she had seen in Yorstone Wood. Even if she saw the newspaper accounts of the block dropped off the bridge and Mavis Ambrose's death, the only connection she need then have made with Amber was that Amber was driving one of the other cars. But when Amber was killed she put two and two together.

'She hadn't recognised the hooded man in Yorstone Wood but some time later, maybe two or three weeks later, she was walking along a street in Sewingbury with her father when they saw Ross Samphire getting out of his car and going into his house. Megan saw him in profile and probably from the back. Now the man in the wood wore a hood and it was growing dark. The only light was from her bicycle lamp. I'm suggesting she saw him only in profile. Ross was also seen by her in profile. He has a mass of thick dark curly hair and he looks healthy, which Rick does not. But – remember this – they were twins. Identical twins. Once they had looked exactly alike, both no doubt with thick dark curly hair and bright eyes and good skin. Time and prison and smoking and probably a poor diet had taken their toll on Rick, a fate from which his brother had not been able to save him. It was Ross whom Megan saw. She saw the same profile as the man in the wood but without a hood and in broad daylight. She took them for one and the same.

'How she made contact I don't know but she knew Ross's address. Probably, as soon as she saw him out on foot, she followed him, told him she recognised him and threatened him with the police. Now Ross could have said it wasn't him but only by exposing his twin brother, his beloved brother. Megan therefore must die but this time Ross didn't dare entrust Rick with the task. There would be no second chance if he messed it up. He would have to do it himself. Perhaps he said there has to be a first time, it's the first step that counts. Whatever it was, he arranged to meet Megan at Victoria Terrace where he would soon be working on refurbishing those houses.'

Hannah put up her hand. 'Why there, guv?'

'I'm almost inclined to take the easy way out and say, why not? But he couldn't have met her in the open in daylight where they might be seen. After dark she wouldn't come. She'd be too afraid. He couldn't go to her place or she come to his. When he suggested Victoria Terrace it seemed all right to her. She went over the night before, remember, to check the place out and no doubt she thought there'd be enough people about to ensure her safety.

'As for Ross, he went to the old bank building with Rick and Colin Fry at eight in the morning. Colin was given a painting job on an upper floor which – and this is important – he couldn't break off halfway through. Once he'd started he had to complete the whole wall. Ross took care of that. He was on the ground floor with Rick. At ten to nine he got into his car, which was parked on the bank forecourt, drove to Stowerton, picked up a brick from the pile stacked up outside Victoria Terrace, met Megan and killed her. He stuffed her body into the cupboard and drove back. The whole thing would have taken him half an hour or, at most, forty minutes.

'Colin Fry had never seen him leave because he had to concentrate on his paint job. Why did Ross put the body in a cupboard? He certainly couldn't take it out in daylight – and remember it was by now between nine thirty and ten in the morning. I don't yet know why he left it there but my guess is that he asked Rick to dispose of it and do so after dark. Rick was alone and this is an important factor. Ross was seldom alone. He has a wife and two children. He runs a business. He also has a girlfriend who must be very important to him for him to go to these lengths for her. But Rick was on his own. No one was watching him. No one at that time suspected him. The disadvantage of Rick was that he was careless and accident-prone. Perhaps Ross impressed on him the importance of getting rid of Megan's body. If her body was hidden or buried somewhere it might not be found for months and never connected with Amber. But Rick didn't carry out his instructions.

'Why not? We don't know – yet. Maybe he didn't know how or where. Maybe by the time he'd decided on a place and a means days had gone by. The weather was still very hot, if you remember. The body had begun to smell. Decay had started. Perhaps he simply couldn't face touching it to get it out of there and reasoned that in time the smell would fade, only he and Ross and Colin Fry would be working in there and Megan's remains could be moved by Ross himself.

'We can all have a break for coffee now and I'll resume in a quarter of an hour.'

Wexford phoned the Assistant Chief Constable's office and asked for an appointment to see him. That day if possible. A date was fixed for four in the afternoon. He drank his coffee on his own and in silence, thinking about things, speculating what might have happened if Rick had removed and buried Megan's body. It might easily not yet have been found. In that case they would never have connected the two girls, the surrogacy scam might never have come to light or Norman Arlen's deception been exposed.

For a moment he let his thoughts dwell on Sylvia and her new baby. Mary Fairfax would be her name. It had a fine ring to it. Dora was already allowing herself to hope once more that Sylvia and Mary's father might get together again. And of course a baby should have a father living with her, though so many didn't these days. Wexford caught himself up. His first priority was this case and explaining it satisfactorily to his team, then to the Assistant Chief Constable, to review the babies incidental to this whole sorry business, motherless African babies – what would become of them? – Megan's adopted baby, the baby Megan never carried to term, the babies longed for by the two German couples and Gwenda Brooks, the baby Brand himself. He went back into his office and the waiting team. A hand went up before he had even begun.

'Who's the third killer, sir?' This was Barry Vine.

'It will soon emerge,' said Wexford. 'I want to go back now to Amber Marshalson,' he continued. 'Poor little Amber was a classic example of what may happen when you give an only child everything she wants. Everything she asks for, call her a princess and tell her she's the most marvellous thing to happen since the wheel.'

'Excuse me, sir.' This was Barry again. 'But shouldn't that be "sliced bread"?'

'We're a non-cliché shop here, I hope, Barry. Back again to Amber. Those of you who have no children but will have, take warning. George Marshalson gave his daughter everything she wanted, everything he thought she wanted, including another mother. Diana had no children of her own, though she was still young enough to have them, but George, of course, wanted no more. He had one and that one was perfect, never to be matched. Probably, Diana tried to be what a parent should be and George had never been: a mentor as well as a mother, an exemplar and teacher or perhaps, worse, a big sister. Nothing worked. Amber hated Diana.

'Amber's pregnancy must have shaken George's slavish admiration for her, if not his love. But perhaps not. In his eyes Daniel Hilland would have been entirely to blame. He told himself this was the result of near-rape, certainly seduction. I don't think giving birth to Brand was particularly traumatic for Amber. In her circle, having a baby in your teens is looked upon as rather dashing. Cool, I dare say, or wicked.'

'Hard-core,' said Damon.

'Yes, thank you, DC Coleman. Amber didn't even have to leave school. The hated Diana, barely spoken to in former days, was handy as babysitter and full-time nanny. Why didn't Diana go? Why didn't she just leave? She no longer loved George and she had never loved Amber. She had money of her own, plenty of it, even without working. But she didn't go. She stayed and looked after Brand. And it seemed as if Amber and Brand would be there for ever. Well, Brand would because Amber would very likely go off to university and after university would come a job. Brand would stay and Amber might possibly go to London or America or somewhere in Europe – or even marry a man who didn't want her child.

'Then the Hillands offered Amber their flat in a London suburb. Not that offer but her acceptance of it accomplished what you would call, Barry, "signing her own death warrant". If she had said no she'd be alive today. But she said yes.'

He looked at the perplexed faces confronting him and at one which wasn't puzzled, one on which light was dawning, causing her to wince. 'Oh, my God,' Hannah said softly.

'Ross Samphire was having a love affair. His much-vaunted happy family life was so much image making. We saw Ross driving away from Mill Lane and then we saw Lydia Burton at her gate. Knowing Lydia Burton "had someone", as they say, we assumed, or we assumed for a while, she was Ross's girlfriend. But if this were so it would have meant Ross had actually been in Mill Lane at half past midnight on the eleventh of August, somewhere he would never have dreamt of being when his brother was due there an hour or so later to do murder. Besides, why would Ross and Lydia have used Colin Fry's flat for their assignations when Lydia was a single woman with a house of her own?

'No, Ross's girlfriend lived in Mill Lane but she wasn't Lydia Burton. She was a rich woman and a married woman who had no wish for her affair to be discovered and she perhaps divorced. Diana Marshalson wanted her affair with Ross to continue but there was something else she wanted far more. Enough to kill for and pay someone to kill for.'

Wexford paused, looking from one startled face to another, all but Hannah's. He went on, 'All the way through this case we've been looking for the reason why. Why? What was the motive for killing Amber? Amber was leaving, she was going to take away the child George and Diana found such a burden, take him to London, and maybe they'd scarcely see him again. So why take the appalling step of killing her? Maybe Diana didn't think of it. It could have been Ross. But Diana handed over the money to be passed on to Ross's poor brother, so dogged by ill luck as he was.

'Why? Diana put up a very good show of finding Brand a nuisance, a bit of a pain to have around. No one would have guessed how she really felt, that though she had had no children with her first husband, the blame for that she thought was his. George didn't want children. She was growing older, by now she was too old to have a baby. But Amber had one and by chance it was she who was destined to look after him, to bring him up. Diana may have found caring for Brand a chore at first. Not for long. She soon came to love him. She loved him, she adored him, as if he were her own. No wonder she didn't want to keep a nanny. And Brand was virtually hers. She was becoming first in his life. His mother wasn't indifferent to him but she was very young and she was careless. Without Diana, where would he have been? She worshipped him – much as her husband had worshipped Amber.

'But Amber was going. She was going to London and taking the beloved child with her. It was a curious situation, wasn't it? There was George wanting Amber and Brand to stay because he wanted Amber, and Diana wanting Amber and Brand to stay because she wanted Brand. And Amber wanting to go because a flat in London meant freedom and life and excitement.

'So Diana paid Ross to pay Rick to kill Amber so that she could keep Brand whom she loved,' said Wexford. He walked behind his desk and sat down, resisted the temptation to put his head in his hands, spoke the final words of his explanation. 'Love doesn't excuse everything. It doesn't excuse anything. This was the worst and the wickedest motive – and I mean wicked in its old true sense, Damon – for murder I have ever known. This was what evil is. Look no further.'

RUTH RENDELL has won many awards, including the Crime Writers' Association Gold Dagger for 1976's best crime novel with *A Demon in My View*; a second Edgar in 1984 from the Mystery Writers of America for the best short story, *The New Girl Friend*; a Gold Dagger award for *Live Flesh* in 1986. She was also the winner of the 1990 *Sunday Times* Literary Award, as well as the Crime Writers' Association Cartier Diamond Dagger. In 1996 she was awarded the CBE and in 1997 became a Life Peer.